# Bill Kirton

# SHADOW SELVES

For Catriona
Thanks for a lovely
evening
X Bill

PfoxChase Publishing

PfoxChase, a division of Pfoxmoor Publishing
4972 Lowhill Church Road
New Tripoli, PA 18066 USA

www.pfoxmoorpublishing.com
www.pfoxchase.com

**Shadow Selves**

Print ISBN: 978-1-936827-18-3
Digital ISBN (PDF): 978-1-936827-19-0
Digital ISBN (EPUB): 978-1-936827-20-6

Cover by Sessha Batto

First PfoxChase electronic publication: October 2011
First PfoxChase print publication: October 2011

Published in the United States of America with international distribution.

# Dedication:

For Max, Christine, Jim, Lili, Linda and David.

*Everyone carries a shadow, and the less it is embodied in the
individual's conscious life, the blacker and denser it is.*
—Carl Jung.

# Acknowledgements

*p 26 demulcent*

Thanks to my friends Donnie Ross, for advice and information on most things medical, David Reid, for insights into structures and remuneration in the world of academic medicine, and Stewart McIntosh for help with surgical procedures. Any flaws which may have crept into any of these areas are mine, not theirs.

Thanks also to Kate Callaghan and Tadg Farrington, whose perceptive reading of an early version of the story led to changes which made it easier to write.

# Chapter One

Sandra Scott was late for classes and trying to get dressed. The man hidden in the foliage of a sycamore tree exactly opposite and slightly above her window saw her growing frustration with her boyfriend, Tom Strachan. Strachan was standing behind her with his arms round her, forcing her shirt back up to her shoulders to cup his hands under her breasts as he munched away at her neck. She was still managing to smile but her struggles were progressively less compliant.

They were in Scott's room on the first floor of block C of the University of Grampian's self-catering student accommodation at the edge of Macaulay Park. Of the five square blocks of flats, all but the two nearest the outer edge were screened by trees. It meant that most of the students looked out onto leaves and sky. It also meant that anyone interested in looking in on them had plenty of cover from which to do so.

The man in the tree sat with his left hand holding the trunk and his right curled into his groin. Since Strachan's arrival earlier that morning, he'd been a silent witness to the sex they'd had, from the kisses and slow fumblings to the manual and oral services they'd performed for one another. There hadn't been any actual penetration, despite Strachan's efforts, but they'd done enough to produce one climax for Strachan and two for the watcher.

The problem was that Scott now had less than ten minutes to get across the park to her ten o'clock tutorial. A final dig with her elbow convinced Strachan that she meant her resistance and the man in the tree watched her tuck her shirt in, grab a bag, blow a kiss at Strachan, who was now sprawled back across the bed, and disappear.

Just a few seconds later, she came round the side of C block and ran along the path and across the grass under his tree. His breathing was shallow and his fingers still moved slowly in his groin.

****

Professor Hayne bent forward and clutched at his chest. The others paused briefly, then continued their discussion. They were used to it. It had happened so many times before. He sucked in short gasps and kneaded his fingers against his ribs, trying to push the pain back down inside him. It was well over a minute before he was able to join in again. When he spoke, his voice was tight and his breathing hard.

"Sorry," he said.

"Are you alright?" said Dr Carlyle.

Hayne flapped a hand at him and nodded.

They were sitting around a long table in a small, stuffy room, with a blackboard and a computer at one end and a locked, glass-fronted bookcase at the other. Outside, the sun was shining and the leaves of two huge rowan trees were hissing in a small breeze, which did nothing to stir the air inside.

It was the usual Thursday afternoon staff meeting. Dr. Christie had just outlined at length a proposal for changing the way students' marks were allocated. The figures he used to make his point were weighted very heavily against the system Dr. Leith had proposed. It made Leith angry, and anger always made him smell even worse as he sweated and scratched, his fingers stirring up the fetid layers from previous tempers and stresses. Christie was far enough away from him to be able to enjoy his distress. Hayne, however, at the head of the table with Leith immediately to his right, was less fortunate and resigned himself to at least another twenty minutes of chest pains and stale sweat.

Christie and Leith contrasted in every way. Christie was nearly fifty but dressed like someone in his early thirties. His skin was sun-bed orange and his blonde hair was long enough to feature in shampoo adverts. Unfortunately, there was very little of it. His dark brown Ben Sherman shirt and green velvet waistcoat suggested that his ideas on fashion had frozen in the eighties. For Leith, on the other hand, fashion was a foreign country. He wore a limp tweed jacket over a green shirt with a filthy collar. His tie had been worn through too many meals involving juices, his face was red and shiny and he had a habit of scratching his scalp with a pencil.

"Perhaps you'd prefer us to dispense with Medieval and Renaissance studies altogether," he said, more concerned with his own hurt than Hayne's heart problems.

Christie smiled.

"I just think we could add more value to our students," he said.

"And singling out my proposal was totally arbitrary, was it?"

"Of course. This isn't about personalities; it's about departmental efficiency."

Leith was about to rise to the bait again when Hayne intervened.

"Let's not make too many assumptions about our value to the university as individuals. Or as a department," he said, quietly.

It disorientated not only Leith and Christie but all the others around the table. There was a silence. Hayne let it drift for a moment, then added, "Changing climates. You've seen the directives. We're all answerable."

It was a typical Hayne interjection, non-specific and yet heavy with implications that they were all under threat and he knew something they didn't. Ever since he'd been appointed head of the department of European Culture, its staff meetings had been closer to the rituals of boxing than to those of academic discourse. Hayne himself, Christie and Leith were the main sources of strife, but each member of staff was touched by the weekly contests. No bones crunched, no blood was let, but hatreds and antagonisms simmered constantly.

It was hard to understand Hayne's continued interest in it all. This was his last staff meeting before being admitted to hospital for an operation on an aortic aneurysm. In the course of the past three years, thanks to cancers of various organs, he'd frequently been absent for long periods, but he'd never lost his grip on the department.

His words had the usual depressive effect. On his left, Ritchie, a big, tidy man, was doodling triangles on the bottom of his agenda. At the bottom end of the table, the three Ms, Drs Miller, Munro and McChaddie, kept their habitual silence. They rarely contributed much and always voted with the majority. In any case, they paid little attention to the items on the agenda, each preferring to think

3

about his own special interest: German Expressionist theatre, Odilon Redon's surrealist legacy and Manchester United.

Hayne showed the ravages of the illnesses he'd suffered. His skin was grey and he looked much older than his fifty-two years. He wore lightly tinted glasses and his graying hair was cut short and combed flat on his head. He let his gaze move slowly across the faces around the table. Only Christie caught his eye. When he did so, he gave a little nod, as if in appreciation of the point Hayne had just made.

Hayne moved the meeting on but the afternoon dragged and it was ten to five before he at last asked if there was any other business.

"Just one point," said Carlyle. "I'm sure I speak for everyone else in offering our best wishes for your operation."

There were soft murmurs of agreement from the rest.

"I've no doubt that it'll be successful and that you'll soon be in harness again," he added.

"I hope so, James," said Hayne. "I hate unfinished business."

None of them would ever know what he meant. It was the last contribution he ever made to a departmental meeting.

****

Susan Jamieson, the acute pain nurse, was in her late thirties but had a young, pretty face which made it easy to see how people might confide in her and trust her to relieve their suffering. Her dark hair fell softly over her forehead and around her cheeks and her brown eyes had a natural gentleness. They'd seen their share of distress and yet they smiled quickly and easily.

She'd spent a lot of time with Hayne in one ward or another over the past three years. Sometimes it was chemotherapy that kept him there, sometimes surgery, but each time the need was for relief from the sort of pain which no one could ever communicate but which was deep inside every patient she had to deal with. She didn't particularly like the man but she respected his fierce resistance to the debilitating conditions and treatments he had to endure. She sat with him for a long time on the Thursday evening after he'd been admitted, listening to his anxieties about what his colleagues might get up to during his absence. The tightness of his face and neck told her that the analgesics were doing little to ease his pain.

When she came back on duty the following day, he had a visitor with him. He seemed to be talking a lot. Hayne was saying very little. When the man left, Jamieson was surprised to see that, instead of turning left towards the main exit, he turned right and went into the Directorate of Surgery. As he passed her she nodded to him and went straight to Hayne's bedside to take his blood pressure.

"Why bother?" he said, rolling up his sleeve.

"You should be used to it by now."

"I am. That's why I'm asking why you're doing it."

Jamieson's smile still held.

"Routine. You know we can't do without it."

Hayne looked into her eyes and she smiled as she looked back at him. Their intimacy was strange. Outside the wards, they would never have come into contact but, over the years, the intense physicality of the services she provided had created a closeness which he didn't even feel with his wife any more.

"I think you need it more than we do," he said.

"What?"

"Routine. It makes us manageable." He touched the band around his arm. "If you didn't have these bits of apparatus to measure us with, you wouldn't know what to do with us."

"Now that's no very nice, is it?"

"I'm not a nice person," he said.

Jamieson was inclined to agree with him but she didn't let it show.

"Well, I'm nice enough for the both of us," she said, unwrapping the band.

"Yes. I think maybe you are," he said.

The remark surprised her. Hayne's compliments were as rare as black pearls.

"Makes you special, really," he went on. "No spite, no ego, keeping well clear of the rush for ... power and the rest of it."

She had no idea what he was talking about and was used to being patronized by him. She tried to keep her lightness of tone and make the usual comforting noises. But as they talked, she knew it was different. Hayne's frustrations had somehow been muted. They were still there, but clouded with something else. It was strange. He told her of the visitors he'd had that day—two colleagues and his wife—and how much they'd disturbed him. In previous months that

5

would have made him angry but now he talked about it with something like sadness. He wondered why the colleagues had come. They had nothing new to tell him and the things they said about the university simply increased his frustrations and isolated him in this white and whispering world.

"That chap who just left, Leith," he said, his head shaking gently as if he didn't believe what he was saying. "Totally untrustworthy. He's been digging away at things for years. I asked him what's going on. Challenged him about it. He talked to me as if I was a first year student or something. Fobbed me off. They're wrecking the place."

"Now you're exaggeratin."

Hayne let his head fall back on the pillow and said, "I wish I were." His voice was so quiet that she hardly heard the words.

Through the night, she came back to him at intervals after doing her rounds or soothing another of her patients. He was always awake. They talked some more and the relentlessness of his many hurts wore down all her attempts to relieve them. By the end of her shift, she was ready for a walk through the morning air across the hospital grounds to the nurses' quarters. She was trained to cope with despair, but she needed to be reminded that there was a big, normal world beyond the agonies of her small group of sufferers.

****

DCI Jack Carston closed the file he was reading and settled back in the sofa. He clicked his fingers, which made his wife Kath look up from her own book.

"Half a minute," he said. "Less, sometimes. Amazing."

"Is this you worrying about premature ejaculation again?" asked Kath.

Carston smiled.

"Listen, woman, you're married to the biggest stud in…"

"…this house," Kath said, quickly.

"Took the words right out of my mouth," said Carston. He lifted the file and dropped it back on his lap again.

"No, this," he said. "Strangulation." He clicked his fingers again. "That's all it takes. Bit of pressure on the carotid arteries, blood can't reach the brain. Bingo."

"Bingo?"

Carston went on, talking not for her but to himself.

"Venous blood can't get away from the head, lips and face get a blue tint to them."

"Jack, what the hell's up with you?" said Kath. "You never do this at home."

"Sorry, love," said Carston. "I just… You know, nowadays I seem to find it more and more difficult to reconcile some things."

Kath noticed the tone.

"Like what?"

"Oh, the usual. People who know each other, love each other even. And even the ones who don't, the ones who just do it to strangers. How can they do all this stuff?" He tapped the file on his lap. "I'm reading statements where they're saying how precious she was to them, how much they miss her and there, right alongside it there's things like…" He opened the file and read. "…sensitivity of the carotid plexus, vagal inhibition, fractured laryngeal cartilages." He closed the file again. "Different world, different language. Maybe I should retire. Maybe I'm getting obsessed with it all."

Kath got up and went to sit beside him. He put his arm around her shoulder and kissed her hair.

"The trouble is," he said, "I still like it. Too bloody much."

"What d'you mean?"

Carston gave a deep sigh.

"It fascinates me—the cruelty, the notion of pain, the details. Opens up depths which … I don't know. I really do wonder sometimes whether it's healthy."

Kath settled more snugly into him.

"I can't imagine what you'd do without it, Jack," she said.

"No," said Carston.

He let his arm drape forward over her shoulder so that his hand was on her breast.

"Mind you," he said. "If I were here during the day, we…"

The phone rang.

"Thank God for that," said Kath.

"Shit," said Carston.

He pushed himself up and went through to the hall, grabbing the phone and saying, "Carston," rather too abruptly into it.

"Sorry, sir. Am I disturbing something?"

It was Julie McNeil. She'd been with his team for a couple of years.

"No, no, it's OK. What's the news?"

"Thought I'd just tell you, sir. I got through."

Carston smiled broadly.

"That's great, Julie," he said. "Or d'you want me to call you Sergeant McNeil now?"

He heard her chuckle.

"I'm glad you phoned, but I'm sorry we'll be losing you."

"Well, that's partly why I'm calling, sir."

"Oh?"

"Yes. I mean, I know I'm supposed to be moved into a different branch—broaden my experience and all that—but I was wondering… Well, I'd rather stay in CID. I think it'd make more sense."

"Well, I'd be all for it, Julie, but it's not down to me."

"I know, but if I went to Superintendent Ridley and pushed my rape counseling stuff, he might … well, what do you think? Specially if he knew you wanted me to stay."

"Not sure about that," said Carston. "If he knew I wanted you, you'd be on dog-handling right away. Tell you what, ask him about staffing levels, they need balancing a bit. It'll be easier for him to fill the gap you've left by just shoving you back into it. That might nudge him the way we want. You know what he's like with budgets and bits of paper."

As he spoke, Carston knew that he was out of order bad-mouthing a superior officer but he trusted McNeil and knew she had the same opinion of the top floor.

"OK, sir. I'll see him first thing."

"Just tell him about budgetary realignment, fiscal imperatives—you know the sort of thing. Invent stuff. Best of luck with it. And congratulations. You deserve it."

He rang off and Kath saw the change in him as soon as he came back into the room.

"Good news?" she said.

"Yep. Julie's got her sergeant's exam. She wants to stay on the squad too."

"That's nice," said Kath.

"Yes," said Carston sitting beside her and cuddling her into him again. "All she has to do is convince Ridley and then deal with all the crap she'll get from Spurle and the rest."

8

****

The following Tuesday, Susan Jamieson was on night duty again, this time in the Intensive Therapy Unit. There were only six patients in the ward but they managed to etch the night air with enough sighing, snoring and moans to make it seem crowded. Stringing through the muttering dimness were the electronic beeps of the machines into which they were plugged. They were discreet, regular and, for the one or two patients who were still awake, reassuring. Basically, as long as they could hear the noises, they were still there and there was a chance of surfacing into another day of light. No sounds came from the streets or skies outside and even the occasional rattle of a trolley or beat of footsteps in a corridor only locked them more firmly into this space. The ticks, whispers and turnings that filled the room were the sounds of half a dozen men and women trying to stay alive for another breakfast.

In the bed next to the door, Mrs Woods was sucking in quick, gasping breaths, fearful of expanding her chest fully because of the pains that dug in on every side when she did. Jamieson sat beside her, talking softly and gently massaging her right hand and forearm. The smell of lemon and thyme from the oil she was using helped both her and Mrs Woods to push aside the other sharp sterile scents of the ward. Mrs Woods had had one of her lungs removed on Monday and, as she was being weaned off the analgesics, her body was beginning to protest about the trauma it had undergone. Sleep was elusive but the comfort of physical contact and the feel and smell of the essential oils helped to defuse some of her stress. For Jamieson, too, the repetitive kneading of the tired old flesh was soothing, hypnotic and certainly preferable to sitting at her desk trying to decipher the pamphlet on psychiatric nursing she'd brought to work with her.

They were slightly detached from the rest of the ward because there was no bed in the next space along. It was due to be taken, in the next hour or so, by a Mrs Rioch. She was in the operating theatre where she'd had to be rushed for an emergency oesophagectomy early in the evening. The operation had gone slowly but well and now the thoracic surgeon was pulling the ribs on her left side back together again with much more substantial sutures than those he'd used to join what remained of her esophagus to the hole at the top of her stomach. Two of the three theatre nurses

9

were beginning to clear away the used swabs and instrument trays and the anesthetist was satisfied with the readings he was getting on her overall blood pressure and the pressure in her pulmonary artery and central venous system.

In the next ward along, the High Dependency Unit, Alistair Hayne's worries were over. He was in a small room at the end of the ward furthest from the corridor. Just before midnight, his aorta split open. He was heavily sedated and so the pain didn't wake him. His blood pressure suddenly dropped, his pulse began to race and, with blood pumping uselessly into his abdominal cavity, he died in a sudden silence.

****

Leith was leaning against the window sill in his room in the university's Selkirk block, his back turned to the view of treetops and the spire of the chapel. His phone was cradled on his shoulder and jammed against his left ear as he used his hands to flick through some papers in a blue folder. The ear piece was slippery with sweat and his fingers left damp patches on everything they touched. The air in his office seemed to have an extra ingredient, thicker than any in the corridors outside, which caught the throat of anyone who opened the door, but Leith seemed totally unaware of his body's reeking micro-climate.

"I've got it here," he said, trying not to shout. "In your letter." He looked at the date. "On the seventeenth. 'Camera-ready copy.' That's what I've given you."

He listened but his patience couldn't hold.

"What do you mean, 'C'est la vie'? It's not 'la vie' at all, it's your specific instructions. I'm just doing what you asked. The grants committee has approved it and publication's been scheduled for October, so don't talk to me about editorial difficulties. I expect the proofs by the end of the month."

He grabbed the receiver and banged it back onto its cradle, leaving smears on both the handset and the desktop beside it. The exchange was the latest in a series of disagreements he'd had with the editor who'd agreed to publish his most recent book. Leith could never accept the possibility that he might be wrong. At work, he insisted that students regurgitate his lecture notes without adding any ideas of their own. In family matters, his was the only voice. In debates in committees he listened to what others had to say then voted according to his initial persuasion. It was something to do with bluffness or some other supposed attribute of the working classes from which he claimed to come. He thought of himself as an old-fashioned socialist and yet it was he who'd spearheaded a campaign to reduce cleaning and canteen staff numbers in order to preserve the departmental publications budget. More recently, he'd turned his attentions to the university's janitors, gardeners and ground staff. He not only specialized in feudalism, he practiced it.

When the phone rang again, he grabbed at it, ready to heap even more abuse on the hapless editor, but it was a different caller.

"Thought you'd like to know," said the voice. "He's dead."

Leith's mood changed immediately.

"When?" he asked.

"Does it matter?"

"No, no." Leith's breath was quicker, shallower, clipping at his words. "Does anybody else know, anybody in the department?"

"No. I thought you'd like time to think about it. Put things in place maybe."

Leith put a hand to his forehead and pressed hard.

"Yes. Thanks for the call. I appreciate it. I'll talk to you again later."

"No need. Better not to."

"Alright. But let me know if you hear anything."

He nodded at the reply he got, then put the phone back and looked out at the soft white drifts of cloud behind the chapel spire. His heart was beating faster and the editor's impertinence was forgotten.

# Chapter Two

The next morning sparkled with the lovely light of late May. With dawn breaking well before five, Carston got up early and played a round of golf with a neighbor, Alex Crombie. As usual, he lost comprehensively but went home with an appetite and a feeling of well-being which irritated Kath all through breakfast. She was always up around seven-thirty but, until about nine o'clock, tended to grunt rather than speak. It wasn't anti-social; she just needed time to settle into the day before having to make conversation. Usually, Carston felt the same and their normal morning routine unfolded in soothing silence. But eighteen holes under a spring sky made him feel that the day was well advanced and that social intercourse was a legitimate pursuit. Kath's frequent stares did little to stem his affability and, when he eventually left just after eight, she felt her tension go with him. She started making fresh coffee and decided to begin the morning all over again.

Carston was anticipating a little tension himself. Mayhem was frequently part of the daily CID routine but McNeil had been clever with Ridley and he'd rung Carston to tell him he'd decided she should stay with his team. That meant that today was her first as a sergeant and there were new sets of relationships to be forged. What remained to be seen was how the colleagues she'd leapfrogged would take to the idea of her outranking them. Fraser, Spurle, Bellman and Thom were all young officers, all able enough to climb at least part way up through the ranks but with a shared attitude to women that was current when Robert Peel appointed his first officer.

Detective Sergeant Jim Ross arrived soon after Carston. He had two very young daughters and it was a few years since he'd had the luxury of choice about how early he woke up or how slowly he eased himself into the day. Kirsty and Mhairi seemed to spring into immediate action the moment their eyes opened and Ross and his wife Jean just had to keep up with them.

The two men were comfortable with each other and settled behind their desks, sipping the coffee that Carston had made when he arrived. Ross was tall and supple, with light reddish hair, an open face and eyes like the young Paul Newman. Carston was in his late forties. His waist was just beginning to spread but there was little extra flesh around his neck and face. His dark eyes were unusually still, fixing frequently on the middle distance as he followed some inner fancies. It was a feature that many of his wife's friends found very attractive.

McNeil arrived at twenty to nine.

"Morning Julie," said Carston. "Big day, eh?"

McNeil nodded, her lopsided grin broader than usual.

"Don't forget, you outrank the Neanderthals now."

"It's going to be hard on them, sir," she said. "I mean, it's my fault for asking to stay in the squad. Puts them in a wee bit of a spot. I was thinking, just to make things easier, I don't mind if they don't call me sergeant."

"Well, I bloody do," said Carston. "If we start letting them get away with that, they'll be calling me Jack and nipping round to my place for a game of darts and a bevy. Sod that."

"Aye," said Ross. "Put them straight right away." He was glad that she'd asked to stay with CID. She had the instincts of a detective and a degree of sensitivity far above that of the other members of the squad. She knew how to handle people.

"Aye, I suppose you're right … Jim," she said, the corner of her mouth twisting further as she added his name.

They heard the familiar sounds in the general office that told them the others had arrived. Carston picked up a bunch of folders and suddenly became brisk.

"OK. Let's get some work done," he said.

In the outer office. Bellman and Thom were looking over Fraser's shoulder at his copy of the *Sun* and, to Carston's astonishment, Spurle was reading the *Guardian*. They all looked up.

"Mornin sir, mornin sarge, mornin sarge," said Fraser.

Carston looked quickly at him but, despite the grin on Thom's face, there seemed to be no ironic intent in Fraser's tone or expression.

"OK, enough of the niceties," said Carston. "It's like a bloody library in here. What're you doing with the *Guardian*, Spurle?"

"Betterin myself, sir," replied Spurle, just managing to keep the sarcasm muted.

"'Bout bloody time," said Fraser.

"Better'n that crap you're readin."

"What's the situation with the outboards?" asked Carston.

One by one, they listed the state of their various investigations. Spurle and Thom had been talking to the staff in two small workshops down by the canal, trying to trace sixty outboard motors which had disappeared from a nearby warehouse. They were only halfway through their list and had so far made no progress. Bellman was working his way through the files of a chemist's shop in Ashby Road looking for discrepancies that would confirm that the shop's owner had been handing out prescribed drugs without authorization, and Fraser was ready to write up a report about a garage which had been fiddling MOT certificates undetected for eight years. None of them described what they were doing with much enthusiasm. When the phone rang, it was something of a relief. Ross picked it up and listened as the team droned on with their reports. There was a lull when he put back the receiver.

"Fiscal's office," he said. "Some guy's died up at the hospital. Needs checking out."

Carston nodded. It was probably a routine affair. Any unexpected death or death associated with a particular medical procedure had to be reported to the Procurator Fiscal and investigated. Usually, it was just for the record and helped to make sure that everything at the hospital was working as it should. In Carston's experience, none of the reports ever amounted to anything. It seemed just right for McNeil's first job as a sergeant.

"OK," he said. "Julie, get on up there. See what it's all about. Take Fraser with you."

Fraser was on his feet immediately, grabbing his jacket and making for the door. McNeil tapped her pocket to make sure she had her notebook and went after him. At the door, Fraser stood aside.

"After you, sarge," he said with a huge smile.

Carston looked hard at him again but there still seemed to be no edge to his voice. He gave every impression that he was pleased to be going with her and unfazed by the fact that she outranked him. Spurle scowled and shook his head as the door closed behind them.

"Smarmy bastard," he said.

****

There were no real slums in Cairnburgh but the houses along the canal and especially around the area of the swing bridge almost qualified. Many of them were student flats and bedsits and some had been squats for longer than anyone could remember. The man who spent so much of his time watching Sandra Scott lived in a single room in one of the seediest tenements of Caledonian Road. His bed was a mattress lying against one wall. Beside it were a lamp, a clock radio and a television set. There were no chairs or table but a tall stool was pushed against a cooker in one corner. The walls were covered in dark green wallpaper patterned with small red flowers and textured by bubbles and ripples in the many damp patches. The single window was covered with a black roller blind.

He was sitting on the mattress, his back against the wall. Beside him, a very old copy of Penthouse lay open at a shot of an oriental girl on hands and knees on a white rug, her buttocks towards the camera and her head turned to look coyly back over her shoulder. The man wasn't looking at the magazine. He'd had it for years and hardly needed to open it to visualize the women, their poses and their apparent invitations. They lived in a world of challenging sexuality which he'd never entered.

He was twenty-four years old, had never had a girl-friend and was still a virgin. Strict, loveless parents and his own shyness had kept him off the streets where his contemporaries, from the age of eleven onwards, had experimented with one another's bodies, aping the antics of the heaving actors on every screen they looked at. The more he'd looked to the soft porn magazines for his pleasure, the further he'd moved from any chance of real involvement. They offered him stunningly beautiful women with gorgeous bodies who were willing to submit to anything. They lay around on fur, silk and satin, permanently ready to be taken and molested. The surroundings, whether boudoirs or hayricks, were closed to everyone but the woman and her watcher. Nothing in the world outside his room could match the riches they brought him.

The women he saw and heard in the streets were flawed, wore ugly, bulky clothes, had rasping accents. He could conceive of no way in which their bodies could unfold the damp treasures or their eyes express the heavy-lidded compliance of the goddesses in his photographs. On pavements and in public transport, he always stayed well away from them, anxious to keep his own space intact. If a bus was too crowded for him to avoid contact, he stayed off it and walked. Women were at once fearsome and compelling. They fascinated him, excited him and yet, when he got near to them, he couldn't speak, was acutely self-aware and longed for the passive company of his paper harem.

His obsession with Scott began when he first saw her walk across her room with no clothes on. Her movements had been natural, sexless and called for no response. Like the women in the photographs, she was displaying herself for him and all he had to do was watch. From that moment, the sight of her, clothed or naked, had always reproduced the same possessive thrill. The days when he had had to work so hard with his magazines to produce an erection were over. In a bizarre way, he was in love. But it was the same sort of emotion that tied him to the photographs. There was no need for Scott to do anything other than be herself. They were connected by his gaze, suspended in a visual embrace that would never be spoiled by actual contact. He was happy to have found her but greedy to have more of her.

He pushed the magazine away from him, closed his eyes and called up the image of Scott lying in her bedroom. Very soon, his breathing had changed and his fist was pumping more quickly.

****

Five students trooped out of Leith's room, gulping gratefully at the stale air in the corridor after an hour of medieval history and armpits. Leith looked at his watch, slid his tutorial notes into a green folder, dropped it into its place in his filing cabinet and picked up the agenda for that afternoon's departmental meeting. It was the first under Carlyle's chairmanship and Leith was eager to make his mark. He went out, locking the door behind him and hurried down the stairs.

16

When he arrived, Carlyle had already started reading out the latest batch of directives from the administration. They were accepted in relative silence and various individuals were delegated to take care of any matters arising from them which were specific to the department's work. Attention then turned to the cases of some students deemed to be "at risk". The expression referred not to any life or identity threatening condition but to the fact that by failing to hand in pieces of work which were due they were in danger of losing marks.

"Ferguson," said Leith, right away. "Hasn't been to a tutorial for three weeks."

"Which Ferguson's that?" asked Carlyle.

"I don't know his other name. First year. In my literature group."

"Gregor," said Ritchie, his triangles already well advanced.

"Didn't show much interest when he did come," Leith went on. "Not exactly enthusiastic."

"Typical larval stagnation," commented Miller. Leith nodded in agreement. 'Larval' was an affectation that amused rather than irritated his colleagues. He'd always defined first and second year students as larvae, and honors students as pupae. When they graduated, they evolved into glittering imagos.

"No, it's not that," said Ritchie, anxious to defend the larva in question. "He's been going home every weekend. His mother's been sick and he's just having trouble balancing things."

"He knows the rules," insisted Leith. "And he's already two essays behind."

"He'll go to hell," muttered McChaddie.

Ritchie started on another triangle.

"Anybody had any trouble with Sandra Scott?" asked Miller. Christie looked up quickly.

"Why?"

"Extraordinary girl. Wrote me a piece about the revolution claiming it failed because it was patriarchal. 'Gender colonization', she called it. Astonishing."

"What's up with that?" asked McChaddie.

"Well, it's rather undisciplined, that's all. I just wondered if…"

"Undisciplined? Christ, at least she's thinking. We should give her a degree right now."

The exchange led them into irrelevant asides about the quality of the intake in recent years and the deplorable failings of secondary education. Fortunately, they were interrupted by a timid knock on the door and the departmental secretary came in. She spoke quietly to Carlyle who got up, excused himself and followed her out. The discussion continued and, when he came back, had progressed to arguments about whether marks should be awarded as grades, letters or percentages. Christie was saying "Take three marks like, say ... B double plus, B minus and C plus. What on earth do they average out at?"

"Fifty-six point three per cent," said Miller.

"Point seven," said Leith.

Some of the others made scornful, dismissive noises and then there was a sudden silence. Carlyle was sitting quietly in his chair. The expression on his face and the stillness with which he held himself told them that something was wrong. He looked round at all their faces.

"We've just had word from the hospital," he said. "I'm afraid Alistair died last night."

"Oh dear," said Leith. "Poor man."

His anxiety not to reveal that he'd already heard the news made the words come too quickly. His timing went unnoticed by the rest of them, however, intent as they were on making sure their own reactions were appropriate. Christie's face was a blank. He held himself as still as possible, waiting for someone else to fill the gap. Ritchie shook his head and gave a single click with his tongue. Carlyle kept his head down, fixing unseeing eyes on the heap of papers before him. The others sniffed, tapped pencils on the table, clicked biros. They were all used to Hayne's absences and knew that he'd actually suffered a lot of pain over the past few years, but first reports had suggested that his most recent operation had been a success.

"I think in the circumstances we ought to close the meeting to give us all time to come to terms with the news," said Carlyle. "It will obviously have repercussions that we can't deal with for the moment and I'm sure we all need to reflect a little before we do anything else."

There were little nods all round and they began to shuffle together the various papers which were spread in front of them.

"How did he die?" asked Ritchie.

"They didn't give any details. Heart failure of some sort. It was sudden. Apparently, he wouldn't have suffered."

"Pity," said Christie, but so low that no one heard him.

As they stood and made their silent way to their own rooms, most of them experienced a similar reaction. Hayne hadn't been a popular departmental head. He'd smiled, been on first name terms with everyone, seemed to agree with the consensus at meetings and then produced minutes which contradicted directly the things which had been decided. His position as head of department gave him a certain power when promotions were being considered and so those who recognized their dependence on him said nothing. But he had very few actual friends and in the silence which greeted the news of his disappearance there was more satisfaction than grief.

Carlyle walked along the corridor to the departmental office, left his files with one of the secretaries and let himself into Hayne's room. He shut the door behind him and looked round. There were books, filing cabinets, tidy heaps of paper, minutes of various meetings stacked in identifiable piles, but nothing remotely personal. There were no pictures on the walls, no ornaments, not even a small family snap on the window ledge.

Lying open on the desk, ready for the return which would not now happen, was a paper Hayne had been preparing for a meeting of the full Finance and Estates Committee. Its title, picked out in his usual yellow highlighter pen, was 'Increased Periodicity of Resource Rationalization'. Carlyle knew that he'd been working on a scheme to identify members of staff who might be persuaded to take early retirement to help the university's budgetary shortfall. The proposals in the paper all came out of the friendly chats he'd had with unsuspecting colleagues in corridors and the senior common room. He'd used these confidences to compile an impressive dossier of 'proofs', as he'd called them, that considerable savings were possible on academic salaries.

Carlyle turned the pages, shaking his head at the statistics and bullet points that Hayne found so compelling and reading the occasional summary at the end of each section. It was soulless stuff, driving with cold partiality over the ambitions and achievements of his colleagues. At last, he picked it up and stuffed it into his briefcase. It would be very satisfying to feed it page by page into the shredder.

# Chapter Three

McNeil thought that the drifts of tulips that bordered the main drive into the Bartholomew Memorial hospital were over the top. They looked good against the pink granite facings of the central buildings and the grey concrete of the newer blocks but she reckoned that, for places full of pain and dying, their affirmation of spring and renewal was a bit insensitive. To her slight surprise, Fraser didn't agree.

"Nah, sarge. It's hope, isn't it?" he said. "Folk wants to think things is normal. They dinna want remindin o' their problems. Tulips is cheerful, bucks 'em up."

"I s'pose you're right," said McNeil, pulling the car into the visitors' car park and starting the crawl along the ranks to look for a gap. "Didn't realize you were such an optimist."

"Aye, there's a lot about me that nob'dy kens," Fraser said. The quietness of his tone made McNeil look at him and she saw that his face had clouded briefly. He caught her look and was immediately embarrassed, adding with a grin, "No that there's much to ken, like".

Fraser worked out. His fair hair and red cheeks made him look younger than his twenty-eight years but, in shirt sleeves, the size of his chest and arms was frightening. He'd been born and brought up in Cairnburgh, was married to Janice, a local lass and, incongruously, they were both passionate Francophiles. The little insight into his psyche he'd just offered was the first McNeil remembered but she'd already noticed that there was something different about him this morning. In the car on the way over, he'd been friendly and somehow respectful—and he wasn't taking the piss either. He hadn't even spoken any French, which was in itself unusual since he was always irritating everybody by sprinkling his sentences with *"n'est-ce pas?"* and *"voilà"*. It made her wary; something was going on and she wanted to be ready for it when it appeared.

Inside, they identified themselves at reception and were sent through to an office at one end of the entrance hall. The woman who greeted them was head of Public Relations, one of the new specializations that proved that NHS Trust hospitals were more than just hotels for sick people.

"Moira Blantyre," she said, her arm angled towards McNeil. Her fair hair, discreetly tinted, was cut in a short, neat style that looked expensive to maintain. She had cool, green eyes made darker by the paleness of her skin. At the corners of her lips were the beginnings of tiny creases, which were accentuated by her smile. She was wearing a charcoal grey suit over a cream blouse. Around her neck, a peach-colored silk scarf took the edge off any formality. McNeil found her fascinating. She introduced herself and Fraser and listened as Blantyre went through what was obviously a prepared statement of the facts. Her voice was low and cultured and slid smoothly over the many convoluted medical expressions that were essential to her explanation of Professor Hayne's death. Fraser pretended to take notes and hoped that McNeil wouldn't ask for them afterwards.

"There's little doubt in my mind that we'll find it was due to natural causes," Blantyre was saying, "but the guidelines are clear and it's in all our interests to investigate any alternative possibilities."

"Yes, we don't want any nasty litigation jumping out at us later on, do we?" said McNeil, with a smile.

Her intention was mischievous, an attempt to ripple the surface. It failed. Blantyre nodded agreement.

"Indeed. It's all anyone seems to think about nowadays. But if things do go wrong—and, as I said, I'm sure in this case they didn't—it means that one or more individuals have let themselves and the institution down. That's much more serious than any lawsuit."

"Yes. Still, we're not talking lawsuits here, are we?"

"No, of course not. It's the statutory reporting of a death under medical care."

"What they used to call anesthetic deaths," said McNeil.

"Yes," said Blantyre brightly. "Much to the disgust of the anesthetists. Mind you, I'm not sure I'm all that fond of the new term, 'medical mishaps'. Still makes it sound as if someone's been careless."

She took a paper from her desk and handed it to McNeil.

"The standard questionnaire. It's been signed by the surgeon and the anesthetist. You'll want to talk to them I imagine."

"Yes," said McNeil, feeling slightly uncomfortable with the way Blantyre seemed to be calling all the shots. "And maybe some of the others involved."

"Of course. I've checked the rotas; the same theatre staff are on duty this morning. Shall we go?"

She was already at the door. There was no impression that they were being rushed and yet McNeil felt the need to establish some sort of control. Already, she'd had the niggling feeling that Carston had only given her the job because it was routine. All she had to do was follow standard procedures, go through the motions and tie it all up. She didn't mind that; somebody had to do it and it was an early display of his faith in her. But this was her first job as a sergeant. She was proud of her promotion and she could do without Boadicea here taking charge.

"Before we go," she said, "I'd like to talk a bit more about the hospital set-up."

There was the briefest of hesitations, enough to convince her that she'd scored a small point. She had to be quick to notice it, though, because Blantyre was smiling again and back at her desk, ready to accommodate any of their whims.

"Fire away," she said.

"We're lucky here, aren't we?" said McNeil.

Blantyre waited for an explanation.

"I've always thought so anyway," McNeil went on. "A wee place like Cairnburgh, Aberdeen just up the road, and yet we've got surgeons and equipment and all sorts."

"Yes, you're right," said Blantyre. "Not many towns this size have their own thoracic surgery facilities. Mostly they're only geared up for extreme emergencies." Her smile slipped as she continued. "Which makes the latest attempts to threaten the department particularly distressing."

"Threaten?" said McNeil.

Blantyre tossed her head dismissively.

22

"Oh, funding nonsense from the Council. Some of the local bigwigs want to close it. They're saying we should concentrate on fewer specializations, leave the rest to Aberdeen Royal Infirmary. But we've got the figures. I'm sure we'll be able to make them rethink. We've had terrific results over the years, supplemented Aberdeen very well. Took some of the pressure off them really. We share some of their staff of course."

"Share?"

"Yes. Lots of their consultants come here for a day, a week, sometimes longer."

"What for?"

Blantyre smiled.

"Efficiency of resource allocation, the board calls it. We've got the best that money can buy. Research facilities at the university, access to their new medical institute, all the…"

"Sounds as if you're just one of their annexes," interrupted McNeil, tiring of the promotional pitch.

Blantyre was unshakeable; the smile just radiated more warmth.

"No, no. The initial finance was all generated here. There were a few legacies to equip the first theatres, then the government chipped in a little and, well, we haven't looked back."

"You don't find yourselves overstretched?"

"Overstretched?"

"I don't know, short of back-up."

Blantyre saw where McNeil was heading. Her smile veered towards indulgence.

"Never," she said. "Double redundancy's built into all our systems. We never undertake any operation unless we know that everything's fully covered."

"So Professor Hayne's death must be a bit of a worry."

Indulgence gave way to concern.

"Patients die, sergeant. You never get used to it but it happens every day. The professor's death is sad but it's not a worry."

"It is for him," said Fraser, surprising both the women. He felt sidelined and just wanted to establish his presence. The expression on McNeil's face and the strain in Blantyre's smile told him that his intervention hadn't been all that brilliant.

"I know it's unpopular," said Blantyre, "but our reorganization of management procedures has made a marked difference to every aspect of our work. We've always had wonderful, dedicated medical staff; now we've got an administrative structure that helps to maximize their effectiveness. The Council are getting real value for money."

It was the sort of remark McNeil was used to hearing from people like Superintendent Ridley at Burns Road. The hospital, the police, everybody nowadays talked as if they were running a private company. People clawing their way up seemed to pay more attention to playing politics than doing the job. Maybe things worked better that way; get your managers right and everything's ace. She wasn't convinced.

They spoke some more about the hospital and its procedures but nothing of much relevance to their case surfaced. In fact, Blantyre was so confident of the Bartholomew's excellence in every respect that McNeil began to wonder whether patients needed to pass an exam or a fitness test before they were admitted.

At last they were taken to a small room near the department of anesthetics which had been cleared for them to use for their interviews. Blantyre left them to it while she went to organize their various visitors. The first was a youngish man who was obviously glad of the chance to sit down. He was the resident doctor who'd been called when the death had been discovered.

"Not much I can tell you," he said before they'd even asked anything. "I filled in the F89 and sent it off. The Procurator Fiscal's ordered a PM. Your pathologist'll be doing it. No point in me trying to guess what he'll say."

"Just tell us what you found though," said McNeil

The man reached up with his left hand and massaged the muscles at the back of his neck.

"I was called to certify the death. I looked for pulse, respiration, heart, pupil reflexes, trucking, all the usual."

"Trucking?" asked McNeil

"Yes, when the red blood cells stick together in the arteries at the back of the eye."

"Oh."

"Didn't take long. He'd obviously been dead for … well a couple of hours anyway. Too close to the operation for me to issue a death certificate. I referred it to the Fiscal."

"Was there anything … well … unusual?"

The massaging stopped as he shook his head.

24

"Not particularly. Standard procedure. If a patient dies after an operation like that, we need to know why. You know, in case of criminality, negligence—stuff like that. Your guy'll do a complete head to toe autopsy and he'll have a very close look around the aorta and the abdomen to see what the surgeon's been up to. If anything's gone wrong, he'll want to know about it so he doesn't do it again."

"So something could have gone wrong?" asked McNeil.

He shrugged.

"Course it could."

"Bloody hell," said Fraser. "Bit hit an' miss, isn't it?"

The doctor sighed.

"There won't be anything, but it has to be checked out."

They talked some more about the hospital's systems but although the doctor wanted to be helpful, he couldn't offer much more than generalizations and he refused to speculate about any aspect of Hayne's operation and death. The same was true of the nurses, the surgeon and the anesthetist they spoke to. They were all careful to stress that they worked according to regulations and techniques that had been very carefully evolved to minimize risk to patients. During premedication, the operation itself and the period in the Intensive Therapy and High Dependency Units, they'd each followed the appropriate procedures. There was never any improvisation or short cutting. They all recognized that no activity was foolproof, but the rules they followed were designed to identify potential errors and eliminate them instantly.

It was nearly midday when they eventually said their good-byes to Blantyre at the main entrance.

"What d'you reckon, sarge?" asked Fraser as they walked through the sunshine towards the car.

"Don't see any problem," replied McNeil "He was just unlucky."

"Aye. Don't take no chances, do they?"

"Can't afford to."

"It's the nurses I admire most."

McNeil looked up at him.

"Why?"

"Just wee lassies like that. And the jobs they do: cleanin up shite, feedin folk, lookin after 'em. They're like everybody's mothers."

"Aye. It's hard work."

They'd reached the car and, as Fraser opened the passenger door and slid his huge body into the front seat, he asked, "Did you ever think o' doin nursin?"

McNeil clicked on her seat belt.

"Never."

Fraser was silent and just nodded his head slightly to acknowledge her reply. Then, as she started to pull out of the parking space, he said, "D'you think the polis is a carin profession?"

It was so unlike anything she'd heard him say before that she stopped the car again.

"What?"

"I mean, you're a woman. You joined up. People like me an' Spurley, it's different."

McNeil was defensive, ready for the attack that seemed to have been in preparation since they'd left the station. She drove on.

"Why?"

"We ken there's goin to be aggro an' that. But lassies like yourself, you shouldna be expected to handle that sort o' stuff."

"Don't worry about me, Fraser," she said. "I can hack it."

"Aye, aye, I ken. But it's the carin bit I was on about."

Once again, his tone and the earnestness of his expression threw her. This was familiar territory but somehow he seemed to be on a different tack. She forced herself to keep silent and listened as he began to try to define what he saw as the basic differences between male and female police officers. Some of it was very surprising.

****

Sandra Scott sat just inside the door of the university's Liberal Arts building re-reading her essay on the *Chanson de Roland* to try to prepare her answers to the criticisms she knew were bound to come. Christie had given her a B--(+) for it, which told her nothing, and his only written comment was 'Cognitively demulcent' in one of the margins beside her analysis of the symbolism of Roland's sword and horn. She'd looked up the words, found that they approximated to 'mind-numbing' and secretly agreed with the assessment. But for different reasons from those which had inspired Christie.

26

She'd been brought up in Fraserburgh. Her father was a trawlerman and her mother worked at the local Presto's supermarket; the symbolic significance of medieval fighting gear had never been an issue in their house. But they were proud of her getting to the university and she was desperate for access to a wider world. So she accepted the rules of the game and pretended that abstract speculations really did belong in the same reality as the prices her mother punched into her checkout register.

She was just twenty-one but sometimes felt a lot older. Her skin was fair, her eyes blue and her hair the color of dark copper. She wore jeans from Next, a Monsoon tee-shirt and a loose, check jacket she'd bought at Gap in Glasgow. As she read, the fingers of her left hand twisted a lock of hair back and forth, drawing it occasionally across her lips. A previous boy-friend who'd studied psychology had told her that the gesture was a substitute for masturbation. She told him that that was more than he was. The conversation stalled and the relationship soured.

A door banging upstairs made her jump. She heard footsteps clicking along a corridor and down the stairs. The person was hurrying and, under the tapping of the heels, Scott could hear another noise. It got louder as the woman approached. She was saying 'no, no' over and over again, sometimes adding 'oh please, no' and she was crying. A door opened and a man's voice called 'Marianne, Marianne', which just made the footsteps quicken and the crying increase in volume as if the woman wanted to drown out the calling. At last, she turned the corner and ran past the place where Scott was sitting. She had oriental features and her right hand was clamped on the top of her head as if to hold in some pressure. She didn't look at Scott but the extent of her distress was obvious from the way she moved and from the sounds she made. She rushed through the outside door, letting it swing shut behind her and Scott heard her footsteps quicken again as she began running away from the building.

She felt helpless. It was just another refusal, another difference of opinion between lovers. Just one of the stories going on around her in the streets and houses all the time. The oriental Marianne was distraught, carrying away a pain which swamped everything else, but there was nothing unique about it. It was her variant of a pain that was repeated daily and nightly all over the campus. Part of Scott's maturity came from her ability to see people and their problems in a fairly broad context. She knew that, eventually, Marianne would be alright and that, anyway, her tiff with whoever he was ranked pretty low on the misery scale. All the same, the spectacle of anyone's distress was disturbing and she wished that it hadn't happened.

At five past three, she shoved the essay back into her bag and went up to knock on Christie's door. He opened it and stood aside to let her in. As she stepped into the room, he put his right hand on her shoulder and waved the other at a chair beside his desk. She sat down, her bag in her lap. He sat opposite her, unbuttoned his waistcoat and leaned back in his creaky chair.

"Well, Sandra, this essay then," he said, his eyes fixed on her face and his mouth lifting into what she supposed was a smile. She waited.

"Any thoughts?" he asked.

"What about?"

"Well, the mark I gave you."

She took the essay out and looked at it again. She suspected that Christie was not the towering intellect he supposed himself to be, but the whole situation made her nervous. It was designed to make her a sort of supplicant and him an adjudicator. The old title of dominie came into her head with all its associations of dominion and domination. That was it; some of the lecturers still behaved as if they belonged to some chosen elite and, with the weight of tradition behind them, they somehow got away with it. She was on the defensive before they'd even got going.

"I don't know what it means. I wondered if you could, well, explain it."

Christie's condescension pulled the corners of his smile a little wider as he leaned forward and his chair creaked again. He tried to make his tone light and jokey. "Well, if A's at the top and C's at the bottom, that puts B in the middle by my reckoning."

"Supercilious bastard," she thought, but said, "It's the double minus brackets plus that's confusing."

The smile slipped slowly away.

"OK, let's break it down, then. B minus is a bit less than B, double minus a bit less again. The plus brings it back up a bit, but the brackets serve to … well, let's say to attenuate that resurgence. All in all, you're marginally ahead of a C double plus brackets minus. That's just in the two two category."

It was crap and it was insulting but Scott had to put up with it. He made the rules.

"Can you tell me ... well, where I went wrong?"

"You mustn't think of it in those terms," he said. "It's all very subjective, after all. Personally, I think you're capable of much better marks." He pointed at the essay. "This time, it just didn't quite cohere."

"In what way?"

"Well, I'm not sure that you make a sufficient distinction between fiction and historical truth."

Scott was surprised. She looked down at the top page of the essay. Its opening words were "Any consideration of the story of Roland's campaign in the Pyrenees must take account of the absence of any reliable historical documentation. For that reason, this study will concentrate exclusively on its fictional representation." She looked up at Christie again. He was still talking.

"...one line, that's all we have. In Einhard's life of Charlemagne. It just gives Roland's Frankish name, Hruodlandus, tells us he's a prefect and..."

She wondered if he'd actually read the essay. What he was talking about was stuff he'd already droned out at them in his lectures; it had no relevance to the line she'd taken. She waited for a pause, then said, "I seem to have got the wrong idea about the symbolism, too."

He stopped. pondered for a moment, then held out his hand for the essay. She handed it across, pointing to the marginal note "cognitively demulcent", and saw his smile reform in appreciation of what he obviously thought was a *bon mot*. He skimmed quickly over her words, then handed the paper back to her.

"Just think. In all these romances, with their gentil parfit knights, chaste and effectively impotent, what's the power of the sword? What does it mean?"

She looked at him to see if it was a genuine question. It wasn't. He was launched on another mini-lecture.

"The only implement with which to imprint themselves on their world. And not just in the Middle Ages. Think of *Manon Lescaut*. Des Grieux breaking his sword when Manon has died. Why? To dig her grave, to bury her. In the sand. Now, if you wanted to dig a hole in loose sand, would you use a sword? Not exactly a practical proposition, is it? No. The broken sword is literal impotence, the disabling of the phallus."

It always came back to this eventually. Before she'd been stuck with any of his classes, Scott had heard the stories about him. He was a groper, little better than a dirty old man who used his learning like a flasher's mac.

"...and with the sword personalized as Durandel and the horn as Oliphant, the specific identification of symbol and function is inescapable. I don't want to diminish the stature of the hero or the resonance of the epic in any way, but the fact that the climax occurs as Roland mounts a rearguard action in the narrow Roncesvalles Pass ... well, it's hardly insignificant, is it? You see, it's not just his blood that bursts out of his temples when he sounds Oliphant, it's his actual essence."

It was laughable really. According to Christie, European literature was awash with semen. The tears of the romantics were nothing less than premature ejaculations, the sensibility of the eighteenth century one long nocturnal emission. One of his standard lectures was based on the fact that, in *Dombey and Son*, Florence Dombey cries 88 times—proof, according to him, of Dickens's repressed sexuality. Even when he was let loose outside his own specialization, he brought his preconceptions and obsessions with him.

Scott knew better than to complain or interrupt. She listened to the lecture and waited. Friends had told her that he was a sucker for tears but she was more angry than upset and the thought of the comforts he might offer were enough to put permanent clamps on her tear-ducts. The ordeal ended when he looked at his watch and said, "Welfare and Academic Services Committee, I'm afraid. Four o'clock. I'll have to be off."

She stood up and hitched her jacket higher on her shoulders. The meeting had taught her nothing. Christie came round the desk and stood by the door. He reached across and brushed at the back of her jacket.

"You've creased it," he said. "Don't want to spoil it, do you?"

She busied herself putting the essay back into her bag as his hand stopped the brushing movements and rested in the small of her back.

"Now, the next essay, the one on Ronsard," he said, his hand still pressed against her. "Come and see me before you start it. I can maybe suggest a structure, give you a few notes."

His hand moved up to her shoulder, its pressure modeling the curve of her back.

"Don't worry about it, Sandra," he said, his face close to hers. "We'll get those marks up for you."

She nodded to hide a little shudder that went through her and said, "Thank you". He smiled but the pressure of his fingers at the side of her neck and the implication behind his words prevented her from smiling back.

****

Carston was bending perilously close to a clump of nettles. He was holding a sort of hoop, over which had been stretched a skin of material, white on one side, silver on the other.

"Angle it up a bit," said Kath, who was on the path bending over her camera tripod.

Carston looked at the side of the gravestone onto which he was supposed to be reflecting the evening light. As he turned the hoop, he saw how the shadows thrown by the stone's carvings lost a little of their depth.

"That's it. Hold it there," said Kath as she began to adjust her exposure time and aperture setting.

"Hurry up, there's a bloody great bunch of nettles here. I'm going to fall into it if…"

"Shut up, Jack," said Kath. "This is art, remember."

"Huh, so's Tracey Emin."

Carston wasn't quite sure why he'd said that but Kath was too wrapped up in her calculations to register it anyway. She looked up, pressed the shutter, changed the aperture twice more and took two more shots.

"OK," she said, picking up the tripod and lifting it onto her left shoulder. She looked at the sky. It was well past nine o'clock but the sun hadn't yet set. The air still seemed saturated with the colors of the evening. Her passion for photography had begun in Scotland and had made her even more receptive to the delicious quality of the light of the north east. Taking shots of the gravestones as the apricot glow slanted across them was the latest attempt to catch something of Cairnburgh's character. But they'd been here since seven and Jack had been very patient.

"OK," she said. "Let's go and have a drink."

Carston took the tripod and put his free arm round her as they walked on through the avenue of stones. The cemetery was well kept, with paths of pink granite chips winding through its plots. Rowan trees, sycamores and even elms were everywhere and the dead lay untroubled by centuries that had long since discarded the simple truths and faiths that had been carved on their tombs.

"Look at that," said Carston, pointing to a monumental edifice at the corner of two paths. "You could house a single parent in that."

Kath smiled. It was true that some of the constructions were real Gothic fancies; pillars, columns, angels and cherubs reared up from the grass, launch pads for the souls of folk like "Captain James Ogilvie Reid, Born 1856, Lost at Sea 1902", "William George Gordon Murray, Granite Merchant, 1870-1943" and "The Reverent Charles Baxter Munro, Called to his Maker 5 April 1772". There were fish merchants, ecclesiasticals, soldiers, farmers and a surprising number of Italians. Generations seemed to have been piled one on top of another since the seventeenth century and, on some stones, despite an already long list of dead husbands, wives, parents and children, blank spaces revealed that there were plenty more to come. Or rather, to go.

Carston had never been religious and found the whole notion of the afterlife an irritating betrayal of normal living. The structures around them were interesting, but they were also a sort of ransom paid to dying, so many attempts somehow to make the process more noble. For Carston they were way over the top as gateways from this life to a place that, if it existed, would be chock-full of American evangelists.

But the place was peaceful and, paradoxically, it was difficult to think negative thoughts as they strolled on. They spoke little until they left by the main gate and began the climb up the hill to their own street, then Kath put her arm through his and said, "How's Alex been recently?"

It seemed an innocent enough question but Carston sensed some concern inside it. The Crombies were near neighbors. Carston played golf with Alex and Kath sometimes went into town with his wife, Jennie. They weren't close but they were friends.

"Alex Crombie?" said Carston, knowing that's who she meant but wanting her to say more.

"Yes," said Kath. "Has he been…" She stopped as she looked for words. "Well … normal?" she finished, lamely.

Carston thought for a moment.

"As far as I can tell, yes. Why?"

Kath shook her head.

"It's just… I saw Jennie earlier in the week. She's… They're…"

This was unusual. Kath was rarely at a loss for words. Nothing ever embarrassed her and yet she was obviously having difficulty finding what she wanted to say. Carston waited. After a short silence, she went on, "D'you think he hits her?"

Carston's instinct was to dismiss the suggestion right away. He knew Crombie well enough and didn't think he was the violent type. But his desk drawers were filled with reports of other peace-loving monsters.

"I'd be surprised if he did," he said. "Why? Has she said something?"

Kath shook her head.

"Not really. Well, not directly anyway. But there's something going on. They're not happy."

"Yes, I know that. But it's hardly GBH, is it? I mean, it's been going on for ages. That bloody job of his…"

"Yes."

Crombie worked offshore and led the pendulum life of two weeks on and two weeks off.

"Did she have any … you know, marks on her or anything?"

Kath shook her head again.

"No. She was just … miserable. Asking strange things."

"Like?"

"Oh, about you. How you cope with the violence you have to handle in your work, how often we have rows, stuff like that."

It didn't sound very significant and, as they walked on, they tried to tease out the signs that their neighbors had real troubles. Apart from the one conversation that Kath had had with Jennie, though, there was nothing. As they turned into their street, Kath said, "See what you can find out, Jack, will you? I don't mean investigate or anything like that. Just talk to him when you play golf, see what's going on."

33

"Is it any of our business, love?"

"It is if he's battering her."

Carston agreed with her but knew that it wasn't that simple. He'd do as she asked but only if he saw the right opening.

They heard their phone ringing as they went through the gate into the front garden. Carston hurried to open the door and pick it up. It was McNeil.

"Sorry to bother you at home, sir," she said. "But this hospital thing, Professor Hayne. It's not as straightforward as we thought."

"Oh?"

"No. I was just in here typing up my report on today's visit and they put a call through from the pathology lab. It's not right. And it seems like it's more than negligence."

"What d'you mean?"

"Well, it's not just the one thing."

"Julie, I expect this sort of roundabout stuff from dumbos like Fraser and Spurle but I appreciate my sergeants being a bit straighter. What's up?"

"Sorry, sir. It … it seems the sutures the surgeon used to sew up his aorta may have given way. That would've killed him by itself. But he's also had an overdose of morphine. The lab says that would've been fatal too."

Carston whistled.

"Yes, sir. Either one could've just been a mistake, but both of them happening together … well, bit too much of a coincidence. Somebody meant it."

Carston no longer minded the call. Working his way through intrigue was an excellent antidote to the job's paper rituals.

"So there are two possible causes of death. Did the lab say which one's the more likely?"

"No, sir. Either one could've done it. And with the sutures thing being down to the surgeon and the overdose to the anesthetist, it all looks a wee bit suspect."

Carston smiled at the understatement.

"OK, Julie," he said. "Thanks for ringing. Get things set up for tomorrow. The lab report, yours and anything you can on Professor Hayne. We'll get onto it first thing."

He rang off and began the tuneless humming that told Kath he was feeling good.

# Chapter Four

It's not about sex, it's about power," said Scott.

"Oh come on, Sandra. It's not a bloody tutorial," said Strachan. He was lying on her bed. She'd just pulled herself away from him and gone to sit in a chair at the window.

"I mean, it, Tom."

"I know you do. That's the bloody trouble. But it's... You're wrong. For Christ's sake, I love you. Don't you believe me?"

She looked out at the trees and shrugged her shoulders.

"Oh, great. Thanks. I'm a liar now, am I?" said Strachan.

"No, Tom. I ... I know you mean it. But ... I don't see why that changes anything."

He pushed himself off the bed and came to stand behind her. He kissed the top of her head and let his hands drop over her shoulders onto her breasts.

"It's part of loving you. If you love somebody, you want them."

"Why?"

"What d'you mean, why? 'cause you drive me bloody crazy, that's why? You don't know how sexy you are."

She smiled and put her hands over his.

"No, you're right. I don't."

Strachan kneeled on the floor beside her and pushed her skirt up to lay his head across the top of her bare thighs. He let his lips nibble at her as he said, "You still fancy me, don't you?"

Her fingers smoothed over his hair.

"Yes."

"Well then."

She let him nuzzle higher and looked out at the evening. It was well past ten but there was still no darkness in the sky. She began to feel the softness coming back into her and the inclination to open herself for him.

"There's a group in the States, you know, men and women," she said, "who're going to stay virgins until after they're married. They've started a campaign. Guess what it's called?"

"Campaign for Sad Bastards," mumbled Strachan, his tongue and lips too busy to form the words clearly.

"No. 'True Love Waits'. See? If you really loved me, you wouldn't want to fuck me."

But she didn't protest as he persisted and her pleasure warmed her again.

It was an argument they'd had many times. Unusually, Scott was still a virgin. In her early teens, under the pressure of her peers, she'd tried not to be, but it had never happened. Now, she put a greater value on herself and took a tiny satisfaction at the thought that she was still intact. However much Strachan (and others before him) protested, virginity was a power issue. It wasn't just a physical condition; it represented more. It was something you "lost", something which was "taken" from you. A trophy. Her sexual hunger was often as great as Strachan's and it was sometimes difficult to refuse him. So far, though, she'd managed to and they were still together. She wasn't all that sure she wanted to wait until after she was married. It made sense to get some practical experience before you tied yourself up to someone who might prove to be nightmarish in bed. And yet she knew that, once she'd given away such a fundamental part of her self, she couldn't get it back and it made her hesitate.

But now, Strachan's tongue was driving the thoughts out of her. Her breathing was long, slow and heavy, cut across with occasional little gasps as Strachan found the places and rhythms that jolted extra pleasures up through her. As her right hand continued to stroke his hair, she lifted her left to brush lightly back and forth over her breast.

The dark eyes of the man in the tree watched her lean back and pull Strachan's head more tightly into her.

\*\*\*\*

36

The next morning, Fraser was the last to arrive in the squad room. As he crossed to his desk and threw his paper onto it, Spurle noticed that he was limping.

"What's wrong with your leg?"

"Nothin."

"Why're you limpin, then?"

Fraser sat down, opened his paper and mumbled, "Reflexology".

"What?" said Spurle, who genuinely hadn't heard.

"Reflexology, OK?" said Fraser, challenging Spurle to take issue with him.

Nobody ever took issue with Fraser.

"OK," said Spurle, raising a hand to show his acceptance. Bellman and Thom, both intrigued by the little exchange, waited for further explanation. When Spurle stuck his nose back into his *Guardian*, Thom risked asking, "What is it, Fraz?"

"What?"

"Reflexology."

"Pressure points on your feet," said Fraser. "You massage 'em and it gets rid of all sorts of problems."

"Oh," said Thom, pretending an understanding he didn't have. "And somebody's been massagin you, have they?"

"No," said Fraser. "You get these special magnets, wear 'em in your shoes. They work all the time then."

The door to Carston's office opened and McNeil came in.

"Mornin, sarge," said Fraser.

"Morning," said McNeil, remembering the previous day's conversation with him and still wondering where it was all leading.

She opened a filing cabinet in which she kept all her old reports and started looking through the folders in the second drawer.

"See this. It's not cars that causes your global warmin," said Spurle, pointing at something in the paper.

"Course it is. 's a well-known fact," said Bellman.

"Not any more, smart-arse. It's termites."

Everybody, including McNeil, stopped what they were doing and looked at him.

"Methane, that's the killer," he said. "Twenty times worse than $CO_2$, accordin to this. And termites fart out up to 80 million tons of it every year."

Bellman and Thom snorted their laughter. McNeil suspected that Spurle had produced his little gem especially for her benefit. She found the folder she was looking for.

"Aye, well," she said, "good job you're not a termite, Spurle, eh? With all the greenhouse gases in your trousers."

She went back to the other office, pleased with the reactions she got from Bellman, Thom and especially Fraser.

"Fuckin dyke," said Spurle.

"Serves you right for readin that poofter shite," said Fraser, indicating Spurle's *Guardian*.

"Yeah, well," replied Spurle, his expression smug, "that's where you're wrong, boy." He tapped the page in front of him. "This is sex—real sex, no just the photos of tits you've got there."

Fraser looked at Bellman and Thom; they were as puzzled as he was.

"What d'you mean?"

Instead of answering, Spurle gave a deep sigh and settled into his smugness as he began reading again. They gave up. He could be an irritating bastard at times.

In the other office, Carston was ticking points off a list he'd made in connection with Hayne.

"D'you want me to go and see his wife, sir?" asked McNeil.

Carston tapped his pen against his lower lip.

"No. You know the score up at the hospital. It'd be better if you came with me for the follow-up. Jim can do the nasty stuff."

Ross' only reaction was to look up from his computer and nod.

"Could be tricky," Carston went on.

"It's OK," said Ross.

"I want to get some sort of idea who he was before we start on details."

Again Ross' only reaction was to nod.

"Come on," said Carston. "Let's get started."

They went through to the squad room.

"Mornin sir, mornin sarge, mornin, sarge," said Fraser again.

"OK," said Carston, "there's real work for you today. That guy who died up at the Bartholomew."

He handed out photocopies of McNeil's report and the pathologist's findings and filled them in on the other details he knew. It didn't take long because there weren't many.

"First, I want the hospital records checked. See if they tally with ours," he said. "Find out how many deaths like this they've had there in the last, say, five years. Maybe more if you think it's worth it. Then see what you can find out about the surgeon and the anesthetist. Where they worked before, what their records are, any problems, anything dodgy about them. Start with the Medical Who's Who or BMA lists of members or something. If you have to contact anybody direct, try to keep it low-key. Medics are worse than priests for protecting each other's arses."

"Right, sir," said Fraser. "We lookin for anythin in particular?"

"Everything," said Carston. "It's wide open. We don't know whether it's a cock-up at the hospital or what."

He went out, followed again by Ross and McNeil. Fraser jumped to his feet then sat down again and started to untie his laces. Spurle stood up and waited as Fraser took the reflexology magnets out of his shoes. Fraser looked up at him and pointed a menacing finger.

"Not a bloody word," he said.

****

McNeil had taken a car from the pool and was standing beside it when Carston arrived. He motioned for her to drive. He liked being a passenger if the driver was good. McNeil was and he could sit back and enjoy the fascination which crowds always held for him: shopping, herding kids, delivering goods.

The hospital was some ten minutes away. As McNeil pulled through the gate into grounds whose mature trees showed that the whole place had once been part of a big estate, Carston said at last, "How do the stripes feel?"

As CID, McNeil wore no uniform but she knew what he meant."

"Not all that different, sir."

"Really?"

"Well, not with the squad, but I must admit, I keep on thinking about it. And it's ... well, it's pretty good."

"You should be pleased with yourself. Your age."

McNeil gave her little smile.

"I am, sir."

"Good."

They'd parked the car and were walking up to the entrance.

"You can do the introductions," said Carston.

"Right, sir," said McNeil.

"Neighbor of mine's an anesthetist here, you know."

"Good job he wasn't on duty the night before last, sir, eh? Could've been a wee bit embarrassing."

"Not with David," said Carston.

The neighbor, David Weston, shared his own cynicism about the running of public services nowadays. His opinions were up-front and, when Carston got the news of Hayne's death, he'd phoned him to have a word about anesthetic procedures. Weston hadn't been keen to say anything specific about the case, of course, but Carston had been careful to keep his questions general. It had been worth it; Carston had at least got himself used to the terminology.

The moment they went through the door, it was clear that they'd been expected. Blantyre enveloped them with smiles and gestures and steered them into her office. As if to counteract the funereal associations of the reason for their visit, she'd opted today for a pale linen shirt-waister. She looked young, summery and seemed to radiate pleasure. There was no need for the introductions Carston had mentioned; right away, she took control. In their opening exchanges, the most extreme opinion she offered about Hayne's death was that it was unfortunate. She was arranging a series of files along her desk, explaining that she'd already classified them for the benefit of the investigation when Carston, as irritated by her bulldozing as McNeil had been the previous day, stopped her.

"Before we get to that, Ms Blantyre," he said, "do you have any figures on the incidence of post-operative hypovolaemic shock over the past, say, three months?"

It stopped her completely but, as before, her recovery time was short.

"Not immediately to hand," she smiled, "but I could let you have them within the hour. There are not likely to be very many."

Carston nodded and went on, "And—I'll check this with the anesthetist, of course—but can you tell me whether Professor Hayne was given the usual epidural infusion—you know, local anesthetics, low dose opiates? I believe that's the customary procedure for post-op aortic patients."

Her smile became a little warmer, less professional.

"That'll be in this file," she said, tapping a pearl-coated fingernail on a green folder. "But I hope the research you've obviously been doing hasn't pre-judged any of the issues here."

"Heaven forbid," said Carston.

"As I told your sergeant yesterday, we all want to know what happened here. You'll find we're completely open about everything."

"Good. I'm sure we'll get on fine," said Carston. "Now then, have you got a ... schedule? For the interviews?"

"Ah yes. I've set up Mr Latimer, the surgeon, Dr McKenzie, the anesthetist and Fiona Brewster. She was the scrub nurse for Professor Hayne's operation. They're standing by for you. You can use my office here if you like."

"Thank you," said Carston. "That'll be very helpful. I'll try not to keep them long. They've got more important things to do than talk to me, I know."

"No, no. We all need to understand what happened," she said, the smile back on full. "We need to show that none of our procedures has failed."

"Who's pre-judging now?" thought Carston.

"And I'd like to take any personal effects Professor Hayne had away with us if that's possible," he said.

"Clues?" said Blantyre, with a raise of the eyebrows and a little intake of breath. "How exciting. I'll see to it myself."

She began once more to plan their morning with suggestions as to places they might need to visit, items they'd want to see and other members of staff who might have contributions to make. Finally, she excused herself and said she'd go and fetch Mr Latimer. Carston wondered briefly why she didn't just phone him but was glad to be left alone with McNeil so that they could settle themselves before the interviews started.

Carston began pushing chairs around.

"OK," he said, "let's get this place sorted. How d'you want to do this?"

"Well, you seem to know what you're talking about. Maybe I'd better just take notes."

"No. Just flannel, that was. That neighbor of mine, last night. He filled me in on some basics."

He put two chairs behind the desk and pointed for her to bring another from the corner and place it opposite them.

"You can take the notes, but chip in whenever you like."

McNeil set the chair down and began to stack the files from the desk on top of a bookshelf under the window.

"Yes, that's it," said Carston. "Best to get them out of the way."

"Yes. So they can't dodge anything."

She was thinking ahead. They needed to hear things straight from the people involved. If they saw case notes and pamphlets on operative procedures lying around, it'd be only too easy to take refuge in referring to them.

"No," said Carston. "If there's anything to be found, we'll only find it in the people. I've been on hospital cases before; they're a nightmare."

"Why's that?"

"Too bloody clean. Not a hope in hell of getting any forensic stuff; everything's scrubbed all the time."

"I never thought of that. What're we looking for?"

Carston spread his hands and said, "Whatever we can get. Normally, I wouldn't expect much, but that report you got—the combination of the rupture and the overdose—not exactly straightforward, is it?"

"No. Makes it more interesting, though, eh?"

Carston smiled. It was a comment he'd never have heard from Ross.

****

Leith had found another reason to be exasperated. This time, it was a janitor who'd arrived in his room to take away a bag of papers for incineration.

"I specifically asked you to bring up an empty bag," said Leith, waving a hand at the open drawers of his filing cabinet. "I haven't finished yet."

The red-haired man shrugged as he picked up the black polythene sack.

"I never got no message," he said.

"Who did I speak to on the phone then?"

The man shrugged again. He was used to being treated like a retard by Leith.

"Oh, for goodness' sake," said Leith. "Take that away and bring me another one right away. An empty one," he added, insultingly.

"An empty one. Yes, sir," said the man, resolving that next time he was on nights and wanted a pee, he'd know where to come for it.

Leith shut the door behind him and began taking more papers from the drawers and adding them to the piles already spread over his desk and the office chairs. A quick glance was usually enough for him to decide where each belonged because he was looking mainly for minutes of meetings, circulars or memos which referred to Hayne's departmental and university projects. The sack which had just been taken away was full of them but there were more to come and Leith was determined to get rid of them all before the next round of meetings. Hayne was no longer a factor in the maneuverings and Leith was getting a lot of satisfaction from erasing him from the records.

He was reading an acerbic exchange of memos between them on the use of native German speakers when his phone rang.

"What?" he snapped into the mouthpiece.

"Sorry," said the voice of Carlyle. "Catch you at a bad time, did I?"

"What is it?" asked Leith, ignoring his question.

"The police," said Carlyle.

"What about them?"

"They want to come and have a word."

"With me? Why?"

"No, with all Alistair's colleagues."

"What for?"

"I'm not sure. But I said we'd be happy to accommodate them. Just thought I'd give you advance warning." He gave a little laugh. "So that you can get your alibi ready."

"Alibi? For what?" blustered Leith.

"A joke. Sorry. Pretty feeble one."

"Well, I'm not sure I can spare the time. I do have some source checking to do in the library and..."

"They've promised me it won't take long," said Carlyle, cheerily ignoring his protest.

"It had better not. Look, while you're on, any idea what happened to that last staff evaluation that Alistair sent round. I remember initialing it, but..."

"Yes. I binned it," said Carlyle.

43

"What? Why?"

"No use to us any more," said Carlyle. "New regime, new priorities I'd have thought." And he rang off.

Leith replaced the receiver and continued to look at it as he tried to balance the news about the police and Carlyle's unaccustomed decisiveness. He was aware of an itchiness around his anus, always one of the signs of stress where he was concerned. He scratched at it, making it worse, then made a decision. He picked up the phone again, dialed the hospital and asked the switchboard operator to page Dr Latimer. While he waited for the reply, he started on his paper sorting once again, this time with a greater urgency. By the time Latimer rang him back, the pile of Hayne-related material was almost big enough to fill another bag.

"Look," he said, "the police are coming to see us. What's it all about?"

"How should I know?" said Latimer. "They're here, too. I'm seeing them myself in a moment."

"Something's up."

"Don't be absurd."

"It must be. What are they looking for?"

Latimer's tone showed his irritation. "It's routine, for God's sake. Any time there's a… Look, what am I explaining it to you for? What's this call all about?"

"Bloody Hayne again. Even now he's gone, he's still got influence…"

"Leith, I haven't got time for this. Don't phone me here unless there's a reason for it, OK?"

"If you don't think the police visiting us simult—"

But he was talking on a dead line. Latimer had already rung off. Leith's itch had become unbearable and he was sweating more than before. This was not the way things were supposed to be; university promotions were calm, reasoned affairs. He went back to his paper-sifting, hoping that the order he brought to his files would transfer into his head.

Downstairs, in his own room, Christie had also been told about the proposed police visit. He, too, had been going through minutes of past meetings and various correspondence files looking for exchanges he'd had with Hayne. Their last confrontation had been particularly bitter and remained hot in Christie's memory. He'd been called to Hayne's room to discuss exam protocols and, as he was about to leave, Hayne had used his usual tactic of disorientation.

"While you're here, Michael," he said, "I've had a sort of warning about your conduct."

Christie stopped, waiting for an explanation.

Hayne pushed his glasses higher on his nose and sat down at his desk.

"Extra-marital, actually," he said.

The blush that hit Christie's cheeks confirmed his guilt immediately.

"Good God," he said. "Who's been spreading that sort of rubbish?"

"The source isn't important. And I don't personally care whether it's true or false. What does concern me is that it could reflect badly on the department."

Hayne's tone was cold, seemingly non-judgmental. Christie would have preferred righteous indignation or some sort of passion.

"I don't see why it should," he said, forgetting already that he'd denied any wrongdoing. "What possible connection could there be between my private life and departmental activities?"

Hayne shrugged.

"All I know is that misdemeanors sometimes call for a separate dossier," said Hayne, swiveling his chair so that he faced his desk. "You have one."

"That's outrageous," spluttered Christie. "Dossiers? What is this, the Third Reich?"

"We're spending public money," said Hayne.

Christie interrupted him.

"Wasting it, I'd say, if people are behaving like tabloid journalists instead of getting on with their jobs."

"We have to be accountable," insisted Hayne, his even tone unchanged and maddeningly reasonable. "And if accusations are put to me…" He paused, seeming to consider his options. "Well, I can hardly ignore them, can I?"

"You can if they're false."

Hayne turned to look at him again.

"I'm not prepared to discuss this any further. I've already exceeded my authority by warning you. You're mature enough to know what's right, I hope."

It was too much for a defensive Christie.

"Oh, stop being so bloody pompous, Alistair," he said. "You know damn well what I'm worth to the department. Without my papers and publications last year, we'd have had a pretty sorry research profile."

It was not a sensitive thing to say. Hayne's own output had been thin for several years. He'd been too busy being a manager.

"This isn't about research," he said, "it's about morality. And I'm not prepared to discuss it further. Please close the door behind you."

Christie was being dismissed like a schoolboy but, infuriatingly, Hayne had the upper hand. Pursuing the topic might uncover more than was healthy. Christie had to accept the rebuke and take away with him the knowledge that Hayne was in possession of something which could be fatal to all his hopes of advancement. It added further complications to their relationship. Nonetheless, he forced himself to draw back from his anger and speak in a controlled voice.

"I see," he said. "Well, thank you for your candor. I can assure you that my conduct never has been nor will be detrimental to the work we do."

Hayne nodded an acknowledgement and Christie went out, closed the door very quietly, took a deep breath and swore violently to himself before going back to his room.

Since that meeting, he'd tried, on several occasions, to get access to Hayne's computer and filing cabinets but, if the dossier did in fact exist, he hadn't yet found it.

Now, he was looking round his room to check that there was nothing to provoke any questions. He had a small lump of cannabis resin in a little box in the top left hand drawer of his desk but he rarely used it during the day. Sometimes, if he'd fixed an appointment for one of his more compliant students he'd nibble a little before they arrived but on the whole, he preferred to stay in control while colleagues were about.

There'd be no question of the police asking to search or anything but, just to be safe, he took out the box and tucked it behind a copy of Rousseau's *Confessions* on the top shelf of his bookcase. He then arranged a few of the larger, more impressive volumes from the shelves across his desk and scrolled through text on his computer screen until he found something of appropriate complexity. If anyone came in, it would give the desired impression of busy-ness. He sat back and considered his next move.

46

****

As Carston and McNeil began to sketch out the broad outlines of the types of questions they'd need to ask, Carston was pleased to notice a difference between her and Ross that had nothing to do with gender. Whereas Ross' insistence on proofs and logic always put the brakes on Carston's guesses and speculations, McNeil was quite happy to indulge and even embroider them. With Ross, results might arrive more slowly but be secure, with McNeil the likelihood was that inspiration would outrun the evidence. It made a change.

When Latimer arrived, they barely had time to introduce themselves before he began to let them know that he was an important man. To begin with, he looked more like a company director than a surgeon. He was in his late thirties and wore a dark blue suit, a soft pink shirt and a tie with motifs on it that implied some sort of royal connection. His black hair was long but neatly styled and, as he sat down and unbuttoned his jacket, Carston caught a flash of gold from some pens in his inside pocket. Before they had a chance to ease into their prepared routine, Carston and McNeil were informed that he was due in theatre in less than an hour and that he had no idea what he could add to the information that was already available to them in the hospital's records.

"Nevertheless, Dr Latimer, I'm sure you'll appreciate the need for a full investigation and the chance to help us find out just what went wrong," said Carston, managing to stay polite even though Latimer's attitude was insulting.

"Who said anything went wrong?" asked Latimer.

"Oh," said Carston. "Hypovolaemic shock's the norm for your patients, then, is it?"

Latimer's glare was the only answer he got. Carston smiled sweetly and referred to a note on the pad on his lap.

"You'll have seen the pathologist's report…"

He looked up for confirmation. Latimer gave one quick nod.

"Perhaps you wouldn't mind explaining for us exactly what hypovolaemic shock is."

Latimer gave a deep sigh and gave what amounted to a recitation.

"It's when fluid's removed from the system and stagnates in the tissues. That reduces the effective volume of blood circulating and the number of oxygen-carrying cells. Tissue oxygenation is impaired, more demands are made on the system—especially the heart. The fluid loss is accentuated and you're into a vicious circle. Eventually, the heart can't cope any more and it fails."

Carston was tempted to applaud. Instead, he nodded.

"And in Professor Hayne's case, the initial cause of all that was a ruptured aorta," he said.

"Yes."

"But I thought you were supposed to be mending his aorta."

"I did. It was blocked. I cleared it. It's a commonplace procedure. There was no reason why he shouldn't have made a full recovery."

"The report says there was maybe some problem with the sutures you used," said McNeil.

"Speculative nonsense. Hardly the sort of observation one expects to find in a supposedly objective analysis. In any case, it's a suggestion I reject."

McNeil persisted.

"Well, it's more than speculation, isn't it? The rupture wasn't in some other place; the actual incision reopened. That means…"

"Have you ever been in theatre?" Latimer asked, looking from her to Carston.

They both shook their heads.

"Then perhaps that should've been your first stop. The sort of tissues we're dealing with are invariably diseased; that's why the patients are in there. When the operation's over, sometimes the strongest feature of the relevant organ or tissue is the part of it that's just been sewn up."

McNeil made to ask another question but he didn't give her the chance.

"Professor Hayne was in a very bad way. He'd had several operations to remove tumors, some of his arteries were almost solid and his whole system had been degenerating for years. When one makes an incision, one discards what is useless. What remains is healthy tissue and that's what holds the sutures. In the professor's case, there were many potential sources of trouble but the site of the sutures wasn't one of them."

"Nevertheless, with great respect," said Carston, stressing the three words in a way that suggested that "respect" could easily be replaced with "contempt", "as Sergeant McNeil said, the report is quite precise in establishing the location of the rupture and it does coincide with the incision."

"I know that," admitted Latimer, "but I still reject the implication that the two are connected."

It was a strange statement, rather like denying that rain was wet, and Carston realized that the man's pride, or something, was obstructing his usefulness. His initial attitude had forced them to take a line that seemed to question his professional competence. He was being defensive and they'd need to change the emphasis.

"Dr Latimer," he said, "as you've noticed, we're completely ignorant of how theatres work. And anatomy isn't one of our strong points, even in the CID."

Latimer waited, not yet mollified.

"What we're trying to do today is understand the practical processes involved." Carston tapped the paper on his lap. "This is all very well but we need your help with it."

Latimer's right hand went to his hair and stroked it back over his ear.

"What about the material you use for the sutures?" asked McNeil.

"What about it?"

"Well, could it be … weak or something? Part of a bad batch?"

Latimer's snorted laugh was unadulterated scorn.

"We don't get it at Tesco's," he said. "Our QAQC procedures are as high as any in Scotland. Check with our suppliers, they'll tell you."

"But there are different types, different strengths, aren't there?" asked Carston, drawing once again on the chat he'd had with David Weston.

Latimer produced another sigh.

"Of course. Some are absorbed more quickly than others. It depends on the age of the patient, the site of the operation, all sorts of considerations. Inside the mouth, for instance, we use very fine grades. You wouldn't want a mouthful of ropes, would you?"

Carston smiled.

"Well, is it possible that they'd get mixed up?" he asked. "That you might use a weaker one when…"

Latimer leaned forward and smacked the flat of his hand on the desk.

"This is absurd," he said. "Are you suggesting incompetence on my part?"

"Of course not," said Carston. "Please believe me, I'm just trying to understand the possibilities here, trying to find out what happens."

"Sutures don't get mixed up. It's more than the sterile nurse's job's worth to hand me the wrong type. And even if she did, I'd spot it right away. They're different thicknesses, for God's sake."

He flopped back in his chair angrily. This was the worst interview Carston could remember for a long time. Usually, it was dealing with suspects that provoked the tantrums, but he was just trying to get some information, for God's sake. And yet it was as confrontational as any of the interviews he'd had back in Burns Road.

"So, as far as you're concerned, there was nothing unusual about any of the circumstances of the operation," said McNeil.

"Nothing whatsoever," replied Latimer, his tone slightly lighter as he spoke directly to her. "Not before, not during, not afterwards. Everything went as it should, perhaps even more smoothly than we had the right to expect, given his medical history. I did my job, the anesthetist did hers, the nurses did theirs and you've got reports and computer print-outs there to prove it."

"What sort of patient was Professor Hayne?" asked Carston.

Latimer looked back at him and let out yet another sigh. If this went on, he'd hyperventilate.

"He was a man with an aortic aneurysm," he said.

Carston smiled and waited. This time, when it came, Latimer's sigh was one of exasperation.

"And a pain in the neck," he added at last.

"Oh?"

Latimer gave what was supposed to be a smile. It sat unpleasantly on his handsome features.

"If you want to know, I'd be very surprised to hear that anyone was very upset at losing him," he said.

Carston's expression obviously conveyed his surprise at the remark.

"I know," Latimer continued, the smile still fixed. "Dreadful, isn't it? Speaking ill of the dead. You did ask, though. The man was a spiteful, aggressive nuisance. Academics. They're all the same. They feel the need to remind everyone how bright they are. They ask questions, quote patients' charters at you." He paused and looked at his watch, then added, "Take up inordinate amounts of your time".

The disdain with which he was treating them and their questions was as evident as his hostility to Hayne. Carston was always quick to sympathize with people who were reticent, apologetic or simply quiet and shy, but people who had a high opinion of themselves really pissed him off. Here was Latimer not only fancying himself but bad-mouthing a newly-dead patient. Carston had expected polite, concerned professionalism. He obviously wasn't going to get it.

****

The Haynes' house was a detached Edwardian villa in Peterhead granite. It was the middle one of a row which curved around the crest of a small hill on the South West edge of Cairnburgh. Between the rose beds at the front, a gravel drive angled its way to a garage and parking bay. Near the road, two laburnums were showing the first signs of what would soon be a spectacular display. They'd been planted to screen the house from the one opposite although the combined width of the two front gardens and the road meant that, if you really wanted to check on the neighbors, you'd need binoculars.

Ross was standing at a bay window looking out at a garden which had obviously been created with love. It folded away from the house in shapes, colors and textures which had been carefully considered but still had the random feel of a natural scattering of species. In a way, the effect was continued inside the room because the terracotta walls were almost covered with prints and paintings of flowers. Not the usual, careful botanical studies, but extravagant bulges of color.

Gillian Hayne came in with a tray in one hand and a cafetière in the other. She was a small, neat brunette, graceful in her movements. Her black dress looked expensive and swung into slow, soft folds as she walked.

Ross was peering at a water color of some white roses.

"D'you like them?" she asked, her voice low and, to Ross' ears, posh.

He turned and went quickly to take the tray from her and put it on the table in the window.

"Very much," he said. "You obviously do, too."

She looked around at the collection and smiled. "Yes. Bit naughty really, but I find it hard to resist them. They're mostly Bob Batchelors. Local artist—well, Aberdeen, I mean. Came from the West Indies originally. It shows doesn't it?"

Ross looked around again and shrugged his shoulders.

"I wouldn't know. The CID's not very strong on art appreciation."

She smiled again but the reminder of the reason for his visit clouded it out of her face almost at once.

"Alistair wasn't a great fan," she said. "Still, I'm the one who spends most of the time here, so…"

As they waited for the coffee, they talked some more about the paintings and prints, then about the garden which was also her creation. It was only when she'd poured the coffee that they began to concentrate on her husband. She didn't seem particularly sad about his dying but Ross assumed that, given his recent medical history, she'd been living with the possibility of it for so long that it might almost have been a sort of relief. In fact, the more they talked, the less she seemed to dwell on her loss.

"He was hardly here, you know," she said at one point. "Lately, it's been hospital visits and so on, but before then, I mean." She stopped for a moment, her slim fingers lifting to stroke her left temple. It was a small, compact gesture, in keeping with everything else about her. "It must be more than ten years. The job changed, you see. He used to be here in the study, writing his books and articles. Then it was committees, trips to Edinburgh and London, meetings with MPs and the like." Her head was shaking. "Not the same at all."

"D'you think that affected him?" asked Ross. "The job changing, I mean."

To his surprise, she gave a humorless laugh.

"Oh yes. He loved it."

Ross waited for her to go on.

"It's hard to believe, sergeant, but he loathed students. Hated teaching. He always said it got in the way of his real work."

"His real work?"

"Yes. Research. 'Pushing back the frontiers of knowledge'."
She intoned the words with deliberate pomposity. It was clear that
she was unimpressed. "Then, as I said, there were the committees,
economics, political games. Very small 'p'. Little power games and
empires, stupid maneuvering. They've all been at it."

"How about the teaching?" asked Ross.

"Students? They just get in the way usually. Necessary evil.
Alistair used to tell his first year groups that half of them shouldn't
be there. Always told them there'd been an administrative error and
that too many places had been offered."

"Always?"

"Every year."

"But the students must have known ... I mean, the second years
must have told the new ones what to expect."

"Yes, of course they did. Alistair was no psychologist, though.
Didn't ever stop to think what might be going on in someone else's
head."

There was a clear edge of bitterness in her words and Ross was
sure that she was talking of herself as well as her husband's
students.

"Did his colleagues feel the same way?"

Ross, watching all the time for nuances in her control, thought
that there was a slight hesitation before she answered.

"What about?"

"Students."

She thought for a moment, giving herself time to regroup fully.

"It depends. Some of them are normal but others are just..."

Instead of finishing the sentence, she raised a hand and made a
little throwing away gesture to indicate that she didn't understand
them.

"It's been a long time since I've had much to do with them. I
used to have to go to dinners and ceremonies and things but I
stopped all that. It made me angry in the end."

It was difficult to imagine how she might express such anger;
her tidiness seemed so complete, so self-contained.

"Why angry?"

For another brief moment, a hint of frustration crept into her
expression. She shook her head, then stroked her temple again.

"Have you spoken to any of them yet?"

"No."

"Wait 'til you do. I don't think you'll need to ask the question then. They give the impression of knowing, understanding. They're supposed to be … enlightened."

"And they're not?"

"Maybe. They're also destroyers—reputations, hopes, people…"

Her voice tailed off and she looked out at the garden. Ross didn't want to exert any sort of pressure but insights like these into Hayne's world were useful.

"Any of them in particular?" he asked.

She gave a small shake of her head.

"They've all got their secrets and flaws. Edward Leith and Michael Christie more than most."

Ross wrote the names on his pad.

"Edward would sell his family if he thought it would buy promotion. And Michael … well, basically, Michael has no conscience."

As she mentioned the two names, her quiet, gentle tone became tense, sharper. There was no hiding the fact that whatever she felt about them, it was personal. She seemed suddenly to become aware of the change in her tone because she turned, smiled at him and said, "Oh ignore me, sergeant. I'm just being cynical. There are some wonderful people there, some very caring people who do worry about education and their students and the value of what they're doing. John Carlyle, for instance, or Dennis Ritchie. Their doors are always open to them.

"But then there are the others, the ones who could never make it in the real world, who publish shopping lists and laundry bills and spend lifetimes excavating tiny areas of knowledge that should have stayed buried. And they're fierce about it, vicious. And they think nothing of colonizing other people's lives."

The anger Ross had wondered about was beginning to show as she spoke.

"As bad as that, eh?" he said.

She looked at him, her face serious.

"Edward, Michael, Alistair—they're all the same." She paused, then continued. "But I suppose Alistair was the king."

Ross sensed immediately that between herself and her husband there had been chasms. She caught his eye and nodded.

"We'd stopped talking about his work. He knew what I thought about it all. It kept us quite separate in the end."

It was an admission which seemed to carry resignation rather than sadness. There was a little pause as she sipped her coffee. She spoke again, her voice so quiet it was almost a whisper.

"When you go there, don't be fooled. There are things going on underneath that blandness."

"What sort of things?"

She raised her hand from her lap in a small, open gesture.

"Staff, students, administrators. There's no … none of it's about idealism any more. Not like in the early days. It's … little. Petty. Personal."

"Personal?"

"Yes. We've had students at the door here threatening to break it if Alistair didn't let them in," she said, as if the information was of no great importance.

"What for?"

She made the same, small gesture.

"Oh, cuts, things like that. He wanted to close down some of their societies, withhold funds. Part of one of his committee jobs. Prioritizing finance or something. I stopped listening. Remember that, though, when they're all smiling at you."

They drank their coffee and talked more about the university. She was an interesting person, with insights into many things beyond the topic of their conversation and, when it was time to go, he got up with some reluctance.

"Well, I shouldn't say so but it's been a pleasure talking to you, Mrs Hayne," he said, slightly embarrassed at himself.

Her answering smile was warm.

"Why shouldn't you say so?"

"Well, the circumstances…"

She nodded, then said, "It must be obvious to you that Alistair and I weren't all that close."

"Maybe."

"Well…" she began but then, seeming to change her mind, she just shook her head and led him to the door.

"Are you married, sergeant?" she asked as they stood beside his car.

"Yes. Two wee girls, too."

"Forgive me for saying so, but keep your priorities right."

She couldn't know that her advice was unnecessary. Ross' protection of his family and their life together was fierce. If he ever felt the job was getting in the way, he knew he'd leave the force without hesitation.

They said their goodbyes. As he drove off, she gave a little wave, then went back inside. Ross thought briefly about the cold world of her marriage and the society she kept and, as he turned out of the drive, he pulled into the kerb, grabbed his mobile and hit the button which dialed his home number.

**\*\*\*\***

The man was sitting on the bench again. Scott had begun to notice him the previous week. Each afternoon, as she walked back through the park from the university to her flat, he was on the first of the benches along the broad central pathway. He didn't try to hide the fact that he was watching her and, the first couple of times, she'd been able to tell herself that he was just another example of the whistlers; workers on building sites or roads whose eyes and comments violated every woman who walked past. But he said nothing, there was no whistling and she began to realize his stare was different. It wasn't just an arrogant appropriation of her body for some schoolboy fantasy. He wasn't just looking at her breasts or legs or hips; he was looking at her. He saw her from a long way off and his head turned to follow her as she walked past him. She'd never looked back to see whether he gave up once she'd gone by but she became progressively more certain that he didn't. This wasn't an idle lecher; it was personal. The problem was that, if she avoided the park, it meant a long detour through the streets around it and she resented the idea that the man could force her to such inconvenience.

When she told Strachan about it, he was angry at first, wanting to walk home with her and confront the man.

"Oh, he hasn't done anything, Tom," she said. "Arguing and fighting with him might make him turn nasty. Maybe he'll get the message if you just come with me. So he sees us together."

Reluctantly, Strachan had agreed and, for three days this week, they'd walked back across the park together after classes. There'd been no sign of him.

"Probably just some deadbeat," said Strachan, on the third afternoon. "Not interested in you at all. After what's in your purse, not your knickers."

"Not like you, then," said Scott.

He put his arm round her shoulders, she tucked her fingers into his back pocket and they walked on, both of them relieved that the problem seemed to have vanished.

But it hadn't. Here he was again. Strachan had a practical which would go on until six, and Scott's last lecture had been from three to four. She'd set off for the flat with no thought of the man in her head. When she saw him on the bench as she turned onto the path, it was a shock. Not only because she would have to run the gauntlet of his stare again but also because it was somehow sinister that he only appeared when she was alone.

The shock grew into anger as she got nearer to the bench. His eyes were fixed on her again but this time, instead of pretending to ignore him, she looked straight back at him. As she got to the bench, she stopped.

"What's this about?" she asked.

He said nothing. Close up, there seemed to be no threat in his expression and he seemed nearer to a boy than a man. The smile around his lips had vanished when she'd approached him and he seemed disturbed by the fact that she'd spoken to him.

"What? Are you watching me or something? Stalking? What is it?"

His eyes dropped away from her. He was confused. His silence made her angrier.

"OK, look. I'm pissed off with it, right? If you don't stop, I'll tell the police."

She stepped back as he stood up. He went past, angling his steps to avoid actually brushing against her, and walked along the path in the direction of her flat. When he got to the third seat, he stopped, sat down and turned to look at her again. Her anger slipped into fear. As she walked slowly towards him, she was careful to take in as much detail as she could. If she had to report him, she wanted to be sure she remembered him properly. He was tall and wore a dark green blouson jacket, black denim shirt, dark blue jeans and white Nike trainers with green flashes. His mousy hair was long but looked clean. She tried to remember the color of his eyes when she'd been face to face with him. She knew they were dark but his face was thin and they were deep set and shadowed so she wasn't sure whether they were brown or deep blue.

He watched her as she came up level with him again and stopped. Still he said nothing and Scott was now afraid to tell him what she thought of him in case it triggered something. Although the sun was still high, there was no one near them in the park.

"Pervert," she said, and hurried away along the path. This time she did turn round and was not surprised to see that he'd leaned forward with his elbows on his knees and was watching her all the way.

# Chapter Five

To the relief of both Carston and McNeil, the anesthetist turned out to be very different from the surgeon. Dr McKenzie was a slim forty year old. Wisps of her red hair had escaped from the pins she'd stuck in it and her animated way of speaking kept making them float down in front of her eyes. She smiled and laughed easily, despite the topic of their discussion, and she was completely open and patient with them when they failed to understand some of the medical terms she used. She'd obviously seen enough death for it to have become an aspect of the job and, while duly respectful of Professor Hayne, she could speak of his passing with a detachment that made their job much easier.

She'd taken them slowly through the pre-med sequence and the setting of the various lines needed to plug Hayne into the anesthetic machines and recorders, then through the four hours of the operation itself, during which her job had simply been to keep an eye on things. There'd been no indications of any problems and the whole operation had been completely routine.

"They took him into the ITU and that was that," she said at last, spreading her hands and lifting her shoulders to tell them that there was nothing else she could say.

"ITU?" asked McNeil.

"Intensive Therapy Unit."

"Didn't you have to go there with him?"

"Well, I went, but there was no need for it. I didn't have to bring him round, you see. He was staying sedated so the ward staff would keep a check on him. He'd come through the operation and all the indicators were good. There was nothing else for me to do."

"Your readings couldn't have been faulty?" asked Carston, feeling that he should apologize for the suggestion.

McKenzie took no offence.

"No. Not with Boyle's machines."

The name sounded horrible to Carston but McKenzie put him straight.

"That's the inventor, Cocky Boyle. Designed his first one in World War One. They give you the mix you want—oxygen, nitrous oxide, $CO_2$, air—the tubes and cylinders can't get mixed up. And you've got permanent displays, read-outs when you want them."

"So we're left with a bit of a mystery then," he said. "I mean, the pathologist's report found a very high morphine concentration."

"Yes, enough to kill him," said McKenzie, almost eagerly. "But don't ask me about where that came from. I've absolutely no idea."

"It was morphine you were using?" asked McNeil.

"Yes and that's what he had in his PCA."

They both looked at her but she was already translating.

"It's a Patient Controlled Analgesic System. A wee machine with a line into a vein in the arm. We give them to patients who're having severe pain. They've got a kind of button which they hold in their hand. If the pain gets to be too much, they push it and the machine gives them an extra dose."

Carston's mind started racing but McKenzie anticipated his question.

"Before you ask, no they can't overdose on them. There's a sixty mill syringe but we set the volume and timings of the doses. For instance, say I set a one milligram bolus with a five minute lock-out, that means that there's got to be at least six minutes between doses—that's a minute for the PCA to pump the dose in plus the five I've set as an interval. You can't over-ride it. And everything you do, all the doses and timings, when the patient uses it, they're all recorded and kept in the machine."

She pointed at the green folder they'd stacked on the bookshelf under the window.

"It'll all be in there."

Her hand flicked at the stray hairs around her forehead.

"OK," said Carston, "but suppose somebody actually wanted to mess around with the machine, deliberately ... I don't know, top up the dose, put a more concentrated solution in it..."

Her head was already shaking and she was smiling—not with Latimer's condescension but with a sort of pride in the apparatus and systems of her job.

"Good try, but no chance. The MEAC, that's the minimum effective analgesic concentration, varies from patient to patient. We know more or less what their systems can take. But guess how many signatures you need to start a PCA?"

"If it's like our set-up, it'll be at least half a dozen," said Carston.

"Nine," said McKenzie, and that's not counting the two from doctors. And when the dose is being prepared, there have to be two nurses there to double check it. No, I'm sorry, but your conspiracy's going to have to find another method of administering the stuff."

"And could anybody other than hospital staff get access to it?"

McKenzie shrugged, thought briefly, then said, "I suppose so. Visitors, anybody. It's there in full view. But I've told you—there's nothing they could do."

"Right. How was it done, then?" asked Carston.

McKenzie grinned and sat back in her chair.

"Done?"

"Well, it doesn't look like an accident, does it? And, if it isn't, somebody's responsible."

McKenzie's face clouded and she lost a little of her bounce.

"Well, if it was me, I wouldn't use an overdose of any sort. And I certainly wouldn't do anything that would lead to me sitting here talking to the CID."

"Doesn't it bother you at all that there's been some sort of cock-up?" asked McNeil, out of the blue.

It seemed to sober McKenzie a little.

"We don't know that there's been a cock-up," she said, a new tightness in her voice. "OK, things aren't right, but I've looked at all the readings, checked the equipment. Everything went as it should. Everything worked, including all the systems."

"And Professor Hayne's dead with a split aorta and a huge dose of morphine inside him," said McNeil.

"Yes," said McKenzie, turning sharply to her. "And I'll be very glad when you find out how it happened so that we can make sure it never happens again."

It was a strange reaction, which contradicted what she'd said before, and yet she seemed unaware of it. She suddenly looked at her watch.

"Yes," said Carston, "we've kept you long enough for now. But I'm afraid we may have to get back to you later."

"No problem," she said, her brightness suddenly back.

"I need to go through the reports again, try to absorb them all," said Carston. "It's all a bit daunting for a simple mind like mine."

McKenzie was on her feet.

"You should come and spend some time in theatre," she said. "That's the best way to slot it all together. See the machines, us, everything that goes on."

It was an idea Carston had already had.

"How much notice would you need for a visit like that?"

"None at all. I'd have to check with the surgeon who's on but I don't think any of them would mind."

"Good, thank you. We'll arrange it soon."

"Fine," she said. "Well, if we're finished for now, I'll go and sedate a few more poor souls." She shook hands with the two of them and was suddenly gone. The stillness felt almost like a sort of relief.

"She could do with injecting some of her stuff into herself," said McNeil, "the rate she goes."

"Yes," said Carston. "Exhausting, wasn't she. I could do with a…"

There was a tap at the door and Blantyre's face appeared round it.

"I forgot to ask if you'd like some coffee," she said.

The words both confirmed and contradicted Carston's mistrust of PR people. They seemed to slip inside your head but they also kept the little comforts appearing.

"You're a mind reader," he said.

"Just doing my job," she said, through a double strength smile.

The door closed.

"Nice woman," said Carston.

"If you say so," said McNeil.

\*\*\*\*

Fiona Brewster was anxious, tired and very grateful to sit down. Carston noticed as she did so that she wore heavy elastic stockings of the type you'd expect to see on older people. She was only just past thirty and still had a young face, but years of standing in theatre had already started to ruin the veins in her legs. When she spoke, her accent had the nasal resonance of Inverness or the Moray district and her voice was quiet. In her answers, she wasted no words.

"Can you tell us exactly what you do?" asked Carston.

"I'm in the green area. Beside the doctor. I hand the instruments to him."

"The green area?"

"Yes, the other nurses don't get as near to the patient. They mustn't touch anything with a green towel on it."

"I see. And so you gave Dr Latimer the suture he used to sew up Professor Hayne's aorta."

"Mr Latimer. Yes."

"Sorry. Mr Latimer, of course. Where did you get it from?"

Her brows wrinkled. The question seemed strange.

"The tray beside me. On the table, over the patient's legs."

"And you put it there yourself?"

"Yes, the floor nurse brought it in from the setting-up room and gave it to me before we started."

"And where's the setting-up room?"

She raised her left arm and gestured off to the side.

"Just beside the theatre. It's like a wee annex."

Carston nodded. McNeil, still scribbling notes, asked, "How d'you know what you'll need before you start?"

"All the surgeons have got cards made up."

"Cards?"

"Aye, a list of all the instruments and types of sutures they like to use for the operation they're doing."

Brewster stopped and smiled.

"Anyway, you just know," she said. "I've done it so many times."

"And you never have to fetch more stuff?" McNeil persisted.

"Oh yes, sometimes. But we make sure there's always more than we'll need on the trolleys in the setting-up room."

"Did you know that there may have been a problem with one of the sutures used for Professor Hayne?" asked Carston.

A slight blush rose in Brewster's face and neck.

"Yes, Mr Latimer mentioned it."

"Any thought on that?"

She shook her head.

"They're all sealed. Brand new. I take them out of the packet myself."

"What sort of packet is it?"

She shrugged her shoulders.

"Wee foil packets, in a clear sealed envelope."

"And it's your job to take them out?"

"Yes."

Carston leaned forward. He was finding it very refreshing getting such straight, simple answers to his questions.

"Tell us exactly what you do with them, will you?"

As she spoke, her hands mimed the things she was describing.

"I take the packet out of the envelope, open it and tear off a wee tab at the end of it. I stick the tab on a panel beside me. Then I give the needle and the suture to the surgeon. And when he's finished with it, he gives it back to me and I put it beside its tab. At the end, I make sure the tabs and needles all tally so that there's no danger of one being left inside the patient."

"So the only people who touch the suture are you and the surgeon?"

"Yes."

"Does he ask for particular ones?"

"Sometimes. But usually I know before he asks."

"What if you choose the wrong one?"

The blush got darker.

"That depends on the surgeon. Some of them shout and bawl at you, others are more normal. But we don't get them wrong."

Carston smiled at the small rebuke in her words.

"How do you know which is which?" he asked.

"They've all got different numbers. One, two, three for the thicker ones, then right down to 8-0 or 9-0. They're the very fine ones, for eye surgery and that. There's different makes, too."

The temptation was to ask her about all the other aspects of the operation. It would be the quickest way of getting the overall picture without having to tiptoe around professional sensitivities and eggshell egos, but since he was planning a visit himself and since

Brewster was obviously not entirely at ease, Carston decided against it.

"What about general nursing care for patients like Professor Hayne?" he asked. "Do they get any special treatment?"

"Well, there's the usual staff in the vascular ward—that's where they go first. Then, after the operation, it's the High Dependency Unit. You should speak to one of the acute pain nurses."

The expression took Carston by surprise.

"Acute pain nurses?" he said. "I never knew there was such a thing."

"Oh yes," said Brewster. "We couldn't do without them."

"And what exactly do they do?"

"They look after patients with acute pain," she replied, not bothering to register the scorn she must have felt for such a stupid question.

"Yes, but how?"

"Check their medication, keep records, tell the doctors if there are problems. Most of all, though, they just spend time with them."

Carston was about to ask another question when, for a change, she developed her answer a bit further.

"Most of these patients are very poorly, you know. Terminal cases or chronic conditions. And part of the trouble is how folk want to avoid them. As if they could catch what they've got. Having somebody spending time with them does them the world of good."

Carston nodded. He could understand how pain and fear would grow in loneliness. Lying on the edge of death and feeling the huge spaces separating you from the living must be terrifying; any hands which reached across the gap would be grabbed at with so much gratitude.

\*\*\*\*

Since the news of the police's intended visit, Leith had been unable to concentrate on any of his usual preoccupations. The fact that they were also at the hospital increased his anxiety even more. He'd tried to put the recent call with Latimer out of his mind but, with no other outlet for his anxieties, he needed to talk to him again. He picked up his phone, dialed the Bartholomew and asked the switchboard operator to page Latimer. When the surgeon answered, his tone of voice suggested that he'd been dragged away from something important. Leith was too involved in his own thoughts to register the fact.

"Well?" he said.

"Well what?" Latimer's tone was one of high irritation.

"The police. What did they want?"

"Oh, for God's sake. It's that bloody man Hayne, of course. He's as much trouble dead as he was alive. And you're not helping."

"Yes ... well..."

"Have they been to see you yet?"

"No."

"When they do, don't tell them I phoned you," said Latimer. "When he died, I mean."

"Of course I won't. It's none of their business."

"They'd think it was, though."

"Anyway, that's not really why I'm calling," said Leith. "I'm off to the REF now. D'you want to go ahead with it or not?"

"Go ahead with it?"

"The REF."

"Oh God, I haven't talked to George about it yet. D'you need to know right away?"

"Well, if we're going to get things started, you'll..."

"Alright, alright. Yes, go ahead. I'll talk to him as soon as I get a chance. As long as those bloody policemen keep out of the way."

"I suspect they'll be around for a while."

"God knows why. There's nothing to find."

"No."

There was a sudden silence. It was Latimer who broke it.

"Look, I'm already overdue in theatre. Do what you can. I'll be in touch."

"Right. It's on this afternoon's agenda. I'll get started on it."

"Good."

They both rang off without saying good-bye. The relationship was obviously not based in friendship. Leith picked up some papers from his desk and went out, locking his door behind him. As he reached the bottom of the stairs, he met Christie who was also on his way to the monthly meeting of the REF. The REF was the Research Evaluation Forum, a body only marginally connected with research, which never pretended to evaluate anything and had none of the public access suggested by the word forum. For Leith, Christie and all its other members, however, it was the most important of all the committees which filled their days because it was here that promotions were bartered. Budgets tended to be weighted in favor of departments whose lists of publications were longest and, when new chairs or senior posts were being dished out, the REF was the place where real influence could be exerted.

When they got there, committee room thirty-two was already nearly full. The two of them sat down and, almost at once, the chairperson, a charmless individual called Menzies who looked like a grown-up rag doll, called the meeting to order and began by expressing deep regret at the loss of Professor Hayne. The murmurs of sympathetic agreement provoked by his words were largely hypocritical.

The usual jockeying and compromising went easily enough until they reached item number four. It was a proposal to expand the REF by increasing the number of medics on it. The university had no medical faculty, but some of the personnel from the Bartholomew were ex officio committee members and there were strong links with the large teaching hospital in Aberdeen. The theoretically independent chairperson, aware that a bigger committee represented a larger empire for him, made a point of expressing his sincere hope that the proposal would find favor. He asked for comments and, immediately, Leith dived in.

"I don't see why we need to discuss this. The figures are here. Medical research brings in huge amounts, grants from all over the place. If golden eggs are being laid, it's our medical colleagues who are laying them."

Menzies was nodding.

"It's refreshing to hear that your department's given this further consideration," he said. "Professor Hayne wasn't at all keen last time it came up, was he?"

"Different priorities," said Leith.

"Of course. Well, there's no gainsaying the fact that our medical colleagues do make a significant contribution to funds. If you'll look at appendix three…"

Papers rustled and Menzies began to drone through an unnecessary reading of the set of figures Leith had referred to. When he finished, a botanist risked suggesting that many medical grants, being privately sponsored, weren't always free of external pressures. This produced a low buzz around the table. Most of the people there knew that the work done in the wards and labs of their medical colleagues had a very high profile. Beside it, some of their own esoteric pursuits looked flimsy. It was never easy to persuade the public that cancer research and investigations of linguistic variables were equally valid. Leith remained sufficiently divorced from that public to have no such reservations.

"I don't know where the Botany department's been for the past ten or fifteen years. Cultivating its Voltairean garden, no doubt."

He allowed a pause for them to appreciate his witticism. They didn't. He didn't notice.

"The simple truth is that, without a flow of funds, we die. And since the drug companies and multi-nationals are so keen to be associated with medical research, then we should facilitate their involvement and make sure that their contributions reflect positively on the workings of this committee."

Everybody wanted a say, and it was twenty minutes before Menzies could call for a vote. To his and Leith's delight, the motion was carried, a sub-committee was formed to work out the implications of the new, improved REF and the meeting wandered on through the rest of the afternoon. Menzies eventually called time at four-thirty. Christie waited at the door for Leith.

"Bit of a surprise, your enthusiasm for the medics," he said as they came out into the sunshine. "What's brought it on? Gratitude that they got rid of Alistair?"

Leith stopped and looked at him.

"That's a rather insensitive thing to say."

"Yes, isn't it?" replied Christie, without stopping.

Leith frowned, then hurried to catch up with him. It wasn't until they'd turned right at the top of the road that Christie spoke again.

"Convenient, wasn't it?"

"What?" asked Leith.

"Alistair being taken out of the reckoning."

Leith was suspicious; Christie rarely communicated at such a direct, seemingly personal level.

"For whom?" he asked.

Christie looked at him and even managed a smile.

"Both of us," he said. "Maybe you're right about medics. Maybe they do have their uses, eh?"

Leith had no idea what he was getting at. He didn't like the questions that seemed to pile up behind Christie's words.

"They bring in the cash," he said. "It makes sense to get them on our side."

"On our side, yes. They can be a great help, can't they?"

Leith was out of his depth. He didn't bother to reply and each lapsed into his own silence. Nothing more was said until they got back to the department. There, Leith disappeared to make another phone call and Christie was pleased to find Sandra Scott waiting at his door.

# Chapter Six

Christie showed Scott into his room with the usual hand in the small of her back, then excused himself. When he came back, the blonde strands around his head had been combed and a smell of peppermint wafted from him.

"I can't tell you what a pleasure it is to see you," he said. "I've just spent an afternoon at the REF. What a collection! Death warmed up, most of them."

There was nothing she could say. She waited. He was at his window, sliding it open a notch. He turned to look at her, sucking in his stomach as he did so.

"It's so refreshing to get away from them all and find someone young and normal here," he went on. "I know I'm not supposed to say so, but you do look very nice. That color suits you."

As he said the words, he walked past her to get back to his chair and let his hand trail across her shoulders. Still, Scott said nothing. Christie smiled and sat forward, leaning his elbows on his desk.

"Right. To what do I owe the pleasure then?" he said, narrowing his eyes and locking them onto hers.

She opened her bag and began to take out some notes.

"The Ronsard essay," she said. "I wanted to ask a couple of questions about it before I start."

As she consulted the notes and tried to get the clarification she needed, she couldn't avoid Christie's unflinching gaze. It was obvious what he was doing. She'd known when she decided to come that he'd make some sort of play, but the essay title was so impenetrable that, if she hoped to recoup the ground she'd lost on the last one, she really had no choice. She was confident that he wouldn't actually do anything unless she let him, but it was difficult to stay focused through the innuendoes and asides in which he wrapped his replies to her questions.

He held his pose all the time, leaning towards her, sliding the forefinger of his right hand up and down the middle finger of his left, keeping his eyes fixed on hers, willing her to return the signals he was trying so hard to give. He saw a young, attractive redhead whose breathing lifted her breasts against the pale green cotton of her blouse. She saw a man with pouches under his eyes, rapidly thinning hair and a loose lower lip which was shining with saliva. The invitation in his grin was insulting, assuming as it did some sort of sexual parity between them.

When she'd got the information she wanted, she was anxious to leave but he stood up and came past her to stand at the window again. She didn't turn to look at him, concentrating instead on tucking her notes and pen away in her bag. She started when she felt his hand touch her hair. He withdrew it immediately.

"Astonishing color," he said. "Especially in the sun. I hope your boyfriend appreciates it."

Her anger flashed and now she did turn towards him. He was silhouetted against the window and she found it difficult to read his expression.

"Dr Christie, I don't really think that's your business," she said, standing up.

"Oh I think it is. It's a purely aesthetic observation. You have lovely hair, full stop."

"But it has nothing to do with Ronsard."

He tapped his fingers against his thigh.

"It could have," he said, adding quickly, "Look, sit down. Just for a moment."

Scott didn't move. Christie's voice lost some of its wheedling quality.

"What are all these essays and exams really for?" he asked. "What difference is it going to make to you if you can quote Ronsard or Montaigne to a prospective employer? It isn't about that, Sandra. It's about people. Making concessions, forming alliances, exploiting the things you have. Do you really think that someone with your sex appeal isn't going to be propositioned? You ought to make it part of your education. It's a gift. Use it."

His words sank into her, expressing alien thoughts of physical couplings in this room lined with evidence of cultured reflections, spiritual truths. Was he right? Was it a surprising acknowledgement of the sort of realism that the books denied? She felt a sudden sadness at the thought that her progress was going to be littered with similar encounters. There was nothing she could say to him. He was talking to someone she wasn't.

"*'Quand vous serez bien vieille, au soir, à la chandelle,'* you won't want to be thinking 'if only', will you?" he said. "*'Cueillez aujourd'hui les roses de la vie'.*"

"Sorry. I have to go," she said, sickened further to hear him using Ronsard's words to strengthen his pitch.

Suddenly, he was the cold tutor again.

"Of course," he said.

He walked past her to his desk, this time making no contact. He sat down and switched on his computer. When he spoke again, he didn't look up.

"I'll need the essay by next Thursday, remember. Good luck with it."

Scott held her bag tightly as she opened the door and left the room. In the corridor, she took several deep breaths, said "bastard" to herself and went looking for some fresh air.

As he heard her footsteps hurrying away, Christie had already switched off his computer and started gathering up papers to take home with him. He chose them indiscriminately because, on the whole, it didn't matter what they were. He mostly used them as an excuse to go into his study and get away from his wife Martha and their children. It helped to preserve the notion of him as a busy academic and spared him the details of domesticity which he found so wearing.

He turned into his driveway just before six, parked his red Toyota in front of the garage and looked briefly at the May colors in the borders. The granite house was semi-detached and worth many times more than the amount he'd paid for it when he'd arrived in Cairnburgh. The excellent condition it was in owed nothing to him. Tending both house and garden was Martha's job. God knew she had plenty of time on her hands to do it.

She was in the kitchen when he went in. He opened the fridge, took out a bottle of Muscadet and poured himself a glass.

"Want one?" he asked.

Martha shook her head. There was silence for a while as he flicked through a pile of letters on the dresser.

"Any news?" she asked at last.

"No," he replied.

"I'm surprised," she went on. "One of your girl-friends was on the phone this afternoon."

"Martha, if you're in one of your PMT phases, I really don't want to hear about it," he said, wearily. "There are some important things happening at the…"

"Gillian Hayne," she interrupted, ignoring his crack.

Christie frowned and looked at her.

"Gillian Hayne is old enough to be my mother," he said.

"Makes a change from being young enough to be your daughter."

"Is there some point to this?"

Martha shrugged, her concentration seemingly on the vegetables she was preparing. "She said the police were asking questions about Alistair. Thought you ought to know. God knows why. Did something go wrong?"

"What d'you mean?"

"With Alistair. At the hospital."

"How should I know?"

"Why are the police involved?"

Christie's face was flushed.

"Didn't Granny Hayne tell you?" he said.

"She wasn't phoning me. It was you she was after."

"So am I supposed to phone her back?"

Martha shrugged again.

"I don't understand," said Christie. "You've got little enough in your bloody head, doesn't your brain ever function normally? Surely you're capable of handling simple phone messages?"

The sudden noise of feet on the stairs signaled that their children had finished their PlayStation game and were about to start making demands. Christie took his glass and went through to his study, slamming the door behind him. He took a sip of wine, looked up a number and dialed it.

"Gillian, darling," he said, when Mrs Hayne answered. "Martha tells me you called."

"Hello, Michael. How are you?"

"Struggling on. Yourself?"

"Free at last, free at last," said Mrs Hayne.

It took him by surprise.

73

"It was a joke, Michael," she said, when he didn't reply.

"I see. What's this story about policemen?"

She told him about Ross' visit, the questions he'd asked, the answers she'd given.

"And did he give any idea of what it was all about?" asked Christie, when she paused.

"They're treating his death as suspicious," she replied.

"Good Lord. Do they ... do they suspect that somebody's responsible, then?"

"Well, I don't think they're treating it as an Act of God," she replied. "However much Alistair might have thought he merited that level of attention."

"So ... is it ... a murder enquiry?"

"They didn't say. Just a suspicious death. I thought you'd want to know."

"Why?"

"He was a cherished colleague," she said, teasingly. "And you're one of the ones who'll profit by his death."

"What d'you mean?" said Christie, the anger he'd felt with Martha swelling up again.

"Oh, stop being difficult, Michael. Things are much easier for you with him out of the way, admit it."

"Gillian. I don't understand this call. I've no idea what you mean by it. And I must say I'm surprised that you're reacting to Alistair's death so light-heartedly."

"Did you cry when you heard the news?"

Her voice was hard, accusatory.

"I'm sorry," said Christie. "You're obviously ... upset. It must be difficult for you."

"It is."

"Yes. Well, if there's any way I can help..."

He let the words hang, unwilling to specify what he was prepared to do.

"I'm sure the police will think of something. Goodbye, Michael."

The exchanges had been abrupt, hostile. As Christie replaced the receiver, he shivered. The brief affair he'd had with Gillian Hayne was in the distant past and had been far from satisfactory. She'd been grateful enough for his attention but had quickly begun to make demands. The only real pleasure Christie had got from it was that of deceiving Hayne because, in truth, she was a lousy fuck. After only three meetings, he'd had enough and, a few tearful phone calls aside, there'd been no repercussions. Now here she was phoning him at home again, after all this time. Why? What did she know about anything?

He emptied his glass and coughed as some of the cold liquid caught in his throat. The thought that Gillian might suddenly be part of the aftermath of Hayne's disappearance was … unwelcome.

**\*\*\*\***

Kath was back in the graveyard by five the following morning. Her idea was to take a series of shots matching those she'd taken on her last visit to catch the difference in quality between the evening and early morning light. When she'd told Carston about it at dinner, he'd offered to go with her and act as her assistant once more.

"I'll be getting up about four," she'd replied.

"So?"

"And leaving the house around quarter to five."

"And? What's your point, woman?"

"My point is that it'll be dawn, which isn't the time for any form of social contact, conversation, interaction…"

She hesitated as she tried to think of more synonyms.

"Sex?" offered Carston.

"Certainly not sex."

"I won't bother, then."

"Good."

She'd left the house quietly enough but the brightness outside and the change in routine prevented Carston from getting back to sleep and he was in the office long before the rest of them. As he'd walked through the empty streets, he'd been aware of the differences that Kath had spoken about. The rose-colored granite of the terraces of houses actually sparkled. In the evening sun, they were muted, warmer, but the early morning light was crisper and seemed to hurry across surfaces, getting them ready for something or other. Carston had let his mind wander over all the things it would be preferable to do on such a day. Being a policeman wasn't one of them.

As he and Ross sipped the horrible office coffee, there was a knock and the door opened immediately. The individual who came in contrasted strongly with both of them. The job required them to wear jackets and ties but neither of them was particularly careful about the process. Ross was the smarter, an impression helped by the fact that he tended to stand straighter than his boss and was carrying no spare weight. The new arrival, though, could have come straight from the board meeting of a merchant bank. He was just under six feet tall, wore a classic double-breasted suit, a white Oxford shirt, a striped Police Association tie and a pair of glasses which looked fashionable and expensive. His cheeks and neck carried a little more weight than they should but he still looked good. He flashed a model's smile at them.

"Morning sir, morning Jim," he said.

"Hi Andrew," said Ross. Carston just nodded and waited. Andrew Reid was one of Ridley's sergeants. Whatever he was doing here, it wasn't going to be something Carston enjoyed. Reid looked from one to the other of them.

"Er... Did you get Superintendent Ridley's fax, sir?" he asked at last.

"What about?"

"Me. Joining the squad."

His words fell between them like a hand grenade. Tension was instantaneous. Ross looked quickly at Carston, who was visibly controlling his reaction.

"What?" said Carston at last, his voice very low, very quiet. "Joining the squad? Our squad? CID?"

"Yes sir."

"First I've heard of it."

Reid's eyes dropped to the papers on Carston's desk.

"D'you mind, sir," he said as he leaned to pick one up.

Carston waved a hand for him to help himself. Reid produced a fax from a small pile with the ease of a magician.

"I think this is it," he said, handing it to Carston.

Carston read quickly through the single sheet of paper. It was true; Reid had been foisted on them "until further notice".

"What's it in aid of?" Carston managed to ask.

"Resource rationalization, sir."

"What the hell's that?"

Carston's annoyance was beginning to break through. Reid rode smoothly on.

76

"Superintendent Ridley's been looking at deployments since Sergeant McNeil's request. He thinks we should create a bigger pool of officers with experience in several disciplines. Multi-skilling. We build up a sort of rapid response force to cope with variations in demand."

"Like Sainsbury's," said Carston.

Reid smiled and said nothing.

"And how much experience have you had in CID work?" asked Carston.

"None, sir," replied Reid. "That's the point. The superintendent thought I might learn more quickly with you."

Carston wasn't flattered. He'd never hidden his distaste for Ridley and everything he stood for. Ever since he'd moved to the West Grampian force, he'd been blocked and hassled at every turn by Ridley's passion for administration, triplicated forms and nit-picking in all its guises. The more likely explanation for Reid's arrival was that he'd been tagged onto them to report back any irregularities and give Ridley the excuse to shuffle Carston out of the way.

"He also thought you could do with the extra pair of hands," Reid went on.

"Oh?"

"Yes sir. You apparently told the last meeting of the finance committee that chronic understaffing was having an adverse effect on clear-up rates."

"Those were my actual words, were they?"

Reid was thrown.

"Well, I ... I mean, I wasn't there. But the superintendent..."

"Yes. The superintendent..."

Before he could go on and no doubt say something that would send Reid rushing gleefully back to Ridley, Ross interrupted him.

"There is the business of the outboards and the MOT certificates to collate, sir," he said. "We need somebody on that."

Carston looked at him, momentarily puzzled by his words.

"You did say we needed to prioritize it."

Ross never used words like "prioritize". He was flashing a signal at his boss. Carston's anger was checked by it sufficiently for him to wave a hand at Ross and say, "OK. Take him through to Thom and Bellman. Fill him in on it all."

Ross got up and flicked his head at Reid to indicate that he should follow him through to the squad room. Reid, who'd taken the word "prioritize" literally and thought he'd been given instant status by it, paused at the door and said, "Thank you, sir".

Carston managed to scrape up a smile. It wasn't a pretty sight.

When the door closed, he swore and went to the window. He picked up his mug, spilled some of the coffee, swore again and looked out at the shining day. It had been soured by Reid's arrival. He felt comfortable with his squad. There were irritations, of course, but working with them had become a pleasant enough habit. The thought that he'd now have to come to terms with having Ridley's man looking over his shoulder kept his anger boiling as he looked at the ordinary things going on in the sunshine.

By the time Ross came back, his boss had managed to suppress his desire to break something or harm somebody. He turned and went back to his desk.

"What d'you make of it, Jim?" he asked.

"What, Andrew?"

Carston nodded.

"He's on his way up. Always had plenty of ambition."

"And he's in Ridley's pocket."

"Maybe."

"Keep an eye on him, will you?" said Carston. "Make sure he doesn't fuck up the squad at all."

"Yes. You'd better watch it, too. You were close to saying something about the super then, weren't you?"

Carston smiled.

"Yes. You're right. I'll prioritize it."

Ross grinned.

"Now then," he said, "about this prof. It's one of the weirdest I've come across."

"How?"

"I don't know. Everything about it. It's all so clean. He dies in a hospital, like thousands of others, but he's been murdered. Nobody seems too upset by it, nobody's going to gain much by it—not that we can see yet, anyway. It's all so bloody airy-fairy."

"Yes, I get the same feeling."

"He's a nasty wee bugger all the same," said Ross.

"Nasty?"

"Aye, if this stuff's anything to go by."

He held up an iPad that had belonged to Hayne. It was one of the things Carston had brought back from the hospital with him. He'd passed it to Ross, knowing that, if he tried to examine it himself, he'd wipe any files it contained.

"Well, what about it?" he asked.

"He uses it to make notes and draft letters. They're all there still, right up to the day before he died."

"What sort of things?"

"I'll do a print-out later. Some of it's work. And there's ideas for changes at the university. And you should see the complaints—about folks at the university, the treatment he's getting at the hospital, the doctors, the nurses. He's not getting a high enough priority, they're withholding information, that sort of stuff. Doesn't think much of the surgeon guy."

"Latimer?"

"Yes. He wrote to the hospital administration about him."

Ross paused as he pressed buttons to call up the document he was referring to.

"Aye, here it is. 'His arrogance and lack of concern for one's psychological welfare do little to alleviate one's apprehensions. His bedside manner is non-existent and he is utterly lacking in professionalism. It pains me to have to write such things about a colleague but there is a public face to health care which Dr Latimer would do well to recognize.'"

Carston whistled.

"Charmer, wasn't he?"

"Aye," said Ross. "And there's bags more like that, too. To the City Council, Health Board, Holyrood, Westminster. He even wrote to the university saying they ought to consider closing down his own department."

"What?"

Ross held up the iPad.

"It's all here. He never let up. Just sat there, day after day, marking folks' cards."

"Latimer said he was a bit of a pain as a patient."

"His wife didn't have much time for him, either. She didn't say so in so many words, but she's not too bothered about losing him."

He went on to tell Carston about his visit to Mrs Hayne and her opinions of her husband and his colleagues. Carston was impressed by her obvious preference for normal, human values and intrigued by the color her words had given to the victim. So far, Carston's own contacts with those involved had concentrated on the mechanics of it all. Hayne had been part of a process which didn't distinguish between scalpels and the tissues they sliced. His venous system had been linked to a set of tubes and become an extra component through which their fluids could circulate. It wasn't that the medical staff were without compassion; it was just that they were understandably concerned about the practical aspects of their routines.

"So she's glad he's out of the way."

"I wouldn't go that far. But she's not very sorry. Why? You looking for motives?"

"Yes," said Carston. "This isn't an accident, Jim. I know they're all saying that everything went the way it was supposed to and his aorta couldn't split open and he couldn't have had an overdose, but…"

"But it did and he did."

"Exactly."

Carston looked at his watch then leaned forward and picked up the phone and dialed.

"I want to see if Brian McIntosh has got anything more to say about it."

"We've got his report."

"Yes, but he might be able to fill in some other stuff. I mean, he…"

He broke off as McIntosh answered.

"Brian. Sorry to catch you so early. It's Jack Carston."

"No bother, I've been here for ages. What can I do for you?"

"The prof. At the hospital. They're all surprised at how he died."

"I bet they are. Double whammy, wasn't it?"

"Is there anything that'd help me get some sort of angle on it? I mean, it is foul play, isn't it?"

"That'd be my guess. It could just be incompetence. But I can't see it."

"How come?"

"The two things happening at the same time. Two major mistakes, in separate disciplines—million to one against. If it was an accident, he was bloody unlucky."

Carston was nodding his head.

"The surgeon and the anesthetist weren't much help," he said. "Just told me point blank it couldn't have happened."

McIntosh gave a little laugh.

"Professionals, you see. Doctrine of systemic infallibility. Trouble is, I'm inclined to agree with them."

"Oh?"

"Aye. I mean, the suture giving way like that. It was too obvious to be deliberate."

"What d'you mean?"

"Well, it's going to show up in the autopsy right away. There's no way of hiding it. A surgeon would know he'd be on the spot."

"Maybe that's why there was an overdose too."

"Eh?"

"Because the suture thing was so obvious, so traceable to him. If he arranges for Hayne to have an overdose, it … well, it confuses things."

"And how would he arrange that without the anesthetist's help?"

"I don't know. You're the medic."

"Hard to see it, Jack. You're talking about some sort of conspiracy now. That's even less likely than an accident."

Carston's eyes were skimming McIntosh's report as they talked. Their conversation was adding nothing to its findings.

"So there's nothing you can suggest to help me out here?"

"Well, you could double check on the actual suture that was used. But I wouldn't hold out much hope."

"Why not?"

"You can't take chances with them—precisely because of what's happened here. I mean, you've got to know that the bloody thing's going to hold. You can't just hope it will. There's so much screening to make sure no dud batches get through."

"But they might?" asked Carston, grateful for the first indication that there could have been a mistake.

There was a pause as McIntosh thought about the question.

"No," he said at last, immediately undermining Carston's hopes. "It couldn't happen. There are too many people's reputations at stake. Especially the surgeon's. Sutures have got to come straight from the packet. That way, nothing can damage them."

"Like what?"

"All sorts of things. The classic is being nipped by instruments."

"How?"

"Well, needle holders for instance. They've got sort of scores on them—they could nip them, make them weaker."

"Really?"

"Aye, but the nurses would never let that happen and the surgeon would insist on a new one anyway. And with the sort that are used for the aorta, you'd probably see that they were damaged. One of the surgeons certainly would. Both of them probably."

That was another difficulty Carston had already considered. Even if Latimer had some homicidal intent, his assistant would be there checking everything. The same applied to McKenzie and the doses of morphine that were being administered.

"Are you going to be depressing about the overdose too?" he asked.

McIntosh laughed again.

"Poor old Jack," he said. "That's even harder to explain. They've got so many safeguards against it. And nowadays they're tending to use lower doses anyway."

"Why?"

"Oh, various things. Muscle relaxants for a start. Once they were introduced, they could lower the levels of narcosis. Anesthesia's improved helluva lot in the last thirty years or so."

"This isn't helping me, Brian."

"It could've been worse. I could have told you about hydroxylation."

"Would it help if you did?"

"No." He chuckled but his voice was serious again when he went on. "Listen, Jack, this beats me. I'm afraid I'm with the Bartholomew staff on it. It couldn't have happened. But it did. I think you've got a crime to sort out."

"OK, Brian. Thanks for your time."

"No problem. You're going to love this one, aren't you?"

Carston knew what he meant. McIntosh's findings had often made the job of detection very easy. Carston preferred a challenge.

"It's a living," he said. "Bye."

As he put the phone down, Ross looked at him. Carston shook his head.

"Nothing," he said. "He reckons it couldn't have happened either."

Ross tapped his finger beside the keyboard of the notebook computer on his desk.

"This is bloody stupid."

"What?"

"All these medics being innocent about killing off a patient. No point in saying it couldn't happen. It did. Their precious bloody procedures missed something. Somebody knew how to get past them."

Carston drained his mug and shuddered at the bitterness of the brew.

"Did you fix Reid up?"

"Aye. He'll be with Bellman and Thom for a couple of days at least. I've told them to fill him in on everything they've got so far. You know how long that'll take."

Carston smiled.

"Yeah. Good thinking. Keep the bugger out of the way."

He stood up, picked up the autopsy report he'd been looking at and lobbed it across the desk.

"Now I reckon this is one for you. You're the logical one. Go through this and the rest of the stuff and find out where there might be chinks, where the safeguards might have slipped."

Ross nodded. Carston went to the door.

"First of all, though, we'll brief the lads and you can keep me company," he said.

"Eh?"

"I think we ought to look in at the university. I want to get to know Hayne a bit better. A chat with his colleagues might change our angles a bit, open up some options."

Ross put the report on top of a neat pile at the edge of his desk and stood up to follow Carston through. Spurle was deep into a paragraph on lesbians and social security in the *Mail*. He'd given up on the *Guardian* after he'd read an article in it which praised Holland's tolerance of euthanasia. Fraser and McNeil were in quiet and obviously private conversation in the corner by the window. Carston had wondered why McNeil hadn't arrived earlier; the serious expression on her face and her evident involvement in what they were saying explained it. But what the hell were she and Fraser so intent about? Carston's curiosity increased when Fraser, seeing him arrive, suddenly sat back from McNeil and blushed. It was a rare phenomenon. Fraser was hard to embarrass. McNeil, too, looked momentarily as if she'd been caught doing something shameful. Never mind, as long as it didn't interfere with their work, it was none of his business. And he was confident that McNeil would soon let him know if it concerned him or the squad at all.

To start the briefing, Ross brought together what Carston and McNeil had learned at the hospital and what the others had found out about Latimer and McKenzie. The anesthetist had been at school and university in Aberdeen and done all her training there and in Cairnburgh. As far as they could tell, she'd made quite quick progress and seemed to be both successful and popular. Latimer's tale was slightly different. To begin with, he was originally from Edinburgh and had spent time in a small hospital in Providence, Rhode Island and then at a private clinic in Glasgow. A rather indiscreet spokesperson there had said that they'd been glad to get rid of him because he was "an obnoxious wee bugger" but that was just a personal opinion and he'd not actually done anything wrong. Nowadays he divided his time between Aberdeen and Cairnburgh, operating but also supervising students on placements.

"What about the list of medical mishaps?" asked Ross.

"Nothing special, sarge," said Bellman. "There've been some, but scattered around. Statistically the same as Aberdeen, Dundee, Perth and the rest."

"You still got a list, though?"

"Yes."

"Put it in the file."

Bellman nodded.

"OK," said Carston, as Bellman flipped his notebook closed, "You all got something to be getting on with?"

Everyone except Spurle nodded.

"Spurle?" asked Carston, putting a challenge into the word.

Without catching his eye, Spurle nodded. He couldn't trust himself to say "sir" with any conviction. Carston didn't push the point. He went back into his office with Ross. McNeil followed almost at once. So did Reid. When Carston saw him appear, he said, "What's up, Reid?"

"Nothing, sir. I thought when sergeants Ross and McNeil came…"

"Don't think. Not here. This is CID. Didn't Jim give you things to be getting on with?"

"Yes, sir," said Reid, not in the least put out by the way Carston was speaking to him. "I'll get back to them right away."

He smiled, went out and Carston went straight to the window and opened it wider. At last, he turned back to Ross and McNeil and said, "What are we going to do about Spurle?"

Ross was at his desk, tapping notes into his computer.

"What do we need to do?" he asked.

"He seems to get worse," said Carston, lamely.

"Aye, but that's just how he is. You won't change him."

Carston knew that he was right. They were lucky to have just one of the kind in their team. Bellman and Thom could easily develop the same way but it was still early enough for Carston to keep an eye on them and he, Ross and especially McNeil knew that in nearly every other force, Spurle clones were in the majority. Carston found it depressing.

"Fraser'll keep him straight," said McNeil. "He won't try anything with him."

Her remark reminded Carston of her tête-à-tête with Fraser but there was no way of asking her about it. He became brisk once more.

"OK, let's get serious with this Hayne business. Jim, give the university a ring, will you? Set up some interview times with the people in his department."

"How about me, sir?" asked McNeil.

"Couple of things up at the hospital, Julie. First, find out who supplies the sutures. Check them, see how stringent their safeguards really are. Then get round the wards, see if you can talk to some others. Get a feel for what goes on. And find out about Hayne's last few days there, what visitors he had, the medication he was on, anything else that seems interesting."

"Right. As long as Moira Blantyre lets me."

Carston smiled.

"Yes. Tell you what, though, you remember Dr McKenzie said we should visit the theatre during an operation? You can ask her to arrange that for us."

Ross looked up.

"Who d'you mean, us?"

"Dunno," said Carston. "Just us, me, you, Julie, I don't care."

"I do," said Ross. "I had enough trouble when Jeannie had Kirsty. Nearly fainted then."

Carston laughed. It was a surprise to learn that this ex-rugby forward was squeamish.

"Fair enough," he said. "If you're that delicate... How about you, Julie?"

"I'll go if I have to," she said, but her expression revealed that she wasn't keen either. Carston suddenly wondered whether there was something lacking in his make-up. He had no qualms whatsoever about watching an operation. The ones he'd seen on television had been fascinating.

"OK, I'll go on my own," he said. "Make a change to see stab wounds on a living body."

"Be careful they don't keep you there," said Ross.

"Why should they?"

"You're sick."

"Only in the head, sergeant."

# Chapter Seven

Sandra Scott had gone to the far corner of the university playing field and was sitting with her back against a tree. The shadows of the leaves moved slowly over the pages of notes on Ronsard she had on her lap. She'd read the lines Christie had quoted to her over and over again. The ones about being old and sitting spinning beside the fire in the candle light. There was nothing difficult about them and they were only the beginning of the verses she'd have to plough through to get the piece of work done for him. The problem was that memories of their last meeting kept getting in the way.

She heard buses and cars speeding along on the other side of the wall and looked across at the small pavilion and the spire of the chapel behind it. The chapel had been there much longer than the university; a couple of hundred years at least. When you looked at things against that sort of time scale, nothing was of much importance. She started to read through her notes again and tried once more to write an opening paragraph. But her hand began to shake and the fear and the anger came back up inside her. It wasn't about an old chapel, it wasn't about passing or failing exams, it was about her, who she was, how much respect she had for herself. She banged the file shut, stuffed it into her bag and leaned back against the rough bark, clenching her teeth to stop the tears.

She sat there for several minutes, her eyes closed and her mind angry, then heard the sound of someone sitting on the grass beside her. It was Carolyn Noble, a postgraduate student in the English department and one of her closest friends.

"Working hard as usual," said Noble.

"That's me," said Scott.

Noble pulled her skirt up to expose her legs to the sun. They were long, skinny and pale.

"Time to cook the celery," she said.

Scott smiled. Noble was tall, thin and, by most accepted criteria, physically unattractive. She knew it, didn't care and, as a result, was open and natural about herself and everyone else. The warmth she generated was worth more than beauty.

It didn't take long for her to realize that there was something wrong.

"What's up?"

Scott shook her head and thought for a moment.

"Men," she said at last.

"Is that all?"

"Bastards, all of them."

Noble was less frequently targeted by the whistlers and their ilk than Scott but she'd been subjected to them often enough to know what she meant. Scott pointed at her chest.

"Why is it, just because we've got these, that we're worth bugger all? They look at your tits and that's all they see. Never bother about who's inside. You might just as well be a leg of lamb."

Noble put both her hands against her own, flat chest.

"With me, they don't even get tits. Still doesn't stop them, though."

"What the hell are they seeing?" Scott went on. "What are they thinking?"

"Thinking? I don't think their brain's the organ they're using."

"It's so bloody relentless," said Scott, and Noble heard that the tears weren't far away.

"What's started it, Sand? Tom?"

"No. Not this time. Oh, he's still trying to fuck me, but I can handle him."

"That's one way of keeping him out of your knickers, I suppose. Who is it, then?"

With a deep sigh, Scott described her meeting with Christie. Little of it came as a surprise to Noble; his reputation was well established. She listened, shaking her head from time to time. When Scott stopped, she just said, "Report him, Sand. You've got to."

"Maybe."

"No. Definitely. The bastard's been at it for years. It's time somebody stopped him. And if you don't, it'll get worse for you every time you have to see him."

"Yeah, well... He's not the only one either."

"What d'you mean?"

Scott told her about the man in the park.

"Bloody hell, Sand. What perfume are you wearing? You must be giving off more pheromones than Beyonce."

Scott didn't smile. Neither did Noble. Both of them knew that the danger represented by Christie was probably minor. He'd pull rank, doctor marks, but he'd never risk any sort of assault. It was impossible to know, though, what was going on in the mind of the stranger.

"You've got to tell the police," said Noble. "They may have him on file. They could show you some photos. You could identify him."

Scott shook her head.

"He hasn't done anything. What could they do?"

"I don't know. Keep an eye on him. Watch out for you as you're crossing the park."

"Oh yeah. An escort. Just for me."

"You can't just wait to see what he'll do," said Noble. "You know what sort of nutters, junkies and pervs hang around there."

"Yeah. Maybe."

"You could do it now."

"What?"

"Tell the pigs. They're here."

"Where? What are you on about?"

"They're here. At the uni. In your department. Something to do with Hayne."

"What? How d'you know that?"

Noble shrugged.

"Everybody does."

Scott was curious.

"Wonder what it's all about? Hayne just died in hospital, didn't he?"

"Yes."

"So what're the police looking for then?"

"Well, you never know with a guy like that. He was never going to go quietly, was he? He'll've left all sorts for them to sort out."

"Like what?"

"Oh come on, Sand, you're not that naïve. He had this place tied up like a ball of string. Societies' grants, postgraduate places, research funding—he was in amongst all that. One of the great Empire builders."

"But that's nothing to do with the police," said Scott.

"Well, something's up. 'cause they're here."

The change of subject was good for Scott. She listened as Noble told her a couple of anecdotes about the antics of Hayne in the postgraduate liaison committee. They seemed silly, lightweight, and yet their effects had been significant. In the second case, Hayne's intervention had deprived two locally based students of funding to allow an American graduate to spend a semester in Cairnburgh interviewing its citizens about Scottish Country Dancing. The American was the son of a top manager in one of the oil companies based in Aberdeen.

"Hard to explain that to folk outside, isn't it?" said Noble.

Scott nodded. The more she heard of such things, the less comfortable she felt in Cairnburgh. Her difficulties with Christie and the man in the park had focused a dissatisfaction she'd been feeling for some time. Every day there was news of more pain and injustice in the world and yet here they all were, staff and students alike, taking the privilege of culture for granted. The enlightenment she was getting from her education seemed to be illuminating some very tawdry truths.

****

As McNeil walked through the corridors and up the stairs of the Bartholomew, she couldn't help thinking of how television colored her perceptions of what she saw around her. The white coats and nurses' uniforms made the people look like actors, and the wheelchairs and trolleys, especially if there was some sort of drip-stand attached to them, seemed to belong to sub-plots. Only when she came across a tottering extra in a dressing gown making his or her lonely way along did the real fragmentation of the place come to her. Yes, it was like a huge, interacting and inter-relating story with

90

a single drive and purpose, but inside it, tiny individual tragedies were dragging along, disappearing and being renewed. On the whole, though, faces were smiling and the general impression was of a place where things were being mended and where there was more good than harm.

She spent almost an hour in ward four just seeing the unfolding of routines that made the whole experience comforting for both nurses and patients. She chatted with various individuals and found the patients especially eager to reveal the sort of details about their conditions which she'd have preferred not to know. One old woman whose name, incongruously, was Annie Lennox, was particularly proud of the progress that had been made with her anal fissure.

"I thought I'd cracked it on my own," she said, "but it went again so here's me back."

"And you're doing fine, are you?" asked McNeil.

"Och aye," said Annie. "Thanks to yon Dr Chandra. And this wee lassie," she added, pointing at a nurse who was taking her blood pressure. "You ken this, when she changes my dressin, I canna feel a thing. See, there's these kind of wee pads…"

McNeil listened to a description involving cotton buds, blood and feces and was glad when the nurse, aware all the time of her discomfort, eventually shut Annie up by telling her that she knew more about medication than most of the doctors and that she shouldn't give away any more secrets.

When lunch had been served, McNeil sat and had a cup of coffee with the nurses before going to see the staff who had been more directly concerned with Hayne during his various spells as an in-patient. As she left the ward, she noticed Annie taking tissues from a box beside her bed and using them to wipe butter from the two slices of bread on her plate. Annie saw her looking.

"They always put on too much," she called, partly for McNeil's benefit and partly for that of the nurses. "Don't know nothin about clestrull."

McNeil smiled and, as she turned to go down the stairs, heard Annie cackle her satisfaction at another friendly point scored. It seemed to McNeil that that was the way things worked; staff and patients lived together here, co-operating, interacting with one another in a regulated, fairly normal context. At the same time, the patients' ailments and diseases were dealt with by physics and chemistry almost as a separate pursuit.

It was an impression that was confirmed in the course of the conversation she had with Susan Jamieson. She told McNeil that she'd not only spent a lot of time with Hayne during his last days at the Bartholomew but also on two of his previous stays with them, including one when a course of chemotherapy had brought him particularly low. As she described how she spent time sitting and talking with him and with her other patients, there was very little mention of medication or treatment. It was as if the pain that was her specialization, although directly caused by some specific physiological malfunction, became an aspect of the patient's psyche. It had to be dealt with as an element of personality rather than as a physical fact.

"So you knew Professor Hayne quite well, then?" said McNeil.

"Yes. As well as anybody here. He kept himself to himself mostly, though."

"Did you see him after his operation as well as before?"

Jamieson nodded.

"Yes. I was on night duty earlier this week."

"D'you stay with patients even if they're still under anesthetic?"

"Yes. Just keep an eye on their pain score, level of sedation. Look for nausea or vomiting, respiration rate, pulse, blood pressure—the usual things."

"What d'you mean by pain score?"

"Anything from nought to four. Nought's none, four's plenty."

"And you give them stuff to relieve it?"

"Yes. After you've spoken to the doctor. Can't do it on your own even if you want to. All the dangerous drugs are locked up in the cupboard. There's two separate keys. Has to be a doctor."

"Isn't it difficult to know how bad the pain is?" asked McNeil, becoming more fascinated by what seemed to her a strange specialization.

Jamieson gave a little laugh.

"Depends. Some of them pretend it's not there," she said. "Blether away, thinking you don't notice their jaws clenching, their fingers digging into the blankets."

There was a small smile on her lips as she said this, perhaps an outward sign of her memories of particular individuals.

"What was Professor Hayne like?" asked McNeil.

"How?"

"I mean, did he pretend, or what? With the pain, I mean."

"Oh, he didn't try to hide things. But he didn't complain either. He'd tell me how bad it was, and I'd know what to give him."

"He was an easy patient, then?"

Jamieson made a so-so gesture with her hand.

"Dr Latimer reckoned he was a pain in the butt," said McNeil.

Jamieson's eyes flicked away to look at the window.

"Aye... Well..." she said.

McNeil sensed that Jamieson had little time for Latimer but that it would be hard to make her say so.

"Did Professor Hayne have many visitors?" she asked.

Jamieson thought for a moment.

"Some. His wife was here most times. And I've seen one or two o' the folks he works with. But not very often."

"How about this last time?"

Jamieson thought again. "Same really. His wife. And one time these two men from the university."

"Were they regulars?"

"Like I said, his wife was. Not the others."

"When did they come, then?"

"Couple o' days before his operation. She was here in the morning and they came later on."

"Together?"

"No."

"D'you know who they were?"

Jamieson nodded then searched her memory for their names. "One was called Carlyle. I know the name 'cause the professor told me. I've seen him before, though.

"Really?"

"Aye, here visiting other folk. In fact, I think he was here today, seeing Mrs Rioch."

"Professional visitor, is he?" asked McNeil.

Jamieson shrugged.

"He only came the once for the professor," she said. "As far as I know, anyway. Stayed for ages, mind you."

"What, with the professor?"

"Some of the time. He went away for a while. Came back just as I was resetting Professor Hayne's IV line."

"Who else was there?"

Jamieson thought a moment, then shuddered.

"One called Leith. The professor didn't have much time for him. Not surprised. He smelt like a midden. Terrible. There may have been others. I wasn't here all the time. I've others to see to."

Again, the thought of having a job which was devoted exclusively to pain and its alleviation struck McNeil.

"Doesn't it get to you?" she asked.

Jamieson's brown eyes fixed on hers once more.

"What?"

"Seeing folk in pain all the time."

The eyes fell away.

"Aye," said Jamieson quietly. "But you can help them. Somebody's got to."

"But, like you said, you can't give them pain killers. Must be hellish."

The smile came back to Jamieson's lips.

"No, no. There's not just injections and tablets. Sometimes you can help by just being with them, talking, holding their hand. There's worse jobs."

"I can't think of many," said McNeil.

"Aye, there are," said Jamieson. "Ask the HIV nurses. Their patients are all younger, and lots of them are dying. And folk treat them like they're kinda untouchable." The smile had faded for the moment. She looked at her hands and rubbed them together. There was a sudden smell of lavender. The silence stretched on.

"Yes," said McNeil, to break it. "I see some sad things, but not all the time, not like that."

There was a pause, then, suddenly, the smile was back on Jamieson's lips, but this time bigger, lighting up her whole face.

"Here, you trying to depress me?" she asked.

McNeil laughed, recognizing that the somberness of the mood had been introduced not by Jamieson or her line of work but by her own awe at the thought of having to deal with terminal pain day after day. It proved Jamieson's point; the problem was not with the pain itself but with other people's attitudes to the causes of it.

"Sorry," she said.

"Fancy a drug?" asked Jamieson.

McNeil looked at her.

"Caffeine," said Jamieson, straight-faced.

They laughed again and set out for the nurses' rest room.

****

Gillian Hayne was in a bottom corner of her garden, adding bundles of papers to a small fire in a mesh container. She'd started it to burn clippings from a pyracantha which was beginning to spread too far over the west-facing wall. The pile had been lying there for nearly a month and, with little wind blowing, it was an ideal day for getting rid of it. When the fire was well established, she'd gone back into the house and begun to work through the shelves and filing cabinets in her husband's study. She'd looked quickly at each bundle, kept a few individual sheets and thrown the rest into a shopping bag on a special wheeled frame which she'd then trundled down the garden path. She watched with the fascination that flames always inspire and was annoyed when the phone she'd brought with her started to ring. The annoyance increased when the caller identified himself. It was Leith.

"Gillian. How are you?" he asked.

"Never felt better," she replied. "What do you want?"

It was a treat to be able to deal with these people in the way she'd always felt they deserved. For years, acting the role of professorial wife had cramped her into a polite pretence of interest. Now, she didn't need to care. The little hesitation on the line showed that her tone had had its effect.

"Er... Just wondered how you were coping," said Leith at last.

"Very well," she said. "Thank you for your concern. Goodbye."

"Er ... there was something," Leith said very quickly, to stop her hanging up.

She waited, saying nothing.

"I wondered if I might come around," he said.

"Whatever for?"

"There are a few things that Alistair and I were ... working on together. I don't have copies of all of them. I'd rather like to..."

"Too late, I'm afraid," said Mrs Hayne, smiling as the curling, blackening pages twisted in the flames.

"What?"

"Too late."

"Why?"

"I'm burning them, having a bit of a clear-out. Anyway, John's already been round. He took away a lot of papers."

"Carlyle?" said Leith.

95

"Yes. I said he could help himself, so there won't be anything relevant left for you to worry about."

"I'm not worried, it's…"

"Look," she interrupted, "if I find anything … interesting, I'll hang on to it. One never knows."

Leith was profoundly disturbed by the control and confidence in her voice, and her asides baffled him completely. How much did she really know about Hayne's contacts with the rest of them? Was she really getting rid of his papers? If so, why? Surely Hayne hadn't been stupid enough to confide in his wife.

"Listen, Gillian," he began, "there are some rather important research findings which need to be substantiated. I could…"

"All gone," said Mrs Hayne. "No point keeping them. Let someone else get the glory. They're no good to Alistair now, are they? And now I really must fly. We'll be seeing you at the cremation, I hope."

She didn't wait for a reply and rang off, leaving Leith in a confusion he had no idea how to handle. She continued to stare at the lively, greedy fire and her lips spread into a smile.

**\*\*\*\***

Ross and Carston set out early for the university and arrived with time in hand. Ross parked in Southside Avenue and they took their time walking up beside the playing field towards the main teaching blocks. A few students were sitting and lying on the grass around the edges of the field in groups or on their own, some reading, some talking. It was all so peaceful that it seemed unreal to Carston.

"Ivory towers, eh?" he said as they walked along.

"Yes," replied Ross.

Carston waved a hand towards the scene on their left. "Wonder what it feels like—being young, sitting around in the sun reading, time to take stock."

"They'd better make the most of it; they'll be looking for jobs soon enough."

Carston nodded. Ross' realism wasn't negative; as usual, he saw things as they were. But Carston himself couldn't help feeling a little nostalgia for his own student days and a tinge of sadness that the apparently carefree individuals lying in today's sun would, in a couple of years, progressively be losing their ideals and having to compromise with people and processes they hadn't yet met. OK, there was always the next generation to take their places, but the way things were going, the lazy spreading of possibilities that a university education had always implied was fast disappearing.

A few minutes later, in Carlyle's study, the feeling of unreality came back to him again. He supposed it came from the fact that the place was dominated by books. Each shelf was crammed and there were more books and papers on every other available surface. There was a computer terminal on the desk but it wasn't switched on and the fact that its keyboard was stuffed vertically into a gap between it and a tray full of files suggested that it didn't get much use. As far as Carston was concerned, it was a point in Carlyle's favor.

Carlyle himself was no stereotype. His grey suit was smart but somehow style-less. He was as tall as Ross and moved with an ease which belied the fact that his was a sedentary occupation. His voice was quiet but, from the outset, he made it clear that they weren't entirely welcome. After clearing papers from a couple of chairs so that they could sit down, it was he who asked the first question.

"We're honored, I suppose," he said. "A visit from the CID. What exactly are you looking for?"

It was, of course, a very good question and Carston had no idea of the answer.

"Well, it's just that Professor Hayne's death was not as straightforward as it seemed," he said. "So, we've got to poke around."

"Poke around?"

There was a smile on Carlyle's lips as he repeated the expression. Carston returned it.

"Yes, while we're waiting for the full medical report. It's not official yet, but I think it's clear that Professor Hayne didn't just die. He was killed."

The smile vanished but otherwise, Carlyle's reaction was barely noticeable. He blinked and looked out of the window.

"Murdered, you mean."

"Killed unlawfully."

"Well, well, well," said Carlyle, his gaze still on the trees outside.

"You don't seem surprised," said Carston.

"I am, in a way. But, after all his illnesses … well … it's been on the cards for a while. Not unlawful killing, of course, but it's certainly no surprise that he's gone."

"Could you tell us a bit more about him? What sort of chap was he?"

Carlyle seemed to compose himself, then decide the line he was going to take. It was surprisingly direct.

"I suppose the classic question is 'Did he have any enemies?' Well, with Alistair it'd be quicker to ask if he had any friends."

"You're way ahead of us, Dr Carlyle," said Carston. "You're saying he was disliked, are you?"

"Universally," said Carlyle, his voice flat, factual, not seeking to create any particular effect.

Carston had skimmed through the print-outs of the letters and notes that Hayne had left on his iPad and experienced the full venom of the man's views of his colleagues and the hospital staff. Hayne had been a vitriolic individual but respect for the dead usually cushioned people's assessments and glossed over imperfections. Not this time.

"That's a pretty damning assessment, isn't it?" said Carston.

Carlyle spread his hands.

"You asked me. Others will tell you the same. There's no point in pretending. Alistair wasn't a popular man. In fact some of us thought that we were just part of his plan."

"Plan?"

Carlyle nodded.

"He was ambitious. He'd've preferred to be at King's in Aberdeen. Had his eyes on an Oxbridge post really though, then perhaps a Vice-Chancellorship somewhere. Sadly, though, he didn't have a great intellect and he was in a rather esoteric field. His research was competent, no more. So he had to go the committee route—the sideways shift into management."

Carston waited, knowing he would explain.

"I think the current expression is moving and shaking. Ghastly idea, but that's what he did. He moved and shook. Met people, volunteered to contribute to steering groups, helped to shape, or as some of us see it, cancel the future."

Now that he was delivering, they were certainly getting their money's worth. He sighed, straightened the edges of a pile of notes on the desk in front of him, then continued.

"Oh, the system certainly needed changing. There were too many passengers, too many parasites. But there was also quality, value. We were helping to show that life was more than a mechanistic progression. But we were out of touch, apparently."

He stopped and spread his hands again at Carston to suggest that that's all there was to it. Carston nodded and thought for a moment.

"Some of the notes we found on his iPad thing were certainly a little … sharp," he said.

Carlyle turned his head to look at him.

"Sharp?" he said.

"Yes. In fact, there was one saying something about closing down your department."

A smile came back to Carlyle's lips.

"Yes, I know all about that," he said. "Alistair's goal was to tailor courses so that students were offered clear, vocational options. None of this aesthetic dabbling or mind-broadening nonsense. He considered European Cultural Studies an anachronism. Wanted it absorbed into the Law faculty."

"His notes mention a paper he'd written on the idea. Would it be possible to get hold of that?"

There was a brief silence, after which Carlyle appeared to have made up his mind about something.

"It's gone," he said.

"Gone?"

"Yes. I've been clearing out Alistair's study. There were boxes of papers, minutes, notes, goodness knows what else. I've been getting rid of … oh, irrelevant things."

Carston was about to protest but Carlyle raised a hand to stop him and carried on.

"I know, I know. Everything's relevant now that you're dealing with a suspicious death, but I didn't know that. My thoughts were for the department."

"I'd prefer it if you left decisions about Professor Hayne's belongings to us," said Carston, with obvious irritation.

"Of course," said Carlyle. "So, are you here to look for potential perpetrators?"

Carston spread his hands.

"A bit early for that," he said. "D'you think we'd find any?"

To his surprise, Carlyle actually laughed.

"Highly unlikely, I'd say."

"Why's that?"

Carlyle paused a moment, the smile slowly dying from his lips. He raised a hand and swept it to indicate the book-laden shelves.

"I think the expression today is 'All mouth and no trousers'," he said. "Words, that's what we deal in here. We 'talk the talk', to use another ghastly modern term. Theories, ideas. Perish the thought that we'd ever have to act on any of them."

"Interesting," said Carston, noting that, for someone who claimed to be "out of touch" with moving and shaking, he was comfortable enough with its terminology.

Carlyle shook his head.

"Not really. We've never had to do anything. No one expects that of us. We discuss things, argue, speculate. And we get paid for it. It's wonderful. Doesn't breed action men, though."

He stopped and seemed to be struck by an idea.

"Except Alistair, maybe."

"In what way?"

"As I said, he moved and shook. I suppose that's doing something. He certainly made some changes."

"Which didn't please you by the sound of it."

Carlyle looked at him and smiled.

"Not in the least," he said. "I'm old-fashioned, you see. I have this strange idea that we're here to educate students."

"And Professor Hayne didn't."

The smile was still on Carlyle's lips.

"I think we're going round in circles," he said.

Carston half agreed with him but felt that he'd like to probe a little more deeply.

"We're taking up too much of your time," he said, standing up. "But I'd rather like to come back some time if I may."

"More poking around?" asked Carlyle.

"That's all I know about," said Carston.

Carlyle in turn got up and shook first his, then Ross' hand. He took them to the door and pointed down the corridor to the room where they'd find the next interviewee on their list, Christie.

Carston stopped and said, "Before we talk to Dr Christie, I'd like to take a look at Professor Hayne's room if that's possible."

"Of course. It's just here."

He took them across the corridor and used his own key to open the door. The room was as full of books and papers as Carlyle's had been, but there were large gaps on some of the shelves. Carston pointed at them.

"Irrelevant things?" he asked.

Carlyle smiled. "I'm afraid so," he said.

"Where's it gone?"

"The incinerator, I regret to say," said Carlyle. "Believe me, it was all esoteric stuff. The library took some but it hasn't room for things no one will ever want to consult. I went to see Alistair's wife and she's not interested in it. In fact, she even asked me to take a heap of files from his study there."

"And they've been destroyed, too?"

"I'm afraid so. Believe me, they're of no use to anyone. Not even the books, not even for charity shops. Rather sad, really." He looked at his watch, and went on. "Forgive me, I'll have to leave you. I have a tutorial…"

"Oh, there's no need for you to hang about," said Carston. "If you don't mind, we'll just have a little look around."

Carlyle nodded and left them.

"What d'you make of him?" he asked.

Ross shrugged.

"He's either naïve or a devious bugger," he said.

"I don't think he's naïve," said Carston. "OK, let's see what we've got."

They began opening drawers, taking books and files from shelves, both of them trying to sense the man who'd spent so much of his time here. There was nothing. It might just as well be a store room.

"Funny," said Carston, after a while. "I thought there was more to him than this."

"What d'you mean?" said Ross.

"I've been looking at the notes from his iPad thing—the ones you printed out. They're like … well, cryptic crossword things."

"How d'you mean?"

Carston shook his head. "Weird expressions, sentences that don't mean anything." He took out his notebook and flipped through some pages.

"Here," he said, before reading, "'I've forgotten what comfort's like. Except the one which ensures a calm passage across many a bad night.' What the hell's that mean? And this bit, about Carlyle visiting him: 'So depressing to hear it coming from him. So inappropriate. The insolence of office.'"

"Academics," said Ross. "They live in a different world."

Carston put his notebook away and looked round the room.

"There's nothing here, is there?" he said.

Ross shook his head.

Carston opened one of the desk drawers. There were just paper clips, notebooks and some colored pens. He flicked through the pages of the desk diary. Every entry was printed in block capitals and they were all committee meetings. Ross had opened the top drawer of a filing cabinet and was looking through the folders in it.

"Lecture notes here," he said, opening a dog-eared pink folder. "'Seventeenth century morals', 'Racine and the Bible', 'Wit and ethics'."

"Holy bugger, wasn't he?" said Carston.

Ross was reading bits to himself.

"It's boring as hell," he said. "Must've sent 'em all to sleep with this. They'd've been better getting it out of a library book. And look at it."

He held up the notes and riffled through the pages for Carston to see.

"None of them hand-written, all off a printer." He dropped the folder back in its place. "Know the feeling I get? It's all empty. There's nobody home."

Carston was nodding.

"Yes. Sterile. Defensive. Didn't want to give anything away."

"If there was anything to give," said Ross.

The bottom drawer was empty but there was no dust inside it. Whatever it had contained had been removed. In the drawer above it Carston found a sheaf of papers. They were the minutes of departmental, faculty and university meetings, each with the relevant agenda. On most of them alongside each item someone, presumably Hayne, had marked a tick or a cross. It was the only sign of commitment he found.

"Maybe he was hiding something," said Ross.

"He was hiding every bloody thing. It's a bugger, isn't it?"

"What?"

"Here we are looking for reasons why somebody might want to kill him but there's nobody here to kill."

102

Ross said nothing. The remark sounded typically oblique. Carston was always taking surprising directions, sometimes well away from the matter in hand.

"In fact, maybe that's it," Carston went on, confirming Ross' suspicion.

"What is?"

"The bloke's absence. Maybe that's part of what we're dealing with."

Ross sighed.

"I know I'm going to regret this, but what do you mean?" he asked.

Carston smiled briefly but his brow furrowed quickly again as he pursued his thought.

"OK. According to Carlyle, Hayne's ... sort of disruptive as far as the department's concerned. Crosses people, upsets them. So how are they going to feel about that?"

"Pissed off."

"Right. So they'll resent him, want to get back at him somehow. So they try. And what do they get?"

"I don't know. Surprise me."

"Nothing." He waved a hand to indicate the room and everything in it. "They get this. He's not there. They just come up against this emptiness, these ... functions. They're like so many barricades, Jim."

"And?" said Ross, still uncertain where Carston was heading.

"And they get frustrated. And maybe that develops into something stronger."

"And that's the motive, is it?" said Ross, his tone revealing what he thought of the theory.

Carston's expression was still thoughtful.

"If you're angry, frustrated, you get rid of it all by punching a pillow or something. You need to release it. What if all you're hitting's a vacuum? Makes it worse."

"And can you see any of this lot actually doing anything?" said Ross.

Carston shrugged. Ross was still skeptical but the coldness of Hayne's room gave him the same uneasy feeling as Carston about the man who'd occupied it. One of the most familiar components of all their investigations was passion; operating in a void was unsettling.

When they eventually finished, they were ready for some real contact again. They knocked on Christie's door and, when he opened it, Carston was, inexplicably, prepared to dislike him right away. There was no welcoming smile, no form of greeting; he simply let them into his office and sat down behind his desk. Carston noticed the subtle shades of the collarless grandfather-style shirt he was wearing under his leather waistcoat and the general neatness of everything around him. For some reason that he couldn't explain, however, the impression that was conveyed was not just one of tidiness but of someone in control of his world, protective of something.

Unlike Carlyle, Christie expressed no interest in why they were there and his answers to their questions on Hayne gave nothing away. He praised the man's skills as departmental head and, although they had had their differences, he was on the whole in sympathy with Hayne's vision of the ideal structure of post-millennial universities.

"He wasn't all that popular, though, was he?" asked Ross. "The sort of changes he was making weren't everybody's cup of tea, were they?"

"Not much room for revolutions in small minds," said Christie.

Carston's attention was grabbed immediately.

"What d'you mean?" he asked.

Unashamedly, Christie launched into very unflattering descriptions of his departmental colleagues. He didn't exactly condemn them, but he did manage to imply that none of them had the sort of stature that would give any substance to their opinions. He obviously thought that Carlyle was an anachronism and, one by one, he consigned the others to an ineffectual level where they played harmless intellectual games remote from the realities of death and progress. As a demonstration of character assassination, it was in the serial killer league. Each opinion he expressed deepened Carston's dislike of him and the tightening of Ross' lips as he took notes and asked his own questions showed that Christie was having the same impact on him.

"You're not painting a very flattering picture of the department," said Carston at last.

"I'm not painting a picture at all," said Christie, immediately. "I'm simply answering your questions."

"So your opinion of your colleagues isn't as low as it seems?"

104

"I have no 'opinion' of my colleagues, at least not one I would wish to articulate for public consumption. Surely you're not here to seek opinions?"

"Well, yes we are at this stage," said Carston. "I've always considered that the process of evidential acquisition presupposes a data-based search pattern against which speculation may be assessed as a relevant adjunct to informational input."

Ross' pencil dug hard into his pad as he kept his face straight and serious. Christie paused and, for almost the first time, looked straight at Carston.

"Only an adjunct?" he said, his expression showing that he knew Carston was talking crap.

"Only an adjunct," replied Carston, his face open, honest and totally innocent. "So you'll understand that your opinions are indeed very valuable to us."

"Really?" said Christie, deciding that Carston was more dangerous than he seemed.

"Yes, sir," replied Carston, holding Christie's gaze and forcing him eventually to look away at the trees outside his window.

"In that case, you may need to establish a wider context against which to make your assessment."

"I'm sorry?"

"You say I seem to have a low opinion of my colleagues' research capabilities."

"Well, it seemed…"

Christie continued to speak as if Carston had said nothing.

"You must judge that against what passes for learning in our community. Alistair himself dabbled away with a writer whose so-called insights have, since Freud and Jung, been revealed as the platitudes they always were. Frankly, Alistair's work was irrelevant. And to be honest, not even very good."

"He was head of…"

Again, Christie continued to speak over Carston's words.

"And the acting head's no better. He isn't even a true European Studies specialist. He started out as a medic but didn't have the stamina."

"Stamina?" said Carston.

Christie sighed.

"Yes. That's all it needs, stamina and memory. Law's even easier; there it's just memory."

"You don't seem to have much respect for your profession," said Ross.

"On the contrary," said Christie. "It's because I value it that I hate seeing it debased."

"Debased?"

"Yes. For example, I don't know whether you're planning to see Dr Gutcheon, but she typifies what I mean. She's produced several papers on the influence of Juliette Drouet on the structure of the poetry collections of Victor Hugo's middle period. Are you familiar with nineteenth century French poetry at all?"

"Peripherally," said Carston.

Well, it was better than telling the truth.

"Juliette Drouet was Hugo's mistress. He kept her more or less as a prisoner, stuck in a room copying out his poems while he had other affairs all over France. Any influence she may have had would have been on his testosterone levels rather than his alexandrines. Now the point is that Dr Gutcheon is a sincere, meticulous academic, but she is celibate. No one who had ever had sexual intercourse could have conceived of the nonsense contained in the papers she writes. The result is that she misses the point completely and so her opinions seem highly original and are deemed to be of considerable significance."

"In other words," prompted Carston.

"In other words, Dr Gutcheon doesn't know what she's talking (or writing) about, nor do most of the people who read her stuff and so her ignorance passes for wisdom."

Carston nodded his head slowly. Wherever you worked, there were people you had to put up with. Back at Burns Road he had Ridley, Spurle, and now Reid to cope with. But, as colleagues, even they were infinitely preferable to this venomous individual.

"Isn't that rather a cynical attitude to scholarship?" he asked.

"It's a realistic analysis of the processes it involves," replied Christie, seemingly unaware of the hostility his attitude was generating. "Some bring genuine insights to their fields of study, some toil away to churn out truisms and some stumble into serendipity."

"What's your field?" asked Ross suddenly.

The question surprised Christie. He paused as he considered whether he might be compromised by his reply then said, "I've tended to spread my net somewhat. My doctoral thesis was a comparative study of imagery in nineteenth century prose fiction in France, Germany and England, I've published papers on topics from Elizabethan iconography to Lorca's *Blood Wedding* and I'm at present researching a book on liquid and its associations in Dickens."

Ross wished he hadn't asked.

"Lot of toil involved in that," said Carston, choosing the word deliberately but knowing it was nothing more than a clumsy gibe.

"It's a privilege to be able to pursue the things which interest me," said Christie smugly.

His company was almost suffocating. His control never wavered and his air of superiority seemed only to grow as the conversation went on. In the end, Carston was glad to cut the interview short and leave him in his cocoon while they went to find Ritchie. On the way up to his office, which was on the first floor, Carston and Ross exchanged just two words.

"Prick," said Carston.

"Aye," said Ross.

# Chapter Eight

The Student Representative Council's offices were on the corner of Southside Avenue and Irvine Place, just a few yards along from the university chapel. Sandra Scott had sat in the sun on the low wall outside for half an hour, watching the groups of students walking to and from classes along the narrow pavements. She was wondering whether Christie was worth the time and trouble involved in making a complaint about his behavior. The fear she'd felt had vanished, swamped by her increasing anger at both him and herself. He was a nothing, full of self-importance and some spurious notion of superiority to which he felt his status as a university teacher entitled him. But she couldn't get him out of her head and was annoyed still to be wasting so much nervous energy on such a specimen.

Enough. Even if she didn't actually make a complaint, she needed to talk about it. She hopped down from the wall and went inside. Once she'd explained her business, she was taken through to a small room by one of the SRC's sabbatical officers who introduced herself simply as Maggie. There was no embarrassment, no false sympathy or specially lowered voices and Scott was able to describe what had happened in quick, simple terms. Maggie just listened, nodding occasionally and interjecting the odd "Uh-huh" or "Yep" to signal her understanding of what she was being told.

"So, he hasn't actually done anything … definite?" she asked, when Scott eventually stopped and opened her hands in a gesture which indicated that that was it. "It's all innuendo."

Scott nodded then said, "Well, no. He's always leaning against me when he looks at my notes and putting his hand on my shoulders and neck and back. OK, he's never grabbed a tit or anything but …

well, it gets to you. There's no rest from it. And yes, he's always suggesting things without saying them straight. Like I could get great marks if I just let him … you know. But you're right, it's not really very definite. That's why I wondered about coming to see you."

"Oh no, you're dead right to come," said Maggie. "The university's hot on this sort of thing. They take it seriously."

"Yeah, but he'll just deny it all and that'll be that."

"We don't know that. And it'll maybe warn him off you."

"Yes, and he'll be marking down everything I hand in."

She was right. Whichever way Christie got to hear about her accusations, even if she just told him directly to his face with no one else involved, he'd make sure she paid some sort of price.

"It's not that I'm a poor wee soul," she said. "I can see how pathetic he is. It just … makes me angry that he's got that sort of power."

"Yes, well, he can't abuse it the way he's doing. Not today," said Maggie.

She was taking some sheets of paper from a file as she spoke. She passed them over to Scott.

"See? The university's policy on sexual harassment. And the procedures to follow. No holds barred. Suggestive remarks or looks, compromising invitations, it covers everything. He can't hide from this."

Scott looked through it. It did seem to take a very tough line and constituted a fairly comprehensive indictment of the things Christie had been getting up to.

"Can you give me a copy of this?" she said.

"Sure," said Maggie. "So what do you want to do?"

The options were clearly laid out on the pages in front of her. She could talk to other people—the head of department, student welfare officer, chaplain, hall of residence warden—and there was a promise of total confidentiality. If she wanted to take it further, it would be referred to a Vice-Principal, who'd investigate it and decide what action to take. The protection was there and it did seem to tilt the balance more evenly than she'd felt it to be when she was sitting on the wall outside.

"I ought to do it, didn't I?" she said. "Just to show the bugger."

"Yes. And to stop him trying it on others," said Maggie. "But there's no point pretending—it could be a hassle."

"Yeah, I know."

They talked some more about precedents in Cairnburgh and elsewhere and it did seem that the old Sex Discrimination Act had changed the climate. But Scott knew that, in the Brave New World, dinosaurs still lurked.

****

In the bedsit in Caledonian Road, the man was agitated. He'd rolled up the black blind and was looking out at the blank windows of the tenement across the alley. Most of them had some sort of curtain or rag across them and the rooms behind them were gloomy enough to need lights on, even though it was late morning. The walls which held them were made from dark grey Aberdeen granite. It was a material that shone and sparkled when used to its best advantage in up-market bungalows or the Edwardian villas of the west end. Here, piled crushingly high on either side of narrow channels, it was a louring, depressing sight, seeming to imprison, not just protect, those who lived inside it.

The man turned back to look at his own room and was struck again by its dreariness. Until he'd seen the bright posters on Scott's walls, the books and bits and pieces strewn on her table and shelves, and most of all, Scott herself, seeming so comfortable amongst them, he'd been unaware of just how miserable his own surroundings were. But the hunger he'd satisfied so quickly and easily before, by using the women in his magazines, was growing and changing its shape. Scott belonged to him. He knew her naked body and the room in which she displayed it. They were both part of his experience and the contrast with this dark hole where he spent so much of his time was beginning to press on him. It wasn't right that he should be here when his real living was done in the bright colors of the room opposite the sycamore trees.

In a way, he regretted having met her in the park. If she'd continued to walk past and just let him look at her, it would have been fine, but she'd stopped. And she'd spoken to him, challenged him. That was wrong. It was too fast. He needed time to prepare for things like that. It had mixed him up completely, brought his hunger to the surface. And, slowly, the hunger had evolved, taking their relationship a stage further. Now he wanted her voice as well as the sight of her body. After their meeting, he'd stayed away from her and her room for a few days but that had only made things worse. She was his. He had to go back to her. She'd called him a pervert. That was OK. There was fire in her when she said it. But he'd done nothing to her and she must have realized that he was OK. Not a threat.

He began to walk to and fro, struggling to contain the pains and fears in his head and trying to replace them with the images of Scott that had once been enough to soothe his excitements. In the end, the pressure was too great. He pulled the blind down again, picked up his cigarettes and lighter and left for the university.

****

Carston and Ross were both beginning to feel the need for some coffee. After the ten minutes with Christie, they'd had something of an antidote in the form of Dr Ritchie. He'd been fairly non-committal about Hayne and mostly generous in his assessments of his other colleagues, even Christie. Brief chats with Munro and McChaddie produced similar results but then spells with a couple of others brought departmental politics back to the fore and egos began to loom larger than educational issues once more.

They'd been at it for almost two hours and were glad that there was only one more person on their list. Unfortunately for them, it was Leith. Even more unfortunately, he himself was, to use a totally inappropriate term, fresh from another altercation with his editor. He'd phoned almost immediately after Leith's call to Mrs Hayne and started by complaining about Leith's "so-called camera-ready material", which had been so bad that it had given him a migraine. He claimed to be "working in a climate of resigned goodwill" which Leith's "arrogant and officious bungling" was jeopardizing. Barely five minutes before Carston knocked at his door, Leith had told the editor that all further communications with him would be through his lawyers, and that it was regrettable that editorial integrity had to be compromised by small-minded bureaucrats. His anger was still gnawing at him as he opened the door for the two policemen.

Carston and Ross stood for a moment, both reluctant to step into the cloud of alien molecules that hit their nostrils. Leith looked at them, then took a deep breath and sighed, "CID, I take it. Come in then. I can give you ten minutes."

They didn't want ten seconds but it had to be done. Carston noticed that the window was slightly open and he went straight across the room and leaned back against the sill, just beating Ross to it. Leith had retreated behind his desk to sit down. He pushed his chair back and clasped his hands together in his lap. He was in shirt sleeves and they saw the damp patches under his arms.

"I fail to see why I'm being questioned by the police," he said. "A colleague dies after years of illness and a major operation and suddenly there's some sort of enquiry. It's damned inconvenient. What's going on?"

"Routine, sir," said Carston. "Just gathering what information we can for a thorough investigation."

"But what on earth is there to investigate? Professor Hayne was effectively an invalid. His condition was terminal. Surely you don't 'investigate' everyone who dies when they're in that sort of state?"

There was nothing approaching sympathy for Hayne in his tone. He was simply irritated that his routine was being interrupted.

"No, sir," replied Carston. "But that's not the way it happened."

"Why not?" Leith insisted.

Carston had no intention of giving in to him.

"Let's just say that sometimes we smell a rat," he said.

Ross spluttered a little as he coughed.

"So," Carston hurried on, "if you don't mind, we'd just like to get some impressions from you of the late Professor Hayne."

Leith seemed to be deciding whether he'd co-operate.

"He had the right ideas," he said at last, "but the wrong way of implementing them."

"Could you perhaps develop that a bit?" asked Carston.

Leith waved an arm to encompass the room and the buildings they were in. Carston regretted having provoked the gesture.

"We were due for a clear-out. Too much dead weight here. Need to concentrate our efforts a bit, get some serious research done. Hayne was working on that but he was compromising all the time."

"Compromising?"

"Yes. Making allowances, using early retirements, playing with budgets. It was going to take ages. Only one way to get a fresh start—cut away the garbage, get rid of the hangers-on, lay down the ground rules so that nobody's in any doubt where they stand."

Carston and Ross both noticed that, as he spoke, his accent became less neutral and moved towards some variant of a Midlands twang. When he stopped, he realized that his words had taken them by surprise.

"It's brutal but it's the real world. We've got to pay our way like anyone else."

He gestured again, this time towards the window.

"Look at the North Sea. You don't see Shell or Chevron or any of that lot indulging their workforce's little whims, do you? They produce the goods or they're out. No reason why universities shouldn't be the same."

"Interesting," said Carston. "And what sort of 'goods' are you producing here, then?"

Leith was ready with his answer.

"Trained minds, ready to contribute. Translators, teachers, civil servants, diplomats—all the obvious things. But more than that, the next generation of managers. Yes, unfashionable amongst some of my colleagues, I know, but that's what'll drive the future."

"And Professor Hayne shared your views?"

There was a slight hesitation before Leith replied.

"Not all of them," he admitted. "He had his blind spots. But on the whole, yes, I think so. He knew that, for most things, he could rely on my support if it came to a vote."

"I suppose it's all on the back burner now, though," said Carston.

Leith picked up a pencil and scratched his scalp with it. Carston tried not to look at the particles which fell onto his collar as a result.

"No, I don't think so," Leith said eventually. "You've got to understand, it's not just a question of opposing factions. There's only one side actively seeking change; the others are just ... well, there. Static, bereft of ideas, hoping the whole thing will go away. It won't."

"But without the head of department to ... keep it moving..."

"It's not just a departmental issue. There are people in the administration who know that things have started. There's an impetus there. They'll make sure they make the right appointments to keep it going."

Carston tried to push him further but Leith was willing to go only so far. At last Carston took the direct route.

"Sort of power game, then, is it?" he asked.

Leith looked up at him, squinting a little because he was looking into the light from the window.

"*Scientia potestas est,*" he said.

They waited.

"Knowledge is power," he translated.

"Depends how you use it," said Carston.

"No it doesn't," said Leith. "And I'm afraid I've no time for any more of this. There's a faculty sub-committee this afternoon and I've got some figures to prepare for it. I don't really see that this is getting us anywhere so unless there's something specific and relevant that I can add…"

He stopped, inviting them to take his hint. Without hesitation, Ross went and opened the door. Carston smiled and followed him.

"If there is, we'll be in touch," he said and, rather to Leith's surprise, the two policemen disappeared before he had time to stand up. He sat for a while, going back over what had been said to try to find what their purpose had been. Their excuse seemed legitimate; the whole conversation had just been about Hayne. There were no accusations, awkward questions or surprises. For that, at least, he was grateful. As far as he was concerned, the sooner Hayne was cremated and forgotten, the better. For now, there were more important matters to be dealt with. He stood up, took a copy of the previous year's diary from the top shelf and started flicking through it, checking very carefully any entry that concerned meetings with Hayne.

****

As Carston and Ross walked down the stairs and outside, there was no need for them to say what was at the front of their minds. They'd both made faces as they left the room and were just glad to be putting distance between themselves and Leith's miasma. As they started down the street, they heard footsteps running behind them and a voice calling "Excuse me". They stopped and turned as a student came up to them. It was Scott. She was carrying her bag over one arm and her jacket over the other.

"Are you the police?" she asked.

"Yes," said Carston. "Is it that obvious?"

Scott managed a smile.

"No," she said. "Everybody knows you're here, though. Can't keep secrets."

Carston smiled back at her.

"Something we can do for you?" he asked.

"I don't know," she said, dropping her eyes away from him. "It's ... it's tricky."

"Try us," said Ross.

She looked at him. He was the sort of guy she might have fancied when he was younger but the fact that he was past thirty put him over the hill. His face, though, looked sympathetic.

"It's about ... sexual harassment," she said, her voice louder than she'd intended it to be.

Carston and Ross were completely thrown. Where the hell was this coming from? Carston looked at her. She was looking from one to the other of them, waiting for a reaction.

"You mean here?" said Carston. "At the university?"

She nodded. Carston didn't want to say anything that might make things worse or lose her confidence, but he needed more information. The one positive feature was that this was no damsel in distress. She looked composed and controlled.

"OK," he said. "First things first. Let's go somewhere where we can talk in comfort. Maybe have a cup of coffee."

Scott shook her head.

"No, I ... I don't want to take up your time. I just wanted to ... well, to find out how often you come across it. I mean, it's not a police matter. It's not assault or anything. It's this lecturer. He's just..." She finished the sentence with a shrug. "I've been talking to people about it here. I just wondered if you've ever had to ... you know ... deal with that sort of thing."

Carston shook his head.

"Usually gets dealt with internally. But it's a serious business. The law's very clear on it."

"Have you reported him?" asked Ross.

"I've talked about it. Nothing formal yet."

"You should," Ross went on, without hesitating. "Don't let him get away with it."

Scott was nodding.

"We can help you, well, advise you, I mean, but, as you say, it's not a police matter."

"Look," said Carston. "I really meant it about a coffee. We're dying for one and we could talk through it all with you and maybe be a bit more helpful. What d'you think?"

Scott looked up at him. He was obviously sincere and wanting to help but there was nothing they could do. She'd intended to say something about the stalker in the park but her recent visit to the SRC had kept Christie at the front of her mind. She hadn't really expected any answers. And they were right, it was an internal university matter.

"It's OK," she said. "I can deal with it."

From the expression on her face, Carston guessed that she probably could but he felt there might be more to say.

"Look, if you won't have coffee with us, just tell us who you are and where to get in touch. You might still need somebody to talk to and I've got a sergeant who's just what you need. And she's worth more than the two of us put together."

Scott smiled and felt glad that she'd spoken to them. She told him that there was no need but she gave him her name and address anyway. In turn, he gave her his card.

"You can ask for me if you like, or sergeant Ross here, but I think you might be better asking for Julie McNeil."

"OK. Thanks," said Scott.

"Are you sure you don't want to tell us about it?"

Scott smiled and hoisted her jacket up over her right shoulder.

"No, really. I'll handle it. But thanks. I'll ring if I need to."

They said their good-byes and watched her walk away up towards the teaching blocks before turning left to go back onto the playing field again. It had all happened so quickly and left them completely disorientated. Carston heaved a huge sigh.

"So much for the ivory tower, eh?" he said.

Ross didn't reply. His face was grim as they carried on down towards Southside Avenue.

"She seemed OK," said Carston. "What do you think?"

"Aye. I think so," said Ross. "Wouldn't hurt to get Julie to give her a ring all the same. Just to show we're with her."

"Right," said Carston. "Now let's go and find some bloody coffee. I'm getting desperate."

\*\*\*\*

The man watched them walk back down to their car. He didn't have to ask to know that they were the police. And Scott had been talking to them. Just as she'd threatened. The misery he'd felt at first when he thought that she was betraying him had drained away as he watched the three of them together. Now, he was just angry. She shouldn't have done that. What was happening between them was their business, no one else's.

****

Latimer was in the middle of a telephone conversation with a senior colleague, George Duncanson. He'd pulled open his desk drawer, taken out a small mirror and was looking at himself as he spoke.

"It's the REF," he said, slowly pushing a finger along the line of each eyebrow. "They're thinking of increasing the number of medics on it."

"So?" said Duncanson.

"So I'm offering my services."

"Like a prostitute," said Duncanson, who was no fan of committees. "What's the advantage?"

"For me, d'you mean?" Latimer wet his lips with his tongue and smiled at himself. "Nothing. I thought it might help to raise the department's profile, that's all. Get some leverage at the university."

"God, Keith, We've got a high enough profile as it is, I'd have thought. What do we want more exposure for?"

"Not exposure, George. Power."

He went on with the argument that he'd rehearsed, making a very persuasive case for being elected onto the REF. Duncanson was right, surgery was still perceived to be at the more glamorous, more visible end of the medical spectrum, but glamour didn't increase staffing or attract a bigger slice of the available funding. That sort of effect only came from mixing with the decision makers. And, of course, although it didn't form part of his pitch to Duncanson, there was the fact that being seen to be involved in an administrative capacity would increase Latimer's own profile and, correspondingly, his chances of qualifying for a merit award. When consultants reached the top of the scale, these awards were the only way of topping up salaries, the "topping up" sometimes being so generous that it effectively doubled the monthly check.

117

He checked his hair and looked closely at the little lines that were beginning to appear at the sides of his eyes.

"I'm not happy if it's going to eat into your timetable even more," Duncanson was saying.

"I can keep a balance, George, you know that," replied Latimer, smiling again to check whether that made the lines deeper.

"Well, if you're sure, you can give it a try. But just give it one session to start with, OK? We'll see how it affects the department."

"Of course. I'll let you know what happens. Bye."

He hung up and put the mirror away. His call to Duncanson had only been a courtesy; he'd been talking about the REF for several weeks with colleagues in other departments. Ever since Hayne had blocked the proposal to increase the REF's size, he'd been working with Leith on a scheme designed to benefit the two of them. Being on the REF would hasten his merit award while his voice and vote would help Leith to the promotion he was desperate to achieve. The demands of long hours in theatre were becoming tedious; research and teaching were a way out. And they were more easily regulated and allowed for a more relaxed lifestyle. By taking this first step towards university involvement, a permanent move to Aberdeen or Edinburgh would be made easier. He'd done enough carving. He wanted more time to enjoy himself; vocational commitment was for new graduates and nuns.

****

From his familiar position at the office window, Carston watched a black mini with two broad white stripes over its roof pull away from the lights. For some reason, it had skis on its roof rack. In May. He shook his head in puzzlement and turned to face Ross and McNeil. It was nearly five thirty and they were tying up the threads of their day.

"So," he said. "What did you get at the Bartholomew, Julie?"

She opened her notebook and pushed it across his desk. It showed a list of names.

"Suture manufacturers," she said. "They use mostly synthetic materials—PDS, Prolene, Vicryl and Monocryl, things like that."

Carston and Ross looked at each other and shrugged.

"Aye, I was impressed, too," said McNeil. "Apparently, they used to use catgut but BSE buggered that up."

She took a small white packet from an inside pocket and handed it to him.

"This is the sort they use."

Carston took the packet and looked at it.

"Unbreakable, is it?" he asked.

"Not necessarily. It seems you can damage sutures by holding them with instruments. Reduces their tensile strength by over fifty per cent apparently. And holding the needle the wrong way can break them, too."

"And none of that happened this time, of course."

"Right," said McNeil. "And I've been in touch with some of the suture people. They all say the same thing. There's no way that any of their stuff could be faulty."

"Surprise, surprise," said Carston.

"I've ticked the ones I've spoken to," said McNeil, pointing to the list. "There's only four left to contact."

"OK, thanks," said Carston. "Jim, you can get onto the others."

"Right," said Ross, copying the names onto a piece of scrap paper.

Carston looked more closely at the suture packet.

"Tell you what," he said, "ask them about heating the things."

"What for?" said Ross.

"Storage instructions here. They give a range of temperatures. I'm wondering what happens to them if they get too hot or too cold."

Ross nodded.

"We could ask Dr Carlyle, too," he said.

"What?"

"That Christie guy said he used to be a medic."

Carston nodded.

"Yes, I clocked that, too. We'll have to ask him about that."

He turned back to McNeil.

"Anything else, Julie?"

"Notes of the medication he was on. Courtesy of Ms Blantyre."

"Anything interesting?"

McNeil shrugged.

"Just a list of drugs. Identical to most other post-op patients apparently."

"How about his visitors?" asked Carston.

"Mostly his wife," said McNeil. She looked at her notebook. "And a couple of guys from the university ... er ... Leith and Carlyle. Carlyle was there quite a while apparently. Went off somewhere then came back for more."

"Went off where?"

McNeil shook her head.

"No idea."

"Were they all regular visitors?" asked Carston, his interest aroused.

"No. Well, the wife was. Not the others though."

"How come you got their names?" asked Ross.

"Hayne moaned to one of the nurses about them. They were there just two days before his op. Upset him a bit."

"Did she say how?"

"No, just that he didn't like them."

"It was mutual," said Carston. "I wish I'd known that before we went to see them today. Could've pushed a bit harder."

"We have to be careful, though," said Ross. "I mean, it must seem like we're accusing some of these folk already. If they take it into their heads to start complaining..." He left the rest of his warning unspoken.

"Yes," said Carston. "They'd know all about citizens' rights, wouldn't they? Love to stir it up for us."

It occurred to Ross that Carston was a fine one to talk about stirring but he said nothing. He just wished they had something a bit more solid to help them concentrate their efforts.

"So," said Carston, "what've we got?"

Ross sat back in his chair.

"Plenty of folk who didn't like him, including his wife," he said.

"Yes, and the surgeon who did his op," said McNeil.

"Oh come on, Julie," said Ross. "From what you said, the guy told you Hayne was a lousy patient. He's not going to top him for that."

"I don't know. With today's NHS, it might be a directive," said Carston. "Make beds available sooner."

"The guy got up folks' noses, that's all," Ross went on. "There's nothing we've heard that says anybody wanted to get rid of him."

Carston didn't entirely agree with him but he let it pass.

120

"And you have to admit," Ross went on, "it's hard to see any of the people we've talked to being murderers."

This time, he was right. The self-satisfactions they'd trawled through that morning, especially those of Leith and Christie, had annoyed Carston but it was hard to think of any of them having the balls to get involved in anything criminal. Mind you, that was exactly the way people got away with things. In what some of them had said there'd been a disdain for colleagues, even specifically for Hayne, which showed no compassion. They'd been ruthless enough not to bother to hide their satisfaction that he'd been taken out of the equation. Ripping at the carcass of his reputation like jackals wasn't so far removed from making the kill. Hayne might have been lingering around death's door long enough for one of them to decide that nudging him through it would be a blameless collaboration in the inevitable.

The door opened and Reid came in.

"We've collated all the data on the outboards and the MOT certificates," he said. "I've processed the material and made out some charge sheets. We can move whenever you like."

"That was quick," said Ross, preventing Carston saying something he would no doubt regret.

"Not really," said Reid. "Bellman and Thom had a lot of superfluous stuff there, lots of duplication. I put it on a spreadsheet, tightened the parameters. The program did the rest."

"And what did the program give you?" asked Carston, his smile ghastly.

"Two names at the garage and three at the outboard workshops."

"Have you got enough to pull them in?"

"Yes sir."

"Do it."

Reid's smile vanished.

"Now sir?"

"Unless you've got some special social activity planned for this evening," said Carston.

"Excuse me, sir," said Ross. "Remember you were telling me to minimize overtime."

Carston looked at him. He'd said no such thing.

Ross went on.

"You were a bit concerned about the budget... I don't suppose delaying 'til the morning will lose us anything. And we'll stay inside the targets you've set."

For a moment, no words came to Carston.

"You did ask me to remind you," said Ross, his tone ludicrously subservient.

"Of course, sergeant. Thank you," said Carston. "OK, Reid. First thing tomorrow morning. I know it's a Saturday, but this is CID. We don't recognize weekends. And let me have your report before lunch tomorrow. And a digest of the material you've been working on today."

Reid reached over and put a folder on the desk.

"It's here, sir. I took the liberty. Thought you'd need it."

"Right," said Carston, suppressing an impulse to put his hands round Reid's throat and squeeze hard. "Goodnight, then."

The suddenness of the dismissal took Reid by surprise. He recovered quickly though, flashed his smile and left.

Carston counted to ten.

"If you don't keep him away from me, Jim. I'll kill him. Slowly."

"You're over-reacting. He's harmless."

"Harmless? He's from Ridley. And it'd help if he wasn't such a smart-arse. Anyway, where were we?"

Ross looked at his notes.

"Finished, I think... Oh, there was that girl..." He flipped over a page and read her name. "Sandra Scott."

"Oh yes. One for you, Julie. Tell her, Jim."

"Student," said Ross, tearing out the page with Scott's name and telephone number on it and handing it to McNeil. "Stopped us at the university. Asked us about sexual harassment. One of her lecturers."

McNeil took the piece of paper. Her mouth had a grimmer set to it.

"Yes. Prime targets," she said.

"Sorry?" said Carston.

"Female students," McNeil explained. "Rape, sexual assault, indecent exposure—helluva lot of them get it. What did she have to say?"

122

Ross sketched the conversation they'd had with Scott and Carston suggested that McNeil should give her a ring just to make contact.

"Low key," he said. "I think she'll manage but maybe a bit of support would help. It doesn't sound like we should be involved. The university's got procedures for things like that."

"Right, sir," said McNeil.

"OK, anything else before we go?" asked Carston.

McNeil in turn looked at her notebook.

"I've fixed for you to see an operation," she said. "There's one tomorrow afternoon. Latimer and McKenzie'll both be there."

"Excellent," said Carston.

"You still want me to look through the procedures for gaps?" asked Ross.

"Yep. The sooner we sort this out, the sooner we can get back to doing what they pay us for."

None of them wanted to hang around. McNeil was being picked up by her fiancé to go and choose paint for their flat, which they were redecorating, Ross wanted to get back to the sanity of Jean and his two daughters and Carston was looking forward to another evening of relaxation and relative silence.

\*\*\*\*

After the hours of vaporous chat at the university, Carston felt he needed to recharge his batteries and fix on something solid again. In his life, nothing was more dependable than to sit with Kath, with a plate of one of her concoctions before him, a bottle of red wine to hand and Channel Four News on the TV. They'd started with a warm goat's cheese salad, moved to a huge dish of roasted mixed vegetables which pumped out a pungent cloud of hot garlic and they were swilling it all down with a Cabernet Sauvignon which Kath had found in Sainsbury's for less than a fiver.

"Guess how many shirts you've got," she said suddenly, as the programme went into a commercial break.

"Dunno. Twenty?"

"Thirty-eight. I counted them this afternoon."

"That means I've got thirty-seven hangers then," he said, taking another swig of wine.

"Why?"

"There's always one too few when I come to hang them up. Anyway, what the hell were you counting my shirts for?"

"Don't know really. I was putting stuff away, opened the cupboard and suddenly saw them all there. I just wondered. Because you only ever wear about five of them."

"It's for when I grow up," said Carston. "I'll need them then."

Kath looked pointedly at his stomach then at the lump of ciabatta he was dunking into his vegetables.

"I think you've grown up enough," she said.

This comfortable mood helped to banish the lingering thoughts of hospitals and operations. It lasted until just after nine o'clock. They'd turned off the television, Carston had done the washing up and Kath had once again brought up the subject of Alex and Jennie Crombie's marital problems. Kath was genuinely concerned because Jennie's early hints that something was wrong had been replaced by silences and a straight refusal to talk about anything connected with her personal life. It wasn't like her and it made Kath even more determined to try to help her (and Alex for that matter) out of the trough into which they seemed to have fallen. Carston was expected to do his share of the marriage guidance work and Kath was pressing him towards some sort of promise when, to his relief, the phone rang. Very badly, he mimed an apology to her and went into the hall to answer it. It was Brian McIntosh.

"Sorry to bother you at home again, Jack," said the doctor. "Thought you should know, though."

"No problem, Brian. What is it?"

"The Bartholomew. Another post-operative death. A woman. Mrs Rioch."

"Christ! What was it this time?"

"Don't know yet. I've just got the call myself. From the sound of it, though, it's internal hemorrhaging again."

"What, the same as Hayne?"

"I don't know about the same, but it sounds suspiciously like it."

Carston had to suppress the satisfaction he felt. It was a totally inappropriate response to the news of somebody's death but it seemed to justify the line he'd taken with the professor.

"So much for Latimer's infallibility," he said.

"Not his fault."

"Oh?"

"No, she was somebody else's patient."

**** 

Scott had played a vigorous game of squash with Noble. For a change, she'd won. Usually, Noble's long arms seemed to reach every shot and, for a tall person, she was quick around the court. But that evening, Scott had played a faster, more powerful game and beaten Noble with speed rather than subtlety. The feeling of satisfaction it had given her was more to do with the draining off of excess adrenaline than any need to win on Scott's part. She was in her dressing gown, rubbing at her damp hair and singing an old Jarvis Cocker number when she heard a knock at the door. It was one of the girls from the downstairs flat.

"Phone call," she said.

"What d'you mean?" asked Scott.

"Downstairs. Phone call. I shouted but you obviously didn't hear."

"I was singing."

"I noticed."

"Who is it?"

"No idea. Mystery man. Didn't know your name."

"What?"

"Just asked for the girl in the upstairs room. Spooky, eh?"

Scott felt a little chill. Nobody used the payphone. Every student living there had at least one mobile. Scott thanked the girl and went downstairs.

"Hello," she said, her left hand still working the towel into the hair at the nape of her neck.

"Wasn't a good idea. Talkin to the polis," said a man's voice.

"What?"

"You heard. Bad mistake. I haven't done you no harm, have I?"

"Who are you? What are you talking about?"

"You know fine what I mean. I saw you. This afternoon. With them bizzies. There was no need for it."

The anger Scott had got rid of in the squash court rushed back into her. She felt the heat of a flush in her cheeks.

"Look, who are you?" she said. "The guy in the park? The pathetic wee bastard who's…"

125

"Don't speak to me like that," he shouted. "Just don't, right? You picked the wrong one this time. Think you're fuckin smart. Fuckin students! They're all the same. Well, I'm tellin you, I've got your number. You can't treat me like…"

Scott put the receiver back. Her anger had gone but the adrenaline was still pumping. She leaned against the wall, said "shit, shit, shit" to herself then ran back up to her room and rang Strachan on her mobile. She got his voice mail and left a message for him to come over. She didn't know what she expected him to do but she needed to talk with someone. In a way, Carolyn would have been a better bet, but she was going to a concert. Tom would get angry and threaten to find the guy and beat the shit out of him. That wasn't the sort of protection she wanted, but at least he'd be with her. There would be two of them for the nameless stalker to deal with.

She brushed the tangles out of her thick hair, looking into her own eyes in the mirror as she did so. She could see the fear there and immediately felt the anger once again that others could have such an effect on her, strangers who knew nothing about her and yet who could dive into her life, into her head and create turmoil there.

"Well, fuck them," she said aloud, still looking at herself in the mirror. She stared hard, looking at the set of her mouth and the tilt of her head and seeing the fear leave her face. She remembered the card that the policeman had given her that afternoon and decided that she'd say nothing to Strachan, but maybe talk to the policewoman they'd mentioned. Not all men were bastards but, in one way or another, not many of them weren't either. She slipped off her dressing gown and began looking in a drawer for panties.

Outside, in the shadows of the leaves, the man had climbed quickly up to his branch, the frustration of his unfinished phone call still burning in him. Scott had not yet turned on her light and the reflections of the evening in the windows made it difficult for him to see inside. But this time he'd brought binoculars and, as he turned their central spindle to find his focus, he began to pick out shapes in the room and eventually stopped on her pale naked body leaning over a chest of drawers. Immediately, his right hand went to his crotch.

"Bitch," he whispered.

# Chapter Nine

They sell drugs over the counter, kill off sick folk like they're bloody flies and now they're lettin poofs get married to each other and adopt kids. And we're supposed to join Europe with dickheads like that," said Spurle, folding his *Mail* and banging it onto the desk.

The paper had played havoc with his stress levels. A feature, illustrated by a photograph of two men locked in a tongue-tangling kiss, reported that the Dutch government had accorded homosexuals the same rights as heterosexuals.

"How are they killin off sick folk?" asked Thom.

"Bloody euthanasia," snorted Spurle. "It's legal over there. Got a sick granny, give her a jab."

"Bloody good footballers, though," said Thom, causing them all to look at him in a sudden silence at the non-sequitur.

"Well, they are," he insisted.

"Anyway, we're already in Europe," said McNeil, who was still in the process of taking reports and papers through to her new desk.

"Some of us," said Spurle.

They'd been told of the second hospital death and were waiting to be briefed on their day's work. Carston was in the other office with Ross and Reid. They were bending over Ross' notebook computer as it searched through records.

"There. That's it," said Reid as some columns of figures began to scroll up the screen.

"OK," said Ross. "I'll print that lot out for you."

He hit two function keys and sat back. Carston went to the window.

"I take it this is really necessary," he said.

"The superintendent was pretty keen, yes sir," replied Reid.

Carston gave a deep sigh.

"It should reflect very positively on your squad," Reid added.

"We've got two suspicious deaths to sort out. Solving them would reflect on us even better," said Carston.

He was right. The print-out was an extra chore. Superintendent Ridley was due to be interviewed on Grampian Television that evening about comparisons between local and national crime rates and, via his mouthpiece Reid, he'd asked CID to collate some statistics for him. Carston's own impulse was to invent them to save time, but Reid's hovering presence prevented that and Ross told him that accessing the necessary data would be very quick.

"Shouldn't you be on your way?" asked Carston, turning to look at Reid, who was looking as immaculate as he had the day before but in a completely different outfit.

"Where, sir?"

"I thought you had some arresting to do."

"Done it, sir. They're downstairs."

Carston's face remained impassive, then broke into a huge smile.

"Reid, your efficiency is breathtaking. You must forgive me if it takes me by surprise; I'm used to Ross and the others heaving their way through cases like carthorses. Good to have a thoroughbred on the team."

"Thank you, sir," said Reid.

"Now what's actually happening with the people you brought in?"

"Er... Nothing yet."

"Have you charged them?"

"No, I was just..."

"Interviewed them?"

"No, I..."

"Off you go, then. Take Bellman with you."

Reid hesitated for a moment but Carston had managed to keep the smile going and his words had, after all, constituted an order. He had no option but to go into the squad room, fetch Bellman and go down to the cells with him to begin the interrogations.

The printer was humming and sliding sheets over its rollers.

"Sorry to be so slow," said Ross.

"That's OK, Dobbin," said Carston. "D'you think he's with us for the duration?"

Ross shrugged.

"If he is, you're going to have to learn to get along with him. If Superintendent Ridley..."

"Oi, oi. What's this, psychotherapy?" said Carston. "If I want to detest somebody, I'll do it, thank you. Don't worry, if he's half as good as he thinks he is, I'll give him credit for it. Until then, I'll treat him like the smarmy little bastard he is. Now, he's away for the moment, so let's get some action going."

They'd already discussed the latest news from McIntosh. His report wouldn't be through until that afternoon but the second death was too much of a coincidence to be ignored.

"It puts a bit more pressure on you to find where the gaps are," said Carston, as he picked up the notes he needed for the briefing.

"By the way," said Ross, "I've been on to the suture manufacturers."

"Good, and... ?"

"I phoned round all the ones on Julie's list. Same story everywhere. Checks, double checks, triple checks. They can't afford even a hint of trouble."

"Yeah, it figures," said Carston.

"One guy told me their shares were fragile enough at the best of times. Companies have folded just because of rumors."

"So?" said Carston, well aware that Ross was leading up to something.

"All the folk I spoke to were desperate to make it somebody else's fault. But I pushed one guy about this whole absorbency thing. With a lot of operations, they don't have to take stitches out any more—they're absorbent, they just kind of melt."

"Yes, I know."

"Well, this guy talked about some of them having an 'erratic absorption profile'."

"Sounds impressive. So what?"

"So it might melt before it's supposed to. Before the cut's healed."

Carston was shaking his head.

"No, Latimer dealt with that one. It's the thinner ones that melt; they don't use absorbent ones for major stuff."

"I know," said Ross, "but he did say that heating it could have a serious effect. Might make them liable to ... well, melting, I suppose."

Carston's interest flashed.

"What, when they've been used?"

"Aye. Simple as that? Heating them makes them weaker."

For the first time, they had a possible breach of the seemingly impregnable procedures and systems that Latimer and the rest kept boasting about.

"So there's the gap we were looking for," said Carston. "It can't happen normally, but it can if somebody makes it."

"Yes," said Ross.

"So we're definitely looking at manslaughter or murder."

"Looks like it."

They'd both felt that that was the case for a while but it was reassuring to have at last found a breach in all the medical confidence.

"I s'pose we can forget about the folk at the university now," said Ross. "With Mrs Rioch, I mean."

"Don't be so sure," said Carston. "She used to work there. That bloke Carlyle mentioned her"

"Any connections with Hayne?"

"Not that we know of. That's what we've got to find out, though."

He leaned across the printer and picked the top sheet out of its tray.

"Right," he said. "I'll take this up to him when we've finished. Come on."

****

For a change, the three students standing in Leith's room had something other than atmospheric pollution on their minds. He smelled as bad as ever but it was the punishment for their alleged misconduct that preoccupied them.

"But if you don't mark it, we miss out on a third of the total for continuous assessment," said one of them, a woman with thick glasses and a mop of black curls.

"Perhaps you should have thought of that before you missed the deadline," said Leith.

"But we've explained. There was…"

"Yes, I heard," Leith interrupted. "There was a picket line and you didn't want to cross it. But whose picket line was it?"

"The T and G," said the woman.

"Exactly. Cleaners and janitors. Nothing to do with you or the NUS. Other students managed to get here."

The students said nothing. Saying what they thought of people who crossed picket lines would add little to their chances of changing Leith's mind.

"That sort of union agitation is ancient history, thank God," Leith continued.

"So there's no way we can get the essays marked," said the woman with the glasses.

Leith shook his head.

"I don't see how," he said. "You had a deadline. They were due on the twenty-first. They weren't here. Others were. Hardly fair on them if I start bending the rules for you. You'll just have to put more effort into the remaining two. And hope that the streets are clear of militants when the time comes to hand them in. Was there anything else?"

The students looked at one another. As they'd suspected, they were wasting their time. The one nearest the door turned, reached for the handle and opened it. As the others turned to follow her, she stopped and said, "Are you sure this is legal?"

"What?" said Leith. It was almost a shout.

"Surely we have the right to choose not to cross a picket line," said the student.

Leith gave a snort.

"Oh yes, of course. Democratic rights and so on. Yes, that's no doubt true. But equally, when I impose a deadline and make it clear that it's not negotiable, you have a duty to meet it. Or suffer the consequences. I suggest you take a little more care when choosing which absolute you subscribe to in future."

He held her glare as she stood at the door deciding whether to pursue the point. The student beside her tapped her on the shoulder and nodded his head towards the corridor. She looked at him, blew out a breath in exasperation and went out, followed by the other two.

At his desk, Leith shook his head in astonishment. Where did these people get their priorities nowadays? They expected exceptions to be made, regulations bent, schedules torn up, just to allow them to play at political correctness. Well, not in his time they wouldn't. He looked at a note in his diary, picked up the phone and dialed Menzies, the chairman of the REF.

"Donald," said Leith, when the phone at the other end was picked up. "Sorry to bother you. Can I have a quick word?"

"Well, I'm just off to Finance and…"

"Good," said Leith. "About the new medics for the REF. Any names been submitted yet?"

"Well, er, it hasn't actually been formalized. We're not sure the expansion will be approved."

"I know that, but it will, won't it?"

"I couldn't say."

"Well, let's just assume that it'll go through. Can I suggest you pencil in Keith Latimer?"

"The surgeon?"

"Yes. High-flyer. He'd be a credit to the committee. Reflect very well on it. Got a lot to contribute."

There was some hesitation at Menzies's end.

"Is he … is he interested, do you know?"

"I took the liberty of checking. I think he could be persuaded."

"Well, I must say, I haven't given it any thought at all."

"No sense in delaying, Donald. You know people will be wanting to foist somebody on to you when the time comes. Better to have your own man, eh?"

Menzies didn't like to point out that Latimer was Leith's "man", not his.

"But isn't there some sort of investigation?" he asked.

Leith was immediately alert. He wondered what rumors had grown around Hayne's death.

"What d'you mean?"

"Well, he was Alistair's surgeon, wasn't he? Isn't there some problem about the operation?"

"Administrative stuff, that's all. Normal police practice. It's nothing."

Menzies picked up the change in his manner. Leith was on his guard, less pushy. He wouldn't force the issue yet.

"Well," said Menzies, "better wait and see, eh? Just in case."

"If you like," said Leith. "But I'm sure you'll find it comes to nothing. He's too good a prize to miss on the REF."

"We'll see, we'll see," said Menzies. "Now I really must get…"

"Yes, OK. Goodbye," said Leith, cutting him off and putting the phone down again.

He picked up a pencil and started digging at an itchy spot on his head. He was confused and irritated. Ever since he'd first started trying to cope with Hayne, there'd been hitches. For each initiative Leith had taken, Hayne had found a counter-proposal, every push for promotion had met Hayne's stubborn resistance. The previous autumn, Hayne had even threatened to report him to the university court for irregularities in his application for a research grant. And now he'd been removed and yet, somehow, he was still blocking Leith's way. Well, it was irritating, but it would pass. As long as Gillian really had burned all his papers, the final links between him and Hayne, and Hayne and everyone else for that matter, would be completely destroyed.

****

McNeil was back at the hospital, this time with Thom. They were greeted as usual by Moira Blantyre, whose distress and concern seemed to have increased significantly with this second threat to her hospital's reputation. Her smiles still came and went on cue, but there were signs of strain in them and she was less ready to brush the whole affair aside as a simple inconvenience. The same seemed to be true of the medical staff. McKenzie and Latimer were preparing for theatre and couldn't spare much time. Latimer was as haughty as before but there were cracks in his confidence and he was less dismissive of suggestions that there might genuinely be a flaw in the Bartholomew's procedures. McKenzie had lost her previous ease of manner and whereas her answers before had been quick and confident, she now thought about them more and took refuge in lots of head shaking and shoulder shrugging.

Susan Jamieson was the worst of the lot. Losing patients was almost part of the job, but McNeil was struck by the fact that, while she accepted Mrs Rioch's death as quietly as she had that of Hayne, she seemed to take it much more personally. With all of them, perhaps it was simply a measure of the difference between the two dead people. Hayne had been with them a long time and had mostly been a thorn in their flesh. Mrs Rioch's admission had been an emergency but, in the very short time she'd been a patient, she

133

hadn't complained, she'd always been grateful for everything they did and had been very easy to like.

The more they spoke to staff and the other patients, the more solid their impression grew of a gentle, self-effacing woman who'd accepted her problems with stoicism and tried to make herself as unobtrusive as possible. Her medical records were cold listings of the things she'd had to suffer and, ironically, the last note indicated that all her early readings were positive and that she seemed to be making a good recovery from the emergency surgery. Where Hayne's death had been complicated by intriguing little insights into his personality and the animosity he aroused, Mrs Rioch's was a harrowing, unadorned tragedy. If there was any link between them, it was beyond McNeil's powers to see it.

**** 

In Ridley's office, the superintendent was jotting notes on a pad on his desk as Carston recited figures at him.

"Nationally, there were 690,300 stopped and searched last year," he said, "and street arrests were up by fifteen per cent, most of them from ethnic minorities. In West Grampian, the figure's way down on that, maybe because the only ethnic minority here are the English."

He knew there was no point either making the joke or expecting Ridley to react to it. The man had no sense of humor and was anyway too busy scribbling it all down.

"Over sixty per cent of all offences are still traffic offences. And eighty-five per cent of all indictable crimes are crimes against property," intoned Carston.

"I know," said Ridley.

Carston increased his pace.

"On average, there are thirty-five violent crimes committed every hour, day and night. We're spending over seven thousand million a year on policing and only two per cent of crimes are cleared up."

Ridley was writing furiously and held up his hand to tell Carston to stop for a moment. Carston waited for him to finish before he took the computer printout out of the folder he was carrying and handed it over.

"It's all in there, sir," he said.

The look Ridley gave him was murderous but Carston sketched one of his Addams family smiles for him.

"So," he went on, "if there's anything else you need to ask about, Sergeant Reid is your man. I've got a hospital appointment, so, if that's all…"

Ridley flapped a hand at him to send him away, hoping that whatever Carston had that needed treatment was serious.

****

Bellman was glad when Fraser eventually pulled up outside the garage on Glasgow Road where Mrs Rioch's husband worked. Fraser had spent the trip there pointing at things, saying what they were in French and getting Bellman to repeat the words.

"*Le garage*," he said, pronouncing it "garridge", as he switched off the engine and pointed across the pavement.

"Give us a break, Fraz," said Bellman.

They'd gone first to Rioch's home address but were told by a neighbor that he'd gone into work. When they expressed surprise that he should do that on the day after his wife had died, the neighbor had simply nodded his head towards Rioch's front door and said, "If he sat in there, he'd go mad. He was cryin all night. Poor bastard's shattered. Needs to take his mind off of things."

Inside the garage, they asked for Rioch and were directed to a man leaning over the engine of a Citroën.

"*Voiture*," whispered Fraser as they walked across to him.

Rioch stood up when he saw them coming.

"Polis, is it?" he said.

"Yes. I'm sorry about the news, Mr Rioch," said Fraser.

Rioch nodded.

"So'm I," he said.

"D'you mind if we ask you a few questions?"

Rioch shook his head and wiped his hand on a rag which was sticking out of one of his pockets. He was a small man and had so much grease and oil on him that it seemed to be holding him together. It was in his hair, around his neck and soaked into his overalls. The darkness of his skin emphasized the whites of his eyes and the redness that was diffused through them.

They talked of his wife's illness and his regular visits to see her. His voice broke several times as he spoke and, although he wasn't actually crying, the tears that came after his first few replies stayed in his eyes all the time and, now and again, ran down one of his cheeks. He was aware of them but fiercely determined not to let them interfere with his words.

"Did they kill her?" he asked at one point.

"Who?"

Rioch shrugged his head towards some distant place.

"Them. At the hospital."

"We don't know. We just need to find out everything we can. Just enquiries, like," said Fraser.

"Aye. Doesna matter anyway," said Rioch. "She's gone. Prob'ly better off."

The discomfort felt by both Fraser and Bellman in the presence of his suppressed grief didn't ease as they talked on. It was only when Bellman asked about his wife's work that they felt that they were doing something other than simply adding to his misery.

"She was a cleaner. At the university," Rioch said.

"Where?" said Fraser.

"Top o' Southside Avenue. Selkirk block. Offices, corridors and classrooms."

"When was that?"

"Oh, a while ago now. Eight, nine years, she was there."

"When did she leave?"

"Year last October. Made redundant."

"Why's that?" asked Fraser.

Rioch looked at him.

"They dinna give no reasons. Just one of their clear-outs. There was a few of them sacked at the same time. Put out the door like bags of rubbish."

"She wouldna still be friendly with anyone there, then?" asked Fraser.

Rioch shook his head.

"One o' them came to visit her, though," he said.

"Who?"

"Dunno. One of the lecturers. A nurse told me. She thought he was there to see somebody else really. No, the only folk she ever saw were the ones sacked the same time as her."

He shook his head.

"She had no severance pay, nothin. She'd been there all that time and they didna even say thanks. It's like she was just nothin."

"Did she get another job?" asked Fraser.

Rioch shook his head.

"No. It was soon after that that she started with the pains. Couldna get out of the house."

The talk had come naturally back to the hospital again and the three of them knew that they were on ground that they'd already covered. Very soon, Fraser had had enough of Rioch's depression.

"OK, sir. We won't take no more of your time for now," he said. "I'm really sorry about your wife."

"Aye," said Rioch.

They shook hands with him and, as they turned to leave, he said, "Will you let me know if you find anythin?"

"Aye," said Fraser.

Rioch nodded and bent over the engine again. The two policemen walked to the door, carrying the sense of the man's sorrow with them. Northsound radio was loud over the sound of revving exhausts, and mechanics in other parts of the garage were singing and whistling along with it. Inside the door was a huge calendar showing a naked woman sitting astride a tire. She'd obviously been the object of someone's attention because there were oily finger marks at the top of the tire between her thighs.

****

By the time Carston arrived at the hospital, the operation had started. McKenzie had left one of her colleagues "looking after the shop", as she put it, and supervised Carston's preparations. He'd then walked through corridors with her past other medical staff and patients, feeling ludicrously important in a short sleeved green shirt, green trousers, boots, a blue hat with a drawstring at the back and a paper mask slung under his chin ready to be lifted. It was the stuff of TV-fuelled fantasies.

In the theatre, John Lennon's "Imagine" was playing quietly in the background as Latimer went quickly, efficiently about his business. He was standing beside a table which was covered in green sheets. Opposite him, his assistant was bending forward, holding two shining implements. To his left stood a nurse. She had instruments, swabs and sutures lined up on a tray in front of her which was fixed across the bottom of the table. A gap in the sheets gave the two surgeons access to a cavity in the patient's chest. To

137

Carston it looked huge. Latimer's hands were brown with blood and little rivulets ran now and again from the lowest point of the incision.

The anesthetist was at the patient's head, surrounded by tubes and pieces of electronic equipment. The two other people in the room were nurses, one of them fetching things from the setting up room as they were needed, the other using cling film to wrap up what looked to Carston like lumps of mince which Latimer had chopped off the patient. There was a pile of them beside her, some deep red, others flatter, paler, but all of them looking extremely anatomical.

"What's that?" he asked McKenzie.

"Used swabs. We weigh them to keep track of how much blood's being lost."

Carston was relieved and watched as the nurse weighed the little bundle and wrote numbers on a board on the wall. As well as a column for these weights, there were others for different sized swabs, needles, blades, tapes, hypodermics and something called newts.

"See? We keep a check of everything," said McKenzie. "So nothing gets left inside."

"That's reassuring," said Carston.

"Come on. Put your mask on and we'll have a closer look."

Latimer looked at Carston and nodded as they came up beside him. On his head he had a contraption that could have been designed for Star Wars, with two black tubes leading to a small, bright lamp on his forehead. As he turned back to his work, the beam was added to the bright illumination of the black, red and brown contents of the gaping hole in the patient's rib cage. Carston saw the heart beating and other organs slipping about as Latimer's fingers probed amongst them but it was difficult to think of it all as a person. The hole was well over a foot across and the skin around it looked grayish, like pork.

"So you couldn't make it yesterday?" asked Latimer's assistant, ignoring Carston and continuing their conversation.

"No. Emergency the night before," said Latimer. "Didn't finish until well past four in the morning."

"Interesting?"

"Not really. That assault victim from casualty. His pal came home and found him in bed with his wife apparently. Set about him with a claw hammer and a knife."

Carston knew of the case he was talking about. It had been passed to DCI Baxter.

"Throat wound through the pharynx which stopped at the trachea," said Latimer, "another at scapula level in his back, and an abdominal wound which didn't quite penetrate the peritoneum. So he had to have three different surgeons; head, neck dissection, and belly."

"Everything OK?"

"Oh yes. Just took a while, that's all."

They sliced, dabbed and prodded as they chatted. But for the subject of their chat, they might have been stacking shelves in a supermarket. Carston was fascinated to see that their fingers moved with precision and care but that organs and tissues were eased aside without undue tenderness.

Latimer held his right hand across to the nurse beside him and she gave him a small, hooked needle with a black suture attached to it. He glanced quickly at it, adjusted his grip on the needle and leaned forward again to dip his hand into the patient's chest.

Carston turned to McKenzie. "Can we have a look at the sutures?" he asked.

"Sure," she said, stepping back and taking him to the end of the table.

He looked at the rows of instruments, piles of swabs and packets of sutures. Most of the latter were still in their transparent coverings. The sterile nurse was taking one out. It was still sealed inside its foil packet like a miniature condom.

"Are they always like this?" Carston asked, pointing at the transparent packets.

"Yes," said the nurse. She nodded her head to indicate the flooring nurse. "Mary brings them through from the setting up room there. They stay in their packets till I'm ready to take them out."

Carston reached his hand across as if to pick one up. The nurse stopped him with a sharp "No".

"Sorry," he said.

"You're not allowed to touch things in the sterile area," she said.

"I know. Sorry," he said again.

"D'you want to have a look at some in the setting up room?" asked McKenzie.

"Please."

They pulled their masks down and she took him into a small room which was a sort of annex to the theatre. Carston noticed that a wedge had been jammed under the door to hold it open. When he asked about it, McKenzie admitted that it should be kept shut really but it made the nurses' jobs much easier if it wasn't. It was a little breach of the system which seemed to go unnoticed.

The room was full of shelves. Just inside the door were three trolleys, each one carrying the same types of things he'd just seen on the tray over the patient's feet. Amongst them there were little heaps of sutures.

"Brand new this morning," said McKenzie.

"Oh?"

"Yes. When Janie came in to check, all the old lot had gone. Mary brought some more up from the store, then they were recalled too."

"Why?"

"For analysis. Precautionary measure. After Mrs Rioch died."

"So you do get bad batches?"

"We've never had any yet, but ... well, just in case."

It was another strangely conflicting response. Like all the others, McKenzie had been insisting that the system was impregnable; now she was allowing that it might not be. Like McNeil before him, Carston had noticed the change in all of them after the Rioch death.

"Who else can get in here?" asked Carston, gesturing to indicate the setting up room.

"Well, anybody," said McKenzie. She pointed to a door opposite the one through which they'd come. "That's the corridor."

Carston was surprised.

"I thought you had a foolproof system," he said.

McKenzie looked at the door and seemed thoughtful for a moment.

"You're a suspicious lot, aren't you?," she said. "If anybody who wasn't supposed to be here came in, we'd see them right away."

Carston looked back at the theatre. From where he stood, he could only see half the room. If he moved to the wall, he'd be invisible to everyone there. He shook his head. The Bartholomew's security seemed to rely more on theory than on practice.

"And what could they do anyway?" asked McKenzie.

"I don't know. Muck about with things."

"Like sutures, you mean?"

"Yes. Why not?"

"You don't listen, Mr Carston, do you?" she said. "They stay in their packets till they're needed. And if anybody's tampered with them, Janie there, or Mr Latimer, or one of the others will spot it."

Carston looked closely at the sutures.

"Can I pick one up?" he asked.

"Go ahead."

He took a small blue packet from one of the heaps and looked at it.

"I could squeeze this between my nails," he said.

"Wouldn't do much harm. And, if it did, they'd see it as soon as they took it out."

Carston nodded.

"What if I tore this outside wrapper? I could, I don't know, contaminate the thread or something. Dip it in something toxic. Get some bugs on it."

McKenzie's head was shaking and she managed a small smile.

"No chance. If the transparent wrapper's damaged in any way, we don't use them. They get sent off to the Third World."

"What?"

"That's right."

"So it's OK if some African peasant gets infected?"

McKenzie's smile faded.

"No, it isn't. To begin with, the suture's still in its foil packet so it's still sterile. And if they didn't get our cast-offs, they wouldn't get any at all. All the ones Janie takes out today which don't get used will be sent off. But there's nothing wrong with them. We're just ultra fussy. Sorry to disappoint you."

The door leading from the corridor opened and a nurse came in. She looked around.

"Mary not here?" she asked.

"In theatre," said McKenzie.

The nurse just nodded and said, "I'll come back later," before going out again.

"Seen enough in here?" asked McKenzie.

141

"I think so," said Carston.

"Right, you can see what I get up to then. Come on."

They went back into theatre. "Imagine" had given way to a bland James Last sound. McKenzie's replacement had been joined by another doctor. They were talking about a visit they were arranging for some medical students from Tokyo.

"OK, I'll take over again, Dan," said McKenzie and the two doctors went to stand at the side of the room leaving her and Carston at the head of the table by the tubes, monitors and gauges, which were giving out regular, reassuring little beeps. They could no longer see the incision; instead, the patient's head was visible. She was an oldish woman with grey hair and Carston was slightly shocked to realize that this was the first time he'd been aware of her as a person. Up to now, there'd been doctors, nurses, equipment and that hole on which their attention had been focused. Suddenly, the object had become someone. Her left arm was held up on a special rest, her head was turned onto its right cheek and her right hand lay across the pillow, near to her mouth as if she'd been sucking her thumb. She looked, and was, frighteningly vulnerable.

"This is Cocky Boyle's machine. Remember I told you about it?" said McKenzie, tapping a construction with cylinders on each side of it. Carston nodded and she took him through the parts of the machine, pointing out the hoses which brought the various gases to the theatre from tanks in the basement.

"And, before you ask," she said, "they can't get mixed up, and nobody can tamper with them, and the tanks are isolated, and the Schrader valves..."

"OK," said Carston. "I believe you." He turned back to the patient and pointed to the various tubes to which she was connected. "What's going in there?"

"Haemaccel. It just replaces the fluid she's lost. It's got bigger molecules than water. That would just seep away. There's hemoglobin too, of course..."

A sudden longer electronic beep cut across her words and momentarily drowned out all the others. It was the first of a series and Carston looked around quickly to see what had gone wrong. To his surprise, McKenzie went on talking and no one else took any notice. He realized why when he saw the other anesthetist take out a pager and check its message. It was another demonstration of how his reflexes had been conditioned by television. On screen, any sudden beeps triggered flurries of activity, cardiac teams galloping through wards, huge electric pads which made patients convulse into yogic flight. To his warped perceptions, the place in which he was standing was one of drama; for everyone else, it was where they worked.

"OK. Ready," said Latimer.

McKenzie turned to face the patient.

"This'll interest you," she said. "Look over here."

Carston peered over the sheet into the incision.

"We collapsed her left lung at the beginning to give Mr Latimer better access. I'm going to reflate it again."

Carston watched, fascinated once more, as she began to pump at a valve and one of the strips of meat inside the incision began to fill out. It didn't inflate like a balloon. Instead, little pink lumps began to appear over its surface, then spread to join up into bigger lumps. McKenzie was watching it to judge when to stop.

"Pretty, isn't it?" she said.

It wasn't the word Carston would have chosen but the pale, spongy looking material was certainly a nicer color than the organs around it.

"You should see the ones we get in Orcadians and Shetlanders, though," McKenzie continued. "They're the nicest. Clean as you like. You could eat your dinner off them."

Carston smiled at the obvious pleasure she was expressing and wondered what they saw when they opened up the many smokers who came through so frequently.

He continued to watch as McKenzie signalled to Latimer that she'd finished and he hauled the ribs back together, sewed them up and stapled the skin into a ridge across the patient's left side. Then, without Carston noticing that any signal had been made, a group of nurses came in, lifted the patient onto a trolley and wheeled her out with a tangled spaghetti of tubes dangling from a stand and linking up to others in her nose, throat and veins. As she went, there was an obvious easing of tension and Carston realized that, despite the apparent calm and ordinariness of it all, there had been a degree of concentration that had given them all an urgency which they were now glad to drop.

After they'd seen the patient properly installed in the ITU, they separated to go to their various changing rooms. Carston had been looking for lapses in procedures, failures of the system which might let mistakes or ill-intentioned actions damage the patient, but as he took off the green uniform, his main feeling was one of respect and admiration for the teamwork and professionalism that allowed these people to invade the bodies of others with such confidence.

****

Teamwork seemed to be a concept foreign to the members of the Department of European Culture. A special departmental meeting had been called for three o'clock and they'd had variously to change schedules, rearrange classes, postpone a game of squash, cancel a visit to the cinema and miss the start of a games seminar on the Internet. Most of them accepted the disruption, although with ill grace, but some resented it and made their feelings clear to Carlyle when he rang to tell them about it. Leith, who'd arranged a meeting with Menzies for three fifteen, told him bluntly that he could only give him ten minutes. He rang Menzies to warn him that he might be late and when he told him the reason, Menzies's reply of "Ah, of course," aroused his curiosity. There was something going on which spread further than Carlyle and his inept attempts to run the department. If Menzies was aware of it, it must be significant.

When he got to room twelve, everyone except Christie was already there. Leith settled himself beside Ritchie, whose pen was already in action on the first of his triangles. Gutcheon looked at her watch and coughed several times. The others were talking about invigilation dates and Carlyle was looking intently at the single piece of paper which was the reason the meeting had been called.

"We'll have to start without him," said Gutcheon at last. "I have a student coming at three forty and I need to prepare some notes before she arrives."

Carlyle looked up at her.

"Michael's not coming," he said, simply.

"Oh. Well, let's get on with it then," said Gutcheon.

"It's all rather unpleasant actually," said Carlyle.

His words created a sudden silence. "Unpleasant" could mean so many things which could affect them directly. Carlyle took a deep breath.

"There's no way of wrapping it up to soften it," he said before holding up the piece of paper and tapping his fingertips against it. It was a letter.

"This is from the Faculty office. There's been ... a complaint."

He stopped. It gave each person present the chance to start a guilty search through their recent activities to check where they might have been remiss in some way.

"It's Michael. Sexual harassment."

The first reaction, suppressed by all of them, was one of relief that they were off the hook. When they then turned their minds to Christie, few of them were surprised at the news. He'd never done anything specific to arouse comment amongst them but it was generally felt that his attitudes to and conduct with some of his female students were less than discreet.

"Who's made the complaint?" asked Kirk.

"Sandra Scott," said Carlyle. "She went to the SRC, then the university counselor. And she's taken it on to a VP."

"So what's happening?" asked McChaddie.

Carlyle put the letter on the table in front of him and held it square with his fingertips as he spoke.

"Michael's been suspended pending investigation of the matter."

"On full pay, of course," said Miller.

"Yes."

There were murmurs from around the table. None of them wanted a colleague to be penalized before there was proof of guilt but the fact that Christie was being paid meant that there'd be no funds to appoint a temporary replacement. That, in turn, meant that they'd have to pick up the tab. Their teaching loads had already been increased as a result of Hayne's death and the prospect of having to give up even more of their time was annoying. However, that was the principal reason for the meeting and Carlyle, having got the unpleasantness of the announcement over, hurried now onto timetables and the reallocation of Christie's tutorial groups and seminars.

As the horse-trading went on, the unspoken opinions of Christie sank even lower. He dressed like a disc jockey but he was on the committees of two local charities, aggressively active in university politics and yet stupid enough to risk it all by making advances to students. The esteem in which the profession was held had fallen low enough in recent years without people like him confirming the public's misconceptions about the job. And, of course, he wouldn't be the one to suffer. Suspension would give him all the time in the world to get on with his research and, if it was just this student's word against his, he'd probably be reinstated.

Only Leith felt that the development might be advantageous. Hayne's death meant that there was a vacant chair and Leith and Christie had both applied for it. Leith's own power base would soon be strengthened by the appointment of Latimer to the REF and, if it came to a straight fight between them, Christie's latest peccadillo would surely weigh heavily against him. The ideal outcome, of course, would be for the Vice Principal involved to find in favor of the student but, like the others, Leith knew that he couldn't count on it. All he hoped, therefore, was that the suspension would be prolonged until his own elevation to professor had been announced.

Wearily, Carlyle listened to the evasions and arguments as he tried to plug the gaps in the departmental timetable. He hadn't been surprised by the letter from faculty. Scott and the SRC representative had come to see him before going through the proper, official channels. Scott liked him and knew that, as acting head of department, he'd be caught in the middle of it all. She just wanted him to know what was coming.

Even before her visit, though, he'd been anticipating some such news. His fears had been provoked by one of the marginal notes in the document he'd taken from Hayne's study when he was first told of his death. He'd read through some of the pages before feeding them into his shredder and come across two paragraphs which assessed Christie's contributions to the department and scholarship generally. As well as being dismissive about Christie's intellectual rigor, Hayne had highlighted one comment about his "unconventional approach to ethics" and added, in the margin, the three letters, "GMT."

To the rest of the population, the initials meant Greenwich Mean Time; to academics, they hid a much more dangerous and potentially damaging formula. The concept of academic tenure meant that a lecturer could be an unqualified disaster at the job and yet still keep it until he retired. Just about the only way that an individual could compromise that security was by committing an act of Gross Moral Turpitude. The GMT which Hayne had scribbled beside Christie's name had nothing to do with chronology but everything to do with termination.

****

146

Carston was intrigued by the notices in the staff room to which McKenzie had brought him for a cup of coffee. Some of them were almost identical to the ones back at the station—golf outings, shows at the theatre, special rates at restaurants—but others were more obviously job-related. Under the section for NESSA, for example, which was the North East Scotland Society of Anesthetists, there was a talk scheduled on the psychological effects of cancer and, just below it, a square piece of paper which bore a single telephone number and the words "Pain interest group, all welcome".

McKenzie came back from the telephone call she'd had to make. They sat together at the low table in the middle of the room. Around them were other doctors, mainly anesthetists, some reading, some talking, one doing the Independent crossword very quickly. Sitting directly opposite Carston were three nurses.

"Any wiser?" asked McKenzie.

"Oh yes," said Carston. "Half the time I forgot why I was there. It's all so … I don't know, astonishing really. Not for you, of course."

McKenzie smiled and reached up to tuck away the strands of hair that were flying about her head again.

"It's a job. Never two days the same, though."

"So you're still learning, too?"

"Yes. All the time."

"Funny, I thought anaesthetizing somebody meant shoving a pad of chloroform over their mouth then waiting for them to wake up."

McKenzie laughed.

"If only. No, there's local, spinal, general, inhalation, intravenous—the works."

"How d'you decide which to use?"

McKenzie stopped fiddling with her hair and looked at him.

"Is this you interrogating me?"

Carston smiled.

"Nope. I just want a complete course on anesthetics in about three minutes."

"Oh, that's alright then," she laughed.

As they talked on, she proved to be a very good teacher. She was enthusiastic about her subject and kept it as simple as possible for him. She didn't mind him taking notes and answered his sometimes silly questions without complaint. Using scribbled diagrams, she showed him how local anesthetics worked by blocking specific bundles of nerves and how sometimes you had to inject substances like adrenaline to reduce the size of blood vessels so that the anesthetic wouldn't be absorbed too quickly. In some places, like the nose and throat, absorption was always very rapid anyway and she spoke of the special care that had to be taken there and the dangers of overdosing, accidentally injecting straight into a blood vessel, hypersensitivity reactions and other things which he didn't fully understand.

All the time she was speaking, Carston was listening for something which could help explain where Hayne's overdose had come from. She'd just described half-jokingly what would happen if there was a sudden discharge of static near the gas bottles in theatre when she was interrupted by the sound of her pager. She checked it and excused herself as she went to make another call.

While she was away, Carston started speaking to another anesthetist who was sitting at the table and who'd overheard their conversation. When McKenzie came back, she found that they were talking about intravenous methods of achieving general anesthesia. It surprised Carston to learn that, once the chosen barbiturate had been injected into a vein, the anesthetist had no control over its effects. The whole dose was absorbed at once with almost instantaneous impact.

"That's right," said McKenzie, as she heard her colleague say this. "Methohexitone's the most common one we use. You just bang it in and hope you've got it right."

Carston looked at her. It was obvious that she was being deliberately provocative.

"Hit and miss, eh?" he said.

"That's right. Then there are the relaxants. They paralyze the respiratory muscles as well as all the others and when it all acts on the respiratory centre, there's a tendency to uncontrolled reflex spasm. The patient just suffocates. It's a wonder they survive at all."

"Some of them don't," said Carston.

She bowed a little acknowledgement with her head then rested her hand on the shoulder of the colleague to whom Carston had been speaking.

"Now Donnie here," she said, "has been at this far longer than I have. So, Donnie, if you wanted to get rid of a patient, how would you set about it?"

**\*\*\*\***

After their own trip to the hospital, McNeil and Thom had gone to supplement the team who were talking to Mrs Rioch's neighbors. They'd all told the same story. She and her husband were devoted to one another, she never left the house, nobody could possibly bear them any grudges. The only slightly negative reactions came when their three children were mentioned. They'd left home in their teens, one to go to university, the others to jobs in the Central Belt. They were now all in their thirties and, although two of them had come back to live in Aberdeen and the third was in Edinburgh, it seemed that they never visited their parents and that both the Riochs made light of it, always found excuses for them but were obviously hurt by their absence. Nothing else rippled the surface of their placid lives and the idea that Mrs Rioch could provoke anyone to murder was absurd.

It was as she was saying her goodbyes to a woman who'd been shopping in the small store at the end of the Riochs' street that McNeil's mobile started to bleep. She walked away from the woman and answered it.

"Is that Julie McNeil?"

"Yes. Who's that?"

"My name's Sandra Scott. Your inspector gave me your name. I phoned the station and they gave me your mobile number."

"Oh, right, yes. DCI Carston told me about you. I'm glad you called."

"Yes, well it's not what I was talking to him about. It's something else. D'you think we could have a chat?"

"Sure. Any time."

"Like this evening?"

McNeil had more or less exhausted the list of the Riochs' neighbors and had already decided to go back to the station.

"Right now, if you like," she said.

"Wow. Talk about public servants, eh?" said Scott, and McNeil could hear the smile in her voice.

"That's what you're paying my wages for," she replied. "Where are you? D'you want me to come over?"

"No. I've just finished a class. How about having a coffee in town? Starbucks?"

McNeil looked at her watch.

"Great," she said. "I'll be there in … say ten minutes?"

"OK. I'll try to get a window seat."

****

Gillian Hayne seemed to have spent a lot of time on the telephone in the days since her husband's death. Apart from calls from the police and his colleagues, she'd had to begin making funeral arrangements and trying to co-ordinate them with autopsies and the continuing investigation into his death. As the time had gone by, she'd become calmer and begun genuinely to enjoy the feeling that she could come and go as she pleased and that the albatross of Alistair and his schemes no longer hung around her neck.

Her latest call was from their solicitor. He was slightly concerned that she'd been unable to find a draft of Hayne's will which he and Alistair had worked on together just a few days before his last hospital admission. She assured him that all her husband's private papers were still intact in his study and that she'd only got rid of documents connected with the university.

"You're sure they couldn't have got mixed up?" said the solicitor.

"Positive. You know how meticulous Alistair was about filing systems. Everything in its place. Well, there's nothing that looks remotely like a will. I even had to contact our insurance people. I couldn't find any of his policies. It's really very strange."

"Well, Mrs Hayne, I'd appreciate it if you could keep on looking. And let me know the moment you find anything."

"But surely you have copies of everything, don't you?"

"Not the latest one, no. It was a draft version we'd only just begun to prepare. He was concerned about getting his latest book published. Wanted to set a sum aside for it in case the publishers … well, you know what's happened to publishing these days. There were a few new clauses connected with his research papers and … well, minor adjustments here and there."

"I see. Well, I'll keep on looking but I'm afraid I don't hold out much hope. It's a puzzling business altogether. As I said, he was always so fussy about that sort of thing."

The doorbell rescued her from a conversation that had already become repetitive and, with more reassurances that she would redouble her efforts, she rang off and hurried through to open the front door. It was Christie. Her surprise was obvious.

"Can I come in?" he said, with a smile.

She hesitated slightly, then gave a little nod and stood aside. He stepped into the hall and, as she closed the door, put his hands to her shoulders and bent to kiss her. She turned her head so that his lips found her cheek rather than her mouth. His arms dropped to her elbows then round behind her, pulling her into him.

"How are you, darling?" he said, his voice ludicrously low and husky.

"Widowed," she said, easing him away and walking through to the living room.

He followed and stood looking out onto the garden.

"Why the visit?" she asked.

He turned to look at her. He was wearing a butter-yellow shirt and pale chinos. His woven leather belt was the color of mahogany and had a Pierre Cardin buckle.

"I'm celebrating the fact that we're both free," he said.

Gillian had a moment of panic.

"You've left Martha?"

Christie laughed.

"No, no. Not that. Not yet anyway. No, I mean I've been spared the daily chore of classes and committees."

"Why?"

"Someone's accused me of sexual predation. So they've asked me to stay away while they investigate."

The news came as no surprise to Gillian.

"And are you guilty?" she asked, knowing his reply in advance.

"Of course not," he said. "More post-adolescent fantasies, that's all it is."

"And why come to tell me about it?"

He walked across to her and put his arms round her again.

"I haven't. I've come about other things."

"Like?" she said, putting her hands on his chest to keep him away from her. To her surprise, he released her and sat in an armchair.

"Shall I be totally straight?" he said.

"Can you be?"

He smiled.

"That's my Gillian. OK, I came for two reasons. One concerns Alistair, the other you. How about a drink?"

Without knowing why she acceded so easily, she went through to the kitchen. As she bent to take a bottle of wine from the fridge, she felt him behind her and his hands were round her waist and on her breasts.

"No, Michael," she said.

"How long is it since you had sex?" he asked, his nose in her hair and his hands still holding her.

"That's not your concern," she said, annoyed to feel a little glow of arousal inside.

He kissed her cheek and let her go. She poured two glasses of wine and they sat at the kitchen table.

"Seriously, Michael. What do you want?"

His smile fell away in an instant.

"The truth? I want to take Alistair's place. I want promotion."

She said nothing. What he was saying was no secret.

"You know Alistair," he went on. "He's got things in his papers which... You know the dossiers he kept. He could make or break any of us any time he wanted to."

"Yes," said Gillian, calmly. "He was boasting about that the last time I saw him."

"What, in the hospital?"

"Yes. On the eve of major surgery and he was gloating about his power like somebody in a cheap play."

"What did he say?"

Gillian noted the change in Christie and was gratified that the power had shifted from him to her.

"He had things to say about everybody, including me. None of them good. I sat beside his bed and couldn't believe what I was hearing. The vitriol—even from him. It was... It just made me wonder why I'd ever married him. And yes, he did have dossiers, and he had lawyers' letters and proofs of the most remarkable things. He was capable of much more than you know."

Christie was listening very intently.

"And what's become of them all, now? All the dossiers, the ... things?"

Gillian's small hand went to her temple and smoothed the skin gently.

"Where have all the flowers gone?" she said.

Suddenly, Christie too was aware of the power shift. There was a smile on Gillian's face and, as her fingers continued to trace light circles over her temple, the folds of her white blouse moved from the point of her breast to her shoulder and pricked in him a desire he'd only been pretending before.

"Gillian," he said. "You're not teasing me, are you?"

She wasn't, but his suggestion made it sound attractive. He'd come for information, to get access to Hayne's papers. She'd been wary because she knew how deeply entangled he was with everything Alistair had been connected with in his last months. To the surprise of both of them, as they sipped the wine and continued their sparring, the secrets they held from one another and the danger of the area in which they were operating began to stir memories of their old affair. The talk was still about Hayne but the questions and answers became less and less probing as each began to realize that they would end the afternoon in bed together.

**\*\*\*\***

The window of Starbucks was a good vantage point from which to watch the not-so-rich pageant of Cairnburgh's citizenry. The pavement outside was broad and the restaurant was more or less in the middle of the busiest shopping area. The coffee wasn't bad and although the individuals on view couldn't compete with those of the Boulevard St Germain or the Piazza San Marco, it was the closest Cairnburgh got most of the time to a continental-style *terrasse*.

McNeil and Scott had quickly struck up a rapport, partly by sharing observations about passers-by, partly by talking about policing and student life. McNeil eased the subject round to Christie and was glad to hear that Scott had reported him. Her obvious understanding of the pressures caused by sexual harassment made it easier for Scott to talk about the man in the park and his phone call.

"It's like a bloody fashion," said McNeil.

"What?"

"Well, one minute, you've never heard of stalking, the next, everybody's at it."

"Is that what this is then?"

McNeil shrugged.

"Can't say, really. I mean, have you seen him anywhere else?"

Scott shook her head.

"No, but he saw me talking to your boss, so it means he's been watching when I haven't known it."

"Yes."

McNeil thought for a moment. Scott was much easier to deal with than so many of the battered wives, rape victims and the like which she came across in the course of her work and yet it could still be a front. She wasn't yet sure of just how fragile the girl was under the reasonable exterior and the throwaway comments.

"When he phoned you," she said at last, "how did you feel?"

Scott looked at her.

"Strange question."

McNeil smiled.

"I'm a strange person."

Scott gave a small smile in return and thought back to the call.

"At the time, I didn't feel scared," she said. "I was angry. Bloody furious, in fact. But not scared. It was after, when I thought about it, that I got a bit … twitchy."

"I can understand that."

"Yes. It's not him. That time I talked to him … challenged him really, face to face in the park. He couldn't look me in the eyes. Walked away. There was nobody around. He could have…" She stopped as she thought briefly of what he might have done to her, then shook her head and went on. "But he didn't. No, it's not him. Not directly anyway. It's just the thought of … somebody watching, somebody out there, something going on that…" She shrugged, incapable of putting a form to the sort of threat which collected around the idea of unseen eyes fixed on her.

"Yeah, it's like you're their property," said McNeil, to whom these nameless fears were very familiar. She'd heard them emerge in all sorts of stammering formulas from other victims, but Scott's ability to look directly, analytically at the experience gave her an edge. The fact that she'd had the courage to make a complaint about Christie was further proof that she was no retiring girlie.

"OK," said McNeil, "I reckon we can handle this officially or ... not." The hesitation she'd put before the last word allowed her to stress it in such a way as to make it impossible for Scott to miss its special implication.

"Not?" she asked.

"Yes. If we go through the channels, there's not much we can do unless he keeps on pestering you, and you can do without that."

"Right," said Scott firmly.

"So, maybe we can ... sort of warn him off in some other way."

"Like what?" asked Scott, intrigued by the new tone of voice McNeil had started to use.

McNeil knew that there was no case against the stranger and that, by the time they'd gathered more evidence, the threat might have become much greater than it was at present. The alternative strategy had its risks but her assessment of Scott and her previous experience of stalkers and flashers gave her a gut feeling that it was worth trying. As the home-going crowds flowed past the window, the two of them talked on about the stranger and McNeil sketched out a way in which, between them, they might get him out of Scott's life.

# Chapter Ten

Tell you what," said Carston. "Next time we get a murder, the first thing we do is round up all the doctors."

Ross looked up from the report on Mrs Rioch which had come through that afternoon and which he'd already read fairly thoroughly.

"This another theory of yours?" he said.

Carston was looking out of the window. He turned and leaned back against the sill.

"They know more ways of killing people and getting away with it than Ruth Rendell," he said.

"What d'you mean, getting away with it?"

"I had a cup of coffee with a few of them after the operation. McKenzie introduced me to some of them. You'd think they'd have been fazed by it a bit. I mean, we're investigating two suspicious deaths at their place but they start listing umpteen ways of murdering somebody without getting caught."

"So one of them's in the frame for Hayne and Mrs Rioch, then?"

"Doubt it. None of that lot would ever be suspected; they've thought about it too much."

He pushed himself away from the window ledge and went to sit down. Ross dropped the pathologist's report onto his desk.

"Nothing exotic about Mrs Rioch, though. Suture failed again," he said.

Carston nodded.

"If it wasn't for Hayne's overdose, it could just be equipment failure. Despite them insisting all the bloody time that it can't be."

"Did you ask them about heating the sutures?"

156

Carston shook his head.

"No," he said. "Didn't want to forewarn anybody."

"So somebody there could've done it."

"Yes. If you'd been there, you'd've seen. They fancy themselves as being watertight but people can walk in and out of the room where they keep the operating stuff whenever they like. Anybody could've had a few packets of dodgy sutures in their pocket and just dropped them with the rest. One second, that's all it'd need."

A memory hit him.

"In fact, I'm bloody sure that's it," he said.

"Why?"

"Somebody got rid of all the ones that were in that room. Apparently, when the nurse came looking for them first thing this morning, there were none there."

"Yes, but you said the hospital had them taken away for analysis."

"No, that was later. Another lot. This was unofficial. Somebody just ditched them. Got rid of the evidence."

His mind was racing now. Suddenly, the looseness and impossibilities of the case had fallen away. He picked up his phone and punched in a number.

"This is better," he said. "A bit of malice aforethought."

A click on the line warned him that he was connecting to an answering machine. He listened to the message and jotted down the number of a mobile which it gave. As he redialed, he said, "I just want a quick word with Brian McIntosh."

McIntosh took a while to answer the call.

"Hullo, Jack," he said, when Carston identified himself. "Up to the elbows in it here, I'm afraid."

Carston didn't ask what "it" was.

"Sorry Brian. Just a quick word about this report on Mrs Rioch. Jim and I were talking about sutures. D'you reckon what happened with her was the same thing that happened to Professor Hayne?"

"Same in what way? I mean, it was sutures both times."

"Yes, but ... well, let's say, could the reasons for the sutures breaking be the same?"

There was just a slight pause before McIntosh replied.

"Impossible to say for sure. They both gave way. There were still traces of suture material in each of them so there must have been a breakage of some sort. The fact that they were both operated on in the same theatre within a short time of each other does rather imply that the same thing's happened to both of them. But I couldn't swear to it in court."

"What d'you reckon, though. Off the record?"

There was only the slightest hesitation.

"My guess is they're identical."

The answer brought a smile to Carston's lips.

"And if we're dealing with foul play, would the fact that it was thoracic surgery for both of them be significant?"

"I'm not with you, Jack."

"Well, it's major organs that are being sewn up, things that'll kill you if they fail."

To Carston's surprise, McIntosh laughed.

"Aye, you're probably right," he said. "But there's major organs and major organs."

"What d'you mean?"

"Leaving aside the usual sad jokes you go in for, what d'you think your largest organ is?"

Carston thought for a moment, then said, "Lungs, I suppose."

"Nope," said McIntosh. "Your skin."

"That's not an organ."

"Yes it is."

"Well, what's it got to do with this case?"

"Nothing. It's just a little reminder for you. Don't get carried away. Leave the medical speculation to the doctors. Did it ever occur to you, for example, to think that your stomach's outside your body?"

"Have you been drinking, Brian?"

"It's true. Technically speaking, the whole alimentary tract is outside the body. We're just a sort of tube really."

"You may be, but I'm one of God's creatures," said Carston.

"That's not what I heard," said McIntosh. "Now, can I get back to my spleen?"

Carston said his good-byes and put the phone back.

"Did you know you were just a tube?" he said to Ross.

"Yes," said Ross.

"You bloody would, wouldn't you? Come on, let's go and pour some beer into it."

****

Although a light haze of cloud had begun to spread down from the Highlands, the weather was still warm. It gave the citizens of Cairnburgh the chance to get into their summer outfits a bit earlier than usual. It was hardly St Tropez but, given the amount of cladding that had been shed, the extra flesh on view was just as provocative. In the case of the barmaid at the Dolphin, who had so much extra to show, it bordered on the alarming.

"Are you still allowed to call them barmaids?" Carston asked after she'd delivered their pints to their table and was swinging her hips back to the bar.

"What else?" asked Ross.

"I don't know. Barpersons, I suppose."

"No idea. Tell you what, though."

"What?"

"I'm going to have to arrest you one of these days the way you look at her."

Carston laughed and picked up his glass.

"Don't worry, looking's all I'm capable of," he said. "Cheers."

The change of location did nothing to alter the way they were both thinking. The short walk from the station had given them time to follow their own separate versions of the circumstances which had led to the deaths of Hayne and Rioch. The reports from the team at the afternoon's briefing had made it fairly clear that temperamentally and in every other way, there were vast differences between the two victims. The fact that the latter had worked at the university would be followed up by the team as soon as possible but the worlds of cleaners and professors were so distant from one another that it was difficult to guess where they might overlap.

"You're sure, are you?" asked Ross, when the conversation came back to the specifics of the case again. "Anybody can get access to the stuff."

Carston was in mid-sip. He swallowed, shook his head and said, "Well, they reckon that they'd notice if it was a stranger. But that still means almost anybody on the staff could walk in. Visitors, too. Sometimes the room's just empty so you or I could nip in and out, no bother."

"Yeah, but why?"

Carston had been asking himself the same question. He shrugged his shoulders.

"I mean, OK," Ross went on, "we know it's easy to do. And you're saying anybody could do it. But who the hell would want to?"

"Yeah, good question, Jim. Nobody liked Hayne. It was all petty stuff, but that can build up. He was well up in the university hierarchy, could have done a lot of damage to somebody if he'd wanted. And the letters he was bunging off to the hospital admin on that bloody machine of his couldn't have made him the ward favorite."

"Yeah, but Mrs Rioch. She wasn't like that. Are we looking for suspects amongst her pals, too?"

Carston shook his head.

"No. When it was just Hayne, it was cozy. We could keep it to the university and the hospital. It's not that specific any more."

Ross was surprised.

"Eh? Surely it has to be the hospital. I mean, everything we've just said..."

"They got visitors, remember."

"Yes, but not the same ones. And where are they going to get hold of sutures to toast? And how would they know how to do it?"

Carston was already nodding.

"I know, Jim. I just don't want to dive into the obvious. We've done that before and come unstuck. Remember Burnham."

The case he was referring to was too recent for Ross to have forgotten it. It had taken them both by surprise. The death scene had been littered with conflicting indicators and it was only Carston's persistence at looking behind appearances that had eventually enabled him to construct a sequence of events which explained them. Nonetheless, Ross wasn't prepared to accept the parallel.

"Oh, come on. Surely this one's got to be a medic. Got to be somebody who knows about sutures breaking and what that'll do."

"We're not medics and we know about it. There's ways of finding out these things."

"OK. But why?"

Carston sat looking at his glass for a while. When he spoke again, his voice was quieter, more reflective.

"Maybe it's not personal."

Ross waited, knowing from experience that Carston was articulating the thoughts as they formed.

"In a way, Hayne and Mrs Rioch were expendable."

"Eh?" said Ross.

"Yeah. Hayne's been terminal for two years at least. Mrs Rioch was pretty far gone, too. It might just be about politics."

Ross suppressed his irritation by taking a long swig at his pint. Sometimes it was bloody hard working with Carston. Especially when he talked like a crossword compiler.

"You're bothered about motives," Carston went on. "I've been worrying about that, too, about how the two of them are linked. Not obvious, is it?"

Ross said nothing. His irritation hadn't subsided.

"Maybe who they are is irrelevant. There were two different surgeons involved, remember. Maybe it's just politics. Aimed at the doctors. Maybe somebody's trying to set up the surgery department, discredit it."

Ross shook his head.

"Hang on," said Carston, "the way things are nowadays, with trusts and budgets and PFIs and Foundation Hospitals down south and all that shit, hospital politics is a game for high rollers. Patients are way down the list."

"Aye, but killing them off…"

Carston nodded.

"Of course, there's another alternative," he said. "We could just be dealing with a nutter. An educated one, too. One who knows about operating procedures and equipment. And he's doing it for fun. That's even scarier."

His words stopped the objection Ross was about to make. Logically, if they couldn't connect Hayne and Rioch in terms of motive, the choice of victims might prove to be random. Carston was right; that was a scary proposition. If the choice really was between motiveless crimes and the cynicism of the political option, politics was the one Ross preferred.

"I think I may nip along there again this evening," said Carston.

"What for?"

Carston shrugged. "Wander about on my own, without PR people and managers calling the tune."

"Looking for what?"

"Bloody hell," said Carston.

"What?" said Ross, looking around the bar to see what had caused the exclamation.

Carston pointed to the door which led through to the other lounge.

"Julie," he said. "She's just gone in there."

"So?"

Carston looked at him, a small frown creasing his forehead.

"With Fraser."

**** 

Kath was one of the few people in their particular group of friends who didn't use Delia Smith recipes. She preferred to invent her own flavors, textures and variations. The main beneficiary, evening after evening, was Carston. Tonight, however, he felt that indigestion was a real possibility. It had nothing to do with the baked aubergines, stuffed tomatoes or fennel with parmesan they'd eaten, nor with the Fronsac they'd drunk with it. No, the gastric threat came from an excess of laughter. They were watching Ridley's interview on Grampian TV and the pressure of the occasion had clearly got to him. He was sweating under the studio lights but trying to maintain a gravitas he obviously thought was demanded of someone in a position as exalted as his. He was, after all, being the voice of crime prevention in West Grampian.

He'd used all the statistics Carston had provided in a burst of nervousness at the beginning of the interview and left himself with no substance for the rest of his answers. Both Carston and Kath thought he deserved a sitcom to himself.

"I think it's possible to think differently than most people think," he said, in answer to a question about government funding. The woman asking the questions waited.

"The fact that there are changes being made is a fact," said Ridley at last. "Integrated resource allocation, for example, that's a … that's a … hot potato. A different kettle of fish altogether."

"I see."

"Or progressively phased devolution of management substructures—you don't get that without breaking a few eggs… Then there's regional policy co-ordination to … er … to co-ordinate."

"And these reservations you seem to have," said the woman, hoping that that's indeed what they were, "are they shared by others in the police hierarchy? Do you talk with your colleagues about them?"

"Only verbally," he replied.

"I'm sorry?"

"Well, it's like decorating a room. You can plan as much as you like, but when you open the tin the colors are never the same as they were on the charts."

Carston had tears in his eyes.

Ridley's ordeal lasted almost eight minutes but as the credits rolled over a close-up of his face, he seemed quite pleased with its outcome.

"What a dickhead," said Carston.

"Your superior officer," said Kath. "Doesn't say much for you, does it?"

As she spoke, the phone rang. The handset was on the small table between their two chairs. Each waited for the other to answer it.

"You know it'll be for you," said Kath.

She was probably right. Carston picked it up. For a change it had nothing to do with work. Alex Crombie was ringing to suggest a game of golf.

"Not this week, Alex," said Carston. "Too much on."

"Pity. I'm offshore again on Wednesday."

He waited, obviously hoping that that might change Carston's mind.

"Sorry. We've got this thing at the hospital. I'm going up there later."

"OK. Well, can't be helped."

There was a slight pause. The call obviously wasn't over.

"What you doing now?" Crombie asked at last.

"Nothing," said Carston. "Just been watching Mastermind."

"Oh... Don't suppose you fancy a drink?"

Carston didn't. Usually, once he was inside the house, he wanted to stay there and just switch off. Kath was always trying to push him into various activities; she thought he needed to move outside the patterns which he found so cozy. Tonight, two things made him think twice about it. First, the weather hadn't broken and the thin feathers of cloud rippled with a warm orange light. And second, Crombie never suggested a visit to the pub, so it was obviously more than a social call.

"Hang on. I'll check with Kath," said Carston.

Kath had no hesitation.

"Go," she said. "I told you. Something's going on. He probably wants to talk about it. I'll be in the dark room tonight, anyway, so you'll be on your own if you stay here."

Ten minutes later, Carston and Crombie were sitting at a white table in the garden of their local. Most of the people around them were young couples, either on their own or in groups. One lot had put three tables together and had obviously already been there for a while. There were glasses everywhere and they seemed to need to shout most of their conversations. At first, Carston and Crombie were relatively quiet and Carston's sense that something was wrong was strengthened by Crombie's unusual nervousness as his eyes flicked over the other drinkers.

Crombie started by asking what Carston was working on. That got them talking about the university and a conference that Crombie had been to there.

"This guy was trying to tell us that we shouldn't accept that accidents were inevitable," said Crombie. "He's never been near a rig in his life."

"Didn't anybody argue with him?"

"Have you tried? They're like bloody eels in a bucket."

Carston smiled.

"He was trying to tell us that we ought to start each day as if we were new on the job. 'Fresh eyes', he kept saying, like a bloody advert. How the hell are you supposed to turn on 'fresh eyes' when you've been on a rig for seven years? There's a guy on our platform been ripping the company off for eighteen months. They've only just found out about it."

"What was he doing?"

"Had his own special recycling system. Nicking tools and parts. We've had this new environmental policy for years now. Waste segregation, different skips for different things, you know. Oil waste, aluminum, steel. He checked them all regularly. When he found something he fancied, he just took it back to the stores, said he'd broken it and they gave him a new one. Then they chucked the broken one away again and if he wanted more, he'd just do the same thing with a different storeman."

"Private enterprise," said Carston. "He should've been promoted onto the board."

Crombie nodded. He'd told the story without much energy or enthusiasm. He was obviously making small talk but something bigger was gnawing away at him. His face showed a tightness that wasn't usually there and his eyes continued to move restlessly over everything even as he spoke of the rig. Carston sensed that he wanted something from him. There'd never been these silences before. Somehow, they had to get through to another level. Carston hated evasions and pretence. He took his usual, direct route.

"OK, Alex. What's on your mind?" he said in the silence.

Crombie looked at him, his eyes suddenly steady on Carston's face.

"There's something, isn't there?" said Carston.

Crombie's eyes fell away again.

"Is that you being a detective?" he said.

"No. Nosy bastard, probably," said Carston.

It drew from Crombie the smile that Carston had hoped for but it lasted only briefly. He'd opened the door. It was up to Crombie to use it if he wanted to. Crombie picked up his glass, lifted it as far as his lips and, just before taking a swig, said, "Yeah, it's Jennie."

Carston remembered Kath's fears and he felt a rush of apprehension. It was an automatic reaction to the thought that he was about to become the confidant of someone guilty of a crime he detested. If that's what Crombie was about to confess, Carston hoped that he wasn't looking for any sort of absolution. Crombie put down his glass and continued to stare into it.

"I think we're finished, Jack," he said.

Carston still didn't want to hear this but he asked, "Why?"

"Fucking job," said Crombie. "Away all the time." He was still finding it hard to get to the point and stayed hunched forward over the table, his arms across it, his hands around his glass. Carston waited.

"She's ... she's got somebody else," said Crombie at last.

Carston was taken by surprise. They'd known the Crombies for four years at least. Jennie was a nice ordinary woman in her forties and, in Carston's eyes, not the type you'd cast as a *femme fatale*. But even as he thought it, he was angry at himself. What did he know about her? Why should she play the role he saw her in?

"How d'you know?" he asked.

"She told me... Wants a divorce."

"Christ. Did you see it coming? Suspect anything?"

Crombie was shaking his head. "Out of the blue. Couldn't fucking believe it, Jack."

Surprisingly, his voice was close to breaking. If this is what had caused the beating, it still wasn't excusable but at least Carston could understand it.

"What did you say?" he asked.

"Nothing to say. I just... It just knocked me back."

Carston felt completely helpless. He'd suddenly been pitched into an intimacy with Crombie which had never been part of their previous acquaintance. He felt huge sympathy for the man and a more general sadness that so many people were racked by the same experience every day.

Now that the first step had been taken, Crombie began to find it easier to speak. With little questions and comments from Carston to help him, he went through the whole story of the past few weeks and spoke mainly of emptiness and pain. There'd been no fight, no rows, certainly no beatings; instead, he and Jennie had been equally miserable as they circled around one another in the place they'd shared but which now felt like somewhere from their past. Crombie was shattered by her betrayal, she was desolate that so much was being lost. Crombie didn't use words like these but the things he did say etched pictures in Carston's mind and made him feel sad and frustrated that there was no answer to it all.

"What're you going to do?" he asked, when Crombie lapsed into another silence.

Crombie shrugged, then shook his head.

"Split up, I s'pose. No point in staying together. Even if she gave this guy up, he'd ... he'd be there. I can't forget it, Jack. He's been fucking my wife, for Christ's sake. You can't put that out of your mind just like that. Christ, I see the bastard at work."

"What, on the rig?"

"No, no. He's got a cushy number in the office. Fucking medic, isn't he?"

Carston had heard enough about medics in the past few days. The buggers got everywhere.

"Have you seen him since ...since Jennie told you?"

"No. I don't want to either. I'd finish up in your bloody cells."

The drink was beginning to get to him but Carston's head was clear. As Crombie drifted towards an inevitably deepening misery, he tried to make suggestions, offer options which Crombie might be able to take, but the fact of Jennie's affair always stood in the way.

It was nearly eleven when they walked home together. The initial relief that Crombie had got from telling someone about the demons that were pressing on his skull began to wane as he got nearer to his house. At the gate, they saw that there were lights in the front room and in one of the upstairs windows.

"You going to be OK?" said Carston.

Crombie was looking at the upstairs window.

"Yes," he said. "Thanks, Jack."

Carston wanted to put a hand on his shoulder to express some sort of closeness but he couldn't.

"No bother," he said. "Any time you want ... you know. Give us a shout."

"Yes. Thanks. I'm sorry about tonight."

"What?"

"Putting it all on you like that."

Carston waved a hand to say that no apology was needed.

"Didn't know who to talk to. Not easy to say, is it?"

"No."

"I'll see you, Jack."

"Yes. Take care, Alex."

Carston walked on towards his own house. When he got there, he looked back down the road. Crombie had turned and was walking away, back in the direction from which they'd come. He was a big man but tonight, in the dusk which had at last started to thicken the light, the heaviness he was carrying forced down on him and he looked defenseless. Carston swallowed back the sadness he felt and put his key into the lock. There was nothing at all he could do. But even as the thought lay heavily in him, some of the things that had been said began to move his mind back to the hospital and his case. The revelation that Jennie had a lover reminded him that the least likely people could be driven by unimagined motives. More than that, though, Carston realized that maybe all the impossibilities could be dispelled by looking at simple mechanics.

Inside, Kath was still in her darkroom. He tapped on the door.

"You can't come in yet," she called from inside.

"No. Just to say I'm going up to the hospital. I may be back late."

"OK," said Kath. "I'll be here for a while yet."

"Night, love."

"Night."

****

At the hospital, he was able to walk unchallenged into the darkened corridors. It was a stark demonstration of how fragile their security procedures were. He was glad, though, not to have to explain his presence to anyone and to have the freedom to sense the atmosphere of the place. As he made his way through to the High Dependency Unit, he was impressed by the sensation that momentous things were going on around him. It was less busy than during the daytime of course, but perhaps for that reason, the pieces of equipment, the waiting wheelchairs and trolleys, the yawning spaces implied a greater expectancy. Although he was walking on the balls of his feet, the clicking of his shoes echoed away into wards and other corridors, sending God knows what signals to fearful patients and weary nurses and doctors.

On his way to the HDU, he had to pass the Intensive Therapy Unit and he stopped briefly to look through the glass panel in the door. The scene was like something out of *Star Trek*; the interior of a spaceship carrying its crew in suspended animation to distant galaxies. This was one journey he hoped he'd never have to make; all of these people had once been independent, active contributors to life, now they were faulty machines, stripped of dignity and self.

He moved quickly to the next ward, the HDU. The light was on at the nurses' desk at the far end of the room but no member of staff was there. He pushed open the door and walked along past the sleeping patients, glad of the chance to see for himself exactly what access visitors had to the people in the beds and their possessions. There were incomprehensible charts, the occasional paperback, bottles of fruit juice and water, glasses, but little that might be considered personal.

On the table beside the last patient on the left, his interest was caught by two small bottles. He picked them up and held them in the light which spilled from the reading lamp on the nurses' desk. Each one carried a hand-written label saying "MRS DICKSON. DO

NOT TAKE BY MOUTH". On the other side of each bottle was another label. One read "BERGAMOT, LEMON, MANDARIN, NEROLI IN APRICOT KERNEL OIL", the other "CYPRESS, GERANIUM, FRANKINCENSE IN SALMOND OIL". He opened the tops and sniffed at their contents. The smell was heavy and concentrated. It contrasted very strongly with the antiseptic freshness that hung around almost everything else in the room.

As he screwed the tops back on, he was suddenly aware of a nurse standing at the door watching him. Rather guiltily, he replaced the bottles and padded up to her. When he got to the door, she put a finger to her lips and motioned him out into the corridor. He showed her his warrant card and, to his slight surprise, she just gave a sigh.

"More questions, I suppose," she said.

"Not really," said Carston. "I was just nosing around."

"Well, I told your lassie everything I know about it."

"My lassie?"

"Aye. A sergeant."

"Ah, Sergeant McNeil," said Carston.

"I think so. I'm Susan Jamieson, the acute pain nurse."

"Ah, right," said Carston. "Yes, Julie said she'd seen you."

"You shouldn't be doing that," said Jamieson, pointing to Mrs Dickson, the patient he'd just left.

"I know. Sorry. I haven't messed around with anything."

"Why're you here at this time of night?" she asked.

Carston shook his head.

"No excuse," he said, his voice as low as hers. "Just looking for help with it all."

"Well, I can't help you," she said. "There's nobody else on at the moment. I can't leave the ward."

Her eyes were tired and he noticed the lines that criss-crossed around them. There was a sudden movement in one of the beds halfway down the room. A thin, white arm was raised and began brushing at the patient's head as if it was trying to get rid of some substance that was clinging to it.

"Mr Kennedy. I'll have to go," said Jamieson, looking at Carston as if she were wanting his permission.

"Of course," he said. "But I'd like to talk to you myself sometime. Is that OK?"

She nodded.

"Good. Thanks for all your help. Sorry to keep you."

He watched her walk quickly down to the troubled patient and lean over him, taking his flailing arm and easing it back under the bedcovers. Carston heard her soothing whispers as she sat on the chair beside the bed and began to settle Mr Kennedy back to sleep. In the dim light, their closeness made them seem like just one body, half in, half out of the bed. Jamieson seemed completely absorbed in her task and didn't look up as Carston turned and went, quickly but quietly, back out to a world where everything was taken for granted.

# Chapter Eleven

Spurle and Fraser were on their way to the university to see what else they could learn about Mrs Rioch. Spurle didn't like being driven but Fraser had got behind the wheel at the station and nobody ever argued with him. The only problem for Fraser was that that left Spurle with more time to look around and chat. What he said was rarely edifying. On top of that, Fraser was preoccupied by things which he wouldn't dream of telling Spurle about. His life was soon going to change and he wasn't sure how he was going to handle it yet. Confiding in Spurle wasn't part of the plan; that would be the first step to disaster.

"What's your game, by the way?" he said at one point, interrupting another of Spurle's moans about something or other. "Readin that fuckin *Guardian*."

"I don't any more," said Spurle.

"Nae surprised. You dinna understand a word of it. Christ, it takes you half the mornin to get through the bloody *Sun*. What was you after?"

"Sex."

"Bollocks."

Unlikely though it seemed, it was in fact sex that had briefly turned Spurle into a *Guardian* reader. The only reason he'd bought it was that one of his mates in the pub had shown him an article the previous week which certainly wasn't easy reading but which was worth the effort. He'd even taken the trouble to write notes about it so that he'd remember. He flipped open his notebook.

"OK, smartarse," he said, "what do you ken about nitric oxide?"

"Fuck all," said Fraser, proud of the fact.

"Well, mebbe you should start learnin about it, 'cause that's what makes sex last longer."

"Bollocks," said Fraser again.

"OK, OK," Spurle went on, determined now to prove his point. "These guys that stick their heads in plastic bags and half strangle themselves an' that, why d'ye think they do that?"

"'cause they're fuckin pathetic, like you."

"No, 'cause they're cuttin off the oxygen. Lowerin oxygen pressure makes sex longer and better."

"I'll stick to my own methods," said Fraser, shaking his head. If Spurle had to resort to reading that sort of shite to turn him on, he was even sadder than everybody already thought he was. As far as Fraser was concerned, Spurle's demonstration of the advantages of the quality press had failed utterly. But, since reading the article, Spurle himself had actually done a bit of research and begun trying to identify substances which had nitric oxide in them. He hadn't yet experimented, but he thought he probably would sometime.

At the university, they talked first to a woman who was in charge of Human Resources. She looked out the relevant records and apologized for being able to add very little to the statistics they contained. Mrs Rioch had worked as a cleaner in the Selkirk block for eight years, ten months. She'd left on October 23rd the previous year as part of a rationalization of ancillary staff.

"What d'you mean, left?" asked Fraser.

"We were downsizing," said the woman.

"She was sacked, then?" insisted Fraser.

The woman was uncomfortable but could only agree with him.

"Did you have any problems with her?"

The woman was puzzled for a moment, then said, "None whatsoever. There's nothing on her record at all. She was a model employee."

"So you sacked her," Fraser said again.

The woman didn't like being forced to defend a position which was none of her making and suggested that, since she had no direct knowledge of Mrs Rioch, they might get more useful information from the head janitor and some of the other cleaners. As they walked downstairs to the janitor's room, Spurle gave an assessment of the Human Resources woman which ranged her alongside most of the women he'd met who were in positions of authority.

"Fuckin dyke," he said.

Only two members of the cleaning staff had been there during Mrs Rioch's time. One of them, who insisted they call her Betty, had known her particularly well.

"Salt o' the earth," was her verdict. "Wouldna do nae harm to naeb'dy. Good worker."

When they asked her why she'd got the sack, she simply pointed a finger upwards and let her facial expression tell them what she thought of those in charge of hiring and firing.

As they talked on, the impression of Mrs Rioch that had already formed in the minds of the team was strengthened. She did her work, never had a bad word to say about a soul, helped out when others were off sick and earned every penny of the tiny wage they gave her.

"Makes no sense to me," said Spurle. "Why'd they sack somebody like that?"

"Easy choice," said Betty.

"How?"

"They knew she'd just take it. Wouldna complain."

"Aye, but if she hadna done nothin wrong..." said Fraser.

"They was clearin out. Just needed one wee excuse," said Betty.

"Did they get one?"

"Oh aye. The usual. One o' that lecturers. Said she threw away important stuff. Papers or some such."

"Which lecturer?"

"In number D26. Dinna ken if it's still the same one there now. It was the one who was there last summer."

Betty had little more to give them so they went back upstairs to check on the room she'd identified. A square of white card in a metal holder below the D26 bore the words "Dr Leith, European Studies." Spurle knocked on the door and, hearing a curt "What?" shouted from inside, opened it.

Leith was at his bookshelves, piling up sheets of paper and holding a black polythene bag. They stepped over three more bags that were partly obstructing the door and Fraser said, "CID, sir. We'd like to ask you about..."

"Oh God, Professor Hayne again, is it?" said Leith, not waiting for him to finish. "I don't know what you expect me to add. He was a first class colleague. Best head of department we've had for ages."

Fraser had noticed that most of the books on the shelves had French titles.

"Raymong?" he said.

Leith stopped and looked at him.

"I'm sorry?" he said.

"Raymong," Fraser repeated. "It's French for 'really'."

"Ah. *Vraiment*. So it is. Well, as I was saying. Alistair Hayne was a wonderful man. Had an awful lot to put up with, what with all his illnesses. The people at the hospital were marvelous with him. Gave him the best treatment available. Made things easier, I'm sure. It's a great loss. Not only to the department; to the university, too. And to European Studies. Such a creative mind. He'll be sorely missed."

"It's no about him," said Spurle, irritated by Fraser's French aside. "It's about a cleaner."

Leith's face changed completely.

"A cleaner. What on earth d'you expect me to know about a cleaner?"

"It's a Mrs Rioch. She used to work here. Used to clean your office."

Leith said nothing, waiting for Spurle to continue.

"She left last year. You complained about her. Something about throwing away some papers of yours."

Leith turned back to his shelves and put the next heap of papers into the bag.

"If I had to remember all the cleaners and janitors who've messed up my papers, we'd be here for days," he said, busying himself again.

"So you don't remember the name? Don't remember anything about her?"

"No and no," said Leith. "Really, I'd have thought that the investigation into Professor Hayne would give you enough university business to keep you occupied. Unless this person's involved in it."

"What papers did she throw away?" asked Fraser.

As usual, Leith was sweating. He brushed a sleeve across his forehead.

"I wish you'd listen. I have no recollection of the events or person you're speaking of at all. If it happened, my mind has not retained it."

His antagonism was clear. They tried a few more approaches but the questions and answers just looped round one another and refused to advance. Eventually, Spurle gave up. Fraser had switched off long before and the stench which Leith gave off was getting to their throats. They listened to one more version of how Leith found it difficult to identify individual cleaners, then cut short the interview and left, swearing, coughing and retching for one another's benefit as soon as they were outside in the cleaner air of the corridor. Leith must have heard them.

****

In the end, sex with Gillian had been as dreary for both of them as it always had been. Christie had been given no access to Hayne's study and no indications whether Gillian knew anything of the specific papers he was anxious about. For her part, Gillian had learned that there was nothing to keep her in Cairnburgh once the whole business was over. She had already started making plans to leave. Of the two, it was Christie whose dissatisfaction was the greater.

For the first time in his university career, he felt powerless. Early on, he'd learned that students and colleagues alike could be kept at bay by words. The longer the words and the more intricate their context, the greater the security they provided. No one was ever willing to admit they didn't understand anything and Christie moved through his days pushing before him a bow wave of verbal pretence and leaving in his wake students who either worried about their own intellectual inadequacy or dismissed him as a wanker.

Since his suspension, he'd set aside his leather waistcoats and Fruit of the Loom shirts for Austin Reed sports jackets and ties. It was a necessary yet futile transformation. In his present isolation, his access to others was severely limited. He could still use his office but, as if fearful of some contagion, his departmental and faculty colleagues stayed clear and always found a way of ringing off fairly quickly if he phoned them. Just when his committee skills might be put to some personal use, he was prevented from practicing them.

He was fully aware that, in a way, Scott's accusations were legitimate. He did find her attractive and he wanted her to know it. But why was that a crime? God, she should have been flattered. It wasn't as if he wanted to fuck her; that always brought complications. Kissing, touching, maybe some oral attentions, those were the things he imagined. So what the hell was she doing bringing a complaint against him? She couldn't hope to make it stick because there was no evidence. He hadn't assaulted her, he'd said nothing explicit and the way he'd touched her could easily be interpreted as contact that was social rather than sexual. The grades he'd given her over the entire period she'd been one of his students averaged out at around fifty-eight per cent and had been consistent. The granting or withdrawing of favors would surely have been marked by some variations.

It was his isolation that began to make him doubt the security of his stance. When the time came to see the Vice-Principal who was dealing with the complaint, he'd be allowed to take a friend or colleague along with him. Now, though, after almost a whole morning on the phone, he still hadn't found anyone willing to fill the role.

His first thought had been to contact his union but, given their strict policy on sexual harassment, he wasn't sure of how strongly they'd support him. Asking the university's own lawyer was obviously out of the question and so he'd tried colleagues in the law department. With each one the answer was the same. Some were aware of his reputation and guessed that there was substance to the complaint, others knew that the Vice Principal who'd been appointed to adjudicate had been an ally of Hayne's and the rumor was that Hayne had already raised the subject of Christie's gross moral turpitude with him. None of them said so in so many words, but there was a possibility that the findings would go against him. In academia, sexism was as embraceable as leprosy.

In the end, he had no choice but to resort to his own lawyer, David Rennie, and, even there, difficulties continued to accumulate.

"It doesn't matter what you meant," said Rennie, after Christie had filled in the outlines of his encounter with Scott. "This woman only has to feel that she's being viewed as a sexual object and she has a right to protest. You've offended her, even if no offence was intended."

"Oh, for God's sake, David, I told her I liked her outfit. How can that be an offence?"

"Listen, unwanted sexual attentions, any undue emphasis on sexual status, anything that creates an intimidating, hostile or offensive environment can be…"

"You're talking like a text book."

"Yes, because those are the expressions that cover what's going on here. That's what you're up against, the sort of thing the university's own written procedures will say."

"So you're saying I've got no chance."

"Certainly not. I'm just trying to make you see that you need to be very careful how you present your side of things. If you charge in full of righteous indignation, you could escalate the thing."

"Escalate. For God's sake, David, I've been suspended. How much further could it escalate?"

"Dismissal," came the reply, fast and intentionally hard. "If you antagonize this woman, and the SRC rep who'll no doubt be with her, you could put the VP in an impossible position. But if we move gently and listen patiently to her claims, we could exploit any weaknesses she has."

"Any weaknesses? Of course there'll be weaknesses. You're talking as if you think I did it."

"It doesn't matter what I think," said Rennie, in the same even tone. "My concern is that we present your actions in the best possible light. My principal aim will be your complete exoneration. Failing that, we'll seek an informal resolution of the matter."

Christie made a noise as if he were about to protest but Rennie didn't falter.

"But I'll need your full co-operation or you may have to face disciplinary action and that, as I said, includes dismissal."

Christie sat back in his chair. Rennie's words were opening sinister options he hadn't so far contemplated. He'd seen the accusation as an embarrassment, an irrelevant but irritating interruption of his progress, not the enormous hurdle that Rennie was making of it.

"You will help me then?" he asked, a little anxiously.

"Of course, Michael. But remember, this isn't trivial. It could be very serious indeed."

\*\*\*\*

Carston looked at the piece of paper which Reid had handed to him and had to check his anger. It was a short note telling him that the people Reid had brought in for questioning about the fraudulent MOTs and the outboard motor thefts had been released.

"What's all this about?" he asked.

Reid, immaculate in dark grey, was standing on the other side of his desk, concentrating hard on polishing his glasses.

"Some of the evidence on the charge sheets was … duplicated," he said, his tone altogether too light for Carston's liking.

"So?"

"There were conflicting dates. Their brief picked up on them and we had to let them go."

As Carston raised his eyes to the ceiling, Reid added, "They may be suing for wrongful arrest."

"Great. Well done, Reid. Welcome to the CID." Carston was finding it difficult to hold back. "I thought you'd collated all the stuff," he said. "Checked through it on your bloody spreadsheets. That's what you're good at, isn't it?"

"Yes sir."

"Well?"

"The spreadsheets weren't at fault, sir."

Reid's tone was smug. He seemed somehow to be enjoying it. Carston saw that there was almost a smile on his lips.

"How come the buggers are free then?"

"Not sure, sir. Some sort of problem when the statements were taken it seems."

In other words, Reid was putting himself in the clear and it all fell back on Bellman and Thom. Carston didn't buy it but, since he'd told Reid to organize it all, there was no way he could check what had really happened. He had no doubt that Reid had already reported the incident to Ridley, whitewashing himself and muddying the squad's procedures. The man was as slimy as he looked. There was only one safe option.

"In future, you're with me," he said.

"Thank you, sir," said Reid.

"It's not a fucking promotion," said Carston, his temper briefly bubbling over. "I want to keep a bloody eye on you till I know I can trust you."

He stood up and went through to the squad room. McNeil and Fraser were in another of their mumbling tête-à-têtes, Spurle, Bellman and Thom were sorting through some report forms and comparing them with a computer print-out.

"Is that the stuff about the guys we had to let go?" asked Carston.

"Yes sir," said Thom. "I don't understand it. We took ages. Everything was kosher."

"Right. Ditch that print-out. Start from scratch. Pull the stuff together yourselves. I want to know what's missing and how we can clean up the bloody mess. The stuff that got chucked away, your original stuff—put it back. You're with them, Fraser. And get a shift on. We've got two murders we're supposed to be solving."

"*Avec plaisir, patron*," said Fraser.

Carston shook his head and went back to his own office, motioning for McNeil to follow him. As she closed the door behind her, she felt the residual awkwardness in the atmosphere. Reid was entering some data into his iPad. Ross was at his desk, his head down, not wanting to make eye contact with anyone.

"Right. Report," snapped Carston.

Ross and McNeil looked at one another. Ross gave a little shrug.

"Er, there's a couple of things, sir," said McNeil. "Nothing crucial. I could leave them till later."

"No, no," said Carston, glaring again at Reid. "It's benefit day for sergeants. What've you got?"

"Sandra Scott, the student you saw at the university. I've had a wee chat with her."

"Oh?"

"Yes. She called me. It's not just the lecturer. Seems some guy's been stalking her."

"A different one, you mean?"

McNeil nodded.

"Sits on a bench in the park. Watches her go by," she said.

"Not much we can do about that," said Carston.

"No. But he phoned her. Saw her talking to you. Thought she was shopping him."

"Bloody hell. What did he say?"

"Nothing much."

"Well, did he threaten her? What?"

McNeil shook her head.

"Not really. Upset her, though."

Carston puffed out a sigh of frustration.

"What's she want us to do about it?"

"Nothing," said McNeil. "Wanted to talk about it, that's all."

Carston detected that there was more to it.

179

"D'you think we need to get involved?" he asked.

"No, sir. I'm keeping in touch. If it changes, I'll ... I'll let you know."

"Very kind of you. What about the other guy? The lecturer."

"She's put in a complaint. To the university."

"Good," said Carston. "Did she say who it was?"

"Yes. One of the ones you've been talking to. Guy called Christie."

Carston and Ross looked at one another and nodded. As well as recalling the poison in Christie's words about his colleagues, Carston saw again the carefully chosen outfit and the air of self-satisfaction that the man gave off. The self image he projected suggested that he found himself attractive. He was no doubt certain that others did too.

"So what's the next step?"

McNeil shrugged.

"She has to see a Vice Principal. He'll talk to Christie too. Then ... well, he'll decide," said McNeil.

"What, on his own?" said Carston.

"Seems so."

"What's his name? Solomon?"

McNeil smiled.

"Well, stay on the case with her, Julie. You may be able to help. Give her a bit of support. Show somebody we're not entirely useless."

"Yes, sir," said McNeil, puzzled at the reference. "We had a long chat. She's OK."

"Good. Anything else?"

"Yes. I've been talking to Mrs Rioch's neighbors. And Fraser's been to see her husband."

Normally, Carston would have thought nothing of getting Fraser's report second hand but the unexplained link that seemed to have grown between him and McNeil triggered a little wariness in him.

McNeil filled in the details about Mrs Rioch's time at the university. None of them linked her death with that of Hayne. They'd worked in the same building, but they might as well have belonged to different species.

"Hard to think that anybody'd want to kill her," McNeil was saying.

"Anything else about the husband?" asked Ross.

McNeil shook her head.

"Doesn't know what he's going to do without her. Cracked up when they were talking about her. Genuine accordin to Fraser."

"Is he a reliable judge?" asked Reid, taking them all by surprise.

"He's been in the CID a long time," said Carston.

It was no answer, but the words had been chosen more for their sub-text than for their surface meaning. Before Reid had time to reply, Carston was active.

"Right," he said, standing up and slipping his mobile into the side pocket of his jacket. "Let's blitz the hospital."

"All of us?" said Ross.

"Yes. I want to talk to all of them again. We've sorted out the sutures. We probably know what happened to them. We need to do the same with the overdose. Find out where the two overlap."

"The two what?" asked Reid.

Carston made a great show of controlling his impatience.

"The two causes of death," he said. "So we check all the possible sources of morphine, find out if any of them aren't controlled, whether it's possible to tamper with doses, that sort of thing. And how does it get into the patient? Are there ways we don't know about? And I want to know a bit more about the politics of the place. Who'd benefit if there's a surgical cock-up? Or an anesthetics one. That's what we do in the CID, Reid, ask questions. We'll sort out who does what on the way there. Jim, get the car organized, will you?"

"Right, sir."

"Go with him, Reid."

The two men went out, leaving Carston and McNeil.

"Julie. Before we go," said Carston. "How come Fraser reported to you and not to me?"

The slight blush that came into her neck and cheeks confirmed that his suspicions had some substance.

She shrugged.

"Don't know, sir. I was in the office. He knew I was coming in here. He just … asked me to tell you."

Carston waited. McNeil wouldn't catch his eye. She obviously didn't intend to say any more either.

"I need to know what's going on in the team," said Carston at last. "It's bad enough that we're saddled with Robocop Reid; I don't want any … secrets getting in the way."

McNeil nodded.

"Don't worry, sir," she said. "There's no secrets. Fraser's just… Well…" Her voice tailed off as she shrugged.

Carston clenched his teeth to stop the anger he'd felt before from returning.

"Julie…" he began.

McNeil looked directly at him, her face open, the blush already gone. Carston could see why Fraser might be attracted to her.

"Trust me, sir," she said.

Carston heaved a deep sigh.

"Bloody hell," he said.

****

When they got to the hospital, Blantyre was at first rather taken aback to see four of them. She quickly covered her reaction, and was very understanding when Carston explained that it would actually shorten the time they had to spend there and was a more efficient use of resources. She excused herself, made two phone calls, scribbling notes as she spoke, then turned to them again.

"Nurse Jamieson's here but she'll soon be going off duty so maybe you should see her first. She's just finishing an aromatherapy session."

"Does the hospital approve of that sort of thing now?" asked Carston.

"What sort of thing?"

"Well, aromatherapy, alternative medicines."

Blantyre flashed him her most caring primary school teacher smile.

"We use any technique that may be of benefit to our patients," she said.

Carston wondered whether the smile would give him a tan.

"Doctors Latimer and McKenzie will be free in about half an hour and Nurse Brewster's on standby today so you can see her more or less when you like. Is there anybody else?"

"Well, there's you, of course," said Carston, aware once again that Blantyre had taken charge and wanting to get the initiative back.

"Me? How can I help you?"

"The broader picture, organizational matters," said Carston. He waved a hand at Ross and McNeil. "Sergeants McNeil and Ross will go through it with you while sergeant Reid and I have a chat with nurse Jamieson. Where will I find her?"

Blantyre made another phone call then took them to a small room off the main corridor.

"She'll be here right away," she said. "I'd better get back for my grilling."

She raised her eyebrows to show them that it was a joke then left them.

"Now then," said Carston. "When this nurse comes in, just sit tight and listen. Don't butt in and only speak if you're spoken to."

"Won't that be rather off-putting for her?" asked Reid. "Me being a sort of silent witness?"

"It'll be off-putting for me if you're not."

****

Blantyre's office smelled of coffee and perfume. It was well insulated against the horrors lurking in the nearby wards and corridors. Ross and McNeil were unimpressed by the bullshit but the coffee was so much better than the stuff they drank in their office that the interview was proceeding fairly smoothly. They'd prompted her with questions about hospital politics and nodded through her encomiums about the management infrastructure. Their interest rose slightly when she spoke of the shortage of nurses in the UK.

"We all got rather complacent a while back," she said, her face serious. "There was a surplus, you see. We stopped training. Now, we're having to rely on temporary staff and overtime. It's very difficult. Members of the board have had to fly to Canada and Holland to recruit new staff."

"Drag, eh?" said McNeil.

"Indeed," said Blantyre, too focused on her subject to pick up the sarcasm. "It's a major headache for Human Resources."

To Ross, that sounded like the sort of problem God might have. He wanted to get back to something more relevant to their case.

"D'you think it affects how things are supervised?" he asked.

"What d'you mean?"

"Well, I was thinking of the problems with Professor Hayne and Mrs Rioch."

"No," she said immediately, giving him no time to go on. "Whatever the strictures, we never allow them to compromise safe working practices."

"But if there's a shortage…"

"Sergeant, there are shortages everywhere. Our job is to overcome them. And, remember, we're a teaching hospital. Our staff not only have to be doctors, they have to be teachers too. Many of them are unhappy about it but they get on with it. A vocation is a vocation."

It was like punching a sponge. Wherever they came from, she absorbed the enquiry and dealt with it. As McNeil's questions became more and more aggressive, Ross' fascination with Blantyre grew. Beneath the patient, smiling, programmed surface, there were obviously significant depths. It was as if Blantyre actually was the hospital.

"How much does this enquiry affect you personally," he asked when McNeil's attack relented.

Blantyre looked at him, a frown crossing her face.

"Me personally?" she asked.

"Yes. I mean, you always have to put the best gloss you can on things. This might make it a bit difficult."

The frown disappeared.

"Yes, I think it will," she said, the smile slowly re-establishing itself. "And you're right. I do take it seriously, even personally. You see, I really do think we're providing maybe the most important service available to this community, and the thought that it could be … compromised … well, I find it very unpleasant."

As she spoke, the fingers of her right hand were playing with the cuff of her left sleeve. It was an unconscious gesture and, for the first time, McNeil felt a little sympathy for her. She was the main point of liaison, the front line of the hospital's defenses and yet she'd treated them with charm and no signs of the stress the investigation must be causing her. McNeil felt a brief touch of guilt.

"Now," said Blantyre, with suddenly renewed energy, "Nurse Brewster, then Dr McKenzie. Ten minutes apiece. Will that be enough?"

McNeil's guilt ebbed. Blantyre's briefly submerged PR persona had resurfaced and, once more, McNeil and Ross were simply units in her schedules.

****

While the two sergeants tried to dig at the surface Blantyre offered them, Carston and Reid were confronting the pains and problems beneath it. Jamieson had brought the scent of geraniums and almonds with her, from the oils she'd just been using.

"Nice smell," said Carston.

Jamieson said nothing.

"Does it help your patients, d'you think?"

Jamieson shrugged.

"Yes."

"How do they work?"

"Some of the oils are bactericidal. They help cells to grow, too. Bergamot's a great one—anti-herpes, reduces edema in limbs after operations, pain relief—all sorts of things."

"You sound like an expert."

"We do a course."

"Where do the oils come from?"

"We've got a stock on the ward. All the basics."

"Are they locked up?"

"No. What for?"

Carston shook his head.

"I was just wondering. Who makes them up?"

"We do. Why?"

Her tone had become defensive. Carston backed off.

"Just interested."

Her expression showed exactly what she thought of his lie. Carston hurried on.

"I remember talking to a friend of mine about them. A doctor. He didn't seem too convinced."

Jamieson gave a sigh and lifted her hand to rub her fingertips across her forehead.

"Aye, well, doctors are sometimes no very bright."

185

"They don't actually prescribe aromatherapy then?"

This time, Jamieson's sigh became a yawn.

"No. That's us. Patient care. It's not just the oils, it's being touched. Contact. Most o' them don't feel very clean. Having us touching them, it's … well, reassurin somehow. Makes them feel a wee bit more normal."

Her voice was tender, far away, remembering nights when a simple massage had eased people back into a momentary self-esteem that every other part of their stay in the wards had taken from them.

"Was that true for Professor Hayne?" asked Carston.

"Yes. He wouldn't admit it, but he was no different from the rest. Peace, he was after. Wantin to … forget it all."

In spite of her obvious tiredness, she was patient as they went over the same ground she'd already covered with McNeil, content to confirm what she'd said then with little nods. It was when they started talking about visitors that things got a little more interesting. There was a catch in Jamieson's throat as she said that none of the Riochs' three children had come near the place at any time during her illness.

"But the husband was a regular, was he?" asked Carston.

"Well, she wasn't here long, but he was here every day without fail," said Jamieson, looking disturbingly close to tears. "That's what kept her goin."

"You must get pretty close to them. I mean the families as well as the patients," said Carston.

Jamieson shook her head.

"Can't afford to. Most of the ones I'm dealin with are terminal. It'd be like losin a friend every week."

"It must be hard not to, though, spending so much time with them."

"Not really. It's a job." She was back in control but Carston knew that her work meant more to her than that. The obvious sympathy she felt for the Riochs made it personal.

Switching the focus to Hayne seemed to restore her balance. She made no secret of the fact that he was mostly unpleasant and had no friends among the staff.

"How about visitors?" asked Carston.

"Yes, your sergeant asked me that. I've thought about it since. He didn't have many. His wife, yes, but even she didn't come all that much. It wasn't like Mr and Mrs Rioch."

"She was here just before his operation, wasn't she?"

"Yes, more's the pity. Her and two others."

"That'd be Dr Leith and Dr Carlyle."

"Aye, that's right. They didn't do him much good."

"Oh?"

"No. Upset him."

"Why? What did they say?"

"Stuff about the university. Things that's goin on there. He told me but I didn't understand it." She stopped and reflected for a moment, her head shaking. "It was bad, though."

"Bad?"

"Yes. He thought they were wantin rid of him. Wantin somebody else to be in charge. Like I said, I didn't understand it."

"You didn't speak to them yourself?"

"No. But the smelly one—Leith—he went into the surgery directorate. Must've spoken to somebody there."

A reflex caused Carston to look quickly at Reid. It was a waste of time; the sergeant's expression hadn't changed since Jamieson first came into the room.

"Any idea who?" Carston asked.

Jamieson shook her head.

"Did he stay there long?"

"Don't know. I had work to do."

"Of course." Carston made a note in his book, more to give himself time than to take down anything of importance.

"Is it normal?" he asked when he looked up again. "I mean, for visitors to go into the directorate? Or anywhere else?"

"Not really."

"But they can go more or less where they like, can they?"

"Well, we don't keep tabs on them. Why?"

"Oh nothing."

Reid seemed to be listening to all this without any of it affecting him. Carston's mind, though, was racing. In Jamieson's simple answers, all sorts of pathways were beginning to appear through the impossibilities that had faced them at first. What business did Leith have in surgery? And exactly what was it about those last few visits that had had such an effect on Hayne? Motives and opportunities seemed to be galloping together. The only difficulty was fitting Mrs Rioch in amongst it all.

Jamieson was finding it more difficult to stifle the yawns that had punctuated their whole conversation. Carston was reluctant to let her go but realized that it might be better to talk to her again at the beginning rather than at the end of a shift. Before she went, though, she had one more surprise for him.

He'd promised that they'd soon be finished, then asked her again about Leith and Carlyle. She couldn't add anything to what she'd already said but, as she stood up to go, she shook her head and said, "After his wife, it was probably just … too much."

Carston looked across at her. Her eyes were fixed on some point near the chair she'd just pushed back.

"His wife?"

"Aye. Have you not spoken to her?"

"Well, yes. But … what about?"

Jamieson looked up at him and let her eyes fall away again immediately.

"Ah, so she didn't say."

"Say what?" asked Carston.

"That last time she came," she said. "She asked him for a divorce."

# Chapter Twelve

Ross and McNeil were having no such luck. After Blantyre had worn them into submission, they'd had ten minutes with the theatre nurse, Fiona Brewster. She was quiet and polite but through her gentle Moray accent came a slight flutter of annoyance. She'd already told Carston about the things they were asking her and quite rightly felt that she had better things to do than repeat herself. She wondered, too, whether she was under suspicion in any way and that made her even less cooperative.

When she was replaced by Dr McKenzie, the tempo immediately increased. She hadn't tied her hair back at all and the result was an electric frizz that sparked about her head like a red magnetic field. Unlike Brewster, she was quite happy to be answering yet more questions about basic anesthetics.

"Well, if I can't tell you about it, who can?" she said when Ross apologized for going over the same ground. "That's what specialists are for. We had an Egyptian doctor in A and E once. He was an expert in anything connected with sand."

They looked at her, unsure whether it was a joke.

"Honest," she said. "Grazes, eczema, conjunctivitis—he was a genius. Show him a fractured tibia, though, and he didn't know where to start."

"Well, what we need to talk about is morphine," said Ross.

"Shoot," said McKenzie, settling back.

"Well, basically, is it easy to get hold of? Who's got access to it? How's it controlled? How's it administered?" Ross spread his hands and shrugged. "The works, in fact."

McKenzie put both her hands onto her head to capture some of the wildness there, smoothed it down and kept her hands clasped behind her neck.

"I've been through a lot of this with your boss. He certainly knows about how it's administered. I told him that you can't get the stuff without about a million signatures, too. So I'm at a loss really to know what to suggest. I mean, it's locked away, in all its forms. And when you get it, it's taken orally or intravenously."

"What d'you mean 'in all its forms'?" asked Ross.

"Well, there are several concentrations. Fentanyl, for example, that's probably the strongest. Or it might be made up in a weaker saline solution."

"Who makes it up?"

"Used to be the nurses. Still is sometimes. But there's a new system now—we get it ready-mixed from the pharmacy and store it in the freezer."

"And who can get at it there?"

McKenzie laughed.

"You don't give up, do you? Nobody. At every stage, it needs several people to get hold of it."

"D'you always take exactly what you need?" asked McNeil.

McKenzie brought her hands down and leveled a finger at her.

"Good point," she said. "No. Because you never actually know how much you're going to need. But if there's any left over, it goes straight into the sin bin." Her hands sketched the size and shape of the thing she was referring to. "It's a waste bin, in theatre. Everything gets chucked in there—needles, bottles, canisters, old syringe bodies. Some of them probably have drops of stuff left in them. Not enough to matter, though. You'd have a job getting it out from amongst all the other stuff, anyway." This time her hand pointed towards Ross. "And, before you ask, sergeant, no, you couldn't save it up until you'd collected a big enough dose."

"Who's responsible for putting it in the bin?" he asked, with a smile.

"One of the theatre nurses, supervised by a doctor. Well, usually. But we know we can trust them. They're better professionals than most of us. Not that you'd think so from the pittance they're paid."

"Hang on," said McNeil. "The procedure says they should be supervised, but they're not?"

For the first time, McKenzie showed a touch of exasperation.

"The place is run by nurses. If their rules say black is white, that's what it is. In theory, yes, we're the supervisors, but in reality, they're the ones in charge."

"But if they're not always supervised, it's a loophole then," insisted McNeil.

McKenzie gave a deep sigh which set the hairs over her forehead floating around.

"I'd trust our theatre nurses more than anybody else in the place." She paused, then smiled as she added, "Certainly more than the surgeons."

"That's a strange thing to say," said Ross.

"No it's not," replied McKenzie, with a shake of her head. "They're like the Egyptian—fine when they stay on their pedestal. But the poor dears don't know very much about anesthetics. Or about tedious things like procedures."

"That's not very reassuring," said McNeil.

McKenzie smiled at her.

"Look, how highly do you rate ... I don't know, dog-handlers or transport police? Not as high as the CID, I bet. It's no different."

"Hardly the same," said McNeil.

"Alright," said McKenzie, suddenly seeming weary. "Surgeons are wonderful. I love them. I don't know what we'd do without them. Now, have we finished?"

\*\*\*\*

Latimer had just been bestowing his wonderfulness on a group of students. They'd come from Aberdeen to spend a day observing in theatre then to attend a seminar on techniques of thoracic surgery. They'd been sent off to have lunch with their vocations intact and with varying ideas about the demigod who'd supervised their morning. Latimer himself was ready for a break and the session with Carston and Reid was more like an audience than an interview.

"You'll be pleased to learn," he was saying, "that the sutures we sent away for analysis after the second post-op fatality were completely clear. As I told you, our procedures leave no room for errors."

"Splendid," said Carston. "Very reassuring. But I don't want to drag you through all that again. Really what I'm looking for is some guidance on … well, the inner workings of this place."

"Inner workings?"

"Yes. Politics, small p, things like that."

"And what d'you suppose I know about that?"

Carston shrugged and gave him an innocent smile.

"I don't know. It's just that you work here and … well, frankly, I haven't the faintest idea what goes on at the decision-making levels."

"But why should you care?"

Carston decided to try being straight with him.

"What if we find that the two deaths weren't accidents? That someone arranged them. That would reflect badly on the hospital, and on your department, wouldn't it?"

Latimer adjusted the knot of his tie with his left hand. He seemed unperturbed by the suggestion.

"There are some three and a half million UK operations every year," he said. "In twenty-odd thousand of them, the patient dies within a month. It's a fact. OK, they're all mainly old or seriously ill, but it happens. That's the nature of the exercise."

"Well, maybe our investigations will help to cut out one or two of them in the future."

"And that's why you're raking over the same stuff again and again?"

"I want to be thorough."

"Well, if you really want to start speculating about internal politics, I'll have to set aside my list for the next two days."

"That complicated, eh?"

"More than you could begin to know. To begin with, you couldn't take us in isolation, you'd need to include the Aberdeen set-up. That opens all sorts of extra issues."

"Like?" said Carston, accepting the imputation that he was ignorant with a smile.

"Like the fact that funding cuts are hitting consultants here and in Aberdeen twice. There are NHS cuts and there are university cuts. We get both."

"I see."

"I wonder. I'm not sure that anyone on the outside can appreciate where it's all going. Academic medicine's anathema. People are deserting it in hordes."

"To go where?"

"Oh, nowhere exotic. Just the NHS. But at least there, they're only clobbered once."

"And why is that such a problem?"

"There are vacant chairs, senior lecturers' jobs for which no one's applying, research is dwindling, the undergraduates are poorer. It's a very sinister spiral."

It was strange; he was describing a very serious situation and yet his tone was almost whimsical, as if it didn't really concern him. Carston wished Ross were with him so that he could help with the questioning and let Carston just be an observer for a while.

"Bugger it," he thought, "let Reid earn his pay."

"D'you mind if my sergeant asks a few questions?" he said, out of the blue. It provoked reactions from both the others, a frown from Latimer and a quick look from Reid. Latimer spread his hands in acceptance of the offer and Carston looked expectantly at Reid.

"Well," said the sergeant, "I was wondering whether the shortfall wasn't being made up in some degree by the fees you get from fundholding GPs."

It was the sort of terminology Carston would have used to take the piss but Reid was serious. Latimer's reaction was instantaneous.

"Hah, the Lilliputians," he snorted. "Now there's politics if you like."

Reid looked pleased.

"The power GPs have nowadays is astonishing. And they exercise it. They send all their easy little operations, the varicose veins and the vasectomies, to smaller hospitals or to their pals in private practice."

"Which frees you for the major work," said Reid, trying to follow his argument.

"Exactly. But the work they're sending to their pals is cheap and quick. There's a turnover. It's only when they need a by-pass or some such, which means sophisticated machinery, extensive post-operative care and so on, that they send their patients here. But they're expensive operations, margins are tighter, so we don't make any profits."

Carston was old-fashioned. He'd never been able to equate balance sheets and illnesses. Reid had no such problem.

"So cost centers are out of step with resources?" he said, bafflingly.

"You could say that," said Latimer. "It's the GPs' revenge. They've always seen us—hospital doctors I mean—as their superiors. Rightly so. Now they can vent their spleen. Is that the sort of political analysis you were looking for?"

Carston's smile was genuinely rueful. He had to accept that Latimer was right; he couldn't have guessed the extent to which politics infected the whole system. If that was just one example, how many motives might he have to plough through before he got anywhere near those he was looking for?

"You're right. It's all beyond me," he said.

"But that's just the beginning," said Latimer, almost triumphant in the power his knowledge gave him. "Try looking for inter-departmental co-operation at the Bartholomew here. But don't hold your breath."

"But I saw it when I was here," Carston protested. "In the theatre, surgeons, nursing staff, anesthetists..."

Latimer chuckled.

"I don't allow anesthetists anywhere near my area or equipment and I wouldn't dream of touching theirs," he said. "We live in different worlds."

"How about people from other departments in the university?" asked Reid suddenly. "We understand that Professor Hayne's colleague Dr Leith came to see you shortly before his operation."

It was a bombshell. Not just for Latimer, but for Carston. He'd been saving it for later. His intention was to soften Latimer up, mislead him a little, then produce the information to test its effect. Flinging it at him without the requisite build-up like this made it more or less worthless. Latimer was obviously thrown by the question but that could just as easily be because of its incongruity.

"Did he?" he said.

"Yes. On the Friday evening."

"Who said so?"

Before Carston could stop him, Reid said, "Nurse Jamieson."

"Strange. She actually saw him with me?"

"Well, no, but he went into your place when he left Professor Hayne's ward," said Reid, apparently unaware of the mayhem he was causing.

"My place?" said Latimer, now totally in control of the exchange. Carston was furious and could only try for damage limitation.

"The surgery directorate," he said. "You didn't see him then?"

Latimer seemed to be searching his memory.

"Not that I can recall," he said.

Carston didn't believe him.

"Do you know Dr Leith?" he asked.

The searching continued.

"Er … yes, I think so. I think he came to see Hayne now and again."

"But you don't know him outside in any capacity?"

Latimer frowned.

"Why should I want to do that? I mean, I may have seen him at university functions or in committees or something but never socially."

"Did you know Professor Hayne's wife asked him for a divorce just before the operation?" asked Carston, deciding that Latimer had had too much of his own way and looking again to disorientate him.

"No. Of course not. How should I know that?"

"I'd've thought an awareness of a patient's pre-operative condition would be of some interest."

Latimer shook his head.

"Contrary to what the songs tell you, an individual's aorta displays no symptoms of his affective condition," he said, with a smugness that bit deeply into Carston's rising anger.

"And the fact that he might be depressed, that his resistance might be lowered, that's not a consideration?" he said.

"Please," said Latimer, standing up. "Leave medicine to the medics. I think this has gone on long enough now. Your questions seem to have very little to do with the deaths you're investigating."

Carston stood to face him. The expression on his face left no doubt that he was furious.

"Please. Leave detecting to the detectives," he said, knowing it was feeble but needing to let his dislike for the man have some sort of expression. "That'll be all."

Latimer smiled and left the room without another word, the slowness of his movements deliberately calculated to let them know that he was still in control.

As soon as he'd gone, Carston swung to face Reid.

"What the bloody hell were you thinking about, telling him all that stuff about Leith?"

"I thought it…"

"No you bloody didn't. That's the trouble. If you ever try anything like that again, you'll be back in amongst your bloody computers, whatever the fucking super says… And," he added, spinning back round after having turned away, "if he gets to hear I called him the fucking super, I'll know where he heard it from, won't I? Just watch your fucking step, Reid. You're on probation."

His anger was directed as much at himself as at the sergeant. He'd always managed to stay cool in the past, but recently, he'd noticed that irritation came more easily, that his tolerance levels were set much lower than before. The constant interference from Ridley and others from "upstairs" was wearing him down. The fascination the job held for him was being displaced by a niggling feeling that he'd had enough. Since a recent harrowing case with a GP, he'd also become more and more aware that having to stay within the limits of the law and its procedures stifled him. It was unsettling. Police work was the only thing he knew about. What else could he do?

****

Scott had spent nearly an hour in the library, looking only occasionally at the open book on the table in front of her. Her last lecture had finished at three but she had to kill time before going home. Perversely, she was delaying leaving in order to give her stalker every opportunity to be in the park as she walked through. Since the first time, he'd always been there, except for the afternoons when Strachan had been with her. But his absence then was too much of a coincidence; it just confirmed that he'd been watching for her and deliberately chosen not to appear. He'd also stayed away for a few days the previous week, but then he reappeared and the strategy McNeil had outlined was back on course. It depended on the two of them innocently meeting him in the park at the same time.

Just after four, she closed the book, crammed it into her bag and set off. The haze had held the day's warmth in and there was a definite feel of summer in the air. The borders in the park were busy with color and there were couples and women with small children sitting on the grass under the big sycamores and chestnuts at its edges. Cairnburgh was looking good, with all the advantages of clean air, open spaces and light and none of the crowds that invaded parks further south.

Scott was so alert that she actually saw the man sit down on the bench as she turned into the central pathway. She didn't see where he came from but their simultaneous arrival was no coincidence. She stopped and bent as if to look at some of the flowers in the first bed, then straightened as she saw McNeil appear at the other end of the path. The man was watching her again but this time she felt neither fear nor anger. Just excitement.

****

At the hospital, McNeil had been conscious of the need to get away by mid-afternoon and Carston and Ross had asked no questions when she told them she had another job to do. She'd parked in the visitors' car park at the halls of residence and come down the steps through the trees to watch for Scott's appearance. She saw the man arrive and sit down and immediately started along the path towards him. She was further from him than Scott but didn't want to hurry for fear of drawing attention to herself. She grinned when she saw Scott bend over the flower bed. She was obviously timing her approach.

****

It was the first time the man had seen Scott bend over like that. The curve of her backside against her light cotton skirt excited him even more than the sight of her naked in her room. There was no need for the usual massaging of his groin; he was already erect. He watched her straighten and move towards him, more slowly than usual it seemed, her skirt swinging and the light from the hazy sun putting a pale gold rim around her hair.

She stopped again, bent over and touched a crimson poppy, cupping its petals in her hand. His breath was quicker and his penis

197

was tight against the front of his trousers. He forgot that she'd spoken to the police. Forgot his phone call. This was what he wanted; the sight of her every day, the easy movements of her body, the flow of her limbs. She was coming closer again, walking with the same languor, actually angling towards him so that he could see the lateral shift of her hips. And there was no anger in her face. Her eyes seemed wide, fixed on him as she walked right up to the bench.

And sat beside him.

She said nothing. Looked straight ahead now at the flower bed opposite them. He turned his own head away from her, unsure how to deal with the new situation. He looked at her profile once or twice and saw that there was a smile on her lips. They were not touching but she was close enough for him to see the soft, golden hairs on her forearm.

There was no way that Scott could know that this was the closest he'd ever been to a woman. His throat felt tight and, having suppressed an impulse to get up and walk away, he concentrated on regaining control of his breathing. As he looked away again, he saw a woman coming from the other direction. She was paler than Scott and her short red hair didn't have the same dark tinge of copper. He had time to register the fact that, although they were both young and female, the stranger didn't have anything like the effect that Scott had. Her figure was OK but her breasts were small and her movements were wrong. Too definite somehow, too strong. Still hotly aware of Scott on the bench beside him and confused about how to respond to her, he waited for the woman to go by. But, as she came to the bench, she stopped and spoke to him.

"Excuse me. D'you mind if I sit here?"

He looked at her, unable to cope with this extra complication. She smiled, waited a moment, then sat down.

Immediately, he knew that this was no accident. He was overwhelmed by panic but, as he leaned forward to get up, McNeil put her left hand on his shoulder, gripped it hard and held him down.

"Sit, boy," she said. "We just want a talk."

"Fuck off," he said, and was instantly rewarded with a tightening of her grip that sent pain shooting down his right arm. He screwed up his face, dipped his shoulder but was unable to move more without increasing the pain.

198

"Now we can sit here like this with me hooked into your nervous system or we can be a bit more relaxed. What d'you think?" said McNeil.

He tried to get away again but her fingers and thumb really were like hooks hard in his flesh. She brought her right hand round in front of his face, lowered it towards his groin and said, "There's still this one too. And my friend hasn't even started on the other side yet."

He turned to look at Scott.

"Bitch," he said, regretting it instantly as McNeil sent the hot pain down his arm again.

"OK, OK," he said, near to tears. "OK, right?"

McNeil loosened her grip but left her hand resting in the same place, her fingers holding him only lightly now. His shoulder was thin. It was easy to find the pressure point under the muscle. She knew she could handle him.

"Right. What's it all about then?" she said.

He didn't answer. She dug at him again.

"I told you, boy, we can either do it the hard way or we can talk. It's up to you. Now then. What's going on?"

The man shook his head. It was quick, barely noticeable.

"Speak up."

"Nothin," he said.

"Oh. An accident, is it? You being here every afternoon? Same time, same bench."

"Yes."

"And how about the phone call?"

"What phone call?"

McNeil gave a deep deliberate sigh.

"Know what, pal? You're getting on my tits. Now stop messing us about. You phoned my friend here, gave her a mouthful of abuse, and you upset her."

He turned to look at Scott. She was watching him, her face expressionless.

"So, first off, you say sorry, then you tell us what's going on. OK?" said McNeil.

"Wasna me," he said, turning back to her.

McNeil raised her wrist to give her more purchase and skewered her thumb hard in under the muscle. It was right on the button. The man gasped with pain and the tears that had been threatening to flow squeezed out onto his cheeks.

"Fuck sake," he cried.

"So talk and I'll stop," said McNeil.

"It's nothin, it's nothin," he said quickly. "I havena done her no harm. Just lookin, that's all. No against the law, is it?"

"It is when you threaten somebody. But I'm not talking law anyway. I'm talking trouble. For you. Heard of the McLures?"

He shook his head. McNeil snorted a laugh.

"Christ, boy, where you been hiding? You'd better find out about them quick, because when they hear you've been bothering my pal here, you'll be Pedigree Chum."

"I'm no botherin her. I just look. She's … I just look."

"Aye well, looking's going to cost you plenty. One guy looked at Billy McLure's sister. In Tesco's. They took him out to the car park, put a Stanley knife up against his prick…"

She stopped as she noticed Scott give her a quick shake of the head. The man's head was lowered. His chin was on his chest and he was crying. His attempts to hold it back forced him to take blocked, painful breaths and just made the flow of tears more inevitable. It was a bigger response than McNeil's empty threat merited and she wondered what she'd unleashed in him.

"Christ, I didna mean nothin," he sobbed. "Just lookin. I havena touched her. Wouldna. But she told the polis about me. What for? I havena hurt her. Just looked. Looked, that's all."

Scott found his breakdown distressing. McNeil had seen too many flashers and stalkers and rapists to be moved. The crying was a surprise, though. She'd have preferred a harder, in-your-face reaction. But it was too late to change tack now.

"OK. Here's what you do," she said. "You never come near my pal again, right?"

The man's upper body still convulsed with his efforts to swallow his sobs.

"Right?" McNeil insisted.

He nodded.

"I don't care whether you're touchin her or not. Lookin is just as bad. She's no your property. You canna do what you like with her. An' if you try to, you won't be hearin from me. Next time, it'll be the McLures. An' they'll make sure you won't be able to look at nobody no more."

200

She'd pushed her accent as far into the rough local idiom as she could manage. Added to the strength and expertise of her grip, it left no doubt in the man's mind that she had access to some evil possibilities. His afternoon had exploded.

"So," McNeil was saying, "that's the last time, right? If she even thinks she's seen you, you're finished."

There was no need to get him to say anything. Before their eyes, he'd changed from a leering menace to a wreck. The perpetrator had become a victim. The speed and extent of his collapse were frightening. McNeil took her hand from his shoulder, smoothed the material of his jacket and gave him a push in the back.

"On your way," she said.

Like a little boy, he pushed himself off the seat, his left hand clutching the shoulder which McNeil had been holding. He was still crying. He didn't look at either of them as he stumbled away up the path down which Scott had just walked.

Neither of the women spoke until he was out of earshot. Scott was twisting a lock of her hair and brushing it against her cheek.

"Wow," said McNeil quietly. "How about that?"

"Did you know he'd be like that?"

"No. I reckoned from everything you'd said that I'd be able to frighten him off, but I didn't think he'd crack up."

Her voice was steady but she wondered whether she'd overplayed the risk. She'd guessed that, if the guy was a watcher and a talker, he'd be all facade. Introducing serious doubts into his mind would be easy and he'd have the option of getting out while he was ahead. But to have him fold so quickly, revert to some sort of childish state, that had never been part of the plan. Her gut feeling told her that he'd stay away, but with the sort of volatility he'd just shown, she didn't want to bet on it. She tried to reassure Scott that it was over but said that, if she had the slightest suspicion that he was still around, she should get in touch and they'd deal with him in more orthodox police ways. Scott was quiet, disturbed still by the memory of the man's sobbing. The man was getting nearer to the end of the path. McNeil stood up.

"Right," she said. "You get on back to your hall. I'm going after our pal there."

"What for?"

"The state he's in, I reckon he'll be going straight home. I'd be happier knowing where to find him. Just in case there's a next time."

Scott nodded and stood up. The man turned out of sight. McNeil started walking away after him.

"Who are the McLures?" Scott called to her.

McNeil paused briefly.

"No idea," she said, then waved and hurried on.

****

Cairnburgh covers both sides of a valley. Macaulay Park runs along the top of the south facing slope and swings down towards the town centre to the west. The crematorium is in the elbow of that bend. From most houses in the town, Cairnburghers can watch their erstwhile neighbors floating away towards the North Sea in little billows of white smoke.

Hayne's body had eventually been released to his widow and she'd quickly arranged the cremation. She would have preferred to dispense with any pretence at mourning but her husband's prominence at the university and therefore in the community meant that there had to be some sort of show. The Cairnburghers got their money's worth. As well as four city councilors, there were twelve representatives from the university, all of whom Mrs Hayne had asked to wear their academic robes. Her pretence was that such a display would be more in keeping with her husband's life's work but in fact it was a way of hinting that his passing wasn't an entirely somber experience for her. Amongst the prevailing black, the colors of gowns and hoods were glorious, dynamic splashes.

Once inside the crematorium, Leith elbowed his way past others to sit beside Menzies and, as the minister began praising Hayne and God alternately, Leith started his own sermon. He congratulated Menzies on his running of the REF in true twenty-first century style. He reiterated the committee's crucial role in the changes that were being forced on them all. He deplored education cuts. Then, after a pause during which he sang that the Lord was his shepherd, he again broached the subject of Latimer's membership of the REF.

"I'd like to say it's a foregone conclusion," whispered Menzies, "but there are two other names in the hat."

"But surely, surgery's got the highest profile," said Leith.

"In general terms, yes," said Menzies, "but one of the others is David Adam, the rheumatologist. He's got an international reputation. Always flitting off to Tokyo or Sydney or Harvard. He'd be quite a catch."

Leith pointed out that, although Adam's status and authority were beyond question, they could hardly rely on getting his support in important votes precisely because he was always somewhere else.

"And anyway, what sort of PR value is there in rheumatology?" he added. "The public at large are going to be as impressed by that as they are by…" He searched for a comparison and saw Carlyle two rows in front of him. "…geriatrics," he concluded.

Menzies still wasn't convinced and they continued their discussion through the rest of the service. By the end, Leith had only managed to bring him round by agreeing to support a proposal Menzies was putting to the next meeting of the Committee on Remuneration of Administrative Personnel. As they began filing out of the chapel, Leith felt that his afternoon hadn't been totally wasted. With Latimer's place secure, he knew that there were now enough voices on the REF to ease through his own accession to Hayne's vacant chair. He had little to fear from the two other contenders for the post. Carlyle might be acting head of department but he had little time for committees and did nothing to cultivate support for himself. As for Christie, whatever the outcome of the vice principal's investigation, his reputation had been severely dented. Leith was rising inexorably.

Back at the house, the mourners ate their sandwiches, sipped their tea or whisky and talked about everything but the dead man. Menzies sought fragrance in the company of others, even the councilors, and Leith, shunned by everyone quick enough to find an excuse to move to another part of the room, had to content himself with Carlyle. They made small talk about the house, the garden and the pictures on the walls. Hayne's name wasn't mentioned once, even when they started discussing the police investigation.

"God knows why they're asking all these questions," said Leith. "What on earth do we know about what goes on at the Bartholomew?"

Carlyle nodded.

"Still, they have to investigate it," he said. "And we're part of his life, aren't we? The main part even."

"Not me. I haven't known what to say to them. They were asking me about some damn cleaner yesterday."

"Ah yes, Mrs Rioch. What sort of things were they saying?"

Leith flapped a dismissive hand.

"Some nonsense. How am I supposed to remember cleaners?"

"We're all going to have to be very clear about what we do and don't remember," said Carlyle. "This is a full investigation. Better get your alibi straight."

"What d'you mean?"

Carlyle shrugged his shoulders.

"Nothing. Ironic, isn't it? Even in death, he's stirring things up for us."

Leith picked another sandwich off the table and took a bite.

"Surely, though, it was an accident," he said, projecting small pieces of egg onto Carlyle's lapels.

"They don't seem to think so," said Carlyle, angling himself out of the direct firing line.

"All the same... Foul play, that sort of thing... It's preposterous."

He waited. Carlyle's only reaction was a small shake of the head and an unheard prayer that Leith would use fewer plosives.

"I mean, persistent police probing. They weren't looking for suspects, were they?"

"Well, they've got plenty to choose from, haven't they?" said Carlyle.

Leith looked at him, not entirely certain what he meant.

"You, me, anyone who had anything at all to do with him really," said Carlyle, a smile in his eyes.

"Oh, I see. Very good," said Leith, "very good."

He laughed to show his appreciation and a well-chewed lump fell unnoticed onto his tie, sliding slowly down it a couple of inches before dropping to the carpet.

"Heard anything about Michael?" he asked.

"Not yet. It'll be a while before they arrange meetings. He'll certainly be off until the vacation."

"Then what?" asked Leith.

"Depends on the outcome, doesn't it?"

"Mm," said Leith. "Well, he's got the department's backing, hasn't he?"

The words surprised Carlyle. It was by no means true that Christie enjoyed much general support and there was no doubt at all that Leith would be the first to wish him ill.

"If the accusation's false, yes," he said.

"Well," said Leith, "even if it isn't, even if he's been tempted, I think we ought to rally round him. There but for the grace of God, eh?"

The thought of Leith making sexual advances to some poor undergraduate was literally nauseating.

"Of course, we'll do what's consistent with professional ethics," said Carlyle. "But if he really has been messing around with students, I for one would find it difficult to work with him."

"Well, never mind," said Leith. "Maybe you won't have to."

And he walked away, leaving Carlyle with no idea what he meant.

# Chapter Thirteen

**R**oss was in the squad room. Carston went through to join him.

"That's it, I think," said Ross.

He was standing beside a chart he'd just completed. It was a breakdown of all the events, people and timings in the case. There were headings, columns and clear, direct arrows indicated link-ups, overlaps and other connections. It was a job that Carston had given first of all to Reid, whose expertise was, after all, in using computers to collate information and produce spreadsheets and flow charts. The result had been a chart an eighth of the size of Ross', covered with printing too small to be read comfortably and criss-crossed with hypertext links and things Reid called interfaces.

Carston looked at the new chart. The name Hayne was on the left and Rioch was on the right. Not surprisingly, it was the former which was the hub of most of the graphic effects. The university and the hospital had their own little boxes and the names of everyone involved in the case were color-coded and arranged under general headings denoting their functions.

As his eyes moved over the information, Carston's head was nodding. It was like children's blocks; arranging things in bold visual patterns made it so much easier to see connections.

"Nice job, Jim," he said. "Everything there?"

"I think so."

Carston followed the various lines, nodding as each ended on a name, a department or some other label relevant to their researches.

"Yep, looks good," he said at last. "The only gap's here."

He tapped a finger on the label "anesthetics". Ross knew what he meant right away.

"You mean the overdose?"

"Yes. Where did that come from?"

Together they looked at the lines connecting the label to Dr McKenzie and, indirectly, to Latimer and the nursing staff.

"I can only put in what we know. They've told us their procedures, you've seen the hands-on stuff for yourself. That's all there," said Ross. "There's got to be an extra something along one of those lines."

Carston tapped the chart again.

"We needed this," he said. "I think I know how he got the overdose."

"How?"

"You played rugby, didn't you? Ever heard of Deep Heat?"

Ross' brows wrinkled. It sounded familiar but he wasn't sure why.

"Liniment," Carston went on. "Dressing rooms reeked of the stuff."

"So?"

They heard voices in the corridor. The tones were unmistakable; Fraser and Spurle were in the middle of another of their arguments.

"You said it yourself, Jim. Hands-on," said Carston as the door opened. "We'll talk about it later."

"…and Madonna's tits are bigger," said Fraser, with some finality as the two constables walked through the door.

"Glad that's sorted out," said Carston. "What's going on?"

"Oh sorry, sir," said Fraser. "I was just wonderin what Pamela Anderson's babies got when she breast fed them with yon implants and Spurle…"

"I'm not interested in your cultural life," said Carston. "I mean what's been happening with the MOTs and stuff."

Fraser beamed hugely.

"All in custody, sir," he said.

Carston looked suspiciously at him.

"What d'you mean?"

"Like he says," said Spurle. "They're in the cells down the stair."

"But we had to let them go," said Carston.

"Aye, but now they're back again," said Fraser. "We went an' had a word wi' one or two folk. They backed us up."

"How d'you mean, backed you up?"

"Remember the things the guys said when we brought them in first time? The stuff they started denyin when their briefs got to them?"

"Yes."

"Well, they're no denyin it any more. Not now there's witnesses."

It all sounded highly suspect and Carston didn't like to think of the methods the two of them had used to persuade their informer to co-operate. Spurle on his own would have made a cock-up of it and landed them in more trouble but he was pretty confident that Fraser had enough sense to stay on the right side of legality.

"What are the guys in the cells saying?" asked Ross.

"They're coughin their guts out. Ready to tell us the lot. Their briefs've said it's OK, too."

"Right," said Carston, eager now to get the business wrapped up before something else got in the way. "Well done. But let's make it all formal while everybody's being friendly. Where's sergeant Reid?"

"No idea," said Fraser.

"Right. Find him and let him sit in with you while you get all the statements. But he's back-up, understand?"

"Aye sir," said Fraser.

"Away you go then," said Carston. "Nice job."

As the two men went out again, even Spurle had something like a smile on his face.

Ross didn't.

"You want to be careful, sir," he said.

"What?"

"Andy Reid. Whatever you think of him, he's a sergeant." He nodded his head towards the door through which Fraser and Spurle had just disappeared. "He outranks them."

Carston knew that he was right and nodded to say so.

"OK, OK, you're right. I'll try to be a bit more ... mature," he said.

"That'll be a first."

Carston felt uncomfortable. There was no excuse for undermining Reid's authority. He was in the wrong and there was nothing more he could say. He was relieved when the phone rang. Ross picked it up, listened, then handed it over.

"Superintendent Ridley," he said.

Carston screwed his face up in annoyance but managed to say a measured "Good morning" into the phone.

"Morning Carston," said Ridley. "Just a quick call. How's the hospital case coming along?"

"None of your business," was the first answer that came into Carston's head. And it was true. Why did Ridley want to know? It had nothing to do with him. His only contact with CID was via clear-up rates, not individual cases.

"Steadily enough," he answered. "We're still getting things together."

"Good," said Ridley. "And how's sergeant Reid shaping up?"

"Not all that great," said Carston, with no hesitation. "He made a bit of a cock-up with some petty thieving stuff we'd almost wrapped up. I think my lads have rescued it alright now. And he hasn't been all that brilliant on the Hayne enquiry."

"I wonder if you're using him properly," said Ridley, as if he hadn't heard Carston's words. "Or rather, making the best use of him? He's got the sort of skills your department needs, you know."

"Oh?" said Carston, wondering what it was all about.

"Yes. Computer literacy. Everybody needs it nowadays. And if we're not used to it, we have to force ourselves to be more open-minded. I mean, the old ways were fine, but we've got more resources available to us now."

The bastard had gone squeaking to Ridley about the business with the chart.

"Do you hear what I'm saying?" asked Ridley, when Carston didn't answer.

"Yes," said Carston.

Ridley waited but Carston had nothing to add.

"Right," Ridley went on, slightly deflated because the explosion he'd expected from Carston hadn't materialized. "Well, see if you can't start applying some technology, eh? A lot of funds are wrapped up in it. We have to optimize resources."

"Exactly what sergeant Ross and I were just saying. Thank you for your support, sir," said Carston.

"Er ... yes ... well, remember, Reid's there for you. Use him."

"Of course, sir. Thank you, sir," said Carston before replacing the receiver. He thumped the desk to release a little of the anger he was feeling.

"That slimy bloody mate of yours has been to tell his pals upstairs that we don't love him."

The accusation that Reid was a "mate" of his brought a frown to Ross' face but he didn't protest. He found the extent of Carston's irritation surprising. Usually, he managed to take things in his stride. In fact, there were lots of times when he'd been too laid back altogether for Ross' liking. His rare bursts of temper were quick flashes which subsided equally quickly and left no residues. His dislike of Reid, though, burned on like a fuse.

"What's the problem?" asked Ross.

"Problem? Reid's the bloody problem. Ridley reckons we should be impressed by his print-outs. How does he know we're not? Unless he's getting dispatches from the bloody front." He got up and went to the window, banging the desk again as he did so. "It's just like the bloody university. And the hospital," he said.

"How d'you mean?"

"The folk who know bugger all about the sharp end are the ones in charge. Bloody managers. They don't give a fuck about the patients or students. As long as nobody upsets their cozy bloody systems."

"I could have Andrew with me for a couple o' days," said Ross.

Carston turned and twitched a quick, humorless smile at him.

"No, it's OK, Jim. It's my tits he's getting on, not yours. I'll handle it."

"So what's on then?" asked Ross, anxious to get away from the pointlessness of Carston's little feud.

Carston took a deep breath and turned to look at the chart once again. He walked across to it and pointed to a name.

"You need to have another chat with her," he said. "Find out why she didn't tell us she asked for a divorce. That last visit of hers must've been a bit traumatic for both of them. Find out more about it. Julie'd better go with you. Just in case."

"Right, sir. How about you?"

Carston was still studying the chart.

"I want to make a call. Tie up the last bit of how it was done," he said. "Then we can concentrate on why."

He pointed to the box marked "university" and slid his finger down the names of Hayne's departmental colleagues.

"I'll go and have another chat with these, too. Find out what their final visits were all about. And, as a special treat for both of us, I'll take sergeant dickhead with me."

"That'll be nice," said Ross.

****

Carston's call was to Brian McIntosh but the doctor was busy and promised to ring back as soon as possible. He also said that he wasn't over-familiar with the topic Carston was asking about and that he'd look it up first to make sure of his facts. While he waited, Carston looked again at the notes from Hayne's iPad. They contrasted very strongly with the arid jottings they'd found in his room at the university. There, they'd seen the function, the absence of self; here, in his private hospital musings, they could hear the man's real voice, the personal edge to his assessments of people and projects, the suffering that gave a new perspective to his planning.

Locked into his pain and into the hospital's systems, Hayne had used the tiny keypad as a sort of escape route. During the earlier part of his stay, the only mention of his condition or treatments came obliquely in withering assessments of most members of the hospital staff. Every few hours seemed to bring another individual to his attention. The nurses were mostly "cretinous", the doctors "charlatans" and Blantyre got a special mention as "that vacuous hag". Most of Hayne's attention, though, was on his colleagues in the department and on arrangements for meetings and tasks to be attended to when he was discharged.

There was just one mention of Hayne's wife. The visits of Carlyle and Leith had been fully documented and provoked the usual reflections, but the only acknowledgement that Mrs Hayne had been near him was a single line entry.

"Gillian was here this morning. Divorce. What timing."

The staff must have been particularly careful or attentive that day because there was no mention of nurses, doctors, cleaners or any of the other irritants that had spoiled every other day he'd spent there. The next entry was made in the late afternoon, after Carlyle's visit, from which Hayne had obviously taken little comfort. Briefly, it had sent Hayne back into planning mode as he speculated on the need to persuade Carlyle to take early retirement. "Little more than a fossil," he wrote. "Totally inadequate, even as acting head. A

211

severe brake on our credibility. And there's something sinister, untrustworthy about him, for all his unctuousness. Merely thinking of the department in his hands is..."

At that point, Hayne had hit the return key twice. The textual space created allowed him to make a new departure.

"Real influence is always going to be compromised by having to accommodate such people. They seem passive, but their presence is as destructive as this damned thing that's eating me away. Scalpels aren't enough. It's a desperate business."

Once again, he left a gap in the text before continuing.

"It was infuriating. He stood there being sympathetic, nodding his head with that feeble concern he pretends to have, weakness personified and yet... He can walk out and leave me here. I find the health of someone like that insulting. It's so easy for him to encourage me. *Nous avons tous assez de force pour supporter les maux d'autrui.*"

"Shit," said Carston, who'd kept on meaning to get the French bits translated each time he'd looked through the transcript. They probably meant nothing but at present they were like holes in the evidence. He hadn't thought of asking Fraser the Francophile to do the job, reasoning, quite correctly, that the little Gallic gems tossed off by Hayne would concern subjects other than asking the way to the chemist's or how much a room with shower and WC cost. He copied the words carefully into his notebook before reading on.

Leith had come shortly after Carlyle and Hayne's mood had not had time to settle. Right from the start, his notes had a sharp personal edge that by-passed departmental functions. He was suspicious of Leith's reason for visiting him at all and clearly derived some savage satisfaction from listing his deficiencies. Naturally enough, the subject of personal hygiene provided thematic consistency to the entry and, if Hayne's judgment was to be respected, Leith's soul was as badly tainted as his body. But as he reflected on the things they'd spoken about—departmental expansion, devolving responsibilities, the elimination of weak links—his loathing of Leith seemed to spread beyond its focus. It was as if, simply by listening to Leith, his remarks had contaminated him.

"And they were my own ideas," he wrote. "There was a despicable logic in it all. He was embroidering on my plans, trotting out refurbished policies that are already in place. I know why he came. He's checking up. He wants to know how ill I am. It's part of some plan. He'd even looked up one of the maxims to quote at me when he left—'*On n'est jamais si malheureux qu'on croit, ni si heureux qu'on espère.*' So depressing to hear it coming from him. So inappropriate. The insolence of office."

Carston reached for his notebook again.

"Bloody academics," he said.

There were only a few more notes. They seemed more general and rambled among non-specific things unconnected with either the university or the two visitors. There was a lot more French and it was only in the last entry of all that Hayne's thoughts returned to the visits.

"Carlyle asked me if I was comfortable," he wrote. "Bizarre question in the circumstances. I've forgotten what comfort's like. Except the one which ensures a calm passage across many a bad night. That's always there. That may be it."

****

When the phone eventually rang, nearly an hour later, Carston felt it as an intrusion into what had become something like a dialogue between Hayne and himself.

He picked the receiver up quickly.

"Carston," he said.

"Jack," said McIntosh. "Sorry to keep you."

"No, I'm sorry to be bothering you again. Any luck?"

"Yes, yes. I've checked it out. Got a few notes here. Why the interest in aromatherapy, though?"

"Down to you partly," said Carston.

"Oh?"

"Yes. You were the one who told me the skin's the body's largest organ."

"Did I?"

"Yes. Made me wonder whether the overdose could get in that way."

"Yes, it could. It's not just that, though. It's smell, too. The skin absorbs the oils but there's also inhalation. Works on the limbic area of the brain; that's the oldest part, the bit where you find things that are vital to survival."

"Don't get technical, Brian. Just tell me about it, eh?"

"It's straightforward. You've got the essential oils and they're diluted in a carrier oil, something like soya, safflower or sunflower. That's for lubrication."

"And these things are absorbed into the body, are they?"

"Yes. Very quickly. Apparently, if you rub garlic oil on somebody's feet, you'll smell it on their breath within ten minutes."

"Feet and garlic," said Carston. "What sort of life do you lead?"

McIntosh laughed.

"Seems it's a classic experiment."

"Impressive. So you could just massage somebody to death?"

"Definitely. Aromatherapists have to be careful what they use. Aniseed, for instance. Highly toxic. It's a narcotic, slows the circulation, damages the brain. And it's addictive." He sounded almost enthusiastic about it. "Wintergreen too. *Gaultheria procumbens*. In the States they use it to flavor chewing gum, coke and things like that. It's just a mild analgesic. It's also an environmental hazard and a marine pollutant."

"Bloody hell," said Carston.

"Yes, but it's still listed with the essential oils. I've got a print out of them all. I'll email it to you if you like."

"I'd appreciate that, Brian. Thanks."

He leaned back in his chair and listened as McIntosh went over some of the points he thought might be of interest. Before ringing off, he asked whether it worked as a treatment.

"Aromatherapy?" replied the doctor. "Well, it does for some. No doubt about it. Chamomile for allergies, bergamot for cell regeneration. And, of course, the aphrodisiacs. Things like jasmine and sandalwood. You making notes?"

"I don't need aphrodisiacs," said Carston.

"That's not what I heard."

Carston laughed, thanked him again and McIntosh went back to his dissections. Carston folded away the notes he'd been looking at and stood up. He was humming the usual little tune which signified contentment. He knew how the sutures had been tampered with and now he'd sorted out the overdose too. Well, possibly. The only little brake on his good humor was the thought that he had to spend the afternoon with Reid.

\*\*\*\*

Sandra Scott could get everything she needed, from shops and launderette to cafe and pub, on the site of her hall of residence. There was never any need for her to go into town, which was precisely why she did, at every opportunity. She enjoyed the privileges that being a student gave her but she knew that academic life made more sense when it was put into the context of what the rest of the population were getting on with.

She was sitting in Starbucks again, this time with Carolyn Noble, who'd spent a lot of time with her since she'd heard about Christie and the man in the park. They were watching a group of four youths walking along the pavement outside. Two of them wore baseball caps the wrong way round, all had tee shirts, baggy jeans and trainers and they pushed each other, spat and swaggered along intent on being noticed.

"Wankers," said Noble.

Scott nodded.

"Must be a biological thing," she said. "Identikit stuff, isn't it?"

It was a conversation they'd had before. Even in the supposedly enlightened student body there were hordes of these throwbacks; brash, aggressive types who marked territories with saliva and vomit and, paradoxically, proclaimed their individuality by wearing identical outfits. Even though Noble had had less to put up with than Scott on the whole, she still shared with her the embarrassment of belonging to the same species as these gobbets of testosterone.

This time, their comments led, inevitably, to Christie and the man in the park. When Scott had gone through all the details of what was effectively McNeil's mugging of her tormentor, Noble's reaction was one of undiluted approval. Scott herself was still not sure and had begun to wonder what the man would do when he'd had time to recover and think about it. About Christie there was less to say. Scott had heard nothing since she'd been told that the matter was under consideration. The only reaction from the department was a note telling her that she'd been moved from Christie's tutorial group into one of Leith's.

"Depressing, isn't it?" said Noble.

"What?"

"To think they never grow out of it. I mean, he's got a Ph.D. for God's sake."

Scott laughed.

"So what? Not a badge of honor, is it?"

"Well …"

Noble was in the first year of her doctorate; she wasn't prepared to dismiss its importance that easily.

"Hang around long enough, scrape together a few thousand words…" Scott continued.

"That's good, coming from you," said Noble, defensively. "Look how long it takes you to do an essay."

Scott smiled.

"Yeah, but I'm thick. Och, I'm sorry. It's just … I've got my priorities a bit … well, off-line."

"Yes. I know."

Scott watched an old woman, wrapped up in scarf and overcoat despite the sunshine, standing at the edge of the kerb, looking nervously up and down the street as cars, buses and motor bikes growled past her. The woman's dilemma was so much more urgent than the choices Scott was having to make about metrical variations in sixteenth century verse. It reinforced a perspective that Scott had kept ever since her first year as a student.

"I'm not sure I want to go on with it," she said.

"What?"

"Uni. Any of it."

"What? That's crazy."

Scott shook her head.

"Not really. It's always seemed like I'm dodging the issue, being here. Like I've stepped aside from commitment."

"Rubbish," said Noble. "What d'you want to commit to?"

"Don't know. But all these lectures, essays … all this talk, it's … irrelevant, beside the point. Folk like Christie, they're out of touch. They're like something out of Disney. Doesn't stop them getting their paws on you."

"That's still rubbish."

"Maybe. All I'm saying, though, is that if anybody's going to mess me about, I want it to be somebody real."

She said it with a fierceness that was very impressive. Noble knew her well enough to know that she wasn't easily upset and that her normal hold on things was secure. This was no weepy female pout. Scott's anger went deeper. For the man in the park, she'd been a shape. Then Christie had, lightly, thoughtlessly, crossed the threshold between professional and private worlds. For him, it was an unimportant excursion; for Scott, it was a violation of basic values.

She felt herself frowning and suddenly laughed at the intensity she was allowing to build inside her.

"I mean, he's not exactly a threat, is he? Probably only makes all these advances because he's insecure," she said.

"Apologizing for him?"

"No. Just being realistic. Look at the pathetic bugger—the gear he wears—he canna be all there. Deprived as a child, I expect."

"Yeah. But don't underestimate him, Sand. It's the ones with gaps in their heads that are dangerous."

Scott laughed out loud.

"Ever thought of doing psychology?" she asked.

"Does it pay?" asked Noble.

Outside, the old woman was still havering, looking as if she might step out at any moment.

"Come on," said Scott. "Let's go and give her a hand across the road."

"What if she doesn't want to cross?"

"Tough, we're good Samaritans, she'll have to."

****

Ross and McNeil were sitting on white folding chairs on the patio outside the French windows of Gillian Hayne's house. On the table between them were three coffee cups, a cafetière and a plate of shortbread biscuits. The early afternoon sun was full on them and it felt more like August than May. Mrs Hayne had been gardening when they arrived but she looked as neat as she had on Ross' previous visit. She'd greeted them with the same quiet charm as before and Ross felt a little discomfort at the thought of having to force on her questions which must certainly bring back unpleasant associations. McNeil was talking with her about a philadelphus beside the patio that was just about to come into flower.

"Come back in a few weeks," said Mrs Hayne. "This corner's full of its perfume. It's intoxicating. I leave the windows open. It fills the room."

McNeil smiled and looked down the garden, comparing it ruefully with the few square meters of earth outside her own flat and wondering whether the scent of philadelphus would be strong

217

enough to cover that of the Indian restaurant at the end of her street. Mrs Hayne looked at Ross, obviously noting his silence.

"But you're not here for gardening, are you?" she said to him. "What can I do for you?"

Her directness was welcome and Ross felt the same warmth towards her that he had before.

"Well, it's about some of the things your husband wrote in that wee computer of his."

Mrs Hayne waited, her face expressing genuine curiosity.

"Look, there's no roundabout way of saying this," said Ross. "It's about you wanting a divorce."

For a moment, the curiosity went from her face, leaving her lips tense and her eyes wary.

"He wrote about that, did he? I'm surprised. It didn't seem to make much difference to him when we spoke of it."

"You'd discussed it before then, had you? Before his illness, I mean."

Mrs Hayne thought for a moment.

"Not discussed it, no. It was mentioned, that's all." Her face suddenly broke into a warm smile. "I had an affair not so long ago. With one of his colleagues." She stopped. "Surprises you, does it, sergeant?" she asked, addressing the words to Ross.

She was right. Her words had thrown him completely. He could only shrug.

"None of my business, Mrs Hayne. Unless it's relevant to the case."

"How do I know whether it is or not?" she said.

"Could we ask the name of the other person?" said McNeil.

"I don't think so," said Mrs Hayne. "He's in enough trouble as it is."

Was she really that disingenuous? She might just as well have written "Christie" in their notebooks.

"The point is that Alistair knew about it but the subject of divorce didn't come up then. It never has."

"What made you bring it up at the hospital? At that particular time?" asked McNeil.

Mrs Hayne shrugged.

"Things we were talking about. Or rather, things that I was saying which didn't seem to be registering with Alistair. There was no special reason."

To Ross, still unsettled by the revelation that she was a bit of a goer, she sounded uncharacteristically cold.

"Wasn't it a strange time to be talking about divorce?" he asked. "With him about to have an operation."

Her head was shaking before he'd finished speaking.

"No, sergeant. You're assuming it would make a difference to him. You're wrong. He had nothing invested in me. There was no love. There was never any love. Since I stopped playing the faculty wife, I was no more important to him than…" She stopped, looked around and waved a hand at the philadelphus, "…that bush. Any of this."

"You can't be sure of that, though, can you?" asked McNeil.

Mrs Hayne looked at her.

"No," she said. "I can't. Not a hundred per cent. But a few years of daily proofs make you pretty confident."

It was said with a smile but it uncovered a powerful bleakness. Before they had time, or the need to respond to it, she was asking her own questions.

"Can I ask why all this is relevant?"

"Good question," said Ross, disinclined to pretend with her. "Maybe it isn't but it's the old story; we need to know as much as we can."

"I see."

She took a sip from her cup and put it back in its saucer without making a sound.

"Well I don't know how much Alistair wrote but I left him in no doubt that I wanted to be free of him. I wasn't cruel or demanding. I just said what I had to say. It was all things that he already knew. I was just … clarifying them. And yes, it was right to say it all then. For me if not for him. The operation could kill him. We both knew that. I wanted to tell him. I didn't want to leave it unsaid."

"How did he react?" asked Ross.

"He laughed," said Mrs Hayne. "Complimented me on my timing. Said he agreed with every word and that we should have done it years ago. He even called it a good career move."

"Who for?"

"Him, of course. What career do I have?"

"So he didn't object?"

"No. Why? Did he say that he did?"

Ross shook his head. Their conversation had shaken her from her tiny, neat role as gardening housewife. She still spoke softly but the words were clearer, driven out by a fierceness that had been unsuspected but which now seemed absolutely natural. The strength Ross had seen in her before had come to the surface. He felt less inclined to shield her.

"D'you know your way around the hospital?" he asked.

It took her by surprise.

"What d'you mean?"

"When you visited. Did you always go straight to the ward?"

"Yes, mostly."

"You didn't know where the operating theatre was, or the intensive care unit?"

Mrs Hayne frowned as she looked at him.

"What a strange question. I ... I must have seen notices ... arrows and things. I'm sure I could find those places if I needed to. Why?"

Ross indicated his notebook.

"Same answer as before. Getting the full picture."

As they talked, the passion retreated and she was soon back to being the neat, rather sad victim of Hayne's obsessive self-interest. She accepted all the questions they asked without trying to see through them to the motives they might betray. Her answers got shorter and Ross once again began to feel protective.

One of her answers did, however, take him by surprise. Before they'd arrived, Carston had rung him on his mobile to tell him his suspicions about the aromatherapy oils and to ask him to find out what Mrs Hayne knew about them. Ross had asked what her husband thought about the treatment.

"I've no idea," she replied. "Personally, I find it obscene."

"Obscene?"

"Yes, young women kneading away at old, diseased flesh. I'm sorry, it just offends me."

With just a couple of sentences, she'd stripped herself of all the charity and humanity Ross had admired in her. Briefly, the full sterility of her contribution to this loveless marriage reared up. Ross shuddered slightly at the thought that perhaps her husband's cancer had simply been inconvenient.

The unpleasantness the exchange had exposed persisted through the rest of their talk. Having revealed her disgust, Mrs

Hayne had become defensive and embarrassed and Ross' sympathy had slipped away. McNeil, who'd had few preconceptions about the woman, was less affected by it all. She asked a few more questions but was sensitive enough to bring the interview to a fairly rapid close. As they left, their small talk about the garden was hollow and all three were glad to get away from the awkwardness which had grown between them.

"Nice lady," said McNeil as she drove down the hill away from the house.

"I used to think so," said Ross. "Before she had hang-ups."

"What d'you think?" asked McNeil. "Was she being straight?"

"Hard to say. I mean, saying she knew nothing about those massage oils when they were beside his bed all the time."

"Maybe she really didn't see them. You sometimes don't see what you don't want to see."

"Aye, maybe."

Ross looked out at the fine detached houses past which they were driving.

"It's all neat and tidy," he said, mainly to himself. "All the wee rows of houses and people. And inside they're all clawing at each other."

McNeil nodded and let a pause stretch between them before saying, "Aye, well, I'll be clawing at my man when I get home if he hasn't finished painting the bedroom ceiling."

It produced no smile in Ross. His mood was still dark and McNeil's mention of her fiancé reminded him of Carston's anxiety about the time she'd been spending with Fraser. Surely she wouldn't be stupid enough to get involved. And with Fraser, for Christ's sake! It would have been easy to bring up the subject and clear the air, but it was none of his business. If Carston thought there was something to be sorted out, he could do it himself. There was enough trouble around without going looking for it.

****

The room was flickering with the silver light of the images on the television screen. There was little enough light in the alley beside the house and, with the roller blind down, the room was filled with its habitual dusk. The variations in brightness from the screen danced an irregular rhythm over the floor and walls, the close-ups and shot changes of the film that was being shown making shadows jump and move unsettlingly. At the foot of the mattress, shoved into a corner where little direct light could reach it, was a bundle of what looked like rags. It was the size of a football.

The man sat on the mattress. Beside him lay pages which had been cut from the two copies of Penthouse. The bundle was simply the remains of the magazines, which he'd screwed up and pushed into the corner. Some of the photographs he'd chosen featured the oriental girl, others were a varied selection of shots, mostly taken from the front, with the models' legs spread wide. Some of them had been sliced into smaller pieces.

He wasn't watching the television. He put down the paper he'd just cut and picked up another. It showed a blonde lying back across a saddle, one leg hooked over the pommel, the other stretched out across the straw which was all around her. She had a Stetson tipped slightly forward on her head, a gun belt around her middle and black leather gloves on her hands. He looked at her, his hands steady, then brought the scissors he was holding to the bottom of the page.

The first cut angled up across the inside of the outstretched leg and bisected the triangle of her pubic hair. It stopped beside her navel. He turned the photograph and cut again, this time in from the left side, going through her forearm in order to target her right nipple. When he reached it, he cut carefully round it, leaving a small, black circle in her breast. He did the same on the other side, then, for his final cut, he lined the scissors up so that they sliced through the woman's smiling, pale blue eyes.

Each cut was made slowly, deliberately and seemed to be without passion. He looked at his mutilations, lay the photograph aside and selected another.

# Chapter Fourteen

The bright afternoon sun had drawn Leith into opening the window of his room. As before, Carston had opted to stand near it, leaning back against the sill. Reid was sitting at a chair across the desk from Leith. Their visit was badly timed. That morning's mail had brought Leith a letter from his publisher telling him that, on his editor's recommendation, publication of his book had been postponed indefinitely. He'd tried to ring them to protest but no one was available and their receptionist had had to listen to several minutes of abuse and promise to redirect it onto those who deserved it. Leith had made it very clear to Carston that they weren't welcome and that he resented both their presence and the nature of the questions they were asking. The effect on Carston was to make him adopt a gentle, smiling tone that infuriated Leith even more.

"You weren't a regular visitor to Professor Hayne, were you?" he asked.

"I have little time for charitable work," replied Leith.

"What made you go on that last occasion, then?"

There was only a slight hesitation before Leith replied.

"I was over there anyway and … well, his operation was imminent. I thought some … solidarity might help him."

"D'you think he was pleased to see you?"

"Probably not. We weren't exactly friends."

"You were there for quite a while, though, weren't you? What did you talk about?"

"Departmental things, university things. Arcane topics, inspector."

The tone of the final comment was insulting, implying as it did that their conversation was beyond Carston's comprehension.

"Like what, sir?" he said, maintaining his smile. "It's alright, if you speak slowly, I'll try to keep up."

"I meant arcane in the sense that they were relevant to internal university matters, not Knights' Templar rituals or anything," said Leith. "They were just things we'd discussed before—expanding the department, restructuring responsibilities, tidying up the status quo."

"Nothing revolutionary, then? Nothing that might upset him?"

Leith gave what might have been a laugh.

"Huh, Carlyle had already done that. He was there just before me, you know. I don't know what he said but Alistair was scathing about him."

"Oh?"

"Yes. Well, understandably. The man's hardly a fit person to run a department, is he?"

"And you think that upset Professor Hayne?"

"Certainly. He was afraid Carlyle would undo everything he'd achieved."

"But you reassured him."

"I tried to, yes. Oh, I didn't say anything new. The ideas we spoke about were basically his. As you say, I was just … well, reassuring him, reinforcing them."

"So it was just a friendly chat?"

"It was an exchange of ideas. To show him that his plans for the department were going ahead, that they were in good hands."

"Dr Carlyle's."

Leith looked at him with something between a smile and a sneer. The effect was very ugly.

"No, mine."

"But Dr Carlyle is acting head."

"Yes, but as I said, he's not exactly a dynamo. Alistair needed to know that his projects were being implemented by someone of the same cast of thought and strength of conviction."

Although he was managing to sustain his sweetness of tone, Carston was repelled by this individual. As Hayne had implied in his notes, the rankness of the air around him was a physical manifestation of the corruption inside. As Leith spoke more of the discussion they'd had, Carston understood a little better what Hayne had been describing. Hayne's own plans had been built on self-interest and so, as far as he was concerned, they were above question. But to be reminded that their champion was as unwholesome as Leith had forced him to reassess them. Leith's answers and Hayne's written notes both suggested that the visit had brought the two men together as allies. To suspect that there was little difference between himself and someone as repulsive as Leith must have undermined Hayne's confidence, perhaps even weakened him. Leith may not have killed him but he might have helped.

Carston took out his notebook, found an entry and handed it to Leith. That necessitated a move into the room. He quickly moved back to the window.

"Professor Hayne made a note of something you said to him. Could you tell me what it means?"

Leith looked at the notebook and read, "'*On n'est jamais si malheureux qu'on croit, ni si heureux qu'on espère.*' Ah yes, I remember. It's LaRochefoucauld, Alistair's specialty. I said it to buck him up. It means you're never as unhappy as you think you are, nor as happy as you hope you are."

"A jolly little reminder for someone with cancer facing a major operation," said Carston.

"Don't be absurd," said Leith. "The pleasure's not in the substance; it's in the formulation."

"Well, that's very reassuring," said Carston. He pointed at his notebook, which Leith was still holding. "There's another … formulation just below that. I wonder if you'd mind…"

Leith looked down and found the words Carston was referring to.

"I think it's LaRochefoucauld again," he said. "'*Nous avons tous assez de force pour supporter les maux d'autrui.*' We're all strong enough to bear the misfortunes of others. Sounds like his sort of nonsense."

"Thank you," said Carston, retrieving his book and retreating once more. He jotted down the two translations, turned to the next page and seemed to be looking through its contents. Suddenly, he flipped it shut and said, "Ah yes, just one other question. Who did you go to see in the surgery directorate when you left Professor Hayne?"

As he'd intended, it took Leith by surprise.

"I don't remember going… Oh yes, maybe I did. Why is that relevant?"

"Please, Dr Leith."

Leith wasn't giving in.

"In fact, I fail to see the relevance of any of this."

Carston sighed, regretting it immediately because it had forced him to take a deep breath.

"Dr Leith, who did you go to see in the surgery directorate?"

The dissatisfaction caused by his publisher's letter helped to fuel Leith's resentment at Carston's insistence.

"I was intending to consult with colleagues on a joint submission to a university committee on research funding," he snapped. "And it has nothing whatsoever to do with you, Hayne or these enquiries."

"Which particular colleagues?"

"They weren't there, so I saw no one."

"But you had someone in mind."

"Anyone would have done."

It was hopeless. Carston gave up.

"I see. And what about Mrs Rioch? What did she do to upset you?"

Again, the question threw Leith. His mouth opened but he said nothing. He took refuge in moving a book on top of a pile of notes on his desk, then said, "I have no idea who you're speaking about. I know no one of that name."

"Oh," said Carston. "So she didn't work here? Didn't clean your room?"

"I have no idea who cleans my room."

"And you didn't complain about her losing some of your papers?"

"Oh, it's that again, is it?" said Leith. "I told your ... people before that I have no recollection of the incident whatsoever."

He was getting more agitated and the stains under his armpits were spreading to join the little patches of gravy and pasta sauce on the front of his shirt. His forehead and cheeks were shiny with sweat. Carston had had enough. For the moment, he didn't care whether what Leith had been saying was the truth or not. It would be easy enough to verify anyway.

"Thank you, sir," he said. "I think that's all for now."

Reid, who'd been careful to follow his instructions and say nothing through the interview, stood up. Carston put a gentle hand on his shoulder and made him sit down again.

226

"My sergeant'll stay with you and go over what you've been saying. Just to make sure we're not misrepresenting you in any way."

Leith pushed himself upright.

"I haven't got time to waste on…"

"The more you co-operate, the quicker it'll be," said Carston, already at the door. He opened it and, with the words "All yours sergeant Reid. I'll see you later," went gratefully out into the corridor.

****

After Leith's brusqueness, Carlyle's ease of manner and willingness to co-operate were almost refreshing. Too much so, thought Carston, as he arrived in the corridor outside Carlyle's room and found him talking with some students who'd just been with him for a tutorial. Each time the police had spoken with him, he'd been all charm and cooperation and yet he'd admitted to destroying Hayne's papers. He'd even been round to Hayne's house and taken things from there. For someone who claimed to deplore political maneuverings, he was adept at shaping things to fit his own preferred vision. He'd also visited both Hayne and Mrs Rioch. And, in his time, he'd been a medic. Carston felt the need to push him a little harder.

Carlyle greeted him and raised his hand to invite him into his room. It smelled of filtered coffee but the students had drunk it all and Carston shook his head when he offered to make more.

"I hear you're a man of many talents," he said.

"Oh?" said Carlyle.

"Yes. Trained as a medical doctor."

Carlyle laughed.

"Oh yes, a long, long time ago. When I first went to Dundee. I did a couple of years, that's all."

"What happened?"

"Nothing. I suppose I expected it to be exciting or glamorous or something, but it was all memory tests."

"Memory tests?"

"Yes. Latin names for parts of the anatomy. Not much in the way of analysis or creative thinking. The only discipline that might have been attractive was psychiatry."

"Oh? Why's that?"

Carlyle gave a little laugh.

"I'm a romantic. Prefer to think we're not just machines or chemical experiments. I loved all the Jungian stuff about archetypes, our dark side, the shadow self."

A recent case had confronted Carston with his own dark side and he was tempted to indulge in a little digression. Scarily, Carlyle anticipated it.

"You must see plenty of it in your line of work."

"Depends what you mean," said Carston.

"Well, according to Jung we all carry a shadow. If we don't drag it up into consciousness, it gets blacker, denser. Some of your clients must be convenient proofs of that."

"Not just my clients," said Carston.

Carlyle looked at him and smiled. Carston would have liked nothing better than to pursue the digression but the image of the inner shadows disturbed him. He still hadn't resolved his own.

"So you ditched medicine?" he said, dragging himself back to the job.

"Yes. Moved over into languages. Why are you interested?"

"Curiosity," said Carston. "It goes with the job."

Carlyle smiled.

"I suppose you've had to make a few changes, because of Professor Hayne dying," said Carston.

"Oh, just juggling some timetables. Hardly rocket science," said Carlyle. "I know Alistair and the others like to pretend otherwise, but it's a tiny chore, that's all."

"Something else I was wondering about," said Carston.

Carlyle waited for him to go on.

"There's been another suspicious death at the hospital."

"Ah yes, poor Mrs Rioch. Terrible."

"You knew her, did you?"

Carlyle paused briefly.

"Yes," he said. "There was an incident. A while ago. Edward—Dr Leith—complained about her. I had to deal with it. Poor woman was dismissed after that. I ... I felt sorry for her. Tried to argue on her behalf but..." He ended with a shrug.

"What exactly was the problem?" asked Carston.

"Oh, the usual sort of thing with Edward. He leaves his notes and lectures in little piles on his desk and chairs. Puts them in sequence. Apparently he'd made some notes on curricular changes for the REF sub-committee and claimed that they'd disappeared. It happened late one afternoon and he was convinced that the only person who could have had access to his room was the cleaner. He put in a formal complaint about her."

"Just like that. No proof, just suspicion? His word?" said Carston.

Carlyle nodded.

"I'm afraid so," he said. "Just another example of... I don't think there was a direct connection with her dismissal but the one followed pretty hard on the other. I understand she was quite ill, however, so her death was maybe a release."

"All the same," said Carston, "something of a coincidence that she and Professor Hayne should be linked this way."

"Are they?" asked Carlyle.

"I don't know," said Carston. "Maybe you could help."

"How?"

"You visited them both."

"Yes. I suppose I'm a fairly frequent visitor at the hospital. Perhaps when you get to my age, it's natural to find more friends and colleagues having health problems."

"D'you think of Mrs Rioch as a colleague?"

"No. I saw that she was due to be admitted for surgery and decided to go and say hello. I think the university treated her rather shabbily."

"And what about the visit to Professor Hayne?"

"What about it?"

"Well, how was he? I've been trying to get a sort of picture of his state of mind just before he died."

"Difficult enough when he was alive," said Carlyle. "Alistair usually kept his own counsel."

"What about the visit, though? What frame of mind would you say he was in?"

"Depressingly normal, I'd say."

"Depressingly?"

"Oh, I'm being facetious. He was trying to run the department from his sick bed, pointing out where I was going wrong. It was all things I'd heard from him before."

"What made you go and see him?"

Carlyle shrugged and shook his head.

"Duty, really. Just thought I'd bring him up to date with things. In the end, he did most of the talking. Maybe that was therapeutic. I don't know."

"Something else," said Carston. "Why did you need to shred his papers?"

Carlyle shrugged.

"D'you want the truth?" he said.

"Of course."

"It was a tiny vengeance. Pathetic, I know, but one which gave me some pleasure."

"Vengeance?"

"Yes. I tell you frankly, if I could destroy Alistair's legacy here, I'd be a happy man. And the university would be a better place."

"So you're as political as he was," said Carston.

Carlyle laughed.

"Oh no. It's an easy enough game to play, but not if you want to preserve any self-respect. And it has been a sort of game, really. Action instead of words for a change. I don't think I can sustain it, though."

"Oh?"

"It's not important enough," said Carlyle. "It wastes time. In fact, it was when I realized that I was getting some pleasure out of shredding Alistair's things that I decided to stop. It's corrosive, insidious."

"You and Professor Hayne didn't seem to have much in common."

Carlyle shook his head immediately.

"Very little. Alistair's motto was 'more students, lower unit costs'. I'm a bit … old fashioned, you see. Still cling on to the idea that students aren't ledger entries. They're here for things other than certificates and diplomas."

"Like what?"

Carlyle laughed.

"Oh, ghastly, subversive things like self-knowledge, an appreciation of the world, culture. A good old liberal education."

"Lighting up the shadows?" said Carston.

Carlyle smiled.

"You'd be a good student," he said.

The smile went as quickly as it had come.

"But it seems that sort of thing's impossible to justify nowadays. I mean what's research into the structure of the novel or medieval verse forms or whatever got to do with homelessness, single parents, poverty?"

"Difficult," said Carston.

Carlyle's eyes, looking over the tops of his half-moon glasses, were bright and quick.

"On the other hand," he said, "keep research wide and it'll produce the unexpected. Penicillin, lasers, even Viagra—they were just accidents, effects other than those the researchers were looking for. If we insist on making it functional, vocational, we'll limit our options. The real danger's in tunnel vision. Our best chance lies in looking at the wider picture, just being aware."

"What did Professor Hayne think of you being in charge of the department?"

"He hated it. I'm not management material, you see."

Carston thought of telling him that that made two of them but instead, he asked, "But you're having to be, aren't you?"

Carlyle smiled again.

"It's minimal as far as I'm concerned. As I said earlier, I won't be able to sustain it. I'll be handing over to someone soon. Probably Dr Leith."

"Who'll continue what Professor Hayne was doing."

"Probably."

"What about the complaint about Dr Christie?" said Carston. "That must be tricky."

It took Carlyle by surprise.

"How did you know about that?"

"Small town."

Carlyle nodded. The ease had gone from his manner. His head was shaking.

"Dreadful business," he said. "For the student, of course, but for the rest of us. And Michael, too."

The last was an afterthought.

"What d'you think'll happen?" asked Carston.

"It's in the VP's hands," said Carlyle. "He'll decide and … well, we'll see."

"Can they appeal?" asked Carston. "Whoever loses, I mean."

"No. His decision's final. No appeal, no review."

"A lot to ask of a single individual, isn't it?"

"Perhaps, but that's the system. Built-in moral rectitude."

He looked at his watch. They'd been talking for over half an hour.

"Look, I'm sorry," he said, "but I've got a Faculty meeting."

Carston stood up.

"Sorry," he said. "I've kept you long enough."

"I can't get out of it, more's the pity," said Carlyle. "Have to play their games."

At the door, they shook hands.

"You know," said Carlyle, "some American comedian defined a meeting as a group that keeps minutes and loses hours. He knew what he was talking about."

As Carston walked back along the corridor, he found it difficult to accept that Carlyle could be responsible for either of the deaths. Hayne, possibly, but certainly not Mrs Rioch. Carlyle might, of course, be a consummate actor, but Carston preferred to see him as a truly compassionate man. His colleagues were less so but the way he'd contrasted words and actions made Carston doubt that any of them were capable of anything as distinct as killing someone. They played games, used fancy words. Murder involved engaging with life, commitment.

He turned to go and fetch Reid from Leith's office. By now, with any luck, he'd have suffocated.

****

Sandra Scott's house always smelled of fish. However hard her father scrubbed at himself when he came ashore, the years of hauling nets and cleaning the catch had forced the odors of his trade deep inside him. It was so much a part of their daily life as she was growing up that she hadn't noticed it but now, each time she came back to it, it was a sweet reminder of a world she loved. Cairnburgh was only forty-odd miles from Fraserburgh but she rarely thought of going home during the term. The whole business with Christie, though, had disorientated her and, knowing her father was ashore, she decided that a day with her folks might help to straighten her out.

She knew how much it pleased both her parents when she was there. Her dad continually boasted about her achievements and was sincerely, even passionately interested in her studies. He'd tried reading, in translation of course, some of her set texts. One of them, Victor Hugo's *Toilers of the Sea*, seemed particularly apt but, after only a couple of chapters, he'd given up, saying that "the Froggie can write OK, but he's never been to sea". She'd once spent nearly two hours in the pub with him, trying to explain the subtleties of the Theatre of the Absurd. When she'd quoted one critic who'd said that the only freedom we have is to crawl westwards along the deck of a boat that's travelling east, her dad had ruminated for a long time before delivering his judgment.

"So what he's sayin," he said at last, "is that there's nothin we can do, we canna change nothin."

"Aye, that's it," said Sandra. "We're stuck."

Her father nodded, testing the validity of the idea.

"Aye, well," he said, "When your prof tells you that sorta thing again, ask him if the boat's a trawler. It's fine for your man, just crawlin along the deck, worryin about life. I never have time for that. I'm always lookin at the waves, or the weather, or the fish I'm chasin." He grinned at her. "Life's too short to think about it too much."

They were in the same pub, sitting at a table on their own. It was early evening, the quiet before the rush. The bus for Cairnburgh didn't leave until half past nine. She looked round at the people on the bar stools and at the small tables. Some of them had been there ever since she'd first started coming in here and no doubt long before that. Billy Petrie was in the same dark blue suit and roll neck jersey that he always wore, Roddy Finlay and Joe Maxwell were at the dominoes, their two pints of ale flat with no head on them, just the way they liked them. Jeannie Ord was dabbing her brownish hankie along her upper lip, mopping up the traces of the snuff she still took. These and the others were reliable, changeless markers; simultaneously proofs and denials of the absurdity Sandra was studying.

She'd told her dad all about Christie and, after a first angry reaction, he'd calmed down, knowing that she could handle herself and that there was nothing he could contribute except his usual support and strength.

"I was thinking," she said. "You know you and Mum are chuffed that I'm at the uni."

"Aye, of course we are."

233

"But ... well, just suppose ... I mean, what if I wanted to leave?"

It was a shock to him but he showed nothing.

"What d'you mean, love?"

She smiled at him.

"Don't worry, I'm just wonderin, that's all."

"What's makin you think like that? This pervert?"

She laughed.

"He's no a pervert, dad. He's a wanker. No, it's no just him. It's ... it's hard to explain but it's the place, all sorts o' things about it."

"Like what?"

"It's no real. Oh, it's fine, and it's interestin most o' the time, but sometimes I feel like I dinna belong there."

Her father was shaking his head.

"Aye, you do, Sandra love." His right hand moved to indicate the scene around them. "This is always here, you can always come back to it. None o' this lot can go where you go. I canna, that's for sure."

"Aye, I know, dad, but Joe, Billy, Jeannie, they're real folk. They know things, they've lived. Some o' these profs... You wouldna believe it. It's two different worlds."

It was her turn to shake her head. Those worlds were so far apart that she couldn't make the comparisons she was looking for.

"You're lucky then," said her father. "You know both sorts."

The door opened and Jimmy Murray came in. Sandra and her father looked at one another and, together, their voices low, said, "Pint o' heavy, packet o' crisps and a nippie."

"Pint o' heavy, packet o' crisps and a nippie," shouted Jimmy obligingly. There was no need; the barman was already getting it all. Sandra laughed and saw the same pleasure in her father's eyes. She was glad again that he was her father. Whatever Christie got up to, however loaded the scales were against her, this love and security would always be stronger. She could stay on at university or pack it all in. Whatever she decided, her dad would be there. The maxims of LaRochefoucauld would never have the power of Roddy Finlay's dominoes.

\*\*\*\*

"Are you pining for something?" asked Kath.

Carston put his plate on top of hers and carried them both over to the sink.

"Why?" he asked.

"You've hardly said a word since you got in. And you've been drinking water."

Carston turned on the tap to fill the washing up bowl.

"Yeah, I think I've got to go out later. I want to give David Weston a ring first."

"The hospital stuff, is it?"

"Yes."

Kath came to stand beside him, pulling the tea towel from its rubber holder.

"Progress?" she asked.

"I think so. It's just an idea niggling away at me. Something Alex was telling me about that night we went for a drink."

They fell silent again, Carston still trying to untangle the strands of his thinking. That afternoon's visit to the university had nudged him further towards a theory that had already begun to form and might explain the lack of coherence about the whole thing.

"They're splitting up, you know," said Kath after a while.

"Who?"

"Jennie and Alex."

"Did she tell you?"

"Yes. Alex is offshore again."

"I know, I've tried to get in touch with him a couple of times. That night in the pub, the poor sod was shattered."

Kath nodded sadly. "They both are."

"I can't say I've got much sympathy for her. She's the one who's been having it off with somebody else."

"It's not that simple, Jack."

"That's what they always say. You didn't see Alex that night, Kath."

They were quiet again for a moment.

"They talked about it before he went, apparently. Decided to get divorced."

"Yes, and he's stuck out there now, thinking about her and this medic guy together... I know it's always a two way thing, but Alex is such a straight guy. Solid. He's just falling apart with this."

"So's Jennie."

There was nothing more they could say. Their sympathies were divided but they both knew that the Crombies were just going through an experience that was being repeated all over the comfortable part of the world. They finished the washing up in silence. When Carston had dried his hands, he put his arms round Kath and hugged her close to him.

"I think we're bloody lucky," he said, his lips in her hair.

"You are, that's for sure," she replied.

"Right."

They kissed and went through to the sitting room. On the way, Carston went to his coat, which was hanging in the hall, and took a package from the pocket. He put it on the coffee table in front of her.

"For you. Later on," he said.

"What is it?"

"A couple of the perfumes of Arabia."

"Perfume?" she said, with genuine surprise. "You know I never wear it, Jack. What are…?"

"Not perfume perfume," he said. "Essential oils. Jasmine and sandalwood."

"And?"

"Aromatherapy. It's good for you. Relaxes you."

"I'm relaxed."

"Not as much as you're going to be."

"If I was any more relaxed, I'd be asleep."

"Ah, that's not really the object. These are supposed to be aphrodisiacs."

"Jack, why don't you just transfer to the vice squad?"

"Couldn't get in, there's a waiting list."

"So you have to practice your perversions on me."

"That's what wives are for, isn't it?"

"That's it. No conjugal rites for a week."

"Mmmmm, conjugal rights," said Carston, in a bad imitation of Homer Simpson.

He kissed the top of her head, then went into the hall and picked up the phone. He felt slightly guilty as he did so because David Weston, the person he was phoning, lived just fifty yards or so up the road and he could just as easily have walked along to his house and got a wee bit of exercise in the process. But Weston would invite him in and he'd be there longer than he wanted to be. When

Weston answered the phone, Carston apologized for disturbing him and said he wanted to pick his brains about anesthesia again.

"Fentanyl," he said.

"Yes."

"Is it fairly common?"

"Yes. If you need a powerful shot, that's the stuff to use."

It was a name that had figured in Ross' notes, which were amongst the things Carston had been reading that morning. McKenzie had told him that it was a hundred times more powerful than morphine.

"What can you tell me about it?"

"Well, it takes a while to clear from the patient's system. It's effective in the circulating volume, that's the blood, of course. But it's lipid soluble so it goes into the fats and there's usually helluva lot of it there."

"What would an overdose do?"

"Kill. That's the short answer. Not right away, but soon enough. You get delayed respiratory depression."

"And is it administered in any special way?"

"Nope, just like all the others."

"What if you massaged somebody with it?"

Weston gave a little cough of laughter.

"Christ, Jack, the job's hard enough without having to massage them into unconsciousness."

"Would it work, though? If it was mixed with massage oils."

"Yep. On the back, that's the biggest area. Or the feet, they've got a pretty high absorption profile."

"But wouldn't the person doing the massaging be affected?"

"No. The skin's pretty thick on your hands. And it's such a small area. What's all this about, though? D'you think you've cracked it?"

"Not absolutely sure but I'm working on it."

They talked a little more, mainly about the news of the Crombies' split, then Carston thanked Weston, apologized again for disturbing him and rang off.

****

For the second night in a row, there was no light in Scott's window. The man could see two of her flatmates in their bedrooms but he had no interest in them. He hadn't seen Scott since the afternoon on the bench with her and McNeil. He'd spent the whole of the rest of that day and the following one in his room, trying to understand what had happened. Up until then, he thought he'd been handling things well, maintaining the distance he preferred. Graduating from watching her unseen to actually appearing on the bench had been easy enough. The day that she'd spoken to him had been difficult but he'd handled it. Then came the humiliation of that last confrontation. It had shattered him. McNeil's threats about the fictional McLures had hardly registered; what mattered was that he'd been reduced to a state of impotence by a woman and that Scott had watched it happen. Their whole relationship had been torn up at the roots. He was confused about it and knew that Scott had somehow set him up. He wasn't sure whether the two of them could get things back to the way they were.

Suddenly, Scott's window opened. It came as a shock to him because he'd assumed that she wasn't there. He focused his binoculars and saw Strachan leaning on the sill and looking down at the grass below. Dimly, on the bed behind him, he saw Scott. She was lying face down, angled across the sheet and reaching for the bedside lamp. She clicked it on and the man saw again the rounded lines of her shoulders, the dip in her back and the rise of her buttocks etched by the yellow light. His hand went straight to his crotch. It was almost a conditioned reflex.

Strachan turned back and went to kneel beside Scott, drawing his fingers down her back and between her legs. She turned her head to the side and the man could see her face, eyes closed, a smile on her lips. His hand moved more quickly. Scott pushed herself against Strachan's fingers and moved her hips from side to side, sliding her body across the sheet. Strachan bent and kissed her shoulder. She turned onto her back, put her arms up and around his neck and looked into his face. He was astride her now, his hands under her shoulders, his weight on his elbows. His head dipped now and again so that they could exchange butterfly kisses, but each time they came back to the same position with his face suspended above hers as they looked into one another's eyes.

The man's hand was working furiously but he was getting no harder. Suddenly, he stopped and put both his hands to the binoculars. The couple were still looking at one another but Strachan had lowered his body onto Scott's and the two of them

238

were moving gently together. He saw Scott's legs part and Strachan settle lower onto her. Her neck arched, her fingers stretched briefly and she gave a shudder. Strachan pushed himself up on his elbows and looked at her. For a moment, they were motionless, then Scott opened her mouth and, her eyes still on Strachan's, nodded twice and pulled him down into her.

The man watched it all, his flesh soft and his body cold and quiet. For him, the couple's movements were no longer sexual. They were clutching closely into one another, denying him access, forcing him further away. He didn't understand or like what he was feeling. He'd seen them touching, caressing and kissing one another before and had always shared in the pleasure. Now, though, it was a betrayal and Scott had retreated to a place where he'd never reach her.

He watched to the end, as the anger, bewilderment and sadness rose in him. At last, the movements stopped and the two bodies lay quietly together on the bed. He lowered the binoculars to wipe tears from his eyes. When he raised them again he was shocked to see that Scott's eyes seemed to be looking straight at him. Her head was on Strachan's chest and his fingers played with her hair. Her left hand was stroking his shoulder. She was crying.

His own eyes filled with tears again and he swung as quickly as he could down through the branches onto the grass. Despite his distress, he was careful to be as silent as he could. He ran away down the path, stuffing the binoculars into their pouch and slinging it over his back. As he got to the steps leading down into the park, he let go of the sobbing he was holding back so painfully and began to shout his anger into the trees. As he stumbled down, he saw someone lower down on the steps turn and start to go back, away from him. It was a woman, a student who'd let the beer she'd drunk in the students' union make her brave enough to use the park at night. He stopped shouting and chased her, catching up with her just at the point where a smaller path branched off the main one to lead through bushes around the edge of the park.

She turned to face him.

"Don't", she said.

He punched her on the side of the head, then again on the cheek. She put her arms up. He swore at her and, the tears hotter still in his eyes, he went on punching and slapping her over and over again.

239

# Chapter Fifteen

**R**eid had managed to get to the squad room without anyone knowing he was there. There was no CID duty officer and Sandy Dwyer, the desk sergeant, was too busy with the nightly parade of drunks to notice his arrival. Carston's obvious dislike of him had come as no surprise to Reid; Ridley had painted an even worse picture of the DCI than the one that had actually materialized. The sergeant's stay in the squad would probably be a short one but it was part of the promotion process. Ridley had left him in no doubt about that.

He switched on a single desk lamp beside his computer and went to fetch the files and statements relating to the MOT fraud and the outboard thefts. They were bulkier than they'd been when he'd first been assigned to the job because the new sets of statements had been added to them. He took off his cashmere jacket, rolled back the cuffs of his Ralph Lauren shirt and sat at the keyboard. He switched on the machine and, as it booted up, opened the top folder. He'd already transferred some of its documents onto discs the first time round; these he put at the bottom of the pile. When he came to one he didn't recognize, he read through it to check that he hadn't actually typed it up and forgotten it, then, reassured that it was indeed virgin material, he pulled the keyboard towards him and began the long process of copying it into the machine.

There was nothing too devious about what he was doing. The case had been tied up, the charges made and there was no more detection to be done. But Ridley would expect a computerized version of it all and, if Reid didn't produce it, his part in the arrests wouldn't be registered. The fact that his only contribution so far had been to put both cases at risk was incidental. There was now a new situation and he had to adapt to it. It was going to be a long night but the print-out he'd slip into Ridley's in-tray would make it worthwhile.

****

The following day proved to be a very busy one in many different ways. For Sandra Scott's father, it started at six when his boat sailed with another for the fishing grounds. So far, they'd been well below their quotas but the sonar suggested that there were plenty of fish to be had on this trip. As the morning developed in a long, slow swell, the boats shot a single net between them and began steaming on parallel courses to scoop up the riches their equipment and their expertise had pinpointed. For the rest of the day, they hauled nets, cleaned and gutted their catches and were grateful that, for a change, it was a pleasure to be out on the North Sea.

The staff of the department of European Culture were equally industrious. Over cups of coffee they were thrashing out a system of moving to a two semester year while retaining the traditional three term structure. The university had willingly embraced things like semesters, modularization, continuous assessment and distance learning to prove its modernity; the problem was that the new forms threatened to squeeze the Christmas and Easter vacations away and make incursions into the summer one too. Leith was particularly keen to project himself as the spokesperson for all his colleagues when he deplored the assault on academic freedom the new structures represented.

At the Burns Road headquarters, the day started with what looked to Carston like some sort of role reversal. When he, Ross and McNeil went through to brief the squad, they found Reid working at his computer and the rest of them sitting and lounging around in their usual early morning postures.

"Mornin sir, mornin sarge, mornin sarge," said Fraser. It was a chant that was getting on Carston's nerves but he was surprised to hear McNeil respond to it by saying, "Fraz". He looked at her and saw her jerk her head at Fraser. The gesture seemed to be one of encouragement.

"What the hell's going on now?" said Carston.

"I think Fraser's got something to tell you, sir," said McNeil.

241

Carston looked at Fraser and saw that the incongruous blush was once again spreading up from his neck.

"Well?" said Carston.

Fraser held up his newspaper. The page he'd been reading carried a large photograph of a woman breast feeding a baby. "It says here that mothers should cradle their babies on the left," he said.

Carston looked at Ross, who shrugged his incomprehension.

"Helps the kiddie's brain to get used to her voice. See," he went on, beginning to read from the article, "'The right side of the brain processes the musical qualities of language which gives words emotion and information to the right side of the brain comes from the left ear.'"

"What the bloody hell are you on about?" said Carston.

"Janice, sir. She's pregnant. We're goin to have a baby."

There was a brief silence then the room suddenly filled with a chorus of congratulations. As the high fives and back slapping continued, Carston shook his head.

"Fraser, I'll never understand you but congratulations," he said. "Is that why you're deep in the paper when you should be working? To be a good father?"

"No, sir," said Fraser. "I just saw the photo of the tit and thought I'd..."

"OK, OK," said Carston.

Spurle's participation in the congratulations had been restrained and his voice was hoarse.

"Anything wrong, Spurle?" asked Carston.

Spurle shook his head and, as a reflex, lifted his hand to his throat. Carston noticed that, as he moved his collar, there was bruising around his neck.

"Just needs to go easy on the nitric oxide," said Fraser.

"Fuck off," croaked Spurle.

Carston had no idea what they were talking about and, leaving Ross to carry on with the briefing, he beckoned McNeil to follow him back into their office.

"So, what's the story?" he asked, as soon as the door shut behind her.

McNeil gave her little crooked grin.

"I've known about it for ages, sir, but I couldn't tell you before. He was confiding in me, like."

"Why?"

"Hard to believe but Fraser's trying to be a New Man. Trying to understand female psychology. That's why he's been treating me so nice. Thinks I can help him."

"So that's what all the cozy little chats have been about?"

"Yes. See, he's read somethin about women getting weird when they're pregnant. He's wantin to know how to treat Janice right. He can't ask her, can he? And I'm the only other one around."

Carston shook his head. He knew the world was a bewildering place, but the thought that it now contained a caring, sensitive Fraser was overstretching its absurdities.

****

After that, McNeil's day turned very bad. A phone call was put through to her not long after ten. It was the university chaplain.

"How can I help?" she asked.

"Sorry to disturb you," said the chaplain, "but I think someone should come and speak to a student of ours. She was attacked last night. In the park, near her hall of residence."

McNeil felt a sudden panic.

"What's her name?" she asked.

"Helen Lawson," said the chaplain.

Inexcusably, McNeil felt a slight swell of relief.

"You say last night?" she asked.

"Yes."

"Why didn't she report it then?"

"She was afraid. A bit confused. She wanted to talk to me about it first."

"I see. Right. I'll get round right away. Where are you?"

"The chaplaincy centre. Off Southside Avenue."

"Yes, I know it. I'll be right there."

It took her less than ten minutes to drive to the university. She parked in the visitors' section of the chapel yard and went straight to a small granite lodge at its south east corner. The chaplain, a tall, thin young man in a pale open-necked shirt, welcomed her and introduced her to Lawson. The student was sitting at a drop leaf mahogany table on which there were two cups of tea and a tray with teapot, milk and sugar. She was wearing casual clothes but each item carried some designer label or other. They were well cut, subtly patterned and helped to mask the fact that she was a little overweight. What they could not mask was the evidence of the severe beating to which her head and face had been subjected. There were strips of transparent tape over cuts on her forehead and eyebrows and along the line of her jaw. McNeil could see the rows of stitches under each one. Both ears were badly swollen, one eye was closed and her face and neck were mottled with the yellows and purples of lots of deep bruises.

Surprisingly, the student seemed embarrassed rather than anything else. She was uncomfortable at the idea of making a statement to the police, but McNeil's skills soon broke through the reticence and Lawson began to speak a little more freely. After a while, the chaplain left the two of them together and McNeil felt able to ask Lawson to relive the attack. Lawson told her of the punches and slaps and kicks. McNeil nodded her understanding.

"And how about sex?" she asked, gently. "Did he try anything?"

Lawson shook her head.

"Nothing," she said, then immediately checked herself. "Oh yes, there was…" She paused and raised her hand to her left breast. "He hit me hard here. A few times. He was aiming for it."

McNeil nodded again.

"He didn't try taking any of your clothes off?"

Again, the shake of the head.

"No. He was shouting at me, calling me a whore, bitch, slag, stuff like that. But it wasn't sex he was after."

"Did he steal anything?"

"No." Lawson paused and thought for a moment. Her eyes filled with tears. "He just wanted to hurt me," she said.

The more they spoke, the more the chill of apprehension spread through McNeil. It had started when she'd first heard where the attack had happened, at the end of the path where she and Scott had confronted the stalker, not far away from Scott's flat. When she eventually got round to asking Lawson to describe the man, the apprehension evolved into fear and guilt. Her memories of a thin face, deep-set eyes and long mousy hair were vague enough to leave some doubts in McNeil's mind. But the dark green blouson jacket, the denim shirt and the green and white Nikes were precise enough to confirm that this could be Scott's stalker. And if it was, how far was McNeil herself responsible for tipping him over the edge into violence?

She kept her suspicions and thoughts to herself as she continued to let Lawson talk out her hurt and begin to come to terms with the experience. Her own thoughts of failure were hidden as her training helped her to bolster Lawson's self-esteem and make her believe that the attack wasn't personal but just a huge slice of bad luck. She even managed to turn the severity of the beating to advantage by pointing out that, if there'd been a personal, sexual component to it, Lawson would have suffered far worse degradations and pain. It was a tiny comfort, but Lawson was intelligent enough to see that it was valid.

When the chaplain reappeared, McNeil took the chance to leave for a moment to phone the station. She gave Sandy Dwyer the Caledonian Road address to which she'd followed the man from the park and an enhanced version of Lawson's description.

"It's urgent, Sandy," she said. "He attacked a girl last night. Get the lads to have a look for blood on his clothes or around the place."

"Right," said Dwyer. "You're pretty sure it's him, are you?"

"Yes, I think so," said McNeil.

"OK, Julie. They're on their way. Well done, sergeant."

The last words were said with a smile to remind her of her new rank. Their effect, though, was simply to bring her anger at herself back into her mind. Her promotion had been helped by the many reports that had been filed praising her handling of victims. She'd always relied on her intuition and usually managed to make contact, especially with women, even when they were severely traumatized. With Scott's stalker, her insights had been badly, badly flawed. She was going to find it hard to forgive herself for this.

****

Carston had been called to Ridley's office. He had no idea what to expect, although Reid's demeanor had made him suspicious as soon as he came into the squad room. Progressively, Reid was beginning to act as if he belonged there, as if the squad room was his area of operations. Carston had no time to wonder whether this was simply paranoia on his part. The summons to Ridley's office had to be obeyed.

When he got there, Ridley gave out a triumphant "Aaah" and reached immediately for a computer print-out in a yellow tray at the side of his desk.

"What're you playing at, Carston?" he asked after he'd consulted it.

"Sir?"

Ridley flicked a hand at the paper in front of him.

"This stuff about MOT certificates and outboard motors. We've had one cock-up by you already. It's happened again."

Carston was wary. Reid had been up to something.

"What exactly is the problem, sir?" he said.

"Exactly," said Ridley, picking up Carston's word and stressing it like a very bad actor, "the same as before. Anomalies."

He jabbed a finger at the document.

"Here. And here. Duplicated evidence, conflicting dates—just like last time. And this time they'll probably sue."

Carston suppressed the panic that he felt and leaned over the desk.

"May I, sir?" he said, pulling the print-out towards him.

Ridley sat back, confident that this time there was no way out. Carston looked quickly at the places Ridley had indicated. They seemed familiar. He flicked to some other references, checked the dates on different pages and suddenly realized what had happened.

"May I ask who supplied the print-out?" he said, with a calmness that immediately disorientated Ridley.

"Does it matter?"

"Well, yes it does. Because whoever it was needs a much more thorough grounding in CID procedures than he or she has got. Most of this is out of date. It relates to the original cock-up, the one orchestrated by sergeant Reid."

"I thought you might try to shift the blame," said Ridley.

"No, sir. If you look here…" He pointed to two statements. "…you'll see that, basically, we've got the same statement, but made on separate occasions and with one or two significant differences. It's the same with all of them. The trouble is, that, between the dates they were taken, constables Spurle and Fraser got some more evidence, and some new witnesses."

"So?"

"So even though two lots of statements are similar, the second lot are supported by the new evidence."

"I still don't see what you're getting at."

"Whoever typed this all up didn't realize that. He—or she—has left all the anomalies of the initial statements in place, so they look as if they're contradicting the eye witnesses. If you stick with the most recent statements, there aren't any inconsistencies. Any of my team would have spotted that right away. This must've been done by some temp the front desk's brought in. Some girl, probably."

Ridley grabbed the paper back and looked at it again.

"Are you sure about this?" he said. "You're not just covering up."

"Nothing to cover up, sir."

Ridley was furious. He'd been looking for ways to puncture Carston's credibility for a very long time and he'd really thought that the print-out would achieve it. He laid the paper on his desk and swiveled around in his chair. He was now side-on to Carston and, when he spoke, he didn't bother to turn to look at him.

"You don't waste a single opportunity, do you?" he said.

"For what, sir?" asked Carston.

"To point out sergeant Reid's supposed shortcomings."

Carston's impulse was to say that there was no "supposed" about it.

"Never occurred to you that the fault might be in you, I suppose," Ridley continued.

"I don't think I'm perfect," said Carston.

Ridley shot him a glance.

"At least we agree on one thing then."

He turned his chair back again and looked straight at Carston.

"Maybe it's time you thought about retraining," he said. "Leading a team calls for proper, efficient man management. I'm not sure your skills are fully developed in that area."

"Our clear-up rates are…"

Ridley didn't let him finish.

"It's all very well working with people you've been with for ages, but you need to be flexible. You've got to be able to adapt. Sergeant Reid's a good officer, intelligent, ambitious. We need young people like that. We need those sorts of attitudes. The way you treat him says more about you than it does about him."

This was astonishing. Ridley was actually stringing words together, following what seemed like a consistent argument. He must have been thinking a helluva lot about it. Carston wondered where all this was going. He was about to find out.

"The truth is," Ridley began, "that you need Reid as much as he needs you. So I've decided there are going to be changes."

\*\*\*\*

Down in the office, Ross had started on the paperwork for the Hayne case, but was as curious as Carston had been about the reason for Ridley's summons. When Carston came in and slammed the door behind him, he feared the worst.

"Trouble?" he asked.

"Trouble? Trouble? Of course not. Your mate Reid nearly dropped us in it again by forgetting to update stuff he sent up to Ridley, that's all."

Carston was walking up and down in front of the window like an angry captain on a very small quarter deck.

"But I put his lordship straight on that. Told him, very gently, that he shouldn't believe everything he reads that comes from a brain-dead, four-eyed plonker."

"Was he grateful?" asked Ross, trying to lighten the atmosphere.

"Grateful? Oh yes. He realizes that Reid needs a bit more experience at the sharp end, doesn't he? And we're short-handed, aren't we? So he's done us a favor. He's made Reid's appointment with us permanent. Isn't that nice?"

\*\*\*\*

Carston needed to get away from the office for a while. He arranged to meet Ross at an American-style diner in Glasgow Road and spent the rest of the morning in the library. He got to the diner at twenty to one. Ross was already there. Carston joined him and ordered a bottle of Molson Dry and a tuna sandwich. Ross had a mineral water and a cheese toastie.

"Did you ask Julie to come?" asked Carston. "I want the three of us to talk it through."

"She can't make it. Something's come up," said Ross.

"OK. What's Reid up to?" asked Carston.

"Doing stuff on the computer," said Ross. "Been at it all morning."

"Good," muttered Carston. "Right, down to business. Hayne and Mrs Rioch."

Ross waited for him to continue.

"We know how it was done—the sutures and the overdose."

"Do we?"

Carston nodded.

"Somebody heated a batch of sutures and put them in the setting up room. And I reckon the overdose was something like Fentanyl which got mixed in with the aromatherapy oils. Hayne was doped to the eyeballs anyway; any extra would be enough to put him over the top."

"Have you checked that that'd work?" asked Ross.

"Yep. And it'd be the easiest thing in the world to do. I was there last night. They leave the bottles of oil beside the bed. All neatly labeled. Patient's name in big letters. I could've put anything I liked in them."

They were interrupted by the arrival of the food and drinks. Carston poked at the tuna filling of his sandwich with his fork. It had the consistency of baby food and was too wet.

Ross was thinking about what he'd been saying.

"I thought their procedures for issuing morphine and stuff were pretty strictly controlled."

Carston tried a mouthful of the goo and swallowed it quickly, washing away the taste with some beer.

"You didn't get to see the sin bin, did you?" he said, dabbing at his mouth with a paper napkin.

Ross shook his head.

"Full of all sorts of things, needles, half used doses of stuff, bits of glass, tubes, dressings. If you knew what you were looking for, you could easily find it there. Friend of mine was telling me about how a guy offshore took broken stuff out of skips and got the stores to replace it with new gear. Same thing could've happened there. Dr McKenzie was confident that it couldn't but she admitted that they didn't supervise stuff being thrown away."

"So who was it?"

Carston pushed his plate aside. Kath's cooking was too good; his expectations of food were too high to be satisfied by Cairnburgh's chefs.

"That's what I want to talk about," he said. "Who'd want to, for a start?"

"Are we including Mrs Rioch?"

Carston shook his head.

"It's possible, but I still think that must've been a mistake. I mean, the dodgy sutures were taken away pretty quickly, weren't they? And with there being no overdose…"

"Well, it could be any of the doctors or nurses. Either for some personal motive or on behalf of somebody else," said Ross. "Or it could just be a bent one, with a grudge against the surgeon or the hospital. Wants to get them in trouble."

"Maybe."

"Well, visitors then," Ross went on. "You said they could more or less go where they liked."

"Yes," said Carston, seemingly prepared to let Ross keep on compiling the list.

"In fact, it's all the people who're already in the frame," said Ross, with slight exasperation.

Carston nodded.

"OK, put some names to them then."

"Well, there's Leith and Carlyle. They were both there. They had the opportunity."

"Motive?"

"I don't know. Politics? Stuff at the university. Everybody who knew him had a motive. Look at the notes and letters he wrote complaining about the staff."

"Yes. So that makes Latimer a candidate, too. And McKenzie."

"His wife wasn't very keen on him either," said Ross.

There was a smile at the corners of Carston's mouth.

"Fair enough," he said. "Now, are you convinced?"

Ross' head was already shaking.

"No. I mean, it's all possible, but it's too lightweight. The guy was a pain in the ass but he was the same to everybody. Nobody had any real personal gripe, at least, not that we've come across."

"Right. So it makes more sense if he's just an accidental victim, somebody expendable."

Ross shuddered slightly.

"That bothers me," he said.

"Yes. So why don't we turn the rules around a bit. Look for sort of reverse motives."

It was the sort of expression that Ross dreaded; it meant they'd be deserting logic to dabble in speculation.

"Reverse motives," he repeated, allowing his skepticism to fill out each syllable.

Carston smiled.

"Exactly. I remember Julie saying how strange hospitals were. Different world, I think she said."

Ross' heart sank. He, too, remembered the exchange, It had reminded him too much of Carston and his airy-fairy musings.

"Yes," he said. "Patients and nurses on one side and all the cures and medicines and stuff miles away somewhere else. As if they're not connected. She's as bad as you are ... Sir."

Carston grinned. He was used to (and appreciated) Ross' skepticism.

"Right. Well, think about what that must've been like for Hayne. Normally, he's in charge of his world, at the centre. And here he is in some fragmented sort of place, stuck alongside people he's got nothing in common with."

"I don't see how that gets him killed," said Ross.

"Read his notes again, Jim. That's what I've been doing ever since you gave them to me. Look inside all the nastiness, all the snide things he's writing about Latimer, Blantyre and the rest. It's frustration. Then he gets people like Carlyle, a man he despises, telling him how he's running the department, his department. And Leith, the walking compost heap, adding insult to injury by suggesting how much alike he and Hayne are. That's the give-away."

Ross was still unconvinced.

"How?" he asked.

Carston had taken out his notebook.

"Leith quoted some French stuff at him and Hayne writes, 'So depressing to hear it coming from him. So inappropriate. The insolence of office.' Ring a bell?"

Ross shook his head.

"Ah, whatever happened to education?" said Carston. "'The insolence of office'. It's from 'To be or not to be' isn't it?"

Ross continued to look at him.

"Suicide," said Carston.

"Oh, I see," said Ross, irony dripping off his words like thick treacle. "He committed suicide. Of course. Obvious."

251

"That's right," said Carston. "Listen to this." He checked his notes and read again. "'Carlyle asked me if I was comfortable. Bizarre question in the circumstances. I've forgotten what comfort's like. Except the one which ensures a calm passage across many a bad night. That's always there. That may be it.'"

He stopped and looked at Ross again.

"Now, does that strike you as a normal sort of thing to write? Even for somebody who works at a university."

"It's a bit flowery." said Ross.

"Yes," said Carston. "So I went online this morning to check it."

"Online? You?" said Ross.

"I got a librarian to help me. Anyway, how about this, from Nietzsche?" Once again, he referred to his notes and read. "'The thought of suicide is a great source of comfort. With it a calm passage is to be made across many a bad night.'"

Ross was impressed enough to feel able to nod some appreciation.

"So it doesn't prove anything," said Carston, "but two separate suicide references and adding 'that may be it' to one of them … well, it's worth thinking about, isn't it?"

"So he crawls out of bed," said Ross, "steals some sutures, heats them up, puts them back, then…"

"Alright, alright," said Carston, cutting across the sarcasm. "It still needs looking at." He snapped his book shut and put it away. "No point in hanging about. I reckon we get straight back up to the hospital and see how it fits."

They finished their drinks and went out. At the door, a small woman wearing a torn overcoat was buying a copy of *The Big Issue* from a young man who looked better off than she did.

"Buy *The Big Issue*, sir? Help the homeless?" the young man asked, offering a copy to Carston. Carston gave him the money and took it from him. It was the third he'd bought that week. When he got round the corner, out of sight of the man, he dropped it into a bin. It was a wasteful thing to do but what was the alternative?

\*\*\*\*

As Ross drove them to the hospital, Carston phoned Blantyre to tell her he was coming and that he'd like to speak to Nurse

Jamieson. When they got there, she was in Blantyre's office waiting for them. Blantyre was once more immaculate in a pale grey silk shirt and a tailored skirt in black cotton. Her smile was more subdued than on previous occasions but still wide enough to read by.

"Susan's a bit nervous about all this. I said I'd sit in on the questions. I take it that's OK?" she asked as they sat down.

Jamieson was sitting beside the desk, her head lowered and an anxiety in her features that hadn't been there before. The change in her was in itself a signal that Carston's intuitions had been correct but it gave him no pleasure to note it.

"Of course," he said.

Blantyre, in charge as usual, organized coffee for them and Carston was content to wait through all the rituals of pouring, passing cups, sugaring, milking and stirring. When there were finally no other niceties to be handled, Blantyre sat behind her desk, still at last.

"Now. How can we help you?" she asked.

Carston turned deliberately to face Jamieson.

"You know I was asking you about those oils the other night," he said.

She gave a little nod.

"Any idea why?"

Jamieson's eyes were lowered, looking at the coffee cup she was cradling in her lap. She shook her head. Again, it was a small movement.

"Well, we think somebody may have tampered with them."

His tone was quiet, gentle, unlike that of Blantyre, who butted in.

"I don't think that's very likely. We…"

Carston looked quickly at her.

"Ms Blantyre, I'd be grateful if you didn't interrupt. I know you prefer to think that your procedures are foolproof, but they're not. In this case, sutures and analgesics were interfered with. It wasn't just accidental."

Jamieson hadn't moved during the exchange. Carston turned back to her.

"That's why I was looking at those bottles. If I'd added anything to them, would you have known I'd done it?"

Jamieson shook her head again.

"So I'm right, anybody could tamper with them?"

Jamieson nodded.

"But, of course, they'd need access to morphine or whatever it was they added, wouldn't they? So that has to be a member of the hospital staff. Unless a visitor brought some in with him. Or her."

He waited. There was no response from Jamieson.

"Could that have happened?"

"I don't know," said Jamieson, a little anger in her tone. "How do I know what visitors are doin?"

"I didn't ask if it did happen. I asked if it could happen."

"Anythin could happen," said Jamieson.

"So Professor's Hayne's wife or colleagues could have…"

"Could, might, I don't know what you're sayin," said Jamieson.

"I'm saying," said Carston, "that somebody helped the professor over the edge. His death was no accident; it was deliberate. Somebody topped up his massage oils with analgesic and…"

Jamieson gave a great sigh and, at last, raised her gentle brown eyes to look directly at him.

"There was no need," she said.

"I'm sorry?"

"For his visitors to bring in anythin."

She seemed to have reached a decision. She put her cup on the desk beside her and looked straight into Carston's eyes again.

"Just bein there was enough. The things they said. That's what they killed him with."

Ross caught the change of mood and remained still and quiet. Carston was nodding slowly.

"Is that what he told you?"

"Not in so many words, but yes, that was it. His wife wantin the divorce. And the other two messin up his work. It's was all too much in the end. Broke him up."

She picked up her cup, took a sip and replaced it. It rattled in the saucer as her hand shook.

"He'd had enough," she added simply. "Usually, he was angry, shoutin the odds, tellin everybody what he thought of them. But that time … it was too much. He was … sort of quiet."

Her own voice was even lower, hushed, and her words began to sound like some sort of confession.

"His mood just changed. He gave up, I s'pose. Accepted it."

Her lips sketched a tiny smile.

"It was the pain that told me. Each time it came, he was different with it. Just turned away from me, eyes closed. He was just fightin it on his own. Just silent."

Carston left a small pause.

"Just tell us what happened," he said.

Jamieson lowered her eyes and looked at her hands in her lap. Then, slowly, quietly, she dragged back her memories of the last evening she'd spent with Hayne.

****

She was supposed to have gone off duty at six but her replacement was stuck in Aberdeen so she had to stay on. The shift had been long and she felt weary but Hayne was more insistent than she'd ever seen him before. She listened to his complaints about Leith and Carlyle, noting the anger and bitterness with which he spat their names. When he talked of his wife, he was no less vindictive.

"She thinks my old will's still in place, no doubt. Well, that's another surprise waiting for her. A pity that one can't see the effect the reading of a will has on would-be inheritors. It'll be such a nasty shock for her. I'd love to see how she handles it."

"That's no very nice. She's your wife," said Jamieson.

"She's a cold, scheming bitch."

"You shouldn't say such things. It's the pain talkin."

"Yes, you have to say that, don't you? But you're wrong. She's been no use to me for years. She was happy enough at the outset but now... It'll be worth dying just for the shock she'll get from the will."

"Stop talkin about dyin."

"Nurse, have the goodness to show some respect for my intelligence. Not only will I soon be dead, I intend to make absolutely sure of it."

"Well, well, well," said Jamieson. "And how are you goin to do that?"

Hayne was silent for a while. Jamieson saw him clench against a new pain that was washing through him.

"I'll need help," he said at last. "And if I can't get it here, I'll fly to Amsterdam or Switzerland as soon as I'm released."

"That's silly talk."

Briefly, Hayne's anger broke through.

"Stop treating me like an idiot," he hissed. "I've had enough of all of them. I haven't the strength to fight them any more, and I loathe what they're doing to the department and what'll happen to it if they take charge. So I don't intend to sit and watch it."

"Well, you've no choice."

"But you have."

"What do you mean?"

"I mean you can help me."

"No way."

"Either that, or some of your wards are closed down. That's your choice."

"What d'you mean?"

"It's not exactly a coded message," said Hayne. "If I don't get your cooperation, I'll make sure that there's enough bad publicity to start an official investigation into what goes on here."

Jamieson looked at him, prepared to smile at his teasing. But Hayne didn't do teasing. He reached across to pick up his iPad and held it in front of her.

"I've seen the wastage here, the inefficiencies, the mistakes that people make. I observe, analyze. It's my job, remember. And the evidence I've got here will have government inspectors rampaging through all your procedures."

"Now why would you want to do that?" asked Jamieson, forcing her voice to stay gentle.

"Because I can. Because you all need something to shake you out of your lethargy. Oh yes," he went on, as Jamieson made to reply, "you rush around and give every impression of being busy, but a lot of it is just panic. Maybe not you, but so many of the others, the surgeons, the high profile 'achievers' get by through luck rather than judgment. Your management structures are a disgrace. Any half-competent audit process would see through them at once."

Jamieson said nothing. The criticism hurt but she didn't know enough to contradict him.

"But the power's yours," he went on. "If you'll help, you can save them all."

She shook her head.

"It's impossible," she said. "You know I can't do that. It's against everythin I do."

"I know. I understand," he said, with no softening of his tone to suggest that he did. "But you can surely see that it's the same for me."

"What d'you mean?" she asked.

He waved his hand down across his body.

"This. This machine. It's letting me down. Have you any idea of the true effects of impotence, incontinence? For you, it's changing sheets, cleaning up mess and baby talking to mature men and women." He paused, his eyes fixed on the sheet over his body. When he spoke again, his voice was lower, his words chosen slowly.

"I hate being part of your routines. It's a betrayal. Leaves no room for pride, dignity, the sort of respect my work has earned me." For the first time, he looked directly into her eyes. "I, me, the person, I've lost nothing. I'm still able to see through their maneuvers, I can still outwit them all." He slapped an angry hand on his chest. "But this ... body has taken over. I can't beat it. And I can't replace it. I can fight the others, but I can't go on fighting myself."

****

It was obvious to Carston that Jamieson's memories were disturbing her. As she told them what he'd said, there was a break in her voice. In a way, she was having to describe her own failure.

"What did you say in the end?" he asked her gently.

She sighed and shrugged her shoulders.

"The usual. Said things'd get better, tried to make him see... Trouble was, I didn't believe it myself. He'd been here too often. And with his visitors ... I knew fine it was all over for him. He'd never been that low before."

No one made a sound. Jamieson looked at Blantyre then down at her right hand, which was tracing little patterns on the desk beside her coffee cup.

"Most of the folk I see ask for the same thing. Well, lots of them. They want out. When it's bad, when they're afraid of another operation. They've had enough."

"So you're used to it?" said Carston.

Jamieson nodded.

"But this time you did help."

She nodded again. He waited.

"You can usually get top-up doses out of the sin bin. I've done it before, for when patients have needed a wee bit more."

"And that's what you did?" prompted Carston. His own voice was as quiet as hers. There was a depth of silence in the room that was more than just a lack of sound. All of them were looking at Jamieson.

"You're right. I mixed it with his oil," she said.

"And the suture?" asked Carston.

"Yes. I knew that'd do the trick, too. And with all the sedation, he wouldn't feel anything."

To Carston's alarm, tears suddenly appeared in her eyes.

"Poor Mrs Rioch," she said, her voice breaking. "One of the ones I'd heated must've been left."

"I'm surprised you didn't say anything when that happened," said Carston.

"What for?" she said, using her right forefinger to brush her tears away. "She was dyin too. She didn't deserve to go but in the end, it didn't make much difference. And if I'd had to leave, I'd've been lettin down all my other patients."

"You were taking an awful lot on yourself, weren't you?" asked Carston.

Jamieson shrugged.

"I could've done the same thing for hundreds of patients over the years. Every week, there's somebody askin…"

"Yes, but you haven't done it before. Why this time?"

Jamieson remained silent, her eyes downcast again. Carston waited. When the answer eventually came, it shocked all of them.

"Because I authorized it," said Blantyre.

# Chapter Sixteen

The man's name was Derek Harvey. When they'd first brought him in, he'd refused to give it, but time on his own to reflect and a growing frustration had made him blurt out that it was typical of "pigs" not to recognize somebody they already had on file. Sandy Dwyer had put a uniformed constable onto cross-checking mug shots and fingerprints. He'd found nothing in the sections on muggers or people convicted of assault but, then, in a wider trawl through their records, he suddenly clicked the man's face onto his screen. He was in the section where the periodic blitzes on Cairnburgh's homeless were logged. If an individual appeared in two consecutive sweeps of the banks of the canal and the bushes of Macaulay Park, he was photographed and put on record. Just in case.

The information they had on him came from Social Services. Actual details of his home life were sketchy, but their broad outlines painted one of the usual stories. His parents were well into their forties when he was born. His father had recently been retired from the army where'd he'd made the rank of company sergeant major. A new son, their only child, had given him the raw material on which to continue to practice his character-building skills. For Harvey, childhood had been something which happened to other people. He and his mother had had to follow precise routines, endure unnecessary hardships and never indulge in anything that might soften their attitudes to life. When his mother was eventually hospitalized after yet another nervous breakdown, his father tried to bring him up alone for two years, then gave up and dumped him onto the Social Services to be fostered. He'd lived in three different homes where love was offered freely and family life was a happy, balanced affair. But he'd never belonged to any of them, the years of suppression making him distrust openness. Feelings equated to vulnerability. You couldn't stop having them, but you could keep them to yourself.

He was now twenty-two and had been living on his own for five years. The shapes and constraints of his youth had prepared him for a reality far removed from that of most of the people around him. He saw them in the streets, shopping, socializing and leading their ordinary, flat lives with ease. They laughed, cried and loved and Harvey saw them as groups, pairs, clans. Nowhere was there any evidence of the disciplines that had been burned so deeply into him. He was a stranger amongst all the crowds, excluded from their intimacy, reduced to observing them and keeping quiet.

When McNeil arrived to question him, all Harvey's details had been printed out and were handed to her. What she read made her feel even worse than before. Her treatment of the man had been as misguided as it could be. She had only seen the threat to Scott, the usual male ego imposing itself on the unwilling female. His appearance, tall, dark, brooding, had confirmed the stereotype and she'd decided to deal with him in a currency she thought he'd understand, that of threat and confrontation. She knew that stalking could lead to violence but there was no text book answer for cases like his. Cautioning him or warning him off weren't options, so she'd calculated the risk and decided that it was worth taking. If the record was to be believed, Harvey was about as threatening as Clark Kent. There was genuine fear in her mind that his move into aggression was a direct response to the way she'd treated him on that bench.

As she sat opposite him, with a detective constable beside her and another officer in uniform at the door, it was obvious to her that he was guilty. His knuckles were skinned and bruised and the blouson jacket they'd taken from his room had spots of blood all over it. DNA tests had been arranged to confirm that they belonged to Lawson, but Harvey had denied nothing, seemed to know why he was there and accepted the inevitable.

What bothered McNeil most was the look on his face. This wasn't the man who'd sat between herself and Scott, his eyes looking down at the path, unable to meet their gaze. This individual had flopped lazily into the chair, an arm hooked over its back, his legs splayed apart, his head on one side and his eyes holding hers.

"Want to tell me about it?" said McNeil, when she'd turned on the recorder and noted the time.

"Nope," said Harvey.

"Not like you, was it?" said McNeil. "You've never beat up on a woman before."

"What do you know about it?" His voice was thin, as if he didn't use it often, but he was making it into a growl.

"You're right. Nothing," said McNeil. "I just didn't figure you for a batterer."

"You didna figure me for nothin. What the fuck do you know?"

"Not much, obviously," said McNeil. "OK, then. You tell me. Why'd you do it?"

Harvey paused, as if deciding whether to answer or not. The change in his demeanor was frightening. When they'd met before, the slightest pressure had been enough to make him cry; the person she was looking at was already playing a hard man.

"Bitch had it comin, right?"

He was making no effort to deny anything.

"Why?" asked McNeil. "You didn't know her."

The thin voice was slow as it separated each word in his reply.

"She ... had ... it ... comin."

"What's her name, then?"

"Who cares?"

"She does."

"I don't."

"So it wasn't her. It was 'cause she was in your way. Just happened to be there."

Harvey gave a little laugh and turned his head away.

"You're not saying you didn't do it, I notice."

His head snapped back.

"I did it," he said, quickly, proudly. "Course I did it. And you know what? Next time, I'll shag her, too."

He looked straight at McNeil. For a moment, she held his stare, but her own guilt and depression made her look away. Something had happened in Harvey's mind. The fragility that had been evident in his crying when she'd grabbed his shoulder on the bench should have warned her that he was volatile. Something, probably McNeil herself, had clicked him into a different gear. This wasn't a man who'd cry; this was one who'd get revenge for having been made to show weakness. He was compensating for God knows what. And

261

the attack had taken him across a frontier. She thought again about his notes. He was no longer an outsider. Beating up Lawson had brought him into the world, committed him. Maybe, as he'd said on the bench, he'd been content just to look. Not any more.

"What happened, Derek?" she asked gently.

"Hey. Fuck you. Mr Harvey to you."

"Sorry. What happened, Mr Harvey?"

"Fuck all happened. I slapped her around a bit. No a big deal, is it?"

"I don't mean that. I mean you. What happened to you? To change you? I thought you said you only liked looking."

This time, his head turned aside and his eyes flicked around, as if trying to avoid seeing something.

"Yeah, well, maybe I did. Maybe I did." He paused, the eyes still restless. "Maybe I did," he repeated.

"So why the change?"

"Lookin doesna get you nothin," he said.

"And what's this got you? Slapping around a girl, a stranger."

Suddenly, the eyes stopped moving. He stared at his hand, which he was holding up in front of him. He smiled.

"She won't forget me, will she?"

"She won't think much of you, either," said McNeil.

"She won't forget me," said Harvey, the smile wider and the voice confident.

McNeil had no idea which direction to take with him. He was unstable but she doubted that a shrink would find much fundamentally wrong with him. She needed space away from him. It was the first time that she'd felt so inadequate. The pride in her new rank had been badly dented. She stood up.

"Charge him," she said to the detective constable. "I'll talk to him again later."

"Fuck you, sister," said Harvey, forming an "O" with the thumb and forefinger of his left hand and sliding it up and down the middle finger of his right.

She went out, preoccupied more with the mistakes she'd made than with the childish insult he'd offered. He'd be found guilty, sent down and punished. The trouble was that the effect of sending him to prison would be to make him into a real criminal. He'd mix with real hard men and be taught that women were objects to be used in whatever way you liked. His newly acquired respect for violent solutions to problems would become a natural reflex. And when he came out again, how would he treat those who crossed his path? McNeil knew that she had to talk to Sandra Scott and tell her everything, including the level of her own misjudgment. She felt very low. Why had she behaved so stupidly? What was she really trying to do that day in the park? Had she talked to too many rape victims? Was she just getting her own back on men?

The questions multiplied and, perhaps for the first time, McNeil's self-belief wavered. In the end, she knew she would get on with the job. But how different would Harvey's transformation make her? Unusually, she felt behind her eyes the heat that meant that tears were not far away.

**\*\*\*\***

Carston's interview at the hospital had had no such personal effects. He'd been feeling his way through it very carefully and the whole picture was still only partly formed in his mind. Then came Blantyre's interjection. It had derailed everything.

She sat unmoving behind her desk, aware of the impact she'd made but not seeming particularly proud of it. The smile had gone and her lips were set fairly tightly but she was still in control. Carston looked at her and she waited calmly for his reaction. The first thing he wanted to do—an action long overdue in the light of her revelation—was to separate her from Jamieson.

"Well, well," he said. "I think we'd better take this quite slowly." He stood up and put his coffee cup on the desk. "Is there somewhere else we could go? Just you and me, I mean."

"What's wrong with here?" she asked.

"I'd like my sergeant to get a formal statement from Nurse Jamieson. It's easier for him to do that here. If you've no objection."

Blantyre stood up.

"Of course not. Let's see what we can find."

As she passed Jamieson, she reached down and gave her shoulder a squeeze. Jamieson looked up and smiled at her. For a moment, it brought the two of them into an extraordinarily close relationship.

Once outside the office, Carston suggested that, instead of finding some other room, they could perhaps go for a walk in the hospital's grounds. The weather continued to hold and, since he hadn't cautioned her and was still trying to understand the whole thing, he thought that a less formal context for their conversation would be helpful. The idea seemed to appeal to her and they were soon away from the wards and car parks and walking along paths between beds of tulips and wallflowers.

"Susan told me that the professor had asked her to help him," said Blantyre, not waiting for Carston to prompt her with questions. "As she said, it happens all the time. Shows how many desperate people we have here."

Carston nodded his sympathy.

"It shows how good a job our people are doing too. Because we deal with these things, we ease their suffering. The Bartholomew's a wonderful institution, you know."

She was back in her PR mode but this time there was an urgency in her voice that showed how much she believed what she was saying. Her words were not just for public consumption; she meant them.

"That was part of the trouble," she went on. "All a question of timing."

"I don't understand."

"The morning Susan told me about what the professor had asked, I'd just received a letter from him. It wasn't the first, but this one was the draft of something he was threatening to send to the Health Minister. It was a list of grievances. About the staff, his treatments, the administration."

She suddenly stopped walking, forcing Carston to stop too.

"He really was a poisonous individual," she said. "Did you know him at all?"

Carston shook his head.

"Not really. I've looked at things he wrote, talked to colleagues... But I couldn't say I know much about him."

"I went to see him as soon as I got the letter. That's obviously what he'd intended. I just wanted to answer some of his complaints, correct some ... misunderstandings. But he wouldn't listen. How can people be like that? You know what he did? He showed me something he'd written on that hand-held computer of his—a letter to Grampian Health Board. It would've more or less compelled them to close down at least seven wards—just to investigate his claims. He said that, if we didn't do as he asked, he'd send it. It was blackmail."

"Yes. He was a manipulator."

"And he knew all the people in the right places. He trotted out a list of names of people he had access to—board members, city councilors, MSPs..."

She made a gesture with her hand to suggest that the list went on and on.

"He was truly horrible. Evil," she said, beginning to move along the path again. "No respect for anything. For anybody. Totally self-opinionated. He tried to reorganize the ward routines. He was critical of everything we did, and incredibly rude to the staff. I don't know how Susan and the others managed to stay civil with him. Anyway, in that letter, he was pulling the place to pieces. And there was no justification for it. It was spite. Uninformed, malicious..." She stopped, controlling the passion the memory of the letter had rekindled.

"I owe you an apology," said Carston in the silence.

"What?"

"In my usual, predictable way, I've always assumed that Public Relations people don't really believe in what they're selling. You do, don't you?"

She didn't answer right away, taking the time to consider her response.

"I'm not selling anything," she said. "We all know what's happening to the NHS. In spite of it all, the Bartholomew's still providing a service. That's what I want people to see."

"And his letter was threatening to undermine it?"

"Largely, yes. When Susan said he wanted to finish it all ... well, she took him seriously. She knew he meant it this time. And the prognosis for him was more or less hopeless. So why not?"

It was a strangely casual way to dismiss a life-or-death decision but Blantyre seemed unaware of that. She spoke some more about the number of times requests for euthanasia were made both by patients and by their relatives who were traumatized by the suffering they were forced to witness week after week. It seemed that most doctors regretted the fact that it wasn't an option. Time, resources and skills were all being used up on patients whose only future was one of interminable pain and who simply wanted a dreamless sleep.

"Didn't it strike you, though," said Carston, "that a post-operative death might reflect badly on the hospital? I mean, you knew there'd be an enquiry."

Strangely, Blantyre smiled.

"Yes, but it was only Susan's thoroughness that caused the problem."

"I'm sorry?"

"Arranging for the overdose as well as the suture failure. Would you have bothered if there'd been only one of them?"

Carston saw what she meant.

"We'd have bothered but not as much."

"You see?"

"But it would still have reflected badly on the surgical department."

Blantyre's smile was still there. It wasn't the one she'd switched on each time they'd visited but one that was stimulated by some deeper thought.

"Probably not, in fact," she said, adding, after a pause, "and anyway, Mr Latimer is a surgeon we could do without. In an ideal world, your enquiry would have found him guilty of misconduct and we could have got rid of him. Hayne would have disappeared and we could have got on with what we're good at."

"Sacking one of your surgeons? A bit drastic, isn't it? Bit of a dubious admission from someone in your position."

She looked at him, seeming to study his face and search for something in his eyes.

"Can I say something off the record?" she asked.

Carston nodded.

"I mean, you won't use it in any way later on. It's a confidence."

Carston gave a little shake of his head.

"I haven't cautioned you or anything but I wouldn't want to be put in a position of having to ignore information that's relevant to the case," he said, rather heavily.

Her head was already shaking.

"It's got nothing to do with Professor Hayne or Mrs Rioch," she said. "I promise."

"OK," said Carston. "But if it sounds doubtful, I'll stop you."

"Latimer talks a fine operation," she said. "He dresses the part, acts the part. The students he gets are impressed. But most of it's show. Oh, he's competent enough. But he does make mistakes. Last summer, we had a patient, Mrs Gallacher. A wonderful person. She'd been in a few times for hip replacements and other minor surgery. She wasn't the healthiest woman around but she lived her life and did an awful lot of good. I know. She was a neighbor of mine."

A softening in her eyes confirmed her fondness for Mrs Gallacher.

"She was well into her sixties and a resolute smoker," she went on. "Came in to have a tumor removed from a lung. Latimer left her till the end of a list. He has very little truck with self-inflicted conditions, as he calls them."

"They are, though, aren't they? Self-inflicted, I mean," said Carston, who'd never smoked.

"It must be nice to be free of vices," said Blantyre, with the lightest touch of irony. "Well, she certainly paid for hers. By the time he got round to dealing with her, he was tired and his mind was elsewhere."

Carston frowned.

"Oh, there was no malpractice," she hurried on. "Nothing specific that you could accuse him of. But he was sloppy, too quick, too careless. She died two days after the operation. And there was nothing that Susan or the others could do to ease things for her. She was in agony for every minute of those two days."

Her eyes had clouded with the memory but her practiced professionalism quickly snapped her back.

"So, as I said, Mr Latimer would be no great loss for us," she said. "The Bartholomew would be able to get on with what it's for—caring for people."

"That still hasn't changed," said Carston.

Blantyre smiled.

"No. The hospital's not to blame. It was just an aberration by a crazy individual, wasn't it? Me, I mean."

They'd reached the edge of the grounds. A line of birch trees marked the border. Through them, Carston saw the familiar shapes of the Cairngorms to the south. The air was good to breathe, the day was full of life. The conversation they were having was a blot on all the vitality around them.

"I still don't understand," said Carston.

"What?"

267

"In spite of what you've said, you're not crazy. So why? Why risk it? Everything you do, everything about you, it's organized, correct. I just can't understand why you agreed to … well, to be blunt, to let nurse Jamieson kill Hayne."

Blantyre gave a different, smaller, more secret smile.

"Did you look back over our records?" she asked after a while. "Pick out other examples of … medical mishaps?"

Carston nodded.

"There is a list. I haven't felt the need to look at it, though. Why d'you ask?"

"How far back did you go?"

Carston had to think for a moment.

"Five years. Ten at the most."

"Ah," she said. "Not far enough then."

Carston saw that, even now, she was teasing him, stretching out this incriminatory conversation. He said nothing, waiting for her to go on.

"If you'd gone back a bit further," she said, "one of the names might have made you wonder."

"Oh?"

"Yes. William Blantyre. My father."

Carston looked at her and shook his head. Once again, she'd short-circuited all his responses, left him adrift.

"You have an astonishing talent for surprising people," he said.

"I know. It's fun sometimes," she replied.

They walked on, Carston trying to absorb this new information, Blantyre deep again in thoughts and memories.

"What happened?" asked Carston at last.

The smile was lost as she brought the memories to the surface.

"He was only forty-four. Had a weak valve in his heart. They tried to repair it but he died in theatre."

Her voice had become very quiet.

"I'm sorry," said Carston.

She nodded.

"And were there any charges?" asked Carston.

"There was an investigation," she replied. "One of your predecessors. They had no case, though. Nobody had made a mistake. There was no Latimer factor. The story was that Dad was just … too weak. Too many years of working on building sites, worrying about jobs, trying to provide for four kids. His heart just … stopped. Nobody's fault."

The event she was recalling had an obvious immediacy for her. Carston felt no urge to speak.

"I was eighteen. Didn't accept it. Dad couldn't die. Not my dad. He was so … such a…" She stopped, unable to pursue the thought. She took a deep breath before starting again.

"I was horrible to everybody. A real bitch. Made their life a misery. Blamed everybody—the nurses, doctors, secretaries—everybody. I thought it was a cover-up. I was always here, trying to…" She stopped for a moment and shook her head, disliking the person she was recalling. "Then one of the sisters started talking to me. Brought me inside, showed me the way they work on the wards, the things they have to put up with. I saw that they weren't…" She gave a little laugh. "…murderers. I saw what they did for people, what they have to see and do day after day."

She stopped walking and looked back at the main hospital building.

"If they trebled their salaries," she said, "that still wouldn't be reward enough for what my staff do."

Carston heard the fierceness of her conviction. Blantyre walked on again.

"They didn't kill Dad. They made his last few days better. Special," she went on. "And I wanted to help them."

Again she stopped, this time turning towards him and forcing him to face her. When she spoke, the fierceness was still in her voice.

"These people are wonderful," she said. "I'd do anything, anything to help them."

Carston looked into her eyes and nodded his head slowly.

"I know," he said.

They turned again and walked on.

"I'm sorry to have messed it up for you," he said.

She looked at him again and saw that he was serious and that he understood. Hayne had been a destructive, negative force. It would have been better for all concerned if his death had generated nothing more than the guilty pleasure that was felt by almost everyone when they first got news of it. But it seemed that, even from the grave, the influence of such barren individuals could reach corrosive tentacles into the world they'd left.

"Shall we go back?" said Carston.

Blantyre nodded and gave him one of her smiles. It made him feel sad.

****

The university's summer vacation was almost over. The long, incident-packed period of Hayne's tenure of the headship of the department of European Culture was history but Hayne himself was still remembered. Carlyle excused himself from his duties as temporary head of department and Leith took over, eager to pursue Hayne's reforms and add his own refinements to them. He was diligent in consolidating his power base and, thanks to the support of Latimer in the REF committee, his confirmation in the post seemed inevitable. Some of his colleagues tried to re-establish systems which Hayne's scheming had undermined, but they were frequently frustrated either by Leith himself, or by delighted administrators who presented them with memoranda drafted by Hayne and countersigned by the university Principal.

The new will which Hayne had been drafting with his lawyer had never surfaced and, as soon as the police had concluded their investigations into his death, his wife sold her house and moved to a detached manse in twelve acres on the Ayrshire coast. She left no forwarding address with anyone in Cairnburgh or Aberdeen.

From July to September, Sandra Scott had been employed part-time at the supermarket where her mother worked at the check-outs. When McNeil had first told her of Harvey's arrest and probable conviction, she'd been relieved. The news that, when he was eventually released, he might be more of a danger than he'd been before, was a shock, but she'd absorbed it and reasoned that she'd probably be away from the north east when it happened. It was just one more piece of unpleasantness to add to all the others that this year had spawned.

There was one bright point. The manager of the supermarket was so impressed with her he'd suggested that, when she graduated, she'd be a welcome addition to the company "at managerial level". It would mean a big salary and plenty of freedom to generate new ideas. She wouldn't have to stay in Fraserburgh and could choose where she did her training. It had made her mum and dad very proud but the prospect of becoming a mover and shaker was too depressing for her to give a definite answer.

It was the end of September and her last week at work before starting a new term. The hearing about her charge of sexual harassment against Christie had been held in the middle of August and the Vice Principal responsible had found in Christie's favor. It had come as no real surprise. The delay before the hearing had been calculated to let passions cool and memories fade and, when pressed on the specifics of what had happened, she found that her scorn for Christie far exceeded any residual distress left by his advances. For his part, Christie had played the innocent, appalled to find that his "genuine interest" in "students as individuals" had been misconstrued and anxious to reassure "Miss Scott" that his attentions were inspired by his duties as a teacher and "circumscribed by the parameters of intellectual enquiry". If there had been any offence, it was unintended and he was "devastated" that it should have given her cause for concern.

On her last Thursday morning, she was restocking the frozen food cabinets when her mobile rang. It was Carolyn Noble. She was phoning to add a simple little footnote to the story. Christie had not only been reinstated, but he'd been promoted to full professor and made head of the Department of European Culture. Scott looked across the cartons of crisps, cereals, sweets and biscuits and wondered what to do.

In Cairnburgh, sweating profusely, Dr Leith was composing a long, angry letter of resignation.


THE END

# ABOUT THE AUTHOR

Bill Kirton was born in Plymouth, England but has lived in Aberdeen Scotland for most of his life. He's been a university lecturer, presented TV programmes, written and performed songs and sketches at the Edinburgh Festival, and had many radio plays broadcast by the BBC and the Australian BC. He's written four books on study and writing skills in Pearson's 'Brilliant' series and his crime novels, *Material Evidence*, *Rough Justice*, *The Darkness*, and the historical novel *The Figurehead*, set in Aberdeen in 1840, have been published in the UK and USA. His most recent publication from Pfoxmoor is a hilarious satire of the spy and crime genres, *The Sparrow Conundrum*. His short stories have appeared in several anthologies and *Love Hurts* was chosen for the *Mammoth Book of Best British Crime 2010*.

Two of his books have won awards. *The Sparrow Conundrum* was the winner of the 'Humor' category in the 2011 Forward National Literature Awards and *The Darkness* was second in the 'Mystery' category.

His website is http://www.bill-kirton.co.uk and his blog's at http://www.livingwritingandotherstuff.blogspot.com/

# BY THE SAME AUTHOR

## THE JACK CARSTON MYSTERY SERIES

### Material Evidence:

"...a fine debut with intense plotting, strong characters and just the right touch of acid in the dialogue ... Fine Rendellian touches ... a cracking page-turner."
—Aberdeen Press and Journal

"...Add to the cast of characters a good sense of pace and an excellent plot that kept me guessing and you'll see why I liked this book."—Cathy G. Cole

### Rough Justice:

"...a thoughtful and thought-provoking book ... It ought to bring Bill Kirton the attention he deserves." (Sunday Telegraph)

### The Darkness:
**2nd Place, Mystery, 2011 Forward National Literature Awards**

"...a wonderful, thrilling, dark, compassionate book"
—Gillian Philip, author of Firebrand

"...clever, tightly constructed, immensely satisfying and peopled with a cast of completely believable characters, who don't let you go until the final word"
—Michael J. Malone

"...a dark, intense ride ... a book that keeps you guessing right until the exciting conclusion."
—P. S. Gifford

### Coming soon: Unsafe Acts

# HISTORICAL FICTION

## The Figurehead:

"Profound, detailed, incredibly written, *The Figurehead* is definitely a kind of book one wants to go back to again and again..."—Maria K.

# SATIRE

## The Sparrow Conundrum:
### 1st Place Winner, Humor, 2011 Forward National Literature Awards

"...The Sparrow Conundrum is the demon love child of Spike Milligan and John Le Carre. I absolutely adore this one—hysterically funny, with this weirdly tender wickedness."
—Maria Bustillos, author of Dorkismo: the Macho of the Dork and Act Like a Gentleman, Think Like a Woman

"...You have combined the elements of The Tall Blond Man with the One Black Shoe with The Biederbecke Affair and thrown in Happer from Local Hero for good measure. It is killingly funny, and for those who love farce—from Scapin to Noises Off—this is utterly brilliant, divine, and classic, and couldn't be bettered."
—M.M. Bennetts, author of May 1812 and Of Honest Fame

# CHILDREN'S BOOKS (written as Jack Rosse)

## Stanley Moves In

"...Stanley in all his obnoxious glory ... it's hard not to like Rosse's charming tale of this out-of-the-ordinary fairy."
—Melissa Conway

## The Loch Ewe Mystery

10439377R00177

Made in the USA
Charleston, SC
04 December 2011